PRAISE FOR *ZERO BOMB*

"Suffocatingly real… An inventive thriller about the increasingly blurred lines between machine and man, animal and AI."
SFX

"Gripping… Grim in places, bitterly funny in others."
SciFi Now

"Hill is a true innovator, a brilliant prose stylist and a writer with a high level of invention. *Zero Bomb* mixes intense human drama and political struggle to show that great SF exists as much on the streets of today's Britain as it does in the stars."
JEFF NOON, author of *Vurt*

"A beautifully written and profoundly dislocating book about a chillingly plausible near future and its discontents. Absolutely essential reading."
DAVE HUTCHINSON, award-winning author of *Europe in Winter*

"Thrilling, audacious and timely, M.T. Hill's visions of the future feel closer to reality than they should."
HELEN MARSHALL, award-winning author of *The Migration*

"Vivid and richly imagined, *Zero Bomb* is a passionate examination of who we are and a warning of what we could shortly become. I couldn't put it down."
CATRIONA WARD, award-winning author of *Rawblood*

"Conceived at the height of an unprecedented national crisis, M.T. Hill's *Zero Bomb* is a violent, vital novel about virtue, loyalty, decency and love, even as we watch these timeless human attributes dissolve in the stomach acids of the World Machine. Think E.M. Forster's *The Machine Stops*, written for the *Westworld* age, and you may just gain a fingerhold on this crazed colt of a book."
SIMON INGS, author *Wolves* and *The Smoke*

BY M.T. HILL AND AVAILABLE FROM TITAN BOOKS

Zero Bomb

THE BREACH

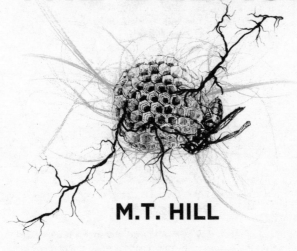

M.T. HILL

TITAN BOOKS

The Breach
Print edition ISBN: 9781789090031
E-book edition ISBN: 9781789090048

Published by Titan Books
A division of Titan Publishing Group Ltd.
144 Southwark Street, London SE1 0UP
www.titanbooks.com

First edition March 2020
10 9 8 7 6 5 4 3 2 1

A CIP catalogue record for this title is available from the British Library.

Printed and bound by CPI Group (UK) Ltd, Croydon CR0 4YY.

For Al

A FIRE IN THE NORTH

The Landowner

The burning starts mid-evening, when Lakeland greens have run to gold and the foxes on heat are shrieking.

Em is on the phone to the solicitor when she notices the smell, a rich and bitter fug, though it doesn't distract her much. After all, people burning stuff is normal up here in the Lakes. Bonfires, barbeques, campfires – walk any which way for miles and count the ash piles with your cowpats. It could be anglers on the tarn, a farmer clearing fallow fields, a young family gearing up for a restless night under canvas… anything like that. And so it's easy for Em to blank it – especially easy given what the solicitor is saying. And when he's done saying it, Em puts down the phone and stares into the grain of the desk.

'Now what?' she asks herself out loud. Now. What. And here it comes, sure as anything: the dread tide, the enormity of losing their home. The life she and her husband Ted have made here. There's no ambiguity, no wriggle-room, because the solicitor has confirmed what they thought unlikely just months ago: the council is seizing land for development, and Em and Ted's property – the farmhouse and its acreage, the barns, the old bunker – is now subject to a compulsory purchase order.

Em reaches for the bottle of red she brought up fatalistically from the cellar, decants the whole thing and starts drinking straight from the carafe. She sits there, looking around the reading room, as if to quantify what they stand to lose. When she gets up, her quiet existence lurches sideways.

The whole house. *The whole thing.* Another swig as Em goes to the window in a daze. The blinds are open, and gauzy smoke rises from the trees at the bottom of the lawn. Is that… is that on their land? Surely not. But Em settles the carafe on the sill and grimaces. What she'd assumed was woodsmoke has turned into a plastic stench she can taste. That, and the fox screams seem much closer than before. Closer and keener. She remembers that their gardener Graham is working down there, and now she'll have to confront him. What the hell's he burning? What's he burning that could drive foxes up towards the house?

A flash of nautical yellow in the thicket. Em's focus narrows, one hand on the window. 'Oh no,' she whispers. A sickening jolt between her ears, behind her ribs. A pain like drowning.

It isn't foxes screaming.

It's the girls.

Em splays her hands and pushes her face against the glass. The girls, sooty and screaming, are running up the garden. Before she can react, they're in the house, tearing through the kitchen and the lounge and the diner and the conservatory.

They're still screaming, the worst kind of screaming, a rabid screaming, when they reach her in the drawing room.

The girls are filthy and stinking and screaming for their mother, and their mother is her. And because Em is their mother – because she *breathes* that sound as well as she hears it – she understands the burning can't be a simple bonfire at all.

'What's the matter?' she manages, biting her lip to try and stop it trembling. 'What's happened?'

She takes them in alternately. Their eldest, Dolly, grey and snotty and blubbing down her yellow cagoule. Their youngest, Damson, staring shock-dumb.

'Tell me,' Em says. 'Tell Mummy what happened.'

She folds the children into her. She cradles Dolly's face by the jawbone and wipes soot and ash from her cheeks with her own spit, with Dolly's tears.

'It was fairies, Mummy!' Dolly says through her sobs. 'It was fairies! We were making a den. We saw them come out. They said we shouldn't look!'

Em swallows. 'What do you mean, fairies? Come out of where? For heaven's sakes, girls, you're scaring me to death.'

But Damson and Dolly, six and eight years old, blinking and stinking of burning plastic, have no more words between them. Instead they take their mother by the sleeves and drag her through the house. She stumbles after them with her guts inside out.

Behind the house, in a panic, Em catches a shin on the handle of an upturned wheelbarrow, sees Graham's hand trowel wedged in the lawn as though he'd thrown it down like an axe. Beside her, the hose reel on the back of the house is unwinding rapidly, the pipe snaking away across the lawn.

'Where's Graham?' Em asks the girls. 'Where's he gone?'

'Down with them!' Dolly shouts. 'He came to save us!'

Em breaks for the treeline, towards the smoke. The girls keep up, still yelling, 'It was them! It was the fairies! They went all over!'

Here the smoke thickens, the same smell as on the children, and Em's world is a chemical fire. First the ride-on mower, motor still going, and then Graham in a clearing. A ragged black line has been seared through the long grass, ending at the greenhouse, which is burning. Graham, in his tweed flat cap and wellies and fishing waders, has the hose nozzle aimed into the flames. He's standing completely still.

'Graham!'

Graham can't hear Em, or ignores her. The girls pull on her waist and cuffs. 'Mummy!' Dolly shouts. She clasps Em's numb fingers. 'The fairies made a fire!'

'That's their *fire*, Mummy,' Damson adds.

Em kneels in dewy grass. The clouds have closed over. She brings the girls close again. 'Did you do this?' she urges. 'Did you set light to the greenhouse? Did you breathe that in?'

'It was the *fairies*,' Dolly insists. 'We *told you*.' She shakes off her mother's embrace and crosses her arms. 'Damson did a wee behind a tree and I was watching for strangers and there was a fizz in the air and the fire came up green and… and I said, "Damson – quick! What's that?" And we only had a look, Mummy, just a very fast look, and they came whizzing about and one of them told us not to – not to snitch! And it called us all these mean things, it said we are so *ugly*, it said we are so small and *useless*—'

'Damson.' Em is staring at her youngest now, this little girl still too young to lie convincingly.

'It was the fairies,' Damson whispers. Then, quieter, 'What if it was Marigold?'

Em's throat catches as she watches her daughter speak. It feels like the whole Lake District has contracted to the size of the clearing. The hiss of water boiling off. Graham standing too still. 'There's no such thing as a mean fairy,' Em tells Damson. 'Marigold's a tooth fairy. She wouldn't light a fire because she's only there to mind your teeth, and she's fond of you. Of both of you. Now, I want to know the truth, and I won't be angry. I won't be mad at all. I'll ask you once more. One more time. Did you take matches from Mummy and Daddy's kitchen? From Uncle Graham's shed? Did you accidentally light a fire? You have to tell me. If you tell me, I can fix it.'

'No!' Dolly screeches, and she starts to cry again. 'Ask them! Go and see the fairies!'

Em looks to her youngest. 'Damson?'

Damson squirms like she needs the toilet. She shakes her head, and her brow darkens the way Ted's does. 'I promise, Mummy,' she says. 'Brownie's Honour. It was them.'

Em's patience runs out. She looks to Graham, the shrinking fire, and points back up the hill, towards the house. 'The pair of you, inside,' she says. 'Lock the back door and shut all the windows you can reach. Then I want you to call Daddy, but no video, okay? I want you to tell him Mummy needs him home.'

The girls blink at her.

'Do it,' Em says, 'and I'll be up to run a bath. Don't put your hands on the walls, either. Go on – scoot!'

The girls sprint up the hill. The back door slams. Em approaches the gardener.

'Graham?'

Graham has the fire down, but the residual heat is immense. The greenhouse frame has deformed and blistered, and the roof glass drips gelatinously into what remains beneath.

'What is it, Graham?'

The gardener doesn't answer.

'Was this the girls, Graham? Was it them?'

'I din't see,' Graham says. 'There were a tearing sound, like a wave breaking.' He points at the strip of burnt grass. 'And this.'

'So it wasn't you, either?'

He glares at her.

'Then what? What the bloody hell's that in there?'

Graham takes off his flat cap and looks at his boots.

'Did the girls do it?'

Graham gestures to the seat of the fire with his hat. A black puddle, smouldering. Em doesn't know why, but she worries it's the neighbour's cat.

'What is that?'

'Best you head inside,' Graham says. He removes his hat, wipes his reddened brow. 'See to them girls.'

'Why's no one *telling* me anything?'

'Nowt worth telling, that's why. Leave me at it. I'll tidy now. Get it shovelled up and sling it down in the old bunker. We'll hold it over till next bin collection day. Can't have it stinking place out.'

14

'I don't understand,' Em says. 'You honestly didn't see anything?'

Graham shrugs. They stand before this black thing in the fire, the stripe of scorched grass, and Em thinks of Damson's face when she asked her for the truth. And she has to wonder – *have you ever believed in fairies?* Has Em ever believed in fairies at the bottom of the garden?

Because as far as Em could tell – assuming she still reads the girls better than anyone – Damson wasn't lying to her.

PART I

LOOK, DON'T TOUCH

The Steeplejack

Not long after first light, Billy Shepherd, Shep for short, wakes up in the back of his work van. It's a harsh start as mornings go. One side of his face is pressed numb against the cabin bulkhead, and overnight he's spilled a tin of cheap lager inside his sleeping bag. He reaches for his phone, still flashing his missed alarm. He opens the back doors and swings his legs out over the bumper. Before him stand the huddled spires of Clemens, Scarborough's new refinery. He should've been up the nearest chimney an hour ago.

Coughing in the chill, Shep rebuttons his damp overalls, gathers his harness, helmet and tools, and staggers over scrubland to the crew entrance. A sign above the security gate reads, WELCOME TO CLEMENS: A SAFE SITE. Beneath that, SILENCE IS CONSENT.

The site engineer is waiting for Shep near the stack's base, clipboard ready. Around her a thrumming, fibrous copse of colour-coded pipework, cylinders and processing plant. Shep recognises the woman from the site's training videos – an old roughneck, nearing obsolescence. Her face weathered, but her eyes still sharp. She watches Shep approach, sizing him up, then nods down at Shep's waist.

'That a real Stillson in there, lad?'

Shep touches the cold wrench in his toolbelt.

'Oh aye,' she says. 'I'd spot one a mile off. What you doing with that?'

'I found it,' Shep tells her.

The engineer snorts. 'You don't *find* a Stilly, sunbeam. Best not be one of mine.'

Shep shakes his head. 'I was on Fawley before here,' he says. 'Couple of old boys robbed some of Heighter's gear. Divvied it out.'

The engineer goes quiet. She doesn't seem to blink. 'Hmm,' she starts. 'That's about all you could say to make it morally right. But don't feed me fibs. If you were on Fawley, how come you're up here now?'

Shep rubs his jaw.

'And don't act daft, neither,' the engineer says. 'Gaping black hole, that place. Greens go in there and don't come out till they're dead or riddled.'

Shep shrugs with one shoulder. 'It was inspection stuff,' he says. 'A fortnight, right through.'

The engineer whistles. 'Two weeks? And then you got off? Think we'd better watch you, hadn't we?'

Shep grins and slides past her towards the chimney ladder. Looks up along its panelling, the gentle undulation of its length. 'Am I good?' he asks.

'Best be,' the engineer says. 'Since you're an hour bloody late.'

The stack they're commissioning is a four-hundred-foot steely, the newest type. On an old refinery it would be brick and mortar, a hardwood strip running to its summit – with maybe a few forgotten iron dogs, access fixings smoothed into nubs by years of weather. These new ones are modular builds, very fancy, with integrated ladders.

Parallel with the ladder runs Shep's shunt line – his fall arrest system. Further round, the heavy-duty hand line the groundsman uses to run stuff up to the crew on top.

'Best start thinking up excuses for them lot, too,' the engineer says. 'They're waiting on you.'

Shep nods once and checks his toolbelt. Podger, quickdraw clips, carabiners, scaffold spanner, hand-welder. His Stillson – the pipe wrench that makes him feel like a proper jack. In his docs pocket is a signed copy of the crew's method statement, and behind that, with the LEDs he prepared in the van with his final beer last night, there's a pouch of tobacco. Not to smoke, but to trade for coffee on breaks.

'Another reason we start early,' the engineer calls over. When Shep turns, she's pointing into open sky. Soft pink cloud filling slots between Clemens' hard lines. 'It'll be a sunny one today,' she says. 'You creamed up?'

Shep pushes in his radio earpiece and sticks the freckle mic to his cheek. He steps into his harness and lugs it up to his hips. With the main belt secure, the biggest clip comes over his head, fastens across the sternum. Then he double-knots his safety rope for luck. He grips the first rung of the ladder, feels the cold alloy bite back. A kind of symbiosis: the ladder rails coursing up through Shep's hands, airstream-silver and clean as wire. Above him, the early light glowing red on the steel.

'Good to go,' Shep says. And he clips on to the safety line and starts his ascent.

Apprentice steeplejacks get the worst equipment by tradition. So while Shep is generally seen as gifted, he's still treated by the crew as a green – and the gear reflects it. Aside from the harness and helmet (new by law), his overalls hang baggy, his boots give him blisters, and through his earpiece he receives static-shot cuts from the crew on the flying stage and about every third word of the groundsman's updates as he fills the supplies cradle.

'I'm on my way,' Shep tells them.

'Ten men!' someone shouts back through his earpiece. 'About fucking time and all!' From nowhere, something pings off the concrete by Shep's boot. Shep squints. A puff of dust reveals a zinc fastener, still spinning.

'Ten men!' the voice cries. 'It's raining nuts and fucking bolts!'

The engineer starts screaming bloody murder at the crew.

'Shepherd!' the jack's voice comes again. 'If you don't have that Thermos on you, you're going straight down the shit-chute.'

Shep shakes his head and continues, mindful not to overgrip. Gloves or not, the cold will quickly work into your tendons, make a start on your bones.

'He ignoring us?' the jack says. 'He's ignoring us! This fucking space cadet.'

22

'I'm not ignoring you,' Shep says.

'I'm looking down the shitter right now,' the jack says. 'Proper minging in there, pal, absolutely hanging. It'll fit you nicely.'

Shep looks past his toes. The engineer is already thirty feet away, the wind starting to whistle. He goes dizzy momentarily, and his insides tighten. The hangover is kicking in.

'Get on with it, squeaker,' the engineer urges. 'And you gorillas best stop chucking stuff, or the lot of you are off my site by noon.'

So Shep shins on. With no laddering required, it's more like an easy route at the climbing gym. In his sinew, he knows he could solo this height without breaking a sweat. He'd only need his chalk bag, a pair of lightweight shorts. The air on his back, the satisfying smell of his body in motion. Soon he'll be high enough to see the North Sea horizon.

'Late bastards get washed!' the jack shouts. And Shep hasn't time to respond before it begins to rain – a warm and heavy rain that gets under his harness and spreads down his back.

Shep gasps for breath. Then he retches. It isn't rain at all – the jack has just tipped the crew's piss bottle down the ladder.

'What happens when you dick us about!' the jack laughs in his ear.

Shep removes his helmet and wipes his face down his sleeve. The smell. The tepid heat on his skin. He takes it, though – takes it because he has to. What else can he do, dangling there? Another glance down. Wind-reddened hands. Liquid falling away from his helmet. He's two hundred feet up now, and the ladder's lower rungs are no longer visible. The surrounding containers, massive from the ground, are bucket rims. Crew cabins and toilets like matchboxes and dice, casting shadows at right angles. Systems of process line, so intricate and precise you could believe they were lifted from a circuit board. And even at this height, that mingling of gases – eggy hydrogen sulphide, sharp hydrogen peroxide – with a whiff of bitumen, rich and meaty, from the gravy lines. Then to the wider refinery, immense and city-like: its glittering tips, steaming apertures, spider-silk trelliswork. Perimeter mesh already patterned with caramel rust, immense sheets of clean, implacable concrete. Contractors whose hi-vis jackets strobe as they move. Lastly, Shep gazes at the semi-circle of tarp around the stack's base, on which the groundsman is prepping their next load.

'Come on, pal,' a different jack says in his ear. 'We're on our arses waiting.'

Drop a tool from up here and it'll bounce a fair way back up. But if you're not clipped in properly, or the ladder somehow fails, you're only one mistake away from the ground yourself – and your head won't bounce at all.

Mallory Limited – Shep's employer – is northern England's most respected firm for high-access jobs. A professional outfit compared to the cowboys and undercutters, the showboaters like Heighter. In digs, trying to sleep, Shep often hears the older jacks fretting about the robots emerging from Heighter's R&D labs. Gear that might eventually score the bigger contracts. But so what if the competition goes fully automatic? Mallory stands loyal to its affordable but highly skilled steeplejacks, who don't ask for much in the way of upkeep. Give your Mallory crew a problem to solve and that's more or less that. Get your engineer to shout them a pint or six afterwards, and they'll be good for the next day, too.

Besides, no site engineer Shep ever met will ever want a machine doing the work Mallory's jacks specialise in. Most are too nostalgic, caring more about strong hands and beastly thighs. And so on that ladder, three-quarters towards the chimney lip, the rising sun in his eyes, soaked in the piss of several men, Shep isn't worried about robots taking his job. Far better to believe there'll always be thankless people climbing gantries behind the scenes, sliding under surfaces, toiling in the gaps – the phobic spaces between. Far easier to think he'll retire someday and see his broadness go to fat or, if he works in a certain kind of place, on a certain type of contract, develop cancer and bow out early with a nice pile of compensation to blow.

Shep's earpiece crackles. 'Caught you daydreaming again?'

Shep cranes his neck. The corona of a hardhat above. He hauls himself up the last few rungs to meet the old jack waiting there. Gunny. Of all the crew here on Clemens, Shep likes Gunny the most; mid-fifties, sallow, but warm and honest. He says to Gunny, 'Got the LEDs. They're all wired, ready to go.'

'Top man,' Gunny says, and he attaches a quickdraw to

Shep's harness and brings him onto the platform, where Shep clips out and back in to the railings.

On the staging, grimacing against the wind, three of the crew are playing cards, carefully weighting those on the deck with carabiners. Two of them are smoking. The third must be winning. A fourth jack – jangling a handful of fasteners – leers at Shep from his perch on the far side. He's the one. Bolt-dropper, piss-pourer. The arsehole whose name he never caught.

'All right?' Shep says, letting on. 'I've got the lights.'

The arsehole leans across the cathead beam and holds out an empty hand. 'Where's my brew?' he asks, dipping his head towards the waste-chute opening. 'Telling you. This hole's hungry for youth.'

'Leave him be,' another jack called Red mutters from the card game. 'He's decent.'

'He still has to learn,' the arsehole says. He spits straight off the chimney's side. 'These greens, man. They have to learn.'

Shep tips the LED units into the bowl of his hand. 'Should be good to go,' he tells Gunny. 'Soldered them last night.'

'In the back of your van?' the arsehole says.

'Yeah.'

Gunny clears his throat. 'Weren't you in the boozer past last orders?'

'Yeah.'

'Aye, and you look like dogshit,' the arsehole says. 'How's this gonna be a clean job? Why aren't you kipping with us in digs, anyway?'

'Leave him be,' Red says again.

The arsehole smirks. 'You better than us? Is that it? That why you reckon you're ten men?'

Gunny sighs. 'Pack it in.'

'I wouldn't trust this muppet to change a light bulb,' the arsehole goes on. 'Or wipe his own backside, come to that. You don't sleep with the lads, you can't be trusted. End of.'

Gunny looks at Shep. He nods at the LEDs. 'Did you test them?'

'Yeah,' Shep lies. 'All good.'

'Telling you,' the arsehole goes on. 'He's a lazy bleeder. Needs a good slapping about, same as the old days.'

'Did you oversleep?' Gunny asks. 'Honest? You'd had a fair few when I turned in...'

Shep shakes his head. 'Safety had me going over the method statement. Ran my bloods.'

The arsehole huffs.

'Clean, I hope,' Gunny says.

Shep nods, and Gunny claps him on the shoulder. 'You only missed me marking up, anyway. Now we can whack these buggers in.'

Shep follows Gunny to the railings. *N* for north chalked on the first LED boss. He looks out to the Scarborough coastline, the dragging sea, the castle ruins on the hill, then a long way down. Seagulls hunting thermals. The dizziness returns, and Shep's legs nearly go. It tells you something, working above the birds. A reminder this isn't your place.

'Pass 'em here, then,' Gunny says.

Shep gives him one of the LEDs. Holds the wires apart to try and help.

'So,' Gunny says, straightening the wires, 'this is your male and that's your female, and they make sweet love. Like this—'

Shep follows the LED unit into its boss. When it's partway in, Gunny hesitates. 'Oh,' he says, surprised, like there's a small amount of resistance. Like there's muck on the wires. When he goes to speak again, there's a sickly purple flash. A hideous, hot smell fills Shep's nose.

Shep rubs his eyes and can't work out why he's suddenly sitting on the staging, or why Gunny is doubled over, mewling, clutching his right arm at the wrist. Like Shep, Gunny is now half a metre back from the chimney's rim, and it looks like he's trying to put on a red mitten.

Shep's ears ring off. Thick, thick ozone. Red and the arsehole have their arms around Gunny's chest, dragging him further away from the edge. Gunny seems afraid. The jacks' playing cards are fluttering over the edge.

Shep swallows. The air rushes in.

'What did you do?' the arsehole shouts.

Shep gets to his feet, thoughts clotting.

'The LED,' the arsehole says. 'What did you do?'

Shep blinks. A small green flame is burning at the north cardinal point. He looks again to Gunny, who's slumped against the cathead's upright, helmet wonky, face drained. A rope of bright saliva hanging from the corner of his mouth. He has his arm limply over one knee, and a parody of a hand dangles from his sleeve.

The arsehole scowls at Shep. Red and the other jacks, who are holding their faces or leaning on their knees, ashen. Shep sees only the mess before him: bright bone,

28

seared flesh. Gunny's hollow stare.

As the other jacks call it in, the arsehole gives Shep a headshake. 'The state of this,' he says in a quiet, stifled voice. 'The state of it. Poor bastard's got kids to feed – what did you do? What did you do?'

But Shep, with bile in his mouth, doesn't respond. He can't remember how to speak.

The Journalist

Freya Medlock tails the driverless hearse through the town and right up to the church. Somehow she's ended up sixth in the funeral convoy, just two vehicles back from the parents. It's pouring down with rain, and owing to her nerves she's grateful her car is driving itself.

The church stands on the jut of a hill overlooking the Manchester basin. It's a cold hill, harrowed and bald, and the church blends right in. Local gritstone gives it an imposing, almost prehistoric profile. A fitting place to bury someone.

Freya's car parks itself uncomfortably close to the hearse, so Freya waits for the relatives to disperse before getting out herself. She throws up her umbrella, sets her Dictaphone recording in her pocket, and heads for the church entrance. The pallbearers stand off to one side, working out who'll take which corner of the coffin.

A middle-aged woman emerges to greet Freya at the church doors. 'Thank you *so* much for coming,' she says, stoic in the crosswind. 'Stephen's aunt. Are you here alone?'

'A friend from uni,' Freya tells her.

The woman's eyes flash. She smirks.

'Really,' Freya says. 'Just a friend.'

'Well, thank you for coming. Get yourself inside and take your pick. It'll be a sad sight from wherever you're sitting.'

Freya leaves the woman with a tight smile. Round a pillar, and the congregation fills both sides of the nave. Black cloth and blank faces. Freya grabs a space at one end of a pew and doesn't look at the person beside her. The vicar steps forward and clears his throat. 'Ladies and gentlemen,' he starts. 'Please stand.'

They do, and between them comes the coffin, glistening with rain. The pallbearers' shoes are saturated, the floor is uneven, and it's easy to foresee a slip. But as the pallbearers reach the vicar and lower the coffin to its bier, only quiet prevails. On the vicar's word, the congregation settles again, skin grey by the morning's thin light. Nobody quite sure what to do, or where to look, or how they've ended up here.

The congregation have this coffin in common, of course. It carries a friend, relative, lover. Freya has done this enough times now to know they'll each be churning with indignation, fear, stinging disappointment. Nothing will have lessened their confusion so far. No words will have rationalised the suddenness of their loss, or stayed its steady, ceaseless reverberations. They all want closure, believe this day will offer that, but no amount of 'soul-searching' or 'looking out for each other' will have worked to balm the shock. Then there's the resignation, the maxims and the clichés: *life is too short*; *live each day as though it's your last*. Regarding a stranger's coffin, stark and still, Freya always pictures her own funeral, lapsing into negative space. *Isn't a healthy, young person's death about as wasteful as it comes?* The mourners here are massed in a kind of group freefall. They share this air as they visit private memories of the dead man, all plotted on a life that bears his name: Stephen Parsons.

All of the mourners, that is, except Freya.

Freya never knew Stephen Parsons, never met him. But owing to the manner of his death, the arrests of two men despite the coroner having already ruled misadventure, Freya's editor thinks there might be a story here worth attracting the nationals, and has despatched her to the church to pretend she did. So as a fresh hymn begins to rise, swells against the old stone with unaccountable weight, Freya wills herself to concentrate. If the Dictaphone's battery lasts the service – if she steals the eulogies her editor wants her to steal – it'll be easier to win a byline. But if the battery doesn't, she'll need to be alert. Otherwise, tomorrow could mean writing another cheap story for a dribble of ad revenue. Shuffling another five-hundred-word, keyword-rich article closer to obscurity.

The vicar gazes among the pews as the congregation sings. Freya fidgets as he loiters on her a beat too long, even if she's surely anonymous. Her scalp tingles at the idea he might understand her place in all this – that she's a parasite, an ambulance-chaser. Like he'll be hovering over her shoulder when she writes up the story tonight.

Stephen Parsons, 29, a data recovery technician and amateur rock climber from Oldham, Greater Manchester, died on a night out in Leeds after falling from the scaffolding of a city centre redevelopment project—

Freya tries to straighten her back. Her bra's too tight, and when she assumes a better posture her blouse just gapes. She's convinced the person on her right is watching her.

If you look back, your eyes will give you away.

So Freya twists left, looks across the aisle. The adjacent pew is stacked with lean-looking men and women. Stephen's climber friends. The way they stand, the stepping of muscles through their clothes, makes her think about the climbing photos she'd scraped from Stephen's social feeds that morning. In every shot, Stephen was a ballet of limbs caught mid-transition. Committed but grinning, regardless of the route – the *problem*, climbers call them. A grin so at odds with his casket. Shouldn't he be here with these mates, or out there in some blissful wilderness? 'Doing what he loved'? Were some of these climbers caught in Stephen's pictures – obscured by a crop, or just out of focus? Did one of them take those photos of him?

Hundreds of mourners, including many of Stephen's rock-climbing friends, gathered yesterday at the Parsons' family church to pay their respects to a popular man whose death is now being probed by—

The hymn ends. The organ's final note hangs heavy. The congregation sways.

'Please sit down,' the vicar says.

And as the congregation does, a woman in the group of climbers notices Freya and returns a flat stare.

Reverend Falkirk led an intimate service that celebrated Stephen's life—

'To start our service,' the vicar says, 'I want to invite Stephen's brother Toby to share a few words.'

Freya swallows – this could be useful. Toby staggers up to the pulpit. His hands are clumsy as he adjusts the microphone, unfolds a piece of paper. His suit, too large, tumbles away from him. His face is bright with sweat. When he goes to speak – 'My brother…' – a knot tightens in his throat.

The church stills. Freya studies her feet, her dull patent heels. A vein pulsing over the leftmost metatarsal. What does Stephen's body look like now? Waxy and blue? Still grinning? She gets the horrible urge to giggle and coughs for cover. How obscene can she be? As Toby struggles to start again, Freya's conscience needles her. She shouldn't be here, hearing this. Let alone recording it. Her face gets hotter and hotter, and she starts to worry the stranger next to her will feel her heat through the bits of them that touch.

But you need to do this. You need it.

'My brother,' Toby tries again, 'was…'

A long exhalation; a rippling through the congregation.

'You know what, right,' he says, 'bollocks to it. This is the first time our Ste's shut up since I've known him.'

A murmur of anxious laughter in the family pews. Freya glances along the aisle, follows the gravestones towards the coffin, the altar. She smiles, desperate to look normal, correct – even as she feels more and more alien to these people, to Stephen. Her distance from his coffin, that silent box, is starting to make the whole church seem false. A stage set. The vicar's figure, his shadow on the organ pipes, only multiplies the dissonance. When Freya concentrates on him, he takes on the aspect of an illusion – as if turning him would reveal a cardboard cut-out. Panic seizes her. Everyone here can tell. They can see her. She holds in a breath.

South Yorkshire police are currently questioning two men seen with Stephen at the scene—

The person next to Freya taps her arm and offers a tissue with a whisper: 'Need these more than I do.' It's another middle-aged woman. Her face is open and her breath smells like make-up. Freya looks down and blinks; an inky droplet explodes between two buttons of her blouse. She takes the tissue.

'Thank you,' Freya says. Sitting outside herself, now. Where the shame and the guilt can't reach.

In the pulpit, Toby has found his grit. He talks about Stephen's obsessive climbing; his strength and ability; their weekends wild-camping; Stephen's 'urban exploring'; and, when they were both a lot younger, their run-ins with the police. Stephen's upcoming project was Mont Blanc. 'He was forever training for that,' his brother says. Then, partway through an anecdote about Stephen climbing a cliff in Anglesey without any ropes, Freya has had enough. She can't do it. She gets up, clammy, and stumbles towards the doors, realising everyone in the church will cast her as one of Stephen's exes after all.

'And Ste was teetotal,' she hears Toby say. 'So it doesn't even make sense. He'd not touched a drop as long as I remember. Never drank, never smoked, never ate meat. Not in the whole time I knew him, and that was quite a while—'

Freya stops, and realises Toby has stopped too. She glances back. He looks disgusted by her.

Teetotal?

They'd missed this back at the office. The coroner's toxicology report, backhanded to the editor, said Stephen

35

was at least seven times the legal driving limit. He'd had too much, got cocky, taken the risk. But if he was teetotal, why would he drink that much? Was this why those men were arrested – because his family had protested about the inquest's findings?

Freya mouths, 'Sorry.' She wants to stay, to hear more, but it's too late: she's made a scene, drawn attention to herself. She pushes outside. Gulps the damp air. Her fringe is stuck to her forehead. She scuffs her shoes on the path as she goes towards the car and wrestles the door open. Her head is full. Who are the men being interviewed? Was there a suggestion he hadn't fallen, but was pushed? Or had he jumped?

Freya tells the car where to drive her. Unable to shake the questions, the tightness in her chest, she slips back into the leaded margins of the north. Maybe this hasn't been a waste of time. Maybe the questions are enough.

The Steeplejack

After long jobs away, a free weekend can feel to a steeplejack like washing up on a strange island. Friday nights are especially disorientating. If a jack isn't pulling overtime on some power station in the arse-end of nowhere – an industrial plant grafted to a post-industrial town – they might seem listless, lost. Having returned to empty homes or weary partners (dumping rancid overalls and safety gear in the hall), a jack will head straight to their local to decompress. In towns near a firm's headquarters, you'll likely find at least one jack at the bar, focusing on something indistinct, something far away. A remembered view – a vista of concrete, a blackened frame, a row of filthy brick megaliths. A power station lit up like an airport at night.

For Shep, though, this Friday is worse than disorientating. After the blood, the sirens and the horror, he'd left Scarborough under a black cloud. He'd desperately wanted updates from the hospital; to call Gunny's wife; to seek forgiveness – or at the very least to be forgotten. To get his inevitable sacking over and done with. But then his phone died a few miles out, and he realised he'd left his charger in his locker. So, he drove straight to the Pea and Ham.

A few double-vodkas have just about dulled the brightest edges of Shep's guilt. It isn't enough, but it's getting there. Luckily, being alone is also a mercy for Shep. He can escape into his own world this way. That, and coming to the Pea and Ham completes a cycle, because this pub is where Shep met his first boss, Mr Mallory himself.

Everyone knew old Mallory was a steeplejack. You recognised him by his flat cap, hunting vest, Dr Martens. He was a hodgepodge of fashions and eras, though not consciously; it was more like he'd stepped out of time to pick the garments he found most practical. Then there was his size: unmissably squat and wide, without definition or tone, yet solid all the same, his skin the rolled steel that held in the mass of him. You'd likely find him holding forth on politics and politicians – particularly Thatcher, whom he admired vocally despite Mallory's older brother being a Sheffield collier, a foot soldier in the Battle of Orgreave.

Back then, Shep was earnest but terminally unemployed. Every week he collected his dole money and came up to the Ham to ask Mallory if there were any apprenticeships going at the firm. In return, Shep would get the stout nod that came to be a simple appreciation of his tenacity. Mallory would rear back and clink Shep's glass and say, 'Not this week! But let me tell you about a place where only knots matter.'

Then Mallory would relate to Shep a short tale about jacking in the good old days. About felling chimneys with prop fires, which involved taking the side out of a chimney and filling the hole with firewood – deadly sounding for sure, but accurate to the metre. A probably apocryphal story about some jack who climbed a flare-stack for a bet, fell inside and didn't come out before they turned it on again. Or a reminder: only respect people who do things with their hands.

So it was a shock when Mallory gave Shep the yes. The old jack eyed him over the table, didn't clink his glass or nod at him or even move his head. 'No more stories from me,' he said. 'Got an opening for apprentices, and I couldn't bloody well say "this lad down the pub wants in", as I've never heard your bloody surname. But if you do, Billy – want in, that is – then you do. The gates to paradise are open.'

Mallory died a few months after that, with his son Mallory Junior taking over the firm. A heart attack, so the barman told Shep. Afterwards, whenever Shep went up to the Ham, he would take his old boss's seat, heir to the bosun's throne.

Still. That's history. That's a story. And right now, there's no one Shep resents more than old Mallory, because Shep has soiled that story by maiming a crewmate he respected.

Which means Shep only has his other life to live.

He turns his glass, picturing Gunny's mangled hand. The pub lights warm and diffuse. What Shep needs now is an opportunity, and some opportunities you have to make for yourself.

Using the pub's payphone, a living relic, Shep dials a number.

'Oh,' a man answers. 'You're eager.'

'Are you working?'

'Not tonight, Josephine.'

'Your other work. Have you got anything for me?'

'Depends. How long can you hang about?'

'I'm not going anywhere.'

The line dies. Shep finishes his drink and orders another. A little after nine, a broad man lumbers up to the bar. He's holding a battered laptop base, and laughs when he sees Shep.

'Christ,' the man says, rubbing his cheek. 'Tough week, or what?'

Shep ignores the question.

'Got a tasty proposition,' the man says. 'One I mentioned a while back.'

And Shep nods like a dog, like he's forgotten Clemens and Gunny already. Five vodkas down and he's finally fit to escape. The broad man has just lowered a ladder.

The thing is, Shep is a spare-time urban explorer. That means he breaks into forbidden places – mansions and bunkers and mothballed industrial plants – then writes about them online. Exploring these places isn't that simple. It's lonely and dangerous and highly criminalised; it takes obsession and preparation; it demands good intelligence. You have to guard your sources jealously.

'Meet me in the bogs,' Shep tells the man. 'Five minutes.'

The broad man is Shep's favourite source of tips. A freelance drone operator who pulls unsociable hours airdropping for Tescaldi, and most Fridays comes up from his festering cell for a gin and tonic. Shep wonders if the droner knows what time it is, if his shift work merges the days into an unbroken line of wakefulness and sleep. But if the droner is tired or vitamin-deficient – he's certainly an off colour – he still finds enthusiasm for Shep.

'I like it when you talk dirty,' the droner says, and he slopes away to the gents.

Shep sucks air through his teeth. Downs his drink. The droner isn't the type he usually interacts with. Not if he isn't using them. Like the old man Mallory, Shep finds remote-working repulsive, pathetic. Over-automated, too removed from what he understands to be proper work. And yet the droner's tips are golden. Thousands of hours of remote-flight time have given him an unmatched knowledge of the north's hidden geography, and helped him develop a knack for the tease. Using hacked map data, he sells illicit images of sites to urban explorers, salvagers, environmentalists wanting to keep tabs on developments. Even the odd doomsday prepper.

The droner had recently told Shep about a rural installation in the Lake District, and Shep had asked for a second look. Now, laptop bag open in the pub toilets, the droner delivers: aerials of the site – hints of concrete, old foundations, sagging walls – with esoteric markings and annotations in wipeable ink. It ticks Shep's boxes, but it's the final print that seals the deal: a ragged clearing in which some sort of light aircraft has crashed and broken up. Vehicle tracks, boot holes. Maybe some attempt to tidy the place up.

'How the hell did you spot this?' Shep asks.

The droner taps his nose. 'Call it the Touch.'

'Implants, more like.'

The droner laughs. 'Your eyes learn. Like screen-burn on an old plasma. I don't see like you normies – not any more.'

'How do I get in?'

'West Lakes,' the droner says, wheezing a little. He produces a ruined A to Z and taps along the Cumbrian coast, then drags his finger inland. 'Go in *here* for a clean run. There's a marina in Whitehaven with long-stay parking. Easy-ish access – there's a hiking trail to here, then you're off-piste to the perimeter.'

Shep pictures the drab bulk and rocky footing of Scafell Pike, England's highest mountain. He sets it against infinite space, with Wastwater Lake below – mirror-flat, long shores hued orange by campfire. Though it feels like years ago, he was bouldering up there recently. 'Is it guarded?' he asks the droner.

'Private, quiet,' the droner says. 'No dogs or sentries.'

Shep grimaces. Quiet doesn't always mean good. The authorities could still stuff you on terror legislation for trespassing or 'preparing an attack' – exactly how they bag tourists taking photos of landmarks. And that's only half the equation. Shep once knew a woman who fell through a rotten roof on a quiet mission and copped for a broken pelvis. It took Mountain Rescue three nights to find her, except animals had found her first.

'Anything else?' the droner asks.

'Nah,' Shep says. 'Unless you've sold these elsewhere.'

The droner tuts. A gleam of wet brown teeth. 'Really? You have to check?'

Shep shakes his head. 'You know how it goes. I'll do this next, anyway. Before some other bastard gets the chance.'

And then, maybe then, out there in the nothingness, he'll forget about Gunny's hand.

'Ace,' the droner says. 'And seriously – on my mam's grave – you've got first dibs.'

'A bunker,' Shep says.

'A bunker. It's a hundred for these exactly.'

Shep pays the droner in dirty notes and leaves the toilet with a map drawn on a paper napkin. He drains his drink, nods bye to the landlord, and heads outside.

Back in the van, Shep sits and memorises the map's lines. Sticks the van in auto and keys in home.

On the way, he chews the napkin map into a paste. Then he throws his dead work phone out of the window with it. What matters now is leaving, heading north to that raw coast, with its blasted grass and filthy beach. No Gunny there – only the roiling green sea.

The Journalist

Home for Freya is her parents' bungalow in Dillock, a dying market town in the elbow of a valley between Sheffield and Manchester. Nothing much changes in Dillock except the cost of charging your car, and being back there makes Freya feel like she's regressed.

Hearing the lock jangle, the door squeak open, her mother peeps around the kitchen doorframe. 'Hiya love,' she calls down the hall. Their little weekday subroutine. 'Good day?'

'Hi,' Freya calls back.

'What's up with you, then?'

'Knackered,' Freya says, coming into the kitchen. A few seconds' silence as she stares at the pallet of milk cartons on the breakfast bar. 'And homesick.'

'Sorry?'

'Just muttering.' But homesick is right enough: she mourns the city centre flat she shared with her ex. The lack of questioning. The absence of an unspoken curfew. Even the freedom to eat whenever. Suddenly angry with

44

herself, she kicks off her shoes against the skirting board. There's a faint smell of soil, and a set of boot prints leading into the study.

'Dad in there?' Freya asks. 'I've got a bit more to do, really.'

'Playing one of his games,' her mother says. 'Eat your tea first. It's in the microwave. Stroganoff...' She gestures to the back. 'Not as good as usual, he tells me, but I'm saying top ten.'

'Mum...'

'What, the milk? It's ridiculous, isn't it? The sodding fridge ordered it without my say-so, and the Tescaldi girl could only goggle when I told her it wasn't us. I still don't understand the future.'

'No. I mean you don't have to fuss.'

Freya's mother frowns. 'I only want to help.'

'I'm thirty.'

'Yes, and you're still my baby. Now, do you want to tell me why you look so preoccupied? Dickhead's not been in touch, has he?'

Freya pouts. Her shoulders ache.

'Come on,' her mother says, patting the stool at the breakfast bar. 'You'll waste away.'

Freya huffs as her mother starts the microwave.

'You're working too hard,' her mother goes on. 'Way too hard. It's not going to... it's hardly going to make things better.' From the study comes the sound of a computer mouse being slammed about. Freya's mother rolls her eyes. 'I keep telling him. Why doesn't he upgrade to all this haptics stuff your cousin prattles on about? He takes chunks

45

out of the desk, then moans at me… Tell me about your day while I load the dishwasher.'

'Court reporting,' Freya says. 'Minshull Street. Bog-standard, really. A carjacking, a retina theft.'

Her mother raises her eyebrows. Lying to her is a bad habit, a means to insulate Freya, a barrier against guilt. It also stops her from indulging a secret excitement. When it comes to seedy assignments like recording Stephen Parsons' funeral, there is – always has been – a sense of getting away with something. Now, with this teetotal thing, she's hungry to find out more, and it's hard to care what her parents are doing. She keeps wanting to—

The microwave dings.

Freya leans over the breakfast bar. She can still smell the coldness of the church on her clothes. Once more she imagines Stephen alive – he's climbing, elongated on a wall, hips twisted and navel turned out.

'Bit of luck,' Freya tells her mother, 'I'm trying to get a byline. Might even be a leader. So then you can read about how my day went.'

Her mother beams. 'Oh, see. Isn't that special?'

Freya flashes a false smile. Her name hasn't been in print since the Metrolink crash in Hyde six months ago – and that was only for 'additional reporting' because she vox-popped some pensioners who'd sat and watched the fire engines for something to do.

After a cheap potted pudding in front of rolling news, Freya kicks her father, grumbling, from the study. She sits at his vintage Mac and spends a while trawling job feeds. As usual, the North West is barren – most writing jobs outside London are subcontracted to content mills in low-rent enterprise parks – but she's too bitter to expand her search to the capital, despite it being the only place to step up career-wise. She resigns herself to transcribing what she recorded at Stephen's funeral, then types up the shorthand she'd jotted down as the car brought her home. She checks her phone: the editor still hasn't replied to her messages about the police interviews.

Why would a teetotaller go out on a bender?

Ten o'clock swings round, and Freya's article sits there half written. There isn't much heft to it – none of the sentiment she wanted to get across, anyway. But no matter. That's not the point, and Freya going to the funeral is only the start of a process. The heavy stuff starts here, when the follow-up teams go hounding Stephen's relatives for magazine features. She rubs her eyes. Does it rankle that she doesn't do death-knocks any more? She'd love the chance to ask them a few things herself. To find out where the tensions are, and where she could push.

Freya prints the doc and checks it for passive language, clunky phrasing. It scans fine. It's fine. She could probably crowdsource something more, some extra ballast, but it's too late and next to impossible from home. She recently deleted her social stream in a fit of isolationism – a protest at narcissism, albeit her own. After she moved back in with her parents, it was feeling like everything she posted online was written by imagined committee, and that anything even remotely controversial – like, say, an

47

opinion – would damage her prospects if she ever went freelance. Or land her on a blacklist. Freya knows plenty of reporters who've been ushered out of press conferences, escorted from swanky dinners, doxxed and threatened with rape and assorted violence. The picture editor, with whom she'd had the brief affair that scuttled her long-term relationship, was actually recognised and beaten up as he cycled home from her flat one night.

And there he is again. Her ex. *Dickhead*, as her mother calls him, not knowing the full truth. Months on, Freya still views what happened to their relationship as a disruption in the surface tension of normality, a corruption of what she expected from the world. Their split came with the resonance of finding a lump, or discovering an unsettling family secret. When it had finished flailing and flensing, and she pawed at her stomach, where the pain was always worst, she found that a kind of hole had been torn there. Somehow, a false life had poured through this hole to smother her. From that point onwards she'd watched as her true, intended life spooled away on a different trajectory.

Through the bungalow's grey windows, she sometimes glimpses a ghost of what they might've been. Freya and Dickhead sitting together on a train that appears from nowhere, runs parallel with the house for a moment, then vanishes again.

Soon it's eleven o'clock. Freya's parents head to bed – flicked light switches, twice-flushed toilet, toothpaste spit – and a dead calm renders the bungalow's windows a shade blacker. She gives up trying to improve her Stephen piece and files it remotely.

Instead of logging off, though, Freya replays the recording from the funeral. Listens again to Stephen's brother. 'And Ste was teetotal,' he's saying, above a clacking that must be Freya's heels on the aisle stone. 'So it doesn't even make sense. He'd not touched a drop as long as I remember…'

Freya kneads her cheeks. It still doesn't sit right, even if there's nothing really to go on. She reloads the browser. Muscle memory for the same sites she'd checked only a couple of hours earlier: her paper's website, her agency feeds, an inbox full of press releases, tomorrow's weather forecast (damp). A list of unaffordable flats and flat-shares back in Manchester. A notification for a dating app on which someone has called her a slag for ignoring his sepia-filtered dick-pic.

New tab. New search. And before Freya can second-guess herself, Stephen's digital life fills her screen again. His public stream, uploads, shared videos and links – mundane statuses that owing to his death now phosphoresce with meaning.

Freya reads the sad messages left by his friends, a community missing one of its own. Very public tributes, lovely most, alongside stunted notices of confusion and shock. The sort of messages she's seen a thousand times over in her job. But no one here appears to challenge what's happened – the oddness of a fit, clean-living man dying such a filthy death. Not the way she *wants* them to, anyway, and certainly not the way Toby had started to in his eulogy. The disconnect is jarring to her, as if the facts have been too readily accepted. Or perhaps it's awkwardness. Everybody's thinking it, but nobody wants to speak ill of the dead.

Deeper she goes – searching her way into archived forums, cached pages – until she begins to make out the scene's boundaries. She's riveted by the language – familiar words used unfamiliarly, slang like 'pumpy' and 'jugs' and 'smear' and 'beta'. She's thrilled by the rigour – so many tutorials on knots and rock types and grades, essays on home treatments for parts of the body she's never heard of. It leaves her breathless, reeling, jealous of the sport's physicality. People honing their bodies as you might a cutting tool. What does she have, except for her regular desk and a subsidised car?

The church recording also reminds Freya that Stephen's hobby crossed into urbex. The overlap is obvious, now she's learning. In his stream, some friends talk about how they went on 'explores' with Stephen. His ballsiness. His sense of fun. That bloody *grin*. And then she's leaning forward to learn another set of terms: 'missions' and 'reports', obscure acronyms for security measures from boards that index mission reports by location, building type and difficulty.

By half-midnight, Freya has a headache coming on. She purges her session and sneaks to her room, thinking about the church as she undresses – her calm deception as she'd spoken to Stephen's aunt outside. From her single bed, she circles back to Toby and the men who'd been arrested. She falls asleep picturing Stephen's face, his brow and jaw, and finds herself wishing Stephen hadn't died at all. This other world – his world – has gripped her. She wants to ask him what happened. Did you fall, Stephen, or did you jump?

The Steeplejack

The Cumbrian coast smells carnal. Shep goes the long way round, leaving the van in Whitehaven's marina before riding his scrambler along the seafront, visor up and helmet full of brine.

Off the main trunk road, away from lapping black seawater and into the Lakes proper, the scrambler's headlamp picks out tight verges on a narrowed beam. Shep threads through country lanes, rattling in and out of villages, skirting farmland trenches, towards the dark mass of Scafell Pike. He crests a hill bounded by starlit fields, and catches sight of the uplands that define the territory. Inscrutable fells like waves at the world's edge.

There, Shep stops at a T-junction to drink water and boot his nav system. His eyes are streaming from the wind, and he's already sweating in his leathers. He retightens his Bergen straps as he waits. It doesn't look like the nav will catch a signal here, so he slides down his visor and sets off again, half an eye on the square of noise the nav projects on the visor's interior. The waterline is now well behind him, and the air has turned bitter. Nettles and berries. He rides deeper into parkland, the road wet and sinuous, and soon the woods' canopy interlaces above – a different kind of nature swallowing him whole.

Forty-five minutes after leaving the marina, Shep meets his first waypoint: a privatised trail. He manhandles the scrambler through a tight stile and floors it over a pedestrianised apron, grinning madly. Beyond that, another stile for a service road that intersects the hiking trail at several points, its fresh surface quieter under the tyres. For a time, he follows the service road with minimal revs. Cautious so far as the rattly scrambler engine allows. While the risk of being caught is offset by the excitement of exploring a potentially virgin site, it's odd to Shep that the site lies so close to a commercial trail. Why weren't there other reports on the forums?

Another mile along, Shep pulls over and leaves the bike idling. The nav's proving useless, so he takes out his OS map and leans over the headlamp to pencil a path. An animal call pierces the night. The sound is muffled and strange through his helmet, so he kills the engine, switches on his torch and scans the treeline for movement.

Nothing. Shep exhales. Shivers a little. The scrambler's motor ticks as it cools, and these might be the only sounds in the world. It's lonely out here, and with that comes the first sharp chill of terror. A primal fear – not only of the dark, the unseeable woodland – but of other people: holed-up drug-runners, bear-headed homeless who don't want moving along, illegal poachers or preppers with twitchy trigger fingers. Never mind the risk of falling masonry, bad roofing, unstable flooring. Fall over, do for your ankle, then what? No phone, nobody in on the act, no means of contact – who knows where you are?

That same strained noise again. Shep's ears buzz with it. An animal call, definitely, and not a bird. There's a rustling, then movement in the near distance. This time behind him, like he's being circled. Warily, Shep goes to dismount the bike and feels a small object, hard and cold, tumble from his neck to the small of his back. He loses his balance and has to hop away from the scrambler, which falls over with a ringing crash. Swearing under his breath, Shep heaves off his helmet, his racing jacket, his overshirt. Drags his T-shirt out of his waistband. There's a faint click as the object comes free and meets the ground.

Shep kneels to the road. Trapped in his torch beam is a large, intricately striped beetle, an inch or so long. It's writhing on its side. It doesn't have antennae, or a head, or even most of its legs at that. Its back arches unnaturally, acutely, the panels of its carapace spaced to extremes, until it stops moving. For an instant Shep thinks it might be playing dead.

'Jesus,' he whispers. And on impulse he draws his boot forward and stamps on it.

Shep stands up, shaken. Checking nothing is embedded in his neck, no mouthparts or barbed legs or otherwise. Checking the beetle is really dead before he sorts himself out. Checking there's nothing watching him from the treeline. He wants to piss, now. Hyperalert, eyes straining and darting from one shadow to the next. His breath ragged.

Nightmares can easily mass in the blackness just out of reach, out of sight: things imagined and things real. Now he's throwing on the shirt, the jacket. Shivers coming on strong. *Was* it just the helmet? Sounds change when your ears are squashed. But the call was so loud. Another glance at the beetle's remains, a paste, and Shep's hairline itches madly. *Jesus Christ.* It was hardly a threat, this stupid creature – but he loathes the idea it touched him, that it got in through the gap between his helmet and jacket collar. And it was of a size as to be otherworldly, definitely a kind he's never seen before. He straps on his helmet with his torch between his teeth and heaves up the scrambler. He needs to move, and now – before he bottles it.

The scrambler coughs on with a firm kick. The headlamp flickers and holds. Shep focuses on the lit-up foliage in front. Leaves and branches. Natural things. Dead things…

Off the service road, the earthen trail winds away in gentle switchbacks. He holds to that ribbon of civilisation like nothing else. He reminds himself that you often see pacemaker detectors at the trailheads; that some officious twat will turn you back if they think you'll keel over on their patch. They'd never let people hike here if there were any real risks involved.

But Shep isn't hiking – he's breaking in. He sniffs hard. His nose is running and his eyes are full. He needs to get on top of this. Get a grip. His next waypoint isn't much further – another few hundred metres before he strikes out into woodland proper. He's too close for second thoughts. Too committed. He sets his jaw and twists the throttle. The scrambler digs in. He pushes up the stand.

A chirpy jingle plays right into his head.

Shep bursts out laughing. Intravenous relief. 'You took your time,' he says.

The nav makes a noise like a seeping fart, then slurs, 'Coordinates unrecognised.'

'Unrecognised' being an understatement. Shep's helmet contains the brains of a driverless car, complete with inboard sensors and head-up display. The sensors will parse his facial muscles, but the brain won't suss that it's been repurposed entirely.

'No response,' the nav says. 'Please confirm: are you driving manually?'

Shep twists the throttle harder.

Another beat, a faint rattling of machine-thinking above the scrambler's whine. 'Anonymity is illegal,' the nav tells him.

'That's the point,' Shep replies.

'This vehicle's warranty and insurance will be remotely invalidated.'

Shep smirks. The transplant means he's fully dark out here, with a kill switch on his phone to brick the system if it comes to it. Whatever the nav thinks it's capturing, it's mistaken. Wherever the nav thinks they're going, it's already lost.

'Shush now,' Shep says, and hits mute. The nav's wayfinder has started to render directly from a satellite, which is enough to go by. He leaves the beetle and the service road for the last section of trail. In turn he slides deeper into his zone, into reduction, driven by base urges towards some personal wilderness. The hiccup back there is soon forgotten, and so too is the stack, Gunny and his hand, and the blood. There's no doubt, then: Shep's basest urge is to be alone, to cross over and seek the stuff left hidden in plain view. Swap his disintegrated work life for the forgotten places, the vaults of memory. Now he can enjoy once more how nature has changed the past.

When the undergrowth gets too thick to ride through, Shep stops the scrambler and starts to push. By his reckoning, the perimeter wall is another hundred feet through the woodland. There, as a last rite, he goes to relieve his bladder against an oak. Except it won't happen. Even as he tries and squeezes and wills himself to go, his erection says he's far too eager for that.

The Journalist

In her single bed in the box room, Freya dreams of Stephen. He comes to her as a loose collage of the images she'd scraped from his stream, which means pieces of his head are missing or deformed. These blank spaces reveal internal edges and planes that don't join up properly; each frame of him crashes into the next, cycling hair lengths and expressions. He glitches towards her, skin gleaming, so that by her feet he lacks all consistency. He smells overripe. He strokes her ankles. His fingers vibrate. 'What grade are you?' he asks, probing her shins and knees, before his mouth seals up completely. He opens a small canvas bag and plasters his hands with chalk, and begins to climb her, fingertips strong and pointed, deep between her tendons. It doesn't hurt so much as it aches. Then his hands are around her waist, his toes splayed on her feet. His face, his sealed mouth, warm and gainful, disappears into her lower abdomen. A tearing sound as he tries to open his jaw, a stuttering as he tries to kiss her on the mound of her pants. She looks away as the kisses grow forceful, sloppy with blood and mucus, and he starts to break open his own face, his whole head. Wider, then wider again.

Freya snaps awake with the fear that a part of her is trapped in another world. The rotting smell lingers briefly, trapped between here and there.

'No,' she whispers, because she's touching herself. Her fingers molten and the sheets stuck to her.

Gritty-eyed, ashamed, she goes to the toilet. By the time she's flushed, dream-Stephen has lost his primacy, her guilty arousal replaced by the cold morning, her mind moving on to the office. A sadness blooms in her, and she clutches her temples like it might stem the spread. Her hair is dense and waxy, like rough fur, and she stamps a foot in frustration. A final vision of Stephen – the contact of their skin with only chalk as a barrier – and the sadness folds away.

Freya goes to the sink. She brushes her teeth warily, because she's been spitting blood for a few days. After the dream, her mouth feels different, senses still glowing. She hangs there in the simplicity of it, naked before the mirror, light drawing around her, and watches her blood expand in the toothpaste foam. She spits again. A red emulsion, bright and elastic. She thumbs her gumline and a wire of pain spreads along her jaw. She looks at her thumb. A perfect rubine print.

Freya swears and showers and shaves. Moisturises while she's still damp. Dresses and eats a slice of dry toast over the kitchen sink, zoning out on the crooked bird table, a wood pigeon watching her from the fence. It's too early for work, for her parents to be up, but she leaves a *see-you-later* note and goes regardless – driving the car manually to the industrial estate with her mouth sore and abdomen still tingling.

The same landmarks. The same signs. The same vague greetings from the car park security man. Yet today is different. She has a line of shorthand in mind: *Stephen climbed my edges.*

Freya wedges the car, clips back her fringe, applies some warpaint.

The office smells greasy, the leftovers from a sub-editor's late night. Freya mouths hellos to a few other early-birds and sits down at her workstation. As her system comes on, she idly rotates her chair from side to side.

A door rattles, and the editor rolls in. Bangles and heels in chorus. Freya glances along the row of desks, then back to her own. Where her colleagues keep family portraits and tacky trinkets, she only has a labelled stapler and a pot of black biros, a sun-bleached crib sheet of proofreading symbols. Even her friend Aisha's desk, vacant since the day after the Christmas party, is still covered in glitter. She'll tell herself it's so she's ready to leave, so there's nothing to miss, but the months keep passing.

Freya prints last night's copy and heads for the editor's office. She knocks on the door.

'Yep?'

Freya pushes in.

'The wanderer returns!'

'Hey,' Freya says, hovering on the threshold.

'How did you get on?' the editor asks.

'Pretty good, yeah.'

'And you didn't feel too dirty.'

Freya shrugs.

'Did much worse for a story in my day,' the editor says. She motions to Freya's hand. 'That your copy?'

'Yeah. I figured you'd want a quick look.'

The editor taps her desk. 'Way ahead of you, actually – saw you file last night. Very tidy stuff, Freya. Spotless, in fact. I'm expecting first syndications in the next half hour. Bunch of nationals on for the ten o'clock briefing. Even got a French mag interested – you know this lad had climbing pals over there? A busy day ahead.'

Freya blinks. 'Really?'

'Why not? There's interest in the man – climbing's like clickbait since that Olympic gold. Add some tragedy, a couple of arrests, and away you go.' Then, with a mocking smile: 'I knew this one had legs. He'll capture the nation's hearts.'

'He was popular, definitely,' Freya says. 'Hundreds at the service.'

'There you are, see. It all goes off when you're an adventuring middle-class boy, killed in your prime. Close your eyes tight enough, and you can actually hear the papers voiding the shelves…'

'So—'

'You'll get your byline, yes.'

Freya gapes, mortified. 'I meant—'

'Anything else you need to run by me?'

'Actually, yes. I was thinking… I thought—'

'Spit, woman.'

'I wanted to try and take the follow-up. I want to dig on the men who were arrested. It's why I chased you last night.'

The editor shakes her head. 'Can't. I spoke to our friends in the force. They were released without charge in the early hours. There's nothing there – the poor blokes were only trying to talk him down. Apparently all the CCTV footage shows Parsons drinking alone. He wasn't spiked, that is. Wasn't led astray.'

'Talk him down?'

'Yes.'

'He looked like he'd jump?'

'Oh God, no. Everybody is unequivocal on that. The witness statements say he was laughing. He slipped.'

Freya shakes her head. 'Then why question these blokes about it?'

'I asked the same. The theory was that they were encouraging him. Goading him. Evidently, some wires have been crossed.'

'Then I need to tweak the copy before you send it out. It mentions the arrests.'

'No. The men are staying anonymous, so their arrests are good colour. Keeps it lively. Keeps it sellable. You'd probably be cutting a good reason we're syndicating.'

'But it's not up to date…'

'It was true while you were at the service, and true while you wrote it. The whole piece is about the service. Come on.'

'What about his climbing buddies? I could interview some of them, get their take. See if he was, you know. Struggling.'

The editor smiles, thin-lipped. 'He didn't jump – he didn't even die *climbing*. He died of bravado. You saw the toxicology. Silly boy gets himself wasted and off he shuffles. Sob stories are best left to the features team.'

'But this is the thing. At the funeral, Stephen's brother said he never drank. Ever. We didn't know that, did we? And I think that's why the police started looking into who he was out with. Why they still picked up these two blokes after the inquest was closed. His parents must've kicked up a fuss. It was clearly out of character.'

The editor raises an eyebrow. 'Should I be surprised by your rigour, Freya? It's still not enough. A man lets his hair down? The mind is there for changing. What's your hook?'

'Okay, fine. But on top of that, he was into this urbex thing. That's fascinating on its own.'

The editor scrunches up her face. 'Urb-what?'

'Just something about it,' Freya goes on. 'I can't properly explain.'

'Yes, but what is it? What's urbex?'

'Uh, urban exploration. Breaking into old stuff – manmade structures. Buildings, towers. All sorts. They share photos, video. Drone footage. You know those tiny fish-eye cameras they use? Picture desk would love it. You could easily do a feature, popular local sites – stuff like that.'

The editor straightens up. 'You're gushing, Freya. Who's "they"?'

'There are whole forums of it, people sharing tips and mission reports. I was pulling tributes from Stephen's stream, and there was—'

'Missions?'

'Yeah. I'd hardly heard of it before, and—'

'On private land? Is that legal?'

Freya shakes her head. 'No. That's my point. The police went zero tolerance on it a couple of years back. Couple of schoolkids slipped off a tower crane in Liverpool.'

'And you think these people would actually welcome the press?'

Freya bites her lip. 'I don't know.'

'Well, we don't mind a challenge, granted. But it's tenuous at best. Why would we ask you to cover illegal activities, in this climate? Never mind that there's a whole team ready to follow up with his nearest and dearest. Why are you so interested, anyway?'

'I just thought if I did a good job, there'd be a chance I could—'

The editor holds up a finger and glances at her desk. 'Looking at the schedule,' she says, 'nobody's covering obits today. We've also got the mayor of Stockport opening a mindfulness spa at two. You'd manage both, wouldn't you?'

Freya looks down at her copy. The paper wrinkling in her hands. 'But on this urbex stuff… did you want me to…'

'Moonlight? Not especially.'

Freya nods.

'Let's catch up in a bit, then, shall we?' the editor says, smiling thinly. 'I'll forward the syndication results when they come in, so you're in the loop. And get yourself a coffee on me, please – it's a good day's work, that.'

'One for the portfolio,' Freya says.

The editor snorts. Freya gets the feeling she doesn't even watch her leave. But where the editor's cynicism usually puts Freya in her place, she doesn't want to recoil this time. In the short walk to her workstation, she makes up her mind. Fuck the follow-up team – and fuck writing obituaries. She'll find out what happened to Stephen Parsons herself.

The Steeplejack

Shep can pull chins on a doorframe with only his little fingers, so the ten-foot brick wall at the bunker's site boundary is as easy as it comes. He runs at the slab of it and springs both-handed to its coping stone, hauling himself up in one fluid motion.

Standing on that skinny border, he already has to manage his breathing. The site beyond the wall is a lightless pool. He pulls on his dust mask and headtorch and quickly double-checks the scrambler and helmet are covered by the bushes. He sweeps his torch across the site. Vague outlines emerge: the ruined foundations and strewn masonry of a levelled outbuilding, the crude parallelogram of the bunker's concrete entrance. His heart is going, and his breath rasps through the mask filter. He shakes out his arms and sweeps the torch vertically. Mechanical parts are scattered between him and the bunker door. He turns off the torch to wait and check. The stars glower through the canopy.

This, then, is the edge. Balanced with one arm, rocking over on himself, Shep twists the torch back on and looks for a place to land on the other side. *Imagine you're standing on a ledge of cold, wet slate.* His toes pulse with strain as he leans over. At the wall's base is a concrete border studded with broken glass, rusty nails and metal offcuts. He nods. Faint nausea like an affirmation. In some ways he expected worse than sharps – substandard measures, really – but figures the bunker being hidden counts in his favour. Dogs and glue traps are standard in more built-up areas, and sonic barriers aren't out of the question. Not that sharps are easy, mind – he's definitely taken some tetanus shots in his time.

Shep sits on the wall and unties his bootlaces. The torchlight falls onto him, jangling between his knees as he swaps the boots for rubber darts, a bit like covered ballet pumps. He stretches out the rubber with his toes, then folds the boots into his Bergen. He turns off his headtorch, transfers his weight over his knees and launches from the wall's inside.

The breach is on.

Shep goes low through the grounds, closing on the sloped concrete lintels of the bunker entrance. A sharp thrill to find its surfaces unspoiled by graffiti. He gathers pieces of machine debris and wraps them with canvas strips, a bin bag for rain cover. He straps this bundle to his rucksack and takes out his ageing camera. Dicey, pausing here, so he reconsiders and continues towards the bunker entrance. Drilled. Trained. Alone by design. There he takes two flashless pictures of the land he crossed, as level as he can manage. The first in RAW format to fiddle with later, the second stabilised but overexposed to get an impression of his surroundings. He reviews them: grainy, yes, but useful. Nothing stands out, even as nothing is familiar. The aerials he saw in the pub toilet have no relationship with the terrain. Then he twists on the torch again. The darkness jumps back thirty yards.

There's a codebox on the door shell, so he applies a skeleton-string. A mechanism stirs and the door clunks open, soil raining from the frame. The smell of must and metal. Shep takes out a wooden stopper and wedges the door.

The bunker's entranceway gapes, wet and warm. Oesophageal. Pale stones under a well-worn earthen path, which in the torchlight resemble fossils. Shep's leading foot brings him out of the wind. He has his hands on the walls, and his skin crawls at the sound of dripping, the wind across the entrance. His tongue thick in his mouth. Now only the habit will keep him down here. Practice and persistence. He can't see what's dripping, and that makes it louder. Another set of deep breaths to try and slow things down before he creeps on. One step. Two. As he rounds a corner the wind dies off completely, and the Lake District is gone. He's crossed a second boundary, and the acoustics change with it. He's vaguely conscious of his eyes watering.

Shep soon reaches a vaulted antechamber, as dark and indefinite as the site appeared from up on the wall. Brown fluid leaks from what might be a run of shower fittings in the roof. The pools beneath crackle and splash. There's still no graffiti.

When he hears a weak scratching, he stops.

To deal with fear, you have to reimagine the threat. So because Shep can't shut his eyes, won't dare, he tries to do just that – remodels the space as the foyer of a hotel, connecting to a corridor that leads off towards its suites. If he holds his headtorch at a certain angle, the rough floor passes for carpet. He puts a hand to the slick wall, and smells again the age of the place, the stagnancy. His breath, condensing on the mask, has started running down his chin.

As Shep goes to wipe his eyes, he stumbles on something soft. He cries out, then gags himself with his sleeve. The scream echoes, travelling deep inside, and his back ripples with cold trepidation. *Look, don't touch.* Just beyond his vision, an animal flutters. It makes an injured-sounding moan of its own. 'Shit,' Shep breathes. And with that, the rasping pinballs from hidden wall to hidden wall, then comes at him. A thought exploding, taking his oxygen: *It's charging.* Shep braces, wanting badly to shit, but the animal veers round him. A glimpse of it moving low and fast. He tries to follow its trajectory, the ticking, and half expects a set of eyes to be glinting back from the gloom – a bird? A cat? Nothing enters his cone of torchlight. He taps the wall to try and coax the creature forward. See it, confront it. He taps again. Nothing. He's twitching, aware of the sweat between his toes, his buttocks, the heat behind his ears. 'Fuck off,' he whispers, and fires his camera flash once to saturate the corridor ahead.

In that whited-out instant, there are no animals. Instead, he glimpses what occupies the bunker. Walls covered with creeping plants and moss, gnarled shadows, flaking paint. Mineral deposits forming tiny stalactites in the pitted roof.

Spider webbing strung wall-to-wall. Is it a blast shelter? Some paranoiac's bolthole? He fights a rising gullet to carry on, loose straps tapping his wrapped salvage. This is the stuff you struggle to put in your reports. The smell. The taste. The way your body will make itself smaller until your back aches with tension. The marble of moulding fabrics. The colour of standing water. The alien heaviness of equipment left in corners under tarp, lost to the appetite of nature's little helpers. Obsolescence and entropy twine and knot in these back pockets of little England. In them brick and vegetation fuse and grow together, form a kind of subterranean nervous system. Exploring is exhilarating because you never know how a changed environment will react to your presence. It scares you in some vital way, and you can never fail to be scared, because exploring is fear itself.

The tapping starts again. Closer. Wet, somehow. Shep is certain of being stalked. Teeth wait in the blankness with a kind of uneven breathing – hoarse and laboured. He listens and knows this. In any sane world, it should be the end of his mission. But he's come too far.

How about I give you a fright?

Shep slaps the nearest wall, hard. To his horror, the wall gives. A plastic beam, a strip light casing, falls down from the roof and sweeps the torch clean off his head.

Shep is dropped into blackness, laid out flat and covered in dust. A wounded howl rises on all sides of him. He wants to get up, but the torch is face down, unfindable, not even a soft halo to place it, and this is both the reality – what can you do when you can't even see your hands? – and the nightmare: thick and humid air, animal musk. And now he

69

wants to stand out in the rain more than anything. He's on his hands and knees, scrabbling to find the torch, which he can't find for the life of him. Beyond him, the animal is closing.

At last Shep's fingers graze a cold buckle, the torch strap; he tips it too fast and blinds himself. As he does, the howl stops with a crack. Dull as a compound fracture. A mass is propelled past him, improbably high, actually brushing his ear. He brings up the light and directs it.

Through a neon smear he sees it. A badger pinned with its belly against the bunker's structural wall, fully a metre off the ground. The badger's mouth, turned out, is far too open and frothing pink, its coat filthy with muck and livid swellings. To Shep it seems *arranged*. It hangs on the wall like a trophy pelt – broken legs splayed at all corners, one shoulder horribly dislocated under its weight. Along with deep claw marks on its flanks, the badger's fur is missing in jagged, mange-like patches. An area of bald flesh, swollen taut across the animal's backbone, is throbbing.

Shep grips the torch with both hands, skin detaching from his frame. How is it stuck there?

The badger emits a series of short, distressed snorts. Shep realises it's trying to escape from the light; when he dips the torch, the badger instantly bites into the joint of its useless leg. The effort of this causes the animal's other forepaw to come free, leaving the creature to swing on the wall, a grim pendulum, from little but the connective tissue of its shoulder. The bulging under its skin begins to calm. The badger stills momentarily before making a final, violent attempt to free itself.

At this – the animal's terrible jerking – Shep is gone. Gone before he can think to stave in the badger's head, catch its last breath and be sure of a small mercy. Gone before he can question what was holding it against the wall.

He runs blind, and the ticking follows. A hundred paces with the torch round his wrist, halogen flickering wildly up the corridor walls, before the light splashes into a wider space. A larger chamber, where Shep's footsteps seem to travel faster and further than he does. He flashes his torch over a low, uneven ceiling. He's come the wrong way. He's standing in a cavernous space with a poured concrete floor, and it's unbearable. 'Hello?' he yells through the mask, desperate for anything, for anyone, for a hint of secondary light; and his echo taunts him. He tries left and he tries right. The torchlight doesn't reach another surface.

So Shep runs onwards.

Much deeper into the chamber with no walls, a new smell reaches him through his mask. He pulls it to one side, gasping, inhaling deeper, and finds himself stooped, as if pulled by some invisible rope. The smell is complex, thicker without the mask. Sweet, like petrol, if not a little more organic.

Shep inhales again. Panting. An island of light straining at the black. 'Hello?' he calls, sure of another person down here with him. A closeness, a warmth, spreads up from his perineum, through his hips, his guts, his lower back, up round his shoulders. Silken and familiar. He thinks he's pissed himself, and he clutches his crotch, and he can taste the petrol. 'Where are you?' he shouts, squatting to steady himself. Hot hands on cold floor. Head down, the taste turning to sharp fruit, caramelised bread. In some memory pocket, his late nan is saying, 'Isn't that yum?'

The chamber closes around him. The ceiling seems to sink. The heat shifts and the smell returns to mouldering. And as he crouches there, ears roaring with blood, the far wall slides into view.

Shep stumbles towards it. Somehow the bunker controls him. A funnelling of surfaces brings him into another corridor, where he finds a run of shelves, inelegantly bolted into place. The shelves are stuffed with damp cardboard boxes and old gardening equipment, most of it spattered with plant matter. An old laundry basket containing waders, boots and thermals that reek of burnt plastic. The text on the boxes is unreadable, blacked out with moisture or missing entirely. But – and this is what fortifies him – it's human. These tools and boxes and clothes are evidence of life, occupation – and so he follows the shelves down the corridor.

'Is anyone here?' Shep shouts.

If they are, they're hiding, and Shep finds it hard to blink, not to check what's at his shoulder. This instinct proves remarkable: at the edge of his vision, right at the edge of the torchlight, one of the cardboard boxes starts vibrating. The ticking sound comes from inside it. Shep backs up against the opposite wall. The corridor is a stricture, ripe and hot, his breathing a phlegmy rattle. He pushes the dust mask tight against his muzzle, headtorch on the box. Then the ticking is replaced by the sound of fibres splitting. He watches the front panel of the box tearing slowly, intolerably, in half. He moves his hand closer, torchlight tightening to a bright white circle. *A tight chimney, a three-hundred-footer, with a coin of white daylight above—*

The box bulges. Through the fissure, the box's contents appear smooth, like a ball. But in the flow of it, Shep realises it's just his torchlight refracting. The ball is more of a translucent shell, or it isn't there at all: an anti-space, an inversion.

A new rustling. Above and to the side. In the walls and the roof. It's urgent, desperate. Clawed. Shep's blood feels frozen and his pulse is fevered, and his feet are so sore inside his darts. The box gives out its own muffled sound, and Shep is sure someone, just along the corridor, is whispering his name.

The box panel breaks. Nothing leaks out, but the wet cardboard shifts aside. If it were anything at all, it would be a globular material sliding down the shelving unit. Those sweet fumes again – more intense – and Shep can't breathe for coughing. Then, as though released by some obscene fallopian mechanism, a dead bird glides out of the box and down the shelves, propelled on this invisible jelly, and slowly twitches across the dirt towards him.

There between his darts, the dead bird begins to rotate, its tiny feet clamped tightly together. The bird is eyeless. Its skull is hollow. It only stops turning when a slit opens in its featherless breast, hairline and precise. The slit wells up with heavy liquid, pushed from within. As if a second invisible ball is about to emerge from the cavity.

'Shepherd—'

His name reverberates. The fumes are overwhelming. His headtorch flickers. A hot sting at his neck. A thick, searing pain through the rubber of his darts. Shep lashes out, falls backwards, catches an elbow on a structural joint

73

of the shelving and brings a ream of slimy cardboard across his body. A length of warm, squirming rope lashes his face.

'Shep!'

Distantly, the walls distorting, Shep swears he *sees* it. It, this anti-thing, takes form as white and yellow, then black. The segments of a hornet's thorax, bald and hollow like the dead bird's, spasming like the beetle he crushed on the road. A single compound eye, with Shep's drawn face reflected in countless cells.

Mass against the wall, suffocating, Shep is rooted there as the sound builds to a frenzy. He grips his face, fixates on the leaking bird through his fingers. He's desperate for the reveal, for this to be an illusion. A fresh and awesome light breaks in the corridor, too bright to withstand. He shields his eyes, and a shape unlike any other sears his mind, imprinting on him a complex, lacy silhouette that deepens into a reticulated structure, like a giant metal hive. His knees give way. Shep drops to his knees on the wet floor and holds his ears as the sound resolves to a word:

'Sepsis.'

Shep screams, and screams. He only stops when a set of fingers wrap his forearm.

'You filthy little bastard.'

Shep uncovers his ears. He tries to see.

It's a man.

A man whose own headtorch renders his face a skull.

And the man says, 'That your dirtbike up there, is it?'

The Journalist

Freya likes to compose her analogue notes in the fake-leather planners her father collected at conferences in the years before he retired. Wherever Freya is in the house, there'll be one of these planners nearby, filling up with thoughts, malformed feature pitches, sentence fragments, or the odd line of fiction she admires.

Sitting on her bed, late again, Freya works in a planner debossed with ENGLAND'S YEAR OF REGROWTH, and the logo of a corporate services firm. At the top of the page she's written *Stephen*, underlined as a title, with *alcohol* under that. The rest of the page is blank.

When the bungalow's central heating clicks off, she gets under the covers and holds the empty page to her face. Stephen… alcohol… *what?* What's her lead? Or, what was his trigger? She flicks back through the planner, hoping some kind of clue might be in her previous notes, a line hiding between sedimentary layers. She often rifles through her planners like this, but tonight it's a craving – a nagging sense that she's lost an important word or fact. And all the while she's absorbed by the idea of there being a lie, a cover-up, even if the editor's dismissal lingers: there's nothing in it; she's reaching because she's desperate; Stephen's family just don't want to accept his death.

Freya goes on staring at the page. Being tired doesn't help, and her untidy shorthand makes it worse. There's definitely a use-by date to her notes. Over time these symbols shed their meaning, bleed together, and sometimes she wonders if she's written them at all.

Still. The past doesn't help. And she can only go deeper if there's a thread to pull.

Stephen. Alcohol. Climbing. Urbex.

This is the first time our Ste's shut up since I've known him.

Suddenly spiked with adrenaline, Freya grabs her tablet and quickly syncs its bookmarks with her father's Mac. She loads up the urbex boards she found in her first dredge.

Had Stephen used these forums? Or was he a lurker? It must be worth a shot. From what she understands of the scene – not to mention Stephen's interest in photography – it isn't far-fetched to assume he was involved. Urbex might be antisocial, lonely by necessity, but it seems social in its competition, its camaraderie. Going by Stephen's friends' public posts, Toby's words, he was surely too enthusiastic, too gregarious, to stay on the fringes.

She only has to find him.

Across each forum, Freya runs a series of searches with keywords targeting funerals and wakes. This serves up several RIP threads, and her screen fills steadily with emojis and memes that crash against the inadequate language of grief.

Then a snag. Alongside blocks on search engine spiders, the forums limit non-members to only a small amount of trawling, which is doubly frustrating when the tools are skittish. Luckily, Freya's years skimming streams for juicy stories count for something. Soon she's lined up recent RIP threads from five forums, each serving as a eulogy to a recently lost member. Most link off to photo galleries as well.

Stephen's remembrance thread is there in the eighth tab, hosted on the UK's 'second biggest urbex report site'. Consider it professional serendipity. In Stephen's thread there are pictures of the church service she'd attended, plus an extra set from his burial, after which they had planted a remembrance tree above his casket. The thread is titled: *Windscale's last problem: in memory of Ste Parsons.*

And there it is. Stephen's username.

'Windscale,' Freya whispers.

Whatever she owes to diligence – Stephen's popularity and the forum's size must have made for good odds – the satisfaction is heady, and she rolls through the thread slightly breathless. Standard stuff – support, grief, memories. But a lead.

New window. User search. Exact word.

Windscale.

Stephen's mission reports spring onto the screen – over a hundred in total. Like his public posts, they're sharply written, scrupulous, well formatted. As Freya reads them, she gives Stephen's written voice his brother's accent, and quickly comes to recognise an approach. Stephen broke into disused factories to shoot decrepit machinery. His pictures, unlike his terse prose, are heavily processed – and their cumulative effect is dizzying. Blacks and browns and golds, struts and gears and holes. Taken together, his reports form an essay on decay, a nod to his own finiteness, a lament for lost industry. Here was a man who knew his obsessions.

Stephen's reports do offer some range, though. Wide-angle shots of fractured landscapes. Close-ups of weeds. Abandoned vehicles from the Second World War. A sleeping barn owl, so close by that Stephen hadn't been able to resist putting a hand in shot for perspective. What looks like an abandoned sewage works. A set of dire warnings tied to the perimeter fence of a royal property, and then a shot of the hole he cut in the fence.

Only one report sticks out as truly different. The screen actually stutters as she scrolls down to it, and does so again when she edges back up. The post has no title or caption, except for a block of Unicode squares under a picture of what looks like a bird's nest. This could mean the text has been pasted in from a foreign language set, or written in characters the browser doesn't support. But this doesn't wash – her tablet is new, and has happily loaded emojis elsewhere on the site.

Under this post, the comments range from exclamatory – '*WTF is this, windscale?*' – to impressed – '*crossposting to cursed_urbex*'. One commenter hints at a minor conspiracy by suggesting Stephen's account has been hacked, and to look out for posts like it on other forums.

Freya reaches the last of the comments. Stephen had replied-all with a single winky face and closed the thread.

She doesn't know what to make of it. The picture is off-style, like it was taken in a hurry, and not with a good camera.

Maybe it *was* just a nest, and his flash had oversaturated the image, and he didn't have time to take any more. But there are colour gradients in the nest material – and Freya's heard enough from the picture editors to know that blown highlights will erase details.

She copies and pastes the block of Unicode squares into her writing app to see if swapping fonts will reveal an answer. No luck. She pastes the whole entry into the forum's search box, looking for reposts, but nothing comes of that either. She reverse-searches the picture for similar images across the web, again without joy. Maybe it's encrypted. Or maybe it's deliberately abstruse, and Stephen wanted this reaction. She checks the image name – 0000001.jpg – and its metadata, which has been stripped. Lastly, she tries to save the image to her desktop, so she can open it in a photo-editing app, zoom in a little. *Unknown error.*

Freya yawns. One in the morning. She screenshots Stephen's profile page and goes for a glass of water. There, at the sink, watching threads of silvery rain crawl down the window, her outline blending with the leylandii outside, she feels sick with exhilaration.

Sleep can wait.

Back in her room, back on her tablet, she picks through Stephen's work once more, the pages and pages of his reports. She enjoys them as she had in the hours before – wonderment, fascination, intrigue. But there's nothing to hint at why he'd posted such a weird picture – and still nothing to suggest what had made him start drinking.

In her planner she writes: *anomalous.*

Come two in the morning. Freya's reached the last of

Stephen's reports – the earliest post. It's basically an intro – the sites he liked, the grades he climbed – with a full-body portrait. It must've been taken a while ago: he's softer round the edges than in his most recent shots. More interesting, though, is the way he has an arm slung round a woman's shoulders, hers around his waist. Their faces are pixelated, but it's telling that they don't mind being so close to each other. From the colour-studded walls in the background, and the way their tops are dark with sweat, they must be standing in a climbing centre. Big Walls, Manchester, at a guess. That's where friends from Stephen's wider network want to hold a memorial.

'Who are you, then?' Freya asks the screen.

The photo caption reads, *Me and my partner in crime.*

Freya wrinkles her nose. Just a phrase? Just a friend? Or was it more? She tabs to Stephen's RIP thread and goes through every message, looking for signs of a relationship, a deeper trust, a more keenly felt pain. Her reasoning being, if you don't mind someone else's sweat on you, you're close. And if you're close, if you share a hobby like climbing, then surely you'll be compelled to say something on your partner's passing. Accidentally reveal, however carefully you do it, your connection.

There are contenders in that thread – a lot of single kisses, a lot of hearts, countless admiring compliments. But she knows when she's found it. A single line with no punctuation or caps. Unassuming, actually – not a post she'd have picked up by scanning. Definitely a comment she'd missed on her first pass. And her heart jumps.

In Freya's bones, in her full throat, she believes this came from the woman in Stephen's picture. And if Freya's own feelings about her ex are anything to go by, she knows this woman is still out there, with a stake in Stephen's life.

Freya scribbles down the phrase in her planner.

'You lost our bet,' Freya repeats. The sentence already indelible. She clicks the woman's username – *freighter*.

This is it. Goosebumps. There, buried in freighter's profile, is a repost of Stephen's nest photo. And beneath it some text:

It drags into its wake proximal asteroids. It bends the also travelling light. A galaxy in span, this journey, under the banner of mitosis and promulgation. The doubling of its image. The path for its replicants is decided, for the extremities of worlds are essential. The health of the inheritors is sought by those with the same journey ahead and all of that fortitude to muster. Carry it for us.

Freya reads the paragraph again and again. Its strange language and syntax give it the feel of an extract, or a poor translation. It causes a prickling that runs deeper than tiredness.

She scrolls to the space below it. *Comments closed.*

'Okay,' Freya says, skin electric blue by the tablet screen. This woman – this is how she gets in.

The Steeplejack

The man pulls Shep from an old Land Rover and marches him towards a building with a collapsing pitch roof. Shep, hazed and foul-smelling, cable-tied at the wrists, is back from survival mode: drained and cold and desperate. Searching the road for markers, for anything familiar. They're on the fringes of a town. Over there a row of pebble-dashed terraces, a bus stop blinking adverts. He desperately hopes it's Whitehaven.

Inside, the building smells of wool and burnt candles. Childish drawings tacked to the walls. A community centre? A nursery? A Scout hut? Shep limps through with syrupy limbs, a thick head. It's worse than a hangover, this, because it feels like it might never end. His visible breath is his only grounding. What did he see back there?

The woman behind a desk in the corner of the room seems unfazed to see them. 'Early doors,' she says, tapping her watch. 'What you in for?'

'Breaking and entering,' the man says. Not local police,

it turns out, but a freelance security ranger. Going by his military-spec equipment, the IR goggles, he's a reservist as well. The kind of person who enjoys the hunt more than the pay. There's every chance he'd followed Shep from the trailhead. That, or Shep's hacked nav wasn't as impenetrable as the grafter had promised.

'This a copshop?' Shep asks the clerk.

'Neighbourhood Watch,' she tells him.

Limited powers, but bad enough. Fingers crossed they don't scan his jaw, or keep up their subscription to the national database.

'Are the police coming?' Shep asks.

'Let's not get ahead of ourselves,' the clerk says. 'What's your name?'

'Shep.'

'Shep what?'

'Shepherd. Like Madonna.'

A patient smile. 'Age?'

'Twenty-eight.'

The clerk pulls a face. 'You're younger than that, Shepherd. Where do you live?'

'Near Manchester.'

'Specifically.'

He gives his mother's old address in Wythenshawe.

'Long way from home, aren't you?'

Shep squeezes his eyes shut. The fog won't lift. The intricate structure he saw down in the bunker is burned right in. The smell of the corridor. The sound of his name. The scale of the place had warped, like it had swollen around him.

'Came up for a night,' Shep says. 'Where's my bike? Helmet?'

'Confiscated,' the ranger says.

The clerk glances over Shep's shoulder. She shrugs sadly. 'Been caught like this before, haven't you?'

'No,' Shep says. But of course he has. Skateboarding on public furniture, tagging a local government building, halfway up a pylon with a camera on his forehead—

'What do you do for a living, Shepherd?' the clerk asks.

'Trainee steeplejack.'

'And what's one of those when it's at home?'

'A labourer who climbs stuff.'

'Like steeples?'

'Like anything high that needs fixing.'

The clerk shoots the ranger a weary look. 'How high?'

Shep shrugs. 'Few hundred feet? Depends.'

'Aren't you scared of heights?'

'No,' he says, and nods at the clerk's hands. 'I'm scared of desks.'

The ranger gives Shep a rough shove. 'Right now you should be scared of blacklisting,' he says. 'Cocky little shit.'

Shep turns to him. The ranger snarls.

'Try blacklisting someone you've watched squatting over a bucket since he was a green,' Shep says. And with it comes a pang for Gunny, and the job he's probably lost. When you're up on a rig, perfect sky, your crew is all you have. You take your power naps under the cathead, you work and eat together, you smoke and drink together, you piss and shit together. It's all shared – the cold-bitten hands, the weeping sores, the cigarettes cupped away from the wind. 'We're family,' Shep adds. 'No blacklists.'

The clerk finishes scribbling in her pad. 'Do you want to call someone?'

'Lost my mobile,' Shep tells her. 'And I'm no good at remembering numbers.'

'It's a brief you'll need,' the ranger says. 'Our client will press charges, trust me.'

Shep doesn't turn around this time. He blinks. 'What charges?'

'Aggravated trespass. Burglary. Desecration.'

'Desecration? Burglary? What you on about?'

'I saw what you did to that badger, you little pervert. I found the wrap on your army bag. Souvenir, eh? One to show your cyber-pals?'

Shep's guts shift. If the ranger knows about the message boards, he has Shep's motive down pat, and this could be the last time he gets away with it. The minimum term is harsh to set examples. No ifs or buts.

'You weren't down that old bunker out there, were you?' the clerk asks.

'The very one,' the ranger says.

'Christ almighty.' The clerk shakes her head. 'What are you kids even *doing* down there?'

Shep can't answer. What does she mean by that? Kids? There were no other reports – he'd checked and rechecked the boards to make sure. There wasn't even much posted from the wider region in the last few months. There'd been nothing to say Shep wasn't the first to try his luck – there was no graffiti – and the idea of being second makes him queasy. He didn't go through all that for leftovers.

'When?' Shep asks.

She looks at the ranger. 'Few months ago, wasn't it? Pair of them. That good-looking couple.'

'Really?' Shep says.

'You heard,' the ranger says. 'And they weren't stupid enough to bring a bloody trail bike with them, either. Who're you working for?'

'Working for?' A flickering bulb behind the clerk starts to fluster him. 'No one.'

'My arse,' the ranger says.

'I swear,' Shep says. 'I was just out riding. I needed a wazz.'

The ranger sniffs, indignant. 'Riders don't dress up like special forces. They don't mutilate wildlife, either. Telling you, mate – they're going to lob the book at you.'

'Sorry,' the clerk interrupts, 'but why *did* you come all this way on your own?'

'To explore,' Shep insists.

'In the middle of the night? Bit weird, isn't it?'

'To you, maybe.'

'Cold, grim hole like that,' the clerk says. 'Condemned as well. What were you thinking?'

'I wasn't thinking about getting banged up afterwards,' Shep says. 'Can I sit down?'

The clerk takes the old phone out of its cradle. 'Let's make our call first, eh? I'll do the talking. Pop some digits in here. I'm not having this can't-remember-numbers rubbish.'

Shep hesitates, then slowly pecks out a number. For better or worse, it's one of the only numbers he knows whose owner might be available right now.

The dialler burrs. A click. Garbling as the call rebounds. A simultaneous intake of breath—

86

Then, clear as anything, a voice through the speaker.

'Mallory.'

The clerk winces. 'Good morning, sir. I'm calling on behalf of a young man I have here with me... Yes, sir, I appreciate it's late. Yes, I know it's Sunday... no. He's called Shepherd. Shepherd, that's right.'

Shep can feel the ranger's eyes on him.

'Sir,' the clerk continues, 'he's been caught trespassing – yes – and he's given us your details. Can you confirm you're his next of kin?'

Mallory Junior's going ballistic at the other end.

'I know,' the clerk keeps saying. 'Okay, okay, then how long has he worked for you?'

'Two years,' Shep whispers.

'You aren't sure,' the clerk says, and she grimaces at Shep. 'If that's the case, he's releasable for a fee... No, no, not bail. It's more like a donation. We invest in the wetlands up here.'

Shep can guess what's being said.

'Sorry, the Lakes. I'm calling from Whitehaven. *Whitehaven*... that one.'

Shep exhales. It is Whitehaven. If nothing else, his work van is nearby. He'd run for it now if his legs felt attached. If the ranger wasn't right behind him.

'I completely agree, sir,' the clerk continues. 'I do know it's Sunday.' She covers the mouthpiece and snaps her fingers at Shep. 'He's asking if you're in tomorrow... no, today.'

'Meant to be,' Shep says.

'He is,' the clerk repeats. 'First thing,' she relays to Shep. Another pause. Then, to Mallory Junior: 'I get where you're coming from. I do…' She puts her hand back over the mic. 'He's saying something about a yard.'

The predictable bastard.

'Sorry, say again? Disciplinary for what?'

The ranger clears his throat irritably.

'The fee comes out just shy of three thousand pounds. Two–nine–nine–five.'

Shep tenses again. Does the sums.

'Two, yes. And we can take that by flash right now.'

Assuming Shep keeps his job, that's the best part of six weeks' salary. Even more if he's stuck in the yard. Plus fines and the retraining that the Health and Safety Executive will slap on him. Plus costs if Gunny decides to take civil action over Clemens. He'd have been better off walking into a police station himself. Shep closes his eyes. Gunny's hand is right there, dripping.

'Course,' the clerk says. 'I'll tell him. And you'll put all that through now?'

A machine chirps on the clerk's desk.

'Oh, great, it's here already. Thank you so much. I'll make sure we get…' The clerk stares at the phone. 'He hung up.'

'How did he sound?' Shep asks.

'Pained,' she says. 'You've got some music to face. Now, I need you to sign this.' Cooler in tone. She taps the desktop with her biro. 'And we need to record your visit,' she adds, producing a sample kit. 'As part of Devo action, we can take swabs.'

'Unless you want to donate a tooth,' the ranger says.

Shep's jaw twinges. But consequences aside, you can still prepare for being caught. He sets his teeth and tongues fifteen beats on the roof of his mouth. A silky film peels away from his palate and dissolves. His mouth fills with the brackish taste of artificial saliva. All he has to do now is hold the liquid in the gullies of his mouth without retching.

The clerk unpacks the tester kit. 'Say ahh,' she says. In goes the swab, woollen and tickling. Shep keeps his tongue wedged back, just like he's practised. He looks at the vial, slime on glass, and knows there's no way they'll identify him.

Then he thinks of a dead bird, shuddering across the floor. A starved-looking badger, pinned to a wall. The taste of petrol. The stench of rot. An insane metallic structure, singing in the wind.

'All done,' the clerk says to him. And the ranger snips the cable ties on Shep's wrists and escorts him back outside.

'Before you go,' the ranger says.

The ranger offers his hand.

Shep takes it, shivering. Before he knows it, he's off balance and the ranger has him up on his tiptoes, face right in his, one fist tight round his little finger. A huge, dark vein snakes across the contractor's forehead. The deepest crimson.

'You don't come here again,' the ranger says. Under harsh security lights, his nostril hair reminds Shep of beetle legs.

'Get off,' Shep says.

'And you don't fiddle about with our animals. Right?'

'I never touched it.'

The ranger takes Shep by the throat. Squeezes under his jaw.

'Say it again,' the ranger says.

'Get off me.'

'One more time and I'll throttle you.'

'Get fuc—'

The ranger wrenches Shep's finger at the first knuckle. Butts him, hard, on the bridge of his nose. Shep's vision explodes. His nose instantly floods. The ranger takes Shep by the scruff of the neck, the seat of his climbing pants, and tosses him to the road.

'These Lakes are ours,' the ranger tells Shep. 'You're pissing about with stuff way bigger than you.'

And the ranger goes inside.

The work van is where Shep left it. In his seat, face ballooning, he smashes his startcard against the reader. Slumps back as the retinal does its cycle, shrieking in pain as he winds climbing tape round his damaged finger, already bruising. When he's caught his breath and cleared the blood from his nose, he has enough sense to check the hackbar in the dash console still works. Before he left Salford, he'd deleted a hundred miles from the odometer – more than enough to cover the journey back, plus a couple of service stops just in case. Mallory Junior might know Shep is here, but headquarters won't know he's in their vehicle.

Shep starts the van to a message from a public toilet asking to rate his recent visit out of ten. He tells it to fuck off.

A good-looking couple. A bird and a badger—

Shep inspects his finger. Swelling and tender. The same deep colour as Gunny's went on the deck. He cradles it. How was he not the first to explore the bunker? How has he missed it? The clock says 3.35 a.m. About two hours till work. He slams the van into gear and drives out to the motorway. The sky has started to lighten, recovering itself by increments. There are things that need sorting out. The scrambler could be returned by courier, at an inflated impound charge. Job or no job, he'll be too skint this month, but the option's there. The helmet he'll lose for sure – which in many ways is harder to take. When he's home he'll be able to activate the helmet's kill switch, hardwipe it, but it's a custom job, if not a prototype, and that'll still give the police plenty to play with.

At least he'd already chucked his phone. And the ranger definitely overlooked the memory card in his camera.

The M6 southbound is lonely at this time. Dawn expands and slides right out across the carriageway. Shep drives in a daze, well past tired. The van's headlights on the glassy road return him to the bunker, its shivering walls. Except now the bunker is more like a fantasy. Does he remember breaking in, or the parts he scavenged? Even his memory of the splitting box feels unreliable with the sun coming up. What if it was all some stress- or light-induced distortion? Mixed-up visual messages, natural phenomena – tricks of the light? But the memory of that petrol smell is still so tangible, so fixed as to be part of him, it can't be explained away so easily. He tries to isolate it, conjure a hint of it. Express it from his pores.

These circles tighten as he travels south. He goes over the breach compulsively – the wall hop, the fragmented equipment, the hanging badger, the panic, the *box*. Stare into oncoming headlights and he can almost make out the splintering hive. Every strut and convergence. Every detail, infinitely rendered. Then he swings to work, his other life an almost comedic counterpoint. The music he has to face, as the clerk put it. What will Mallory Junior have him doing in the yard? Sweeping, litter picking, checking harnesses for damage?

And back once more: the mission – the thought it was all for nothing – becoming an albatross. The disappointment of missing another report. Even if the report was hidden on a different board, he has alerts running, and loads of people cross-post their content on the biggest sites. So when did those other bastards get in there?

Someone beeps at him. Shep drops out of blacktop dreams, shocked to realise he's been following the road unconsciously for miles, and the van is straddling two lanes. He checks his mirrors. No other vehicles. Heart on a hair trigger. The beep was the fuel gauge. When signs appear for the services, he leaves the motorway and parks under the petrol station canopy. His hands carry a faint scent of vinegar. His mouth full with old iron. Before he gets out, he tethers the van to the forecourt Wi-Fi and brings up the contact details for the Pea and Ham.

'Call it,' he says.

After a few rings, a woman answers groggily. 'Hello?'

'Is he there?' Shep asks. 'Sorry?'

'Is he there?'

'What? Is who here? It's five o'clock in the bloody morning!'

'Is he, though?'

'What? Who the hell's this?'

'Is he *there*?'

'Who! It's five o'clock on a blasted Sunday morning!'

'That bastard did me over,' Shep says.

'If you don't tell me who you are—'

'Just tell that big twat, that drone-man at your bar, tell him I know. Tell him I'm never buying his shite again.'

'Andy, Andy – wake up! Some nutter's on the phone—'

Shep hangs up and gets out of the van.

It's the kind of service station you can visit for a coffee and leave with a kitchen. An entire out-of-town shopping centre hanging off the back of it. Through its doors, the interior is kaleidoscopic: sleek messaging crawling every edge-lit surface, and people bumbling past, morning-vacant, but smiling. On a panel to Shep's side, an androgynous face materialises and crows special offers at him. This disembodied thing, crawled straight from the uncanny valley, makes Shep feel ill, and the enduring taste of the DNA strip isn't helping.

Shep pays up front for fuel with cash. In the queue, flashes of the bunker still with him, no less alarming under these bright lights. The word *sepsis* like a warning. He's paid up, and he's burning through again. He's back at the pump, with the petrol dispenser nozzle deliberately angled right through the driver-side window. He squeezes the trigger gently, ignoring the sharp pulses from his injured finger, enjoying the sound of the fuel splashing on his seat.

Several people stand and watch him.

Shep smiles. 'I don't smoke,' he tells them. 'No worries.' He takes the nozzle out of the window and slides it into the van's fuel inlet. When the tank's full, he hangs up the dispenser and gets in. 'Mallory Limited,' he tells the mapper. 'You drive.'

By now the sun has fully emerged, shimmering behind a dragging westerly rain. Shep closes his eyes and concentrates on the sensation of petrol soaking through his trousers and underwear, alcohol-cold on his thighs. The heavy fumes as they rise from between his legs, from the footwell carpet.

The Journalist

Big Walls climbing centre occupies an old textile mill near central Manchester, its brickwork varicose with tatty rope and fire service training gear. Freya sits in the car park, geeing herself up to go inside, unsure about her choice of clothing.

The forums say weekdays are busiest at Big Walls, so on this Saturday morning she hopes fewer people will present more opportunities to chat, ask questions. Ideally, she'll recognise one of Stephen's climbing friends from the funeral, though it's unlikely she'll try her luck – asking questions can make people edgy when you're still so close to the fact. That, and it's not a death-knock if you're there on their terms.

Always saw Ste down at Big Walls on Thursdays, someone had posted in Stephen's eulogy thread. *Fingerboard magician that lad.*

Freya has no idea what a fingerboard involves, but everything else on the forums, especially on the RIP thread, points to Stephen being a regular here. Drawing closer, she imagined him cycling along the same roads. Come the weekend, hitting real rock over the tops. Dovestones, Stanage Edge, the Woolpacks on Kinder – all these mystical-sounding places she's been reading about.

Freya pushes hard on the mill door, and the smell comes first: sweat, rubber, hot minerals. There's a wiry, sullen woman on reception. To the rear of the building is a run of slabs – short walls knobbled with painful-looking shapes. Then the taller walls, folded into themselves like half-constructed nets of vast packaging boxes. Watching a climber leap effortlessly between two slivers of neon, Freya wonders how many parts of the body you can tense. Just the sound of exertion makes her palms clammy. In any case, she'd been right to question her clothing. Her ex's board shorts should really be yoga leggings, her oversized T-shirt a regulation sports bra and crop-top.

Freya approaches the staffer and explains she's new, has never done this. In return she receives a withering look and a photocopy of *Things to know before you climb at Big Walls*.

'On your tod?' the staffer asks coolly. 'That's brave.'

Freya squeezes her forearm. She nods.

'Won't get your money's worth, is all. And, like, I have to give you an induction.'

Freya takes a pen, sits down on a scruffy settee to read the paperwork. Plenty of warnings to get neuroses about. Too many points of weakness on a single limb. Why doesn't she tell the staffer she's a reporter? If only it were easier to say she's here to get info on Stephen.

Professional detachment.

Except this isn't just about getting a story any more. Freya knows herself better than that. Not least because rooting through Stephen's life has put her own inertia in sharp relief.

The staffer has Freya wait on the crash mats while she logs the application. Freya surveys the angular walls, surfaces patterned in garish paint, smeared with chalk and moisture and fainter streaks of what might be skin.

'Need a quid for your locker,' the staffer says when she's done. 'You'll want to grab yourself a pair of shoes from the bucket.'

'Ta,' Freya says.

'No danger,' the staffer says. 'But keep your socks on, yeah? We're growing potatoes in some of them.'

Freya climbs like a spider in a bathtub. It's a gangly, frantic technique that the staffer tactfully ignores. Through sheer belligerence, though, Freya completes a few easy routes; by her sixth or seventh, she begins to appreciate where stronger muscles might be useful. Going up and down the wall, palms stinging from the holds' rough handles, hands clawed owing to the lactic build-up in her forearms, she senses how it might feel to be good at it. What Stephen must have loved so much.

'See what I mean?' the staffer asks.

Freya hasn't listened. The surroundings keep drawing her focus. Into the roof travel all these different bodies, each with staggering fluidity. Like the topless young guy making his way up a high wall, completely by himself.

'Okay with that?' the staffer asks.

Freya nods tentatively. Holding her breath.

'So have fun, yeah? Maybe try the traversing walls, if you want to get your extremities used to it. Your toes will suffer tonight.'

Freya motions across the matting. 'The sideways ones?'

'Sure,' the staffer nods. 'Get a bit, like, fingery, but they're rad for warming up.'

'Cool.'

Then the staffer is gone.

Alone, Freya listens. Noises both angry and sexual: grunting, self-willing groans; the odd surprised shout when a hold fails, gear slips, or a hand misses. A painful-sounding bang as one girl comes off the wall and swings hip-first into a slab. She watches the half-naked climber with fascination, some inner sense of matronly disapproval. It's hot in here, but the man's body is more of a statement, a diary of investment. He climbs up, slaps the top of the wall, and descends on a pulley system that emits a distinct keening. Then he starts again.

Next time he's down on the matting, Freya goes over to him.

'Shouldn't you have a partner?' she asks.

The man turns to face her, dazed. Stringier up close, his waist improbably narrow. 'Say again?'

'For belay.' Freya gestures behind her. 'Is that the word? Everyone else is paired up.'

The man tilts the compact device on his climbing harness. 'Belaying. This is an autobelayer.'

'Oh,' she says. 'I didn't know you—'

98

'You can. Miles better on your own.'

'Right,' she says.

The man grins sheepishly and looks away. Freya stares at his nipples. The perfect handprint chalked on his stomach. The little finger of his left hand is strapped to the finger next to it.

He glances back, catches her looking. Her eyes snap to his, and she can't tell if he saw. 'Do this a lot, do you?'

The man wobbles his head. 'I try to.'

'How long's it take to get good?'

He chuckles. 'Depends how hard you go at it.' He looks Freya up and down. 'You're a decent build for it.' He grins again. 'Lanky.'

Freya snorts. 'Says you.'

His brow and eyebrows soften. 'It takes graft, obviously. Your muscles get strong fast, but it's a while till the ligaments catch up.' He rotates his wrist until it pops. 'Hear that?'

Freya nods, horrified.

'Knees are shot to shit as well. You have to learn how to climb back down, not jump. Even harder than going up. And stretch out when you can.' He touches his shoulder. 'Get too carried away and you'll knacker a rotator cuff, or a hip.'

'All a bit risky,' Freya says.

The man looks up the wall. 'That's half the fun.'

'So can I watch?' she asks.

'Watch what?'

'Your next climb.'

'Uh, if you want?'

Freya shrugs. 'I learn better by watching.'

The man cocks his head.

'If you don't mind,' she adds.

'Might be more useful if I watch you.'

'Nah,' Freya says. 'I don't like being patronised.'

The man laughs. 'Fair enough. But look.' He wiggles his fingers. 'We've both got four limbs.'

The man dips a hand into his chalk bag and sits down at the base of the wall, carefully rubbing his fingers. He extends his arms to full lock and expands his hands to grip two different holds, nails scraping the backboard as he adjusts for purchase. 'And you kind of go with it,' he says.

His movement from seated to climbing is explosive. His back bulges with the strain of it. He rocks up, down, then jumps – his toes seeming to stretch, angled into the wall, fingers splayed. From Freya's perspective he hovers there briefly, before his feet dig into what looks like thin air above a pair of tiny sloping holds, and his fingertips secure him.

'Crimps,' he calls down to Freya, 'are a bastard.'

'Blimey,' she says. 'Now where?' She can't see his next move at all. There's a feature with two holds a metre or so above him, but that's it.

'Dyno number two,' he says, twisting a hip into the wall. From there, squatting almost, he uses the handholds to bounce over his knees, readying for another jump. Freya keeps one eye closed. Then the man is off and level with the feature. One hand landing, latched. The other flailing. He loses his grip, resigned to it. The rope screams through his gear as he falls back to the matting.

Freya squeals and hops back.

Flat on his back, the man splutters and starts to laugh.

'And that's... decking it.'

Freya stands over him. 'Oh my God. Are you all right? Wasn't your belay thing meant to stop that?'

He rolls to his belly and pushes himself up, dusting loose chalk from his chest. 'I don't... sorry, winded. I don't use it. It's only so they don't kick me out...' Now he's holding out the rope for her. 'Your turn,' he says, coughing. 'You can use my harness, if you want. You'd flash the green route.'

Freya shakes her head. 'I was going to do some short routes over there.'

'That's not climbing,' the man says.

'Sorry?'

'Bouldering. It's not climbing.'

'How come?'

'Because.'

He smiles. She finds it inviting. 'Mind another annoying question?' she says.

'No?'

'Did you know Stephen?'

The man's expression changes. 'Come again?'

'Stephen.'

'Ste? Ste Parsons?'

Freya nods.

Now it's harder to read him. One eye partially shut, like he wants to remember. In a suppressed voice, he adds, 'You a journo, or something?'

Freya doesn't reply.

The man sighs. 'Seriously.' He starts to pull the rope back through his belay device, but doesn't tie it off. 'You'll not hear a bad word about him, if that's it. He had this big cheeser on him, all the bloody time.' Then a slight hesitation. 'He didn't deserve...'

'No,' Freya says. 'That's kind of why I'm looking into it.'

'Into what?'

'Whether he boozed a lot.'

The man holds up the autobelayer. His corrugated stomach is tensed. 'Oh,' he says. 'Must have, given—'

'Because I don't think he did,' Freya says. 'Not normally.'

'Oh,' the man says again. 'So you're saying... what?'

'Did you climb with him?'

'Sometimes. I prefer it alone. Not really wired for spotting people.' He holds up his splinted finger. 'Don't really trust myself. But we weren't that close, me and Ste. Might've gone out as a group now and then... He'd always let on, ask me how it was going, whatever. If we *were* bouldering near each other...'

'I thought bouldering wasn't real climbing.'

'It's not. It's conditioning.'

'Okay. Were you at the funeral?'

'I was away with work. Were you?'

This wrong-foots Freya, and she doesn't deflect it well.

'Not many of us here made it,' the man continues. 'Not even his missus, from what I heard. Only his closest mates.'

Freya nods, making a mental note. 'And there's a memorial day being planned for here.'

The man frowns. 'How do—'

'You know any of his good friends?'

He shakes his head. 'They're on the Sheffield side.'

'Then what about his girlfriend? I didn't know he had a girlfriend.'

102

'Not much of a hack, are you?'

'I'm curious.'

'Professionally curious?'

'No, I meant why wasn't she there—'

'I don't know. She used to climb here. Stopped coming a while back.'

Freya clears her throat, trying to stay casual. 'She must be in ribbons.'

The man shrugs. 'I guess.'

'What's her name?'

'Ha, *that's* shameless. Can I get on?'

Freya wavers, then lets it slide. A different tack: 'You know Ste did urbex?'

The man drops the autobelayer. 'What?'

But Freya can tell he knows. 'Never mind,' she says.

Does he look relieved, now? 'All right,' he says, motioning to the wall. 'I've got this 7B to boss. Just be careful who else you chat to in here, yeah? It can be a closed shop. Loads of rawness around Ste. I don't mind much, but it won't go down well, you sniffing about. We all join up somewhere.'

Freya gets that. And even if his assumption annoys her – she has *some* discretion – she smiles gratefully. 'Some other Saturday?'

'Maybe,' he says, and pulls an awkward smile. 'What's your name? So I know where to kick off when you start posting your fake news.'

'Freya,' she says.

'Freya what?'

'Medlock.'

'All right, Freya Medlock,' the man says, sitting down to face the wall. He looks at her over the bulb of his shoulder. 'I'm Shep. See you around.'

The Steeplejack

Shep's too weary to notice his colleagues staring across the car park when he arrives at headquarters. It's harder to miss the shape of Mallory Junior leaning against the yard's chicken-wire fence. As Shep approaches, head low, the boss clears his throat, but he doesn't greet him. Much less mentions the swelling and caked blood on Shep's face.

'Happy Sunday, arsehole,' Mallory Junior says, holding the yard gate open for Shep before locking him in. 'Crack on,' he says. 'We'll chat later.'

Left there alone, Shep paces. When the yard isn't a cell for misbehaving greens, it goes unused: a museum for the firm's antiquated safety gear, a catalogue of the random stuff a jacking firm accretes as it updates its training regimes. One of these retired artefacts is a grubby first-aid dummy that lives on, limbless, in the bucket of a dead cherry-picker. Everyone calls it Harold, and there's a rumour IT have installed a camera in Harold's mouth.

Out of custom, Shep flicks Harold the Vs. The dummy gawps back, thin-lipped and bovine. Shep feels a flicker of rain on his scalp. This isn't the first time they've met.

Before he gives in to labouring, Shep sits on a pallet out of Harold's sight and stretches out. The tiredness is catching up, and little wonder: a clock on the wall reads 6.30 a.m., which makes it twenty-five hours awake. Shep yawns in kind and tries to ignore the slop bucket in the corner. He staggers around unsurely for a while, retrieving a bag of toothbrushes from the shed, some wire wool and rags, foam chunks for knee padding. Under Harold's catatonic gaze, wincing every so often at his taped finger, his sore face, Shep starts scrubbing rust from a box of fall arrest gear.

Come ten o'clock, the back door lock jangles. Mallory Junior opens it a crack.

'Boss?'

'Get a hot drink,' Mallory Junior says. 'You've got fifteen minutes.'

Except Shep doesn't go to the canteen. Lightheaded and hollow, he slinks to the server room, where the IT manager has his feet up and is sucking on a bulky e-cigarette.

'Oh,' the IT manager says, swivelling idly in his chair. He glances back to his laptop. 'Heard you'd been a naughty boy. Who lamped you?'

'No one,' Shep tells him.

'Right. So what, then?'

The room smells of peaches. A hazy pall hugs the ceiling tiles.

'You still a first-aider?' Shep asks.

'Yeah, why?'

Shep dangles his injured finger over the IT manager's shoulder. 'I need some first aid.'

The IT manager sighs and draws on his e-cig. It crackles warmly. Another big cloud of vapour. 'How'd you manage that?'

'I don't remember.'

'You don't remember.'

'No.'

The IT manager stands up. 'Let me check what I've got.'

'Cheers,' Shep says. 'And I wondered if I could have a blast on your laptop.'

The IT manager looks at him.

'Your other laptop.'

'No chance,' the IT manager says, pulling a green box from a shelf. 'Whatever you did last time borked the whole rig.'

Shep shakes his head. 'You still owe me for that VR set I scored for you.'

The IT manager tuts. Pulls out a bandage roll and points to the server stack. 'Five minutes. Or a splint. Choose one.'

Shep snatches the bandage roll and squeezes past the server cabinets. It's hot and loud behind them. Stacked on the floor is an array of Chinese crypto-miners running at full tilt, a heavy-looking laptop as the controller.

'Aren't you better off doing this at home?' Shep shouts over the racket. 'Stay cosy through winter with this lot.'

The IT manager's face appears in the gap between two of the cabinets. 'Four minutes,' he says. 'Gobshite.'

Shep opens the laptop, unsmiling, and pulls up an encrypted search program. He navigates to a webapp that aggregates reports from every major urbex board. When it loads, the search terms tumble out.

Bunker, Whitehaven, Lake District.

Lakes, dead bird, petrol.

He scans and scans. No sign of his bunker, nor any recent visits or reports with hits in the right context. A few results mentioning waterworks and unfinished developments near Whitehaven, but not the same place. Not *his* place. He refines and tinkers and continues until there's a kind of relief pushing behind his stinging eyes.

No posts match your search.

Shep closes the app and comes back round the stack, wiping the sweat from his face. The Whitehaven clerk must've had it wrong. The lifting of that burden is perfect.

'Ta for that,' Shep says. The IT manager grunts, and Shep heads back to the yard. There, kneeling on the foam, he peels the climbing tape from his finger and bandages it properly. His next job is to run the frays off a crateload of training ropes.

Mallory Junior fetches Shep at one-thirty in the afternoon. The boss seems preoccupied, and they walk in lockstep towards the canteen.

'Tasty shiner you've got there,' Mallory Junior comments. 'Or two, let's be honest. Who weighed you in?'

'No one,' Shep tells him.

'I do know why you do it,' Mallory Junior says.

'Do what?'

'Don't play the smart-arse.'

Shep stares dead ahead.

'My old man hired kids like you for good reason,' Mallory Junior says. 'So I'm asking, on a level, that you don't pull this again. Wife's going to kill me later for the time that woman in Whitehaven called. On top of that, you're meant to be in Redcar this week, and now I've had to pull another green out of Fawley.'

Shep rubs his neck. 'That green'll thank me for it. And Redcar's fine. Sea views.'

'I'm not asking for more opinions, Billy.'

'Then I'm sorry about your wife.'

'I bet. And doing a runner from Clemens was worth it?'

'The yard time? Or these shiners?'

'The lack of bloody sleep.'

Shep shrugs.

'It's not a game, this. Get some grub in you now and see me after. We need to talk about what happened up that stack.'

Shep stops walking. 'Is he going to be okay?'

'Gunny?'

Shep looks away as he nods.

'They saved his hand, if that's what you mean. He's off sick with full pay for a few months. Isn't far off retirement anyway.'

'It was an accident,' Shep tells him.

Mallory Junior says nothing.

'I feel shite about it,' Shep adds.

'If it's anything,' Mallory Junior says, 'he thinks you're all right. Doesn't want to press charges. He said you were getting shit off the other lads, might've been distracted. I'd say you're forgiven.'

'That makes me feel guiltier.'

Mallory Junior snorts.

'If you're sacking me, I can go now.'

Mallory Junior keeps his head very still. 'Come to my office after your scran. Like I told you. We've got stuff to talk about.'

And Shep watches him go. A heavy, heavy feeling.

In the canteen. Shep says hi to the chef, but the chef ignores him. A plate of chips, a slice of bread, half a round of quiche. When he's done, he wipes the plate clean with the bread and rifles his pockets for a pen and paper. Then he starts writing, bad finger burning.

Abandoned military, Lake District, unnamed bunker e/ of Whitehaven.

Burrowed a nice one this Sunday gone. Night mission so I took the scrammy for the country leg. Aim to go that way while there's still light and take a big lens for the views. Route is national limit so a good clip into blind corners. Ditched van on the coast and biked rest. Standard tyres do the job but you'd manage with an MBT. Facility security is standard: HW and spiker. Wore thermals, torch and darts. Hopped HW nice and easy but the spiker line was nasty.

On site there's debris all over, ruins, weeds, nothing you haven't seen in the wild before. No burns or tags. I bagged a few parts. Here's the main site scene [picture here?]. The parts looked like alloy, burnt. Bunker is

old school, maybe Cold War, in good nick. Guessing at
gardening/tool storage. Main room could hold a lot of
people. Field hospital or fallout shelter? Last section I
found was a corridor with mouldy boxes on the shelves. I
got rumbled when—

Shep stops writing and absently sucks the salt off his
fingers. It's uncomfortable to leave out what he thinks really
happened. And there's a bigger issue: does he really want
someone else to be intrigued, head up there? He scrubs the
line and continues:

I poked about but there was nothing much. Wasn't a
wasted trip because I got a buzz, but I can't recommend it.

Shep rocks back and reads his draft from the top. Not
bad, but at the same time all wrong, dishonest. No point
lying to himself: he doesn't want to expose the bunker to the
wider community. And even if this instinct isn't in the spirit
of exploring, isn't the sport of it, he knows if he isn't careful
there'll be nothing left there to pick at. That's a certainty
– he's seen it happen time and time again. He stands up.
His breaths have shortened. Maybe that's what the couple
did, too. Maybe that's why he couldn't find their report.
He screws up the paper and heads back to the yard with it
stuffed in his pocket, digs a lighter from the stash and puts
the flame to the paper, a finger to his lips. He whispers to
Harold, 'This one's between us.'

Viewed sidelong, it's possible to believe the dummy's
expression has changed, its lipless mouth set into a smile.

When Shep looks back to the burning paper, the flames working towards his thumb, he frowns. Something new and unexpected. Beneath the final sentence – *I can't recommend it* – another line has been scrawled on, as though he wrote it with his other hand. The flame draws close to his skin, and he drops what's left. Flame becomes ash, and the ash disperses. Shep kneels and bites a thin strip of skin away from his thumb. He can't be sure – no, he doesn't want to be sure. Because he thinks the extra line said: *our blood ladder.* And he doesn't remember writing that at all.

The Journalist

On Sunday morning Freya agrees to accompany her father to the splicers' market at the garden centre a few villages along. Conversation in the car doesn't move beyond clipped small talk, and while Freya smiles in all the right places, nods along, she isn't fully there. Her back and shoulders ache from her session at Big Walls, and her stomach is unsettled. Regret she missed her chance to ask the climber – Shep – more, if she were to guess. At the very least she should've taken his number.

'It's a life, this,' her father says. 'Best decision we ever made moving out here, I'm telling you. Then you turned up, with all your little ways...'

Looking out on these higgledy-piggledy houses, their wonky slate roofs, to Wracklow moor looming above, slopes of heather burnt into black patchwork, Freya couldn't disagree more. To become her parents would be to fade away.

Suddenly the dread is overwhelming. She needs a break, to get out of there.

'Eggs the size of fists in here last time,' her father carries on, parking up. 'Yolks like a cow's bloody eyeballs. Imagine the hens they fell out of!'

Freya climbs out and readjusts her blazer in the passenger window reflection. She rolls her shoulders like Shep did. The joints feel crunchy, and the muscle resists.

A dark shape ghosts across the car's paintwork. Another person, close by and getting closer. Freya turns just as a man in a tweed flat cap and waterproofs rustles past, knocking her slightly off balance. He doesn't even break stride.

'Hey!' she calls after him. 'Sorry'd be fine!'

The man disappears into the garden centre without a glance.

Freya turns to her father, incredulous. He's shaking his head.

'Know him?' he asks.

'No? Do you?'

Her father makes a face. 'You sure, duck?'

'Why wouldn't I be?'

'He followed us.'

Freya holds the back of her head.

'Don't look so worried,' her father says. 'Not that many roads out here, are there?'

Freya stares back into her reflection. Her distorted face.

Her father comes round the car. 'Get a wiggle on, then.' And they go into the garden centre hand in hand.

Market stalls line the garden centre's walkways in neat rows, steam drifting from hot food containers and coffee machines.

Every stall displays a range of grotesquely outsized vegetables, fruits, or combinations of the two. Freya and her father stroll along the thoroughfare, pausing to steal nibblets of over-engineered bread to dip in oils, and to smile graciously at the young splice-farmers with their artisanal haircuts. It's hardly her father's scene, and Freya doesn't know what he wants here aside from freakish eggs. Probably it was just a reason to get out of the house, much as it was for her. But as good as the change of scenery is, it's hard to feel like her patience isn't wearing thin – aided in no small part by the wearying chalkboard messages at every stall: '100% inorganic'; 'horticulturally appropriated'; 'Johnny Hydroponics'.

'All these braces,' her father comments under his breath. 'Bloody underwear, that is.'

Freya touches her father's waist. 'I think I'm going to find a cuppa. Meet you back here in half an hour?'

Her father's eyebrows arch, but Freya sidles away before he can respond.

At the end of the row sits a greenhouse-styled ganja cafe. Inside, a table of women giggle into flutes of green prosecco. Freya goes straight to the counter for a fresh mint with honey, demurs on the offer of THC oil, then sits down under the awning to watch the crowd.

As Freya sips her drink, her thoughts settle on Stephen and Shep. In a weird way, it's possible to blend their features, to view them almost as the same person. Superimpose Stephen's smile onto Shep's rigid body, for instance, then conjure the smell of chalk from their combined form. She rubs her thumb and forefinger together, trying to invoke the tackiness of chalk and sweat. It draws her back to how she'd felt in Shep's presence. He hadn't seemed to notice her reddened chest and neck, her lack of gear. He was only there to climb. So was Stephen like that, too? So single-minded? Did he climb to shut something out?

Lost in the spiral, Freya realises her ex is a fogged-up memory, cooling and distant. Where he was self-obsessed and needy and never took the lead, Shep had a quiet confidence that makes him more magnetic in hindsight. He didn't patronise her, or try to flaunt his superiority on the wall. He didn't feed her lines in the hope they'd go for a drink and half-enjoy a casual fumble a few weeks later. In fact, Freya had liked his single-mindedness *because* it focused him elsewhere. His priorities were the slabs, the puzzles between coloured holds. When he smiled at her, he looked embarrassed. Even a bit vulnerable.

Freya shakes her head. Here she is, overanalysing an encounter with some bloke who's likely forgotten her name already.

She watches the splice-market punters. A stall selling enormous mutant flowers, a man sniffing round a bucket branded MEGAFAUNA. A space-brownie seller handing out tasters with glee. There was a time Freya might've captured this, this jarring future-village scene, and shared it on her stream. As an old habit, the impulse tugs gently at her, but knowing herself – that it'd be her seeking validation for leaving the city – she lets it slide.

It's then that she notices the man in the tweed flat cap from outside. He's standing on the far side of the brownie stall. His hat obscures his features, but she can tell he's staring back. She breaks his gaze on impulse, legs and back seized.

Something in her squirms. She looks again. The man's arms are by his sides. Chin raised. He's absolutely rigid.

'Is that you?' Freya hears.

A woman's voice, off to one side.

'Hey! It *is* you! Freya?'

Freya startles and turns. Aisha, her old colleague, is racing towards the cafe barrier. Freya blunders to her feet, face flushing.

Aisha hugs Freya warmly, squeezing with both arms. 'Hey-y-y!' she goes. 'Oh my days! Small world!'

Over Aisha's shoulder, the man's still there.

'Hey,' Freya says. About all she can do to sound normal.

'What are you doing here?'

'Oh, a breather,' Freya tells her. She holds up her mug. 'Parents are only up the road, aren't they?' She swallows. The man hasn't moved an inch, and her back is on fire. 'It's been ages!' she adds, overcompensating. 'Why are you up?'

'Oh, visiting some of Sabine's mates. They live near your folks. We—'

'How's London?'

Aisha sits down at the table, pulls her chair in. 'Great, great. Just a *great* place. Busy-busy, though. Crazy-long days. There's *so* much down there – it's worth the eye-bags. Only wish I'd gone sooner: a *lot* of work, lots of clients. There's all the *food* to get through.'

'Mm,' Freya says, and it's such an effort to keep her eyes on Aisha, to listen. She puts down the mug in case Aisha notices it vibrating.

'You doing okay?' Aisha asks. 'Out here in the wild, breathing this nice fresh air…'

'Coping with the slowest internet in the country.'

Aisha chuckles. 'But really? How's the office? I heard about you and—'

'I'm good… I'm good,' Freya says, blocking it off. She glances past Aisha again; the man is gone. Freya scans quickly: no hat, no one standing too still. She tries to relax. Wills herself to concentrate on Aisha. 'Still there,' Freya says, 'finally focusing on digital. Board won't admit which way it's falling, even if *we've* known for donkey's years. You know how it is – snail's pace. When the old dudes clock off, the curtain will crash down. And, uh, I've got some plans to travel, so I'm saving for then. It's… yeah. It's fine. It's okay.'

'Home comforts though, right? And is the dragon still editing you all to death? I can't imagine still working on actual pulp, actual paper…'

'She's mellowed a bit since the group was sold on,' Freya says. 'I guess she's part of the furniture.' Freya pauses. 'Like me. And they keep trying to nudge me out of the nest…'

Aisha beams. 'So we'll get you down in the Smoke soon?'

'To visit, sure,' Freya says. She exhales, and it seems to help. 'Which reminds me: I'm meant to be catching up with Siobhan before Christmas – if you're about, you should join us.'

'Sweet,' Aisha says. 'That's a plan – just let me know. I meant *work*, though. Good to hop into a bigger pond, and you're such a fab writer, Frey. I know recruiters, if you want a leg-up. So many jobs, like I said. And I don't mean *content*.'

Freya smiles quickly. 'I know. I know. I'm not rushing. Been good to see more of Mum and Dad. Spend some time getting my head together.' She looks at the marijuana leaves printed on her mug. Her hand has almost stopped shaking, so she picks it up. 'You wanna grab a brew and sit with me? They've probably got normal coffee in there somewhere.'

'Best not,' Aisha says. 'Sab's out here somewhere having French practised on her. You two haven't met yet, have you?'

Freya shakes her head, though there are plenty of pictures of Aisha and Sabine online. In truth she hasn't even messaged Aisha since she left the paper, and doesn't want to remind her of the time elapsed. Time – life – runs differently in London.

'You *must*,' Aisha says. 'You'd really get on. She's got your taste in stuff.'

Freya shrugs. 'I'd love to,' she says. 'Ah, you look great, Aisha. You look really happy.'

'Thanks! And I mean it, I was sorry to hear about you and—'

'It's grand,' Freya says. She drains her mug.

'Great.' Aisha squeezes Freya's shoulder. 'I mean, it'll get better.'

'Yeah.'

'Well, I'd better go find this one.'

Freya nods. Relieved on two counts, now – and still unsure how she's held it together. 'Lovely to bump into you,' she says. 'I'll message about those cocktails. You're on the same number, I'm guessing…'

'Sure,' Aisha says. 'And all the usual places. Take care, yeah?'

• • •

It isn't long before Freya's father finds her, paper bag under his arm. Seeing him again makes Freya feel like a little girl. That quiet impression of safety.

'Got the buggers!' her father says.

Does she tell him about the man?

'A dozen bloody *Godzilla* eggs,' he says, hovering at the cafe barriers. 'Seen anything else you want? My treat?'

'Let's head off,' Freya says, shaking her head. She rounds the barrier, waving thanks to a barista who's too stoned to notice. 'Could do with a glass of wine.'

Her father grins. 'On a Sunday? I like it. Mum should have some in the fridge – if it's not full of milk.'

They move through a busier crowd, Freya's father ahead of her, her wrist in his hand. She spots Aisha and Sabine at a distance, stoops lower. The last thing she wants is to make awkward introductions, watch her father bumbling air-kisses, or to feel any more inadequate about her life choices.

Deeper in the crowd, Freya loses her father's hand momentarily. The crowd thickens. She's several inches shorter than the people hemming her in, but her father tugs solidly to get her through. She bounces between shoulders and chests, clips an elbow with her bag. Alarm when a woman huffs and calls her a snotty bitch. She spots Aisha and Sabine again, and slouches in the gaps between the people and stalls. Concentrates on staying on her feet, on not being seen.

From nowhere, a hawker steps out and severs Freya's link to her father. 'Fresh ganj!' he bellows in her face. 'Green vapes!' Freya pulls up, face spittled, head on a swivel, and notices they're back outside the weed cafe again. How? Her father reaches back for her. She takes a step round the hawker, and her belly floods with worms. There's a roughness to her father's hand on her skin. It has the coolness of turned soil—

She looks at the back of her father's head. It isn't him.

Freya shouts out, tries to wrench herself free. The crowd scatters. The man in the tweed cap is right there, one of them, anonymous among them, even as he grips her tightly. He pulls his tweed cap to his chest. His pate has a sickly glow.

'Get off me,' she spits.

The man resets his grip around Freya's wrist and opposite shoulder. There's a sweetness about him, notes of petrol and mowed grass. His deep-set eyes are milky with cataracts. His mouth sags into a jutting underbite, as though his bottom row of teeth is all that stops his face sloughing off.

'Don't worry,' he tells the people closest. 'She's one of mine.'

Desperate, Freya draws back a knee. The crowd, shockingly, churns on. Freya goes for the connection, but only glances the man's thigh.

'Freya—'

She tries again. He takes this one hard but doesn't flinch.

'Who the *fuck* are you?'

'Come on, love.'

'Get away from me!'

'I seen that story,' he says. 'What you wrote.'

The crowd jostles them, amorphous and uncaring.

'You know what's good for you, you'll steer well clear of Parsons,' the man goes on. 'Stay right out of it—'

A fresh warmth at her back. Tension on her bag strap. Her father is right there, beside her. 'Frey? Frey? What happened? We were all the way over here—'

And the sweet-smelling man is winking and backing away. Her father, starting to drag her in the opposite direction, is oblivious. Freya is torn between them; wanting to follow, wanting to know. Only she's lost her voice, and the man's hat is back on his head, and he's blending away.

She allows her father to pull her with him. They stop by the exit. She's hollow and trembling and he's clueless. 'What a smashing morning,' he says.

'You didn't—'

'Hmm?'

A gust of wind blows the garden centre doors open. In fresh light Freya notices the age of her father's face. The delicateness of him. She resents it – and him for leaving her alone in the crowd. But she is alone, and what can her father do? Beyond childhood, when your carers seem invincible, there are times you're reminded that mortality is written in wrinkles and moles. Death has a texture. Cells break down in ways you can follow. Freya isn't a little girl now, her father is an old man, and soon he won't be here at all.

'Forget it,' Freya says.

Back in her father's car, warm and dry, Freya takes out her phone and reactivates her social profiles, her full stream. She settles her head against the cold passenger window, aware of this being a direct, impulsive response to fear, to seeing Aisha. And something hanging over her does lift away. Affirmation, acceptance – there's nothing gained from self-imposed isolation. Somehow the sweet-smelling man, however frightening, however *calm* he'd been, has proved to her that being lonely is no way to be.

She replays their surreal face-off. It feels like staring over an edge. On one hand it's terrifying: it happened so quickly, and the implications – violence, abduction, worse – are too grim to think about. On the other hand, the man's warning feels like proof that Freya's instincts about Stephen's death are right. She resolves to carry on. There'll be no staying away. There'll be no staying out of it. She knows what will be good for her.

'Can already smell that roast beef,' Freya's father says. He prods Freya's knee. 'Can't ask for better.'

'Sorry, Dad,' Freya says. She wipes her eyes, looks ahead.

The Steeplejack

Mallory Junior's office is all pastels, delicate porcelain and vases of dried flowers. The effect is startling to greens like Shep, especially taken alongside the big man's scars and dented knuckles. It makes even less sense when you've heard the anecdotes from his anti-fash days. Mallory Junior, though, doesn't care what the jacks think of his taste. He likes what he likes, and sod the rest. If that intimidates or confuses you, that's your problem.

Shep edges through the door. 'Boss,' he says.

Mallory Junior is perched on his desk, cradling a framed monochrome picture of a well-muscled jack. The jack stands harnessless on what looks like the rim of a cooling tower. 'Shepherd,' Mallory Junior says. He places the picture face-out on the desk and folds his arms.

'Hi,' Shep says.

'Are you on speed, or what?' Mallory Junior says. 'I don't get how you're still standing.'

'I've felt better.'

'So grab a pew.'

Shep sits down in the chair beside him.

'For a kick-off,' Mallory Junior says, 'this isn't a disciplinary. If you were crap, you'd be long gone. The way I see it, a day in the yard does more good than sending you off to the pub. That said, what you managed to do on Clemens was... impressive.'

'I know,' Shep says. And he winces.

Mallory Junior rubs his hands on his thighs. 'My old man had a word for lads like you. Precocious. And when you're precocious, you're given to cutting corners. Now, don't get me wrong – you're okay. But you're not as good as you think you are. Definitely not good enough to cut corners.'

'No,' Shep says.

'So tell me. Was it the booze? Was it distraction? Some bird keeping you on your toes?'

'I got careless,' Shep says. 'It was a long stretch. I didn't get on that well with the crew.'

'This isn't a nursery, lad. You're a big boy now. I've had to pay a hefty fine to cover this trespassing nonsense you're wasting your weekends on. You busted a finger, so you're not even a hundred per cent. And yard time doesn't faze you much. If you being sloppy is the reason I have this pain in my fundamental orifice, what do we do about it?'

Shep stays quiet.

'While I'm at it, you can quit using your work van for these adventures of yours, too. And why you thought it was a good idea to flee Clemens and dump your phone...'

'I didn't.'

Mallory Junior shakes his head. 'We're not bloody thick.'

'No.'

'No. So here's how I see it. I've got a half-functioning jack who's three grand in my debt, and who my senior jacks'll think twice about crewing when they get wind of what he did to a colleague they hold dear. I'm asking myself, how can we make the most of him?'

'Okay,' Shep says tentatively.

Mallory Junior stands up, stretches. 'Have you ever heard of diamondoid, Shep?'

Shep hasn't. He stares at the photo on the desk.

'To me it's a lot like "cementitious", so far as daft engineering words go. Some frustrated poets in our field.'

'I guess,' Shep says.

The boss tips his head. 'Diamondoid is an experimental material. Kept shush beyond the trade. Well worth knowing about as we look at new markets. Which is to say, I had to sit through a bastard-long conference to bring you this. The deal's simple, mind. Diamondoid spins the finest carbon filament imaginable. It helps you make super-strength cabling systems. Okay?'

'Okay.'

'Next question,' Mallory Junior says. 'You know what a space elevator is?'

'A space elevator.'

'Elevator. Lift. Not powered access, see – an actual elevator. Like the ones you get in hotels.'

Shep scratches his head. 'I'm lost,' he admits.

'Hold the thought,' Mallory Junior says. 'Final question. You ever met a treehugger? People who like to chain themselves to fences and wallow in muck?'

'Like the people outside Fawley?'

'Aye. Like that bleeding mob outside Fawley.'

Shep nods. 'They threw paint on our crew transport.'

'They did. As is their right. Except we're talking *pro* treehuggers, here. Top tier. Because there's a particular family of crusty-backers called the Vaughans, see. Made their fortune in digital storage, encryption, cloud tech. Bought a bunch of ancient North Sea rigs to make them bloody "data principalities" or whatever they're called. Solar, wind, bio. We've had the odd contract with them.'

'Name does ring a bell,' Shep says. 'Think some of the Fawley crew worked on a Vaughan wind farm.'

'Right. They bang on about blood-oil and fracking and energy monopolies and the rest of it. Except they go in harder than that. The Vaughan estate's so deep, they actually bankroll these mobs we see on the ground. Sponsored disobedience to put off Chinese investors – that kind of thing. Fun and games. It's tough at the top. But what people don't know is, it's all a ruse. Deflection. Right? And genius at that. What the Vaughans are really doing is clearing the decks so they can go top–dog. Smear the trad-energy market, undermine shale gas extraction, shaft their competitors, shift into the vacuum. And trust me, they're ballsy about it.'

'But how are they competitors if they're in different markets?'

'Because,' Mallory Junior says, 'they're actually not. The Vaughans want to create maximum distraction so they can get on with mining the moon.'

The office falls silent.

'On my old dear's life,' Mallory Junior says. 'Lunar

127

mining ops. Future of energy. They're saying—'

'Hang about,' Shep cuts in. 'As in the *moon* moon?'

'Oh aye. Helium-3 mining. You can't keep flying shuttles out from bloody Guiana and back. Expensive business, getting private rockets off the ground – escape velocity's a sod. Dirty job too, is rocketry – unreliable, dangerous. So, what they're planning is a bona fide space elevator. Powered lifters going from an Earth-surface tower to a platform out towards the stratosphere, where gravity doesn't trouble you so much. From there you get to launch your shuttles, ferry lunar minerals back down to Earth, and, I don't know... Have tea parties with what's-his-name – that tuneless Irish wanker – and the rest of your rich pals.'

Shep sniggers.

'Not even funny,' Mallory Junior says. 'They're cracking on with it.'

'What does that have to do with me?'

'Feasibility studies, Shepherd. And a bit of hard graft.'

Shep goes on staring.

'The Vaughans bought up a whole bloody island in the Pacific. Proper Tracy Island stuff. They're flat-out on the base tower's beta frame right now – a big-arsed scaffold, just to see how it all hangs together. Whether it'll work. We got the call last year. They want safety sensors on it, the lot.'

'They want *us* to work on their space lift?' Even the question is ridiculous.

'Not quite,' the boss says. 'The scaffolding system for it, at least to start with. And it gets better. This space lift won't work on an island. It needs to be on a mountain – right? It needs all the altitude they can get.'

Shep nods slowly.

'They bought a mountain as well. In the Himalayas.' Mallory Junior sucks in a breath. 'A mountain. When the beta scaffolding's signed off, they're going over there for the gold build.'

'But—'

'I know,' Mallory says. 'I know. And the thing is, you'd be right. The project's surely doomed. Probably only come this far thanks to Daddy Vaughan's aides paying engineers to hear the right things – old bugger must be surrounded with yes-men. Even if they get a *quarter* of the way up on a mountain, the weather'll raze the structure. Or before they even need to think about crampons, some tropical storm or typhoon or tornado'll come wash the beta scaff off the island. And all these gullible whapnecks going along with it, investing their millions, they haven't clocked it's a massive Ponzi scheme. The longest con. And yet – and *yet* – it might still be lucrative for us. At least in the short-term.'

'We're already out there, aren't we?'

Mallory Junior's mouth tightens to a line. 'The island beta stage, yes. Only for NDT at the minute. Small crew went out through Los Angeles last month – they're analysing the rig. Next up is flight warning systems, gyros, lightning protection. Your bread and butter. The Vaughans are offsetting their setup costs by letting the US Navy field test new drones out there. It's on us to make sure they don't crash into the structure.'

'Christ,' Shep says.

Mallory Junior breaks eye contact to consider the picture on his desk, then angles it back towards Shep. 'They'll never make it,' he says. 'No chance. It's the fucking Himalayas. Fucking *Everest*. Never mind that you've got to get the cable down from orbital space, land the bastard's nasty end – bearing in mind it'll whip about like nobody's business – and stick it all together. I got eyes on plans for their counterweight, too – might as well be an extra moon floating over us. Good bloody luck towing that into place.'

Shep shakes his head slowly. The whole thing sounds like it's been lifted from a book.

'That said…' The boss holds his arms apart, palms facing each other. 'The engineering's sound. Your satellite, the counterweight – my right hand, see – goes in geosynchronous orbit around the Earth, right above the Vaughans' mountain, with the cabling connecting to the peak, my left hand. When it's online, you run your lifts out to a midway point in near-space, launch your miners, snap your selfies, all that shite. But this means the magic's in the cable, because the stresses up there are plain daft. And that's where your diamondoid comes in – it's the only material strong enough. And the crux of Daddy Vaughan's lie is here, because as far as I can see, nobody can make anywhere near enough of the stuff. No one.'

'Lofty, then,' Shep says.

'Can you imagine insurers signing off on it? Amount of testing it'll take? You're talking sixty, seventy years to get close to that kind of tech, easy. A hundred, even. How many deaths, accidents, cock-ups? Never mind the brains and resources you'll burn through – paying for food and board alone is a nightmare. And what if some mad fucker comes along and manages to cut the cable free? It'd be like sending a cheese-wire round the planet. And that's before you talk special tooling – 'cos your twenty-one-mill spanners'll do bugger-all when they compress in the cold. And what do your contractors wear? Spacesuits? Don't tell me those Heighter twats'll have their robots ready in time.'

Shep, alert now, focuses on the photograph. The cold void of space seems appealing. Soon things slide into place; he's looking at a picture of Mallory Senior. The old jack from the Pea and Ham. Here on the desk as a message.

'The island beta would be perfect experience for someone like you,' Mallory Junior says. 'Keep you out of trouble, get your debts clear – it's good money, being in the remote Pacific and all. Warm, to boot. And who knows. By the time you're as old as me, you might land a contract for the Himalayas.'

'I haven't even got my full jacking ticket yet,' Shep says.

Mallory Junior laughs. 'That's bureaucracy talking – thought you were better than that. We put in a good word here and there, you get the training you need. Box ticking. You're better on the job, like the olden days. Not like offshore stuff, either. None of that chopper dunking malarkey.'

'How soon?' Shep asks.

'Well, we're still pulling together a subcontract abseil team.'

'Not Heighter…'

'No, Shepherd, not Heighter. We'd bunk you apart regardless. Plus, you'd get the rep back here. You know this industry – incest isn't far wrong. You'd be the envy of many. Crawl back into your elders' good books, anyway.'

'How long's the contract for?'

'Few months.'

'Months?'

'With theory and practical training down in Portsmouth on the training stage. While your finger's mending itself.'

Shep clenches his fist. The bunker with the ache of an old injury; a stab in the guts; phantom pain in his ears. A misremembered dream.

'Can I think about it?'

'Can't do much else when you're out in that yard.'

'I don't know…' Shep says. 'How far up would that be?'

Mallory Junior shrugs. 'Don't look a gift horse in the mouth.'

'I'm not. I'm asking about height—'

'Listen,' Mallory Junior cuts in. He taps the picture of his father. 'Do me and this old codger proud. Go home. Go to bed. Get down the hospital and get that finger seen to – on our insurance. We'll firm the rest up soon. Sound good?'

Shep looks away from the photo. He owes the old man for all of this. 'I'm going to the climbing wall,' he says.

Mallory Junior shakes his head. 'You must be mad,' he says. 'But aye, go on. And pick up a new phone from IT on your way out.'

The Journalist

Freya has new momentum after the garden centre. All she thinks about over their Sunday roast, on her Monday morning commute, is the strange man in the crowd. Of how she'll stay right out of nothing.

To get started, she plans to build a sort of case file on Stephen. She'll have to systematically message the people behind the tributes on his public stream, join the dots between family members, dig for relatives' contact details. Send a freedom-of-information request to her father's motor insurance company, so she can check the footage from his car's rear-facing camera and hopefully ID the staring man's registration plate. Approach the Parsons family direct. And, most importantly, find out more about the woman in the picture.

But as the week unfolds, her day job keeps getting in the way. Thursday is the paper's publication deadline, which means her shifts run late and hectic. There are no gaps in which to properly research Stephen on the side, and her compulsion to investigate turns into low-level anxiety, complete with uneasy guts, jittery legs. It's a kind of suffering, to be held back. To have to wait.

Stay well clear.

In bed, after work each night, she immerses herself in Stephen's reports. It relieves some of the pressure. Like method acting. A new ritual, too, of poring over his words, the picture of the nest.

A galaxy in span, this journey, under the banner of mitosis and promulgation.

Of course, this isn't simple curiosity. And Freya isn't naive. Lying there, she's all too aware of something unhealthy taking root: of becoming a voyeur. She's starting to obsess, and she can't help herself – she's too adamant there's a story. Or too scared there might not be one.

On the Tuesday and Wednesday nights, Freya tries to do press-ups in her room, remembering what Shep told her about muscles, about practice. She's still given to wondering how she might've spoken to him differently. In the night stillness, it's like Shep had been a conduit for Stephen in Big Walls. She projects onto Shep her impression of the dead man, so that Shep carries both of them. He'd spoken for Stephen as well as himself. Yes, bizarre and ridiculous – not least because she's only met Shep once – but that's the generosity of private thought. And, again, she can't help herself. It makes her want to go back to Big Walls and practise on the traversing walls. Climb until her fingers are so raw that when she sucks on them, she can taste the salt and chalk and iron.

• • •

When Thursday finally arrives, Freya sits agitating at her workstation. She only has to keep herself busy until the paper goes off to print. Then she'll be free. Then it can happen.

After subbing and uploading her pages, she mucks in with the news desk juniors and their news-in-brief – typing up petty crimes, lost cat stories, other mundane flotsam. In the gaps, she slips into daydreams: climbing a blank wall whose monoform shifts behind an intricate lattice of rope. No obvious route up this wall, no extremes. Freya grows long, tapering hands that seem over-articulated – an extra set of joints, a hinge at the first set of knuckles. Shep – or is it Stephen? – climbs way above her, and she follows.

Still, these daydreams aren't fantasies by the fullest definition. While Shep was friendly enough, it's hard to imagine sex with him. His body was over-forged, mechanical: a system going up and down a rope. Even if he appealed in some archetypal way – a body like Grecian sculpture, a swimmer's build – the idea makes her uncomfortable.

The afternoon passes. The paper goes to print. The office turns mortuary-still. Febrile with purpose, Freya clocks off and heads into Manchester.

From the park-and-ride at Middleton, Freya catches the Met towards Altrincham. The tram takes her through the city centre via Mosley Street, where she notices some freshly installed bollards and barriers. She'd seen the press release – 'hostile vehicle mitigation' spun as postmodernist seating. Party political conference season is close, and the city tends to hunker down. In the coming weeks they'll be flooded with

PR about 'unprecedented security measures' and 'police operations involving personnel from across the region'.

Freya alights at St Peter's Square, where the vast cylindrical body of Central Library stands opposite the tramway. The library's stone is clean yet stubbornly of an older world, its rounded aspect a warming sight. It's no small miracle it hasn't been inhaled by private developers and turned into flats yet.

She comes off the platform and crosses the tracks. It's quiet in the square for a weekday evening, her heels loud as the tram draws away. She goes under the library's portico, held aloft on its white columns, and towards the stairs to the entrance. She fishes in her bag for her membership card and takes out her phone to turn on flight mode.

As she unlocks her phone, a familiar red coat catches her eye. She looks at the owner and lets out a soft gasp. Her ex is crossing St Peter's Square towards her.

Freya reels against the nearest column and doubles over, convinced she might collapse across the damp slab steps. She edges around the column as if letting go will hurt, trying her hardest to melt.

Did he see her? She peers round the column, chest tight. She recognises the gait, the bag, the thinning crown. He hasn't. She wills him on.

A whole galaxy of conflicted feelings about to pass beyond an event horizon. He pauses and kneels down to tie his laces. Another man, sprinting to catch a tram arriving on the square, trips over her ex's bag. Her ex stands to apologise.

It isn't him. The nose, the height of his forehead – not him. And now she sees what else doesn't tally: his height, the direction of his parting, the longer chin, the width of his shoulders. *Dickhead*. Confirmation bias isn't a new concept to her, but its effects are always stupefying.

Ruffled, Freya heads straight for the front desk. The librarian recognises her and smiles questioningly. Freya offers her library card to be scanned.

'After a quiet spot?'

'Please,' Freya says, worrying at her sleeves.

The librarian pinches her nose as she searches the booking system. 'You're in luck,' she says. 'Few rooms up in Mauve.'

Freya nods and flashes a smile.

'All sorted for you.'

Freya takes back her card and hurries to the nearest toilet, her neckline damp and bits of hair sticking to her face. In a cubicle, bag on her lap, she sits on the lid and lets it out. Angry, stinging tears, owing more to frustration than sorrow. She's spent so many months retrenching, consolidating and rearming that her reaction to the man she thought was her ex has upended her. Does it mean she misses him? If it does, it's only because he represents a broken habit. Does she still love him? Can she imagine forming new memories, fresh domestic routines? Will they ever sit together on a sofa again, or go out for a meal and promise not to look at their phones during all three courses?

She doesn't have it in her. Going back to their failed project would be devastating. A harder regression than moving back into her parents' bungalow. Not that it's possible: the recession of emotional tissue is too great. If they meet in the future, there'll only be small talk. Everything else will be held back.

Freya blots her forehead, reapplies her mascara. In the mirror, the red eyes of someone afraid of dreaming. A stress rash up to her neck. She wraps herself in a light scarf and holds in a breath until the cubicle darkens, sparkles.

Freya's library card unlocks the study room. The door's window is covered with a piece of paper reading NO INTERNET. She settles at a computer and plugs a slim USB stick into the tower. She waits.

After a spate of gang fights turned into countrywide riots, a change in the law made it much harder for ordinary people to use social networks anonymously. Not all was lost, though: loopholes exploited by newspaper offices – mainly on the grounds of protecting sources – still afford some degree of privacy. Senior editors continue to enjoy backdoor access to social networks when there's a front-page-worthy event, or an obit to write, or information to 'cascade' across the news floor. It's how Freya was able to access Stephen's public stream without worry. But if you're a reporter who comes up short when you're at home, in the field, or working out of contract, you're bound by the same rules as everyone else. Which means if you go looking for somebody on a social network, the network will tell them.

For Freya, these changes initially required her to create fake profiles she could switch between. Then the mobile providers agreed your handset could only be tethered to one account, locked to its IMEI. Here, sophisticated proxies did the job – deepweb devs always a step ahead – and Freya learned how to run a profile sweep without much hassle.

These exploits were eventually shut down when it was decided you could only log in from a preregistered phone, and so the mainstream userbase capitulated. Now, if you want to find someone, you're better off trying in person.

So why is Freya at Central Library? Because its legacy public-sector-developed IT systems offer a useful workaround. The North West's last remaining libraries continue to operate non-internet connected machines on which people like to write essays or dissertations or stories, distraction free. These unlinked machines, effectively dead spots, 'no-internet zones', have become a phenomenon in the happy-shiny world of ceaseless connectivity. Together these machines form an anti-network, complete with its own subculture of evangelical users, who share tips on locations and swear by the 'productivity gains' enabled.

By their nature, unconnected computers don't need updating to comply with the new laws. In turn, they don't hold software certificates for social apps, never mind traffic records. If you can link them to an external connection, you have a way to get online without checks. For Freya, this is an essential tool for information gathering – and the reason she carries a tiny burner modem, which can siphon nearby Wi-Fi. The results can be unreliable, the connection unstable, but most of the time she can get a crude browser to run, and most of the time it does the trick.

This particular machine is definitely hit and miss. She hard resets the tower four times before it works. When the connection goes live, she opens her browser, tabs to the Big Walls social page, its member list, and begins. First, she searches names beginning with S. Stephen's private profile is there, but so too is Shep's – unlocked – which proves a surprise. She clicks through and explores his stream. It's empty, save for a single picture of him at the bottom. An uneasy smile, focus above the camera. A muted city flowing around him. Possibly taken through a cafe window. Freya exhales. To see him in normal clothes, a loose T-shirt and old-school skater jeans, alters her perception of him. He's more human, more... susceptible. She takes a long breath and checks the picture is really the only one. It is. Then she notices his friends list is also wide open. She hesitates – it feels too easy. She clicks. Too easy for sure. She now has sixty-odd connections to make her way through. Sixty-odd faces staring back.

No Stephen. No Ste. But there – a woman against a familiar background. A woman in a climbing centre, arm draped around someone.

Freya's fine hairs lift away from her skin.

'Freighter,' Freya whispers, and clicks. It loads a close-up, high def. There's Stephen. There's the woman – there's freighter. And there's her real name – Alba. She goes into Alba's profile. Languages: Spanish (mother), Catalan, English. Current location: Reykjavik, Iceland. Freya goes through her profile pictures. Black, black eyes, like storage ponds. Bright teeth. Her nose is straight, skin snare-tight. Her face is freckled. Her top lip carries a hint of blond down.

Feeling queasy, even a gentle remorse, Freya scrapes the rest of Alba's profile: a frenzied intake of information. All of it goes into a plain document: Alba's engagement with comments; her liked stories; hints at radical politics. Her profile, unlike Shep's, is almost too full, and active until just a few months ago. Freya pulls up the most recent picture.

'Oh my God,' Freya says.

Alba is standing against a tundral background with an infant in her arms. The baby's facial structure is unmistakably Stephen's. Its eyes are unmistakably Alba's.

From there, Freya logs and searches in a frenzy, copy-pasting images to her USB stick – screengrabs of profiles, the algorithm's clunky translations of Alba's friends' posts. With a name in hand, it's easier to search beyond social sites, and she throws the dragnet wide. Soon she has partials of Alba's education record, past addresses, a small business entry on the English commerce database – some sort of homemade jewellery venture, long since closed. A notice of the baby's birth on a community site – a boy called Oriol. And all the while Freya recognises the perversity of this, her cataloguing of Stephen and Alba's life. There'd be no justifying it, should she get caught, and yet she continues anyway: she needs to understand what on the surface looked to be a normal relationship, now riven by the emotional shrapnel of Stephen's death. What was their wager? What bet had he lost in death? Why had they each posted the same image of the nest?

Or is their separation what drove Stephen to spiral? The loss of his son?

Freya reloads the urbex boards. Stephen's reports page now a URL she knows by heart. All that familiar writing. And again, shuddering into frame, that unexplainable image, its empty squares.

When Freya next checks her watch, ninety minutes have slipped.

She swears and pulls the USB stick and gathers her stuff. The door is stubborn and the lights in the corridor are dim. Her eyes itch, her mascara has clumped up in the dry air. She darts through the library and onto the street.

When she opens her phone to tell her parents she'll be late back, she nearly collapses. Horror, cold and sliding. When she thought she saw her ex, she must have forgotten to change her settings. The phone isn't in flight mode, which means it won't have been in flight mode the whole time she was inside. Which means, owing to past usage, her modem will have automatically tethered to the mobile, not the library's corporate Wi-Fi.

Which means her activity was unencrypted, findable and quantifiable. Which means Shep and Alba will know she's accessed their streams.

Before she can even lock her phone, a notification pings on her messaging app.

did wonder when you'd come digging

Freya freezes. Who's this? she replies.

don't be a nobhead
is it that you want to play out?
i can show you why ste did urbex
your choice where

Freya sits down on the step, a lump in her throat. She turns the phone's Wi-Fi off and on, scans for local spots. Every SSID name reads SHEP. 'Shit,' she hisses. He's airjacked her.

you still there?
one time offer
you'd love it
freya
see me waving?

Freya gets up. St Peter's Square is heaving – commuters, bikes, joggers. Her phone buzzes again.

haha only messing

What are you doing?

only messing

Freya comes off the library steps and searches left and right. The messages still rolling.

i get it tho
more than you know
why ste did it

Stop. You're scaring me.

don't mean to. invites are where everyone starts.
you wouldn't be on my profile if you weren't digging

Get out of my phone. Stop texting.

chill
let's go together

How did you get my number?

doesn't matter
good site i can show you
don't be stressy

I swear, I'll call the police.

143

why?

all I say is no writing about it

no fake news

freya

come on

                      Why would I go anywhere with you?

cos you're alright for a hyena

                                      Seriously.

meet at salford mcdonald's, saturday next, 3pm

pack light, waterproofs, running shoes. thermals if

you got them

don't bother with recorders

i'll show you some cool stuff

                            I don't even know you.

you sharked my stream haha

strange woman

3pm mcdonald's

white trader van

i'll help you see

Shep's airhack subsides. Freya stands there shivering. A tram begins to peel out of the square. As it leaves, she hears a distinctive tapping. She stumbles off the kerb. Out from beneath the portico. There's a narrow-waisted, broad-shouldered man pressed against the tram's door glass. He's waving.

The Steeplejack

Shep still doesn't know whether to say yes to Mallory Junior, to the beta scaffold out on the island. The thought of the heat there is one thing, the distance another. But the office computer isn't programmed for ambivalence – Shep needs more laddering hours to qualify for the trip, and the scheduler can only fudge the numbers if Shep takes a laddering-intensive job this week. So off he's sent to Manchester Airport for a few days hanging off the Terminal 2 building.

The crew there is upgrading lightning protection, which means stripping away old fittings and lines and installing a suite of instruments the mayor's office ordered in from Beijing. Monitoring the airport's microclimate, or something. Prep-work for another runway expansion, if you ask a cynic. Either way, it's what the jacks call a shitter – icy wind and spells of hail, persistent drizzle, fiddly bits you can't do with your mind disengaged. But take what you can get: Shep's happy to be out of the yard and, for once, close to home. Plus, it's lively out here. There's satisfaction in following the planes as they come in to land, the rough squeal and smoke as the tyres make contact.

'You're on a go-slow today,' the lead jack shouts over the roar of another take-off.

'Say again?' Shep did a few shifts for this woman on the Ferrybridge decommission and he's grateful she doesn't seem to know about Clemens.

'Your laddering,' she says. 'Lot slower than usual. What's eating you?'

Shep can't answer. He is slower, and apart from his finger, he knows roughly why. Between second-nature judgements on fasteners and lashings, adjustments for balance (he's shagged his wooden ladders into the wall so tightly they've warped towards the structure), Stephen Parsons plays on his mind. Little vignettes of them together at Big Walls: Stephen beasting a rockover, slipping off a greasy crimp then catching his fall with a quick redistribution of weight, legs reacting with impossible style. Stephen's hand stuffed deep in a crack, no delicacy about it. Stephen, clinging to an arête by just the tip of his index finger, scanning casually for a toehold. Shift it up, Shep, shift it up. *I've got you spotted…*

Shep's ladder grows before him. Sweat stinging his top lip, his eyebrows. Why think about Stephen? Why out here? But it's simple, it's her again – the journalist he met at the wall. Freya. Standing on the crash mats with him, expectant, entitled, a deep V of sweat in the swell of her top, clavicles shifting under the skin, neck viscera flaring, mascara starting to diffuse. It's her fault he's thinking about Stephen.

Shep's earpiece blips, pulling him back. 'Come on, gents.' The lead jack, again. 'We'll break at four o'clock. Shep, let's get access finished so we can chill on the roof with a brew for ten.'

Shep turns his wrist. Two forty-five. If he gets the laddering done, he'll be able to clock off early for sure. 'It'll be right,' he tells her.

And it is, give or take a few minutes. The crew tops out. They unfold their pocket stoves and gaze at the runways, walkways, baggage trucks bustling below.

'When you off to the island, then?' the lead jack asks.

'What?'

She laughs and lights her stove. 'Gaff wants me to give you a hard time so you don't change your mind.'

Shep rolls his eyes. 'I haven't agreed yet.'

'Not what he reckons. Shame, really. Quality of that laddering, I'd have you with me in Ellesmere Port next week.'

'Stanlow?'

The lead jack mock-shudders. 'Even the name goes through you...'

Shep doesn't mind Stanlow. A big refinery, a fine tangle of a plant. Proper concrete chimneys. When you drive past on the M56, there's an instant where the pylons all line up perfectly.

'I'm in Newcastle next week,' he says. 'Our scheduler said.'

The lead jack grins into her tea. 'Oh, that'll be a treat as well. Then you're down to Portsmouth for training, aren't you? Actually, we had another bloke on crew last week who's heading that way. Proper technician he was. What was his name?' She nudges the jack squatting behind her. 'Who was

147

that bloke last week – the big one with the old-school gear?' The jack grunts. 'Kapper,' the lead jack relays to Shep. 'That's the one. Kapper.'

Shep shrugs.

'It'll be fun,' she goes on. 'Pissing about with aircraft warners? For drones?'

'That what Mallory told you?'

She nods. 'Why?'

Shep tries a mysterious look. 'No reason... I just don't get why we need the extra training.'

The site lead laughs again, tilting her face into the drizzle. 'When you're working that far off the ground, you'll be—'

A plane landing mutes her; he watches her lips finish the sentence. A word he thinks might be 'freezing'.

He shakes his head. 'It's all right,' he says.

'Not like here, anyway...'

'No,' he says.

The lead jack claps her hands and stands up. 'Right, gents! Ladderers – Shep, Frank – you've done your bit. Get off home. You can give these muppets another masterclass tomorrow.'

Shep washes in the airside Portakabin's toilet sink, applies a squirt of deodorant, and decides he'll head over to Big Walls. He's more confident in his finger after his last session, and thinking about Stephen all day has got him in the mood. As he pulls on his T-shirt, his phone starts going off in his pocket. He ignores it, assuming from the vibration pattern that it's a spam call. He bags his overalls, harness and hi-vis, and signs out at contractor security. His phone goes off again. He takes it out, annoyed. It takes another beat for him to realise what's happening on the screen.

Freya Medlock searched for your account
Freya Medlock accessed your stream
Freya Medlock enlarged your picture taken on

Heart pounding, Shep swipes open to drill into the hits. Activity from a single IP, a winking dot on a map, with a name attached: Central Library Services, Manchester. Then a pop-up: *Do you want to block Freya Medlock?*

Shep shakes his head for the front-facing camera.

Do you want to suspend your stream?

He shakes his head again. He has the feeling of both relief and power. Unexpectedly, suddenly, in control. A quick, fast-holding idea, some fantasy of connection. Wasn't he only thinking about her an hour ago?

At the same time, he wants to know for sure. He weighs it. The library is probably an hour from there. Airport traffic will melt away soon enough, and the driverless commute doesn't clog the M60 orbital till gone six. Even then, the manual carpool lanes are free-flowing. If all else fails, he keeps an inflatable passenger in the back of his van. Stick a helmet on it, strap it in, and off he goes.

Not that he holds any real doubts. He's exhilarated by the idea she's hunting him. That, perhaps, he occupies her mind in the way she has staked territory in his.

He gets in the van and grips the wheel. His bad finger pulses. A second fantasy takes hold. What about a mission? Remembering the bunker gives him palpitations, and his bad finger trembles. As much as he wants to return there

– as much as it's calling – the thought of exploring it alone repulses him. It has done ever since he drove south from the Lakes with his van seat and carpets soaked in petrol.

But if there's someone to go with… Why shouldn't Freya be the person to confirm what he experienced down there? Why should he have to confront that alone? And why should it matter that she's never done it before? If she really wants to know what it's like, who's going to be a better guide than him?

Shep's journey only takes forty minutes, his van's tachometer flashing speed warnings the whole way. He'll sort all that later: a simple wipe, a rolling back of the figures. He parks in a Gilper bay near the Midland Hotel, listens as the compound scans pretty much everything but the contents of his underwear. When it's done, he gets out and sprints down Lower Mosley Street to the busy junction with Oxford Road.

Here the cloud relents, and a golden line slides across Central Library's slatted windows to reveal silhouettes of people moving inside. It reminds Shep of angling – standing on some slippery bank, peering into still water, marvelling at the suggestion of thick, slow fish rubbing together in the shallows. Trout, or carp. A shuttering of blue-gold scales, gone the next moment. He inhales as the clouds close up again, Mancunian half-reflections desaturated on the glass, before he bounds up the library's portico steps and into reception. The counter seat is empty. His phone is still buzzing with notifications in his pocket.

'Can I help you?'

He looks up. A middle-aged woman is leaning over the first-floor balcony, neck muscles like bungee cord.

'I'm after a computer,' Shep tells her.

'Give me a sec,' the woman says, and vanishes.

Shep stands tapping the counter. A smell of cleaning products and coffee and books. Too delicate, too clerical, for his taste.

The librarian emerges through a door behind the reception desk. He unconsciously mirrors her changing expression when she puts on her glasses and blinks at him.

'A computer room,' she says.

'Please.'

The librarian gives an upward nod. 'Let's have a gander…'

Shep marvels at her swift typing. The librarian squints. 'Research suites are all booked up,' she says. 'We have the tablet stack, though, and there are other quiet spaces around the building.'

'Oh, I've just had a message,' Shep says, holding up his phone. 'My friend's here already.'

The librarian's cheek twitches. She touches a finger to one nostril.

'Have you seen her?' Shep asks. 'About my height. Hair down to about here. Freya, she's called.'

The librarian narrows her eyes.

Shep plays it cool, nodding along. He focuses on the wall behind the librarian. The last dregs of sun give it a coppery burnish.

'Can I see your card?' the librarian asks.

Shep shakes his head. 'I forgot it.'

'Then what's your surname? I can find you on the system.'

'I'll just pay,' Shep says. He flashes his debit fob before she can protest. 'Did you see her at all?'

The librarian nods hastily, in case anyone should see. 'Mauve section. The disconnected machines. She really shouldn't be using her phone in there.' She taps the top. 'Pop your fob on here, please.'

Shep realises what's happened, and grins. Freya's forgotten to mask herself.

'Sir?' The librarian motions to the reader.

Shep holds down his fob. The reader turns green.

'And just so I've told you,' the librarian adds, 'tablet rental's cheaper if you take an analogue book home with you. Know where you're going?' The librarian angles her head. 'Up there and round.'

Shep gives her the thumbs and slopes off.

The library's interior has a tactile finish, brassy details and squashy carpet. The books in the tapering walls are kept with a standard of care approaching obsessive. In one section, Shep pauses to admire a machine tidying several shelves at once, its stacking arms taking misplaced volumes, shuffling them like cards, and reseating them at uniform depths. In the central study area, readers sit at every table. He clocks an oceanic bank of manuscripts wound tightly over spools, like carpets in a wholesaler's warehouse. It's dizzying to think of all those words.

Shep finds the dead zone corridor, moving away from the central domed room into the library's outer ring. Silent over the corridor's thick carpet, between the hardbacks waiting in trolleys to be re-shelved. The walls engineered to deaden sound.

When the walls turn mauve, Shep slows. There are five rooms to his right. He approaches the window of the first room and swallows, surprised by his nerves. He peers in. Beige and vacant like a museum exhibit. He half expects to see labels on mundane objects, a waxwork overachiever in the corner. The next room contains three students crawling across a spread of yellowed newspapers, faces rumpled with concentration. The third room is empty, the fourth closed, lights off. Freya's in the fifth, then. Christ, his heart. Maybe he should knock? Pretend not to realise it's occupied and make a fuss of the door? He hangs there, then changes his mind.

Shep slips back into the third room and locks the door. Freya is two rooms over. He empties his pockets and rolls up the hems of his jeans, the sleeves of his top. He goes to the window and looks down on an alley. A few people walking by. Blank windows opposite, streaks of rainbow in the bomb-blast film that coats them.

Shep opens the window, pulls up his hood and climbs onto the ledge. From there, he lowers himself into the gaps of the brickwork, every finger but his damaged one stuffed into the mortar. He traverses beneath the fourth room's window, toes tight on slender edges until a good stretch brings his leading hand up to the fifth room's window ledge. Stone powder grinds under the callused pads of his fingers. His other hand follows gracefully. He controls his body's natural heft, swings from the core and heaves himself up. The blinds open and the room is revealed to him. Freya

Medlock sits at a desk, side-on but face mostly visible, her neck extended. There's a picture of Ste Parsons' ex-girlfriend enlarged on her screen.

Maybe it's a kind of validation that makes Shep lose his grip. Maybe it's his weak finger. The hand comes off the ledge and he barely compensates for the swing, then his feet lose their hold. His body locks up. His stomach leaps into his throat. In one instant he notices a few people beneath him, a shower of dust dispersing. Time decelerating. Somehow, he doesn't fall. His other hand stays solid, arm fully locked out, and with a grunt, he puts the weaker hand back in place. 'Fucking hell,' he rasps, trying in vain to get his toes back in. He can't see, and it's no good. Someone below shouts to him. He needs a different perch. Down is too far, traversing impossible without footholds. The only option is the downspout over to his left, so in desperation he swings his legs and jumps for it. His knees connect first, wrap the pipe monkey-like. His hands and forearms follow. Momentum carries him out to full extension beyond the pipe, which shivers mortar dust, and somehow doesn't break. He brings himself back into the stonework. Someone on the ground claps. He waits, expecting Freya to appear at the window having heard it all. No angle here except on a plane of the inner wall. He wipes his face on his shoulder. He waits there, panting. But the wall remains as it was. No change in the shadows of the room. How? Is it that she isn't coming, or that she won't come? How has she not heard him?

Shep takes his chance. A small crowd is starting to form now. Phone camera shutters sounding out. He checks his hood is covering his face, unpockets his mobile and holds it up to the window until it locates Freya's handset. When a little vibration confirms it's lifted her number, he descends the pipe, her expression an afterimage. That was her natural state, sitting there in front of the terminal. She was leaning in, lost in it, totally oblivious. And she'd looked so upset.

Sirens bear down. By the time Shep reaches the ground, jostles through the bystanders and sprints across St Peter's Square, his jaw aches from laughing. He vaults the tram platform, heads behind an office block, and stuffs the hoody in his bag, double-checking that nobody near the library can see. Then he darts back towards the square. He knows now what Freya must want. He knows because it's what he wants. The pull for both of them is too great.

He sits on a bench and preps an airhack.

The Journalist

Freya wakes from dreams of ice-climbing, ropeless and frightened. She dresses and eats breakfast like an automaton, phone in one hand, rereading her exchange with Shep in partial disbelief. His sender details now display a ghost emoji, signalling he's used a throwaway account, a burner phone, or simply blocked her. It comes across as paranoid, if not plain childish. She'd write off the whole thing if the idea of going on a mission wasn't so powerfully linked to Stephen, and her investigation. If finding out Stephen had fathered a son with Alba didn't feel so significant.

As Freya is about to leave, her mother shouts from the computer room. Freya pauses by the door as her mother storms to the kitchen sink with three mugs. 'You need to *sleep*,' her mother says. 'Working late and drinking this crap'll do for your heart.'

Freya placates her with a wave and fastens her blazer.

'And you need to stop obsessing like you do!' her mother calls after her.

Freya unlocks the door. The sharp air stings her nostrils. She has her car drive her to work while she listens to Stephen's eulogy again. Turned up loud, there are new details: a woman's huffing sobs, rhythmic like a click-track, a baby mewling, a piercing tenor during the first hymn. 'My brother,' that broken voice begins.

She cuts it there and enters the office. The speech is almost taunting, now there's a concrete lead to follow.

When she gets to her section, her colleagues break into quiet applause.

'Here she comes,' one says.

Freya frowns at them, confused. She hurries past, into her bank. And stops. Her workstation is covered with cuttings from various papers, some of them national. She unsticks a Post-it note from the top of the run-outs. A smiley face, a thick tick, the editor's initials. She sits down to poke through the pages, slightly woozy. Every article is derived from her piece about Stephen's funeral, now-irrelevant arrests and all. The recognition alone should feel better than it does, but after what happened with the man at the garden centre, Freya feels even more exposed by it. Never mind that Alba will already know that Freya plundered her stream.

'It's done quite well,' the editor says behind her. 'Monthly targets smashed in a day. Online impressions *way* up. And that's not even counting the fact that the *Mail*'s subs forgot to update the photo links, so all their traffic came to us for a few hours.'

Freya swivels, closes her eyes. Stephen's family will now be fending off requests from countless British journalists, not to mention Americans, Australians, or reporters from expat communities in any number of places. It's the nature of a story snowballing, but it makes her feel strangely protective. Worried, in fact. Expat journos in particular are vicious about things back home – a fixation that keeps them rooted, or reassured.

'Maybe you should consider features after all,' the editor says, arms folded. 'If you think anything's got legs.'

Freya sees the value, now, of writing under a pseudonym. What would hers be? *Sneaky bitch*, she thinks. *I'm a sneaky bitch.* 'I've had a few more ideas,' she tells the editor.

Stephen never drank. Stephen had an estranged partner. Stephen had a son. And someone doesn't want her to dig.

'Tell me,' the editor says.

Freya has a planner in her desk with useful numbers for helpline operators, outreach centres and service-sector businesses, salons and massage parlours included. After pitching to the editor, she takes the planner into a meeting room and calls the local children's services branch.

'Hello, GMCS?'

The desk phone shows a smartly dressed woman in her early twenties.

'Hi there,' Freya starts. 'Hoping you can help. My name's Esther, and I'm a relative of a man who passed away recently.'

'Oh,' the woman says, friendly enough. 'So sorry to hear that. How can I help you today?'

'Actually,' Freya says, 'I'm trying to amend the child maintenance arrangements he had in place for his son.'

The woman's expression is unreadable. Freya clears her

158

throat. It'd crossed her mind to message Alba directly, try to set up an interview. But they lack mutual connections, so the message wouldn't hit Alba's main inbox. Even if Alba did see it, she'd likely delete or ignore it. Or, if Alba received the notifications about Freya accessing her stream, she'd have grounds to cry harassment. It wouldn't take much to search Freya's name and see her duplicity in full – to realise that Freya wants info on Stephen. And that's assuming Alba hasn't already spotted Freya's piece on Stephen's funeral.

All of which means Freya has to play this differently.

'Amend them how?' the woman asks.

'So, the problem is that only his ex-partner has access to the account, and we don't know any of the security details. We think she's moved abroad, possibly to Iceland.'

'I see, okay. And you don't have a case number?'

'Nothing,' Freya says, cringing to herself. 'Not right now.'

'Could you tell me your full name, then? For data protection…'

'Parsons,' Freya says. 'It's Esther Parsons.'

'Thank you, Esther. And the child's name?'

'Oriol…' Freya hesitates. 'Parsons.'

'Hello? Ms Parsons? Did you say Orion Parsons?'

Freya freezes.

'Ms Parsons? We'd need Orion's date of birth, too.'

'Maybe we could resolve this without having to pay fees,' Freya tells the woman. 'If you could confirm the address you have on file.'

'I'm very sorry, but we can't share information like that.'

Freya's blown it. Of course she has. She mutes the phone. 'Shit,' she says quietly. '*Shit*.'

'Hello, Esther?'

Freya hangs up. Now she'll have to go the other way.

Freya arrives outside Stephen's parents' cottage with a bunch of garage forecourt flowers on the passenger seat. The village is wealthy. Verdant and orderly. While she's still in the car she applies heavier make-up and takes her hair out of the same high bun she'd worn for the funeral. She pulls her layers around her chin to try and soften her face. She gets out, smooths her blazer. Unlatches the front gate and skulks up the path. After ringing the doorbell, she admires the front lawns and bedding, which are bursting with coordinated neon flowers. Her bouquet seems bleak in comparison.

'Come on,' she says under her breath. There's a sign pinned to the front door that reads NO PRESS, NO PHOTOGRAPHY, because the cottage has been fenced off by judge decree.

The door latch clanks, and a man peers out. His father.

'Hey,' Freya says. She holds up the bouquet.

'Afternoon!' he says cheerfully. She was ready for frost, abruptness, and his response throws her. Not that she knew what to expect. A harried-looking couple? Vacant stares, Freya blinking expectantly at them, being spat at, the door slammed in her face? She'd deserve as much. She's had as much before. *Sneaky bitch.* In her mind it was all that or nothing at all – a doorbell ringing, curtains drawn, a sad stillness.

'You look familiar,' Stephen's father says. 'Were you at his funeral?'

There's no shakiness in his voice, no discernible sorrow. He looks bright – he looks energetic. On the surface, at least, he's bearing up well.

'No,' Freya says. 'I…'

The man smiles. 'It's fine duck, but Helen's out today. I can still put the kettle on if you like.' He nods at the flowers. 'She'll love them.'

Freya tilts the bouquet fractionally. 'I wanted to…' she says. 'A cup of tea would be nice.'

She steps into the house expecting a faint mildew smell, but it's warm. Cream walls, pristine white furniture, slender technology. Functional items hidden in the walls. Very few chairs, books, collections of anything. The shelves are empty save from a stack of newspapers. No visible wires, either – though she does spot red error blips firing on an old wireless hub and wonders if Stephen used to deal with such hiccups, if he served, like most of their generation, as his parents' IT consultant. Maybe the hub has been in spasm since he died. Maybe he'd popped out with the promise to fix it later. His lingering presence bears this out. A technical-looking jacket hangs in the hall. A filthy roll of climbing tape and a set of chalk marks at one end of the shoe rack. A solitary picture of his – she knows it by the colours alone – on the mantelpiece.

'He did take such bizarre pictures,' Stephen's father says, following her gaze. He's standing in the kitchen doorway.

Freya edges closer. The picture describes a dusty, abandoned warehouse. A rhombus of light falling through the roof.

'Please make yourself cosy,' Stephen's father says.

Freya breaks away from the picture. 'I'm Claire, by the way,' she tells him. And she sits down like she's forgotten why she's here. Like she's as entitled to grief as any of them. Like she really knew Stephen.

Stephen's father slides out a tray from some unseen alcove. He stops, fleetingly, by the stack of newspapers on the shelves. Suddenly she knows why they're keeping them.

'Milk and sugar?' Stephen's father asks.

'Just milk,' she says, then listens as he fills the kettle. The sound of it, so ordinary, makes her wonder if Stephen's death will ultimately separate his parents. Her own parents always said they'd turn into husks if anything happened to her. Is it possible to still love the person with whom you created a life you then lost?

Stephen's father returns, cups rattling on the tray.

'Sorry,' he says. 'It's the tiny things that keep eluding me. Where's the sugar? What did I open that cupboard for? Here you are.'

Freya takes her tea. A lipstick mark on one side of the cup. She carefully rotates it, blows and takes a sip. 'Lovely,' she says, though it tastes sour. 'Ta.'

'So, how did you know him?' Stephen's father is pacing the lounge, eyes to the carpet. 'Was it climbing?'

Freya looks into her tea. A curd of milk pushes against the surface tension. She swallows thickly. 'Sort of,' she says.

'Oh, the exploring,' he says.

This surprises Freya, and she can't hide it.

'We hardly approved,' Stephen's father says. 'Constant cuts and bruises, pulled muscles, sprains. Came home panting most nights, in the wars. I waited in that bloody

162

A&E department more times than I care to remember. I suppose in the end we needn't have fretted. It's the stuff you don't worry about that gets you, isn't it? That boy climbed like we pick our noses. He wasn't made to fall.'

Freya nods, but his ruse is thin. He's desperately trying to keep it together. 'I don't think exploring ever harmed anyone.'

'No. And that's what I'm saying. Laws are laws and all, and he was extremely lucky to get away with some of the things he did, but... we know it did him good. One of his pals got five years, if I recall. That's a madness. But all this? This wasn't him.'

Freya nods.

'And we keep wishing we could say he died doing what he loved,' Stephen's father says. 'Because he didn't, did he? He didn't. Now we're... I'm sorry.'

Freya gives him a sympathetic smile. 'I can't imagine how hard it's been.'

'It's these questions. You just keep asking yourself, over and over. And Helen hasn't slept since they released those men. She's convinced the coroner missed something. Were you close to him?'

'No,' she says. 'Not massively.'

'Oh.'

'I mean we used to be,' she says. 'Once.'

'And you're certain we've never met?'

'Yes.'

Stephen's father sips his coffee. He doesn't seem to notice the spoiled milk, and Freya wonders how many cups he's gone through in this state. 'What was your name again? Claire?'

'Claire, yes.'

Freya needs to break the thread. This can't be about her.

'Have you heard from Alba?' she asks him. She does it casually enough: concerned but deliberate.

Stephen's father stops pacing. 'Alba,' he says, then hesitates, as if he's weighing whether to go there. 'And you said you weren't close to Stephen?'

There it is. She pushes. 'Have you spoken to her?'

'She has nothing to say to us. She ran off before he... Before.'

'I didn't realise.'

'No one did. Something happened there. Neither his mother nor I can understand what. She took off with Oriol, and that was that.'

Freya shifts, tingling. Something new is forming, but with flaws in it.

'Was he much of a drinker?' she asks.

His father frowns. 'Surely you... No. He'd have been a lightweight. All that exercise.'

'He took the split badly, though.'

'Not at all.'

'What?'

'No,' Stephen's father stresses, as if at last noticing her questions. 'Not in the ways you'd think. I think it was a liberation. I know everyone blames that... thinks he might have, you know. But it was all going this way before their break-up. Her third trimester. That whole time he was... how to put it? Delirious? And I mean he was *arrogant* with it, quite unbearable. How would I describe it? Excruciatingly... happy. Helen found him insufferable.

His brother had to stop having anything to do with him. He was constantly *on*. Constantly wanting to *do* things. Dance, climb, run, playfights, whatever. Like a toddler – and this was even after Alba left with Oriol. Even after she took off with his son. I can't work out why he'd start drinking any more than I can understand his behaviour during that whole period.'

'So it wasn't just that one night out?' Freya feels deeply sorry for Stephen's father, whose loss, whose frailty, is showing in his sideways glances. And yet this is all confirmation to her that something changed Stephen before he climbed that scaffolding, stopped him caring about the absence of his own young son. That his parents saw it, however unconsciously. That Freya *is* right.

'I don't know,' his father says. 'We don't know.'

'Why weren't Alba or Oriol at the funeral?' Freya asks.

Stephen's father sighs. 'You'd have to ask her. Not that a funeral's any place for little ones.'

'You're not in touch?'

'We wrote to her. She's the mother of our grandchild.'

'But nothing back?'

Stephen's father shakes his head.

'Has anyone else tried to contact her? I mean, I could try for you. If that would help.'

Freya holds her breath. Stupid, *stupid*. She's pushed too hard, and now Stephen's father will sniff her out. Call the police, even. For so much as being here, she deserves that and more. *Sneaky. Bitch.*

Only Stephen's father doesn't react. He just says, 'Have you got your phone?' So Freya nods and passes it to him, and when he returns it to her, case damp from his hands, he says, 'Maybe you'll have better luck.'

Freya looks at the screen. He's entered Alba's address in a fresh note.

'You don't have a number? An email address?'

'The number's disconnected, and our messages bounce. We don't even know if she's online. I thought about flying over there, but Helen needs me here, and her heart... You understand. She's aimless. There's all this paperwork... Perhaps in time I might. Or perhaps that bloody woman will come to her senses.' He looks away, eyes red. A hand on the shelves by the papers to steady himself.

'I'll do what I can,' Freya tells him. And for so many reasons, she means it.

The Steeplejack

Shep would take another month in the yard over the next week dangling from a concrete plant roof with his knackered finger. Mallory Junior knows this, so has the scheduler send him anyway.

Shep's first day on site sets the tone. A taxi out to an industrial estate on the fringes of a quarry, up towards Newcastle, where he'll support a crew of subcontractors as they cut sections from the roof's steel joists ahead of a full renovation. The labour is dull, heavy on the forearms. Frustrating because the roof beams are spaced just widely enough that he has to reset his protection for every movement. Doubly trying because the repetition makes it easy to forget where he's up to with his gear. Is he on? Is he off? Is he only suspended by a lucky knot, or by his foot coiled round that bar, or by the crook of his elbow as he grazes cold knuckles on rough welds for the millionth time that day? A ruthless draught sweeps through the gaps in the plant's cladding. Shep's nose runs, his toes are numb, and he never feels far from a grim death in the block machinery running beneath him. Tonight, he'll sleep on a rough bunk in a dosshouse up the road.

The site safety rules and meta-rules pile up for his second day. Hypnotising reminders within and without. DO NOT BACK-CLIP. Watch you don't dash your brains on the poured floor. BEWARE FALLING OBJECTS. Don't overgrip. DO NOT SMOKE. Ignore the engineer calling you a twat because you didn't hear him ask you to brew up while he went for a dump. DO NOT REMOVE HEAD PROTECTION. Don't mind the crew sniggering between themselves because your Stillson went missing yesterday. The crew laughing at your Stillson being in your sleeping bag come morning, because you'd been 'poking at your arse with it'. Sneering at you, calling you a *little bender* because you admitted you don't have a partner, because you haven't been in the kind of broken relationships that to their minds turn young greens into real jacks.

Don't take it to heart when they compare you unfavourably to 'the birds' they've had on crew; when they say you've got your head up your arse along with your Stilly; that you think you're smarter than them, or better than them, or worth more than being here, a tiny fly stuck in the steel webbing of this roof, taking their insults over the relay while knowing if you try to give it back, you'll only get your pay sanctioned for reasons obscure.

Don't rise to it, with your temper like it is. Don't reveal the heat in your face, the way your eyes can sometimes well up when your anger rises, so that people accuse you of balling, or being a 'wee fanny', et cetera. Don't lash out or break something. Don't bust another finger thumping a wall. You can't show your weaknesses in sight of them, and you know exactly why.

Don't miss your regular crew, the regular work, and the rare occasions when you've earned the right to backchat. The crew you've forsaken by blowing old Gunny's hand off. Don't reminisce about the last time you were working in a concrete works – roped up and fully masked and dangling inside a preheater tower with five other jacks gouging bad lagging from the wall, laughing at the state of it, at the danger and the heady buzz.

Don't miss being outside, the winter sun on your face, dry rope in your hand, your shunt planing up its line. Overalls damp and grimy and stinking, ears weeping with the cold. The wood of the bosun's chair reassuring under your backside. The view from a big old stack, where nothing else on the ground matters or even really exists.

Don't pause to think about a badger, a bird, a bunker in the Lakes—

The thing you saw within yourself, that structure, that hive—

Don't think about a reporter called Freya who broke into your world without a care—

Don't think about where you're going back to, the place only you know, the only place you want to be—

And don't let Mallory Junior break you.

But do expect this feeling to last for days. Do break through your second night, your third day. Fight through the tiredness. Tackle the fourth day head-on despite the aches all over, the flu coming on. Take that cold shower without a squeak. It's grey out there and it's grey in here, but you'll be back there, soon. You'll be back.

By the fifth morning on site, Shep has all but forgotten the allure of the petrol smell, the tension of his near-arrest, the darkened Lakes. The flayed badger that, in hindsight, served as fair warning. Though his finger continues to heal, he's convinced his lungs are filling up with grey particulate, that he's sneezing ready-mix up his sleeves.

But at least nobody talks to him now. At best, the crew simply tolerate his presence. All the same, he stays alert. He reads and rereads the site's method statement in case they question him – the day before, the site engineer had taken him to one side because 'head office' wanted drug tests. He's also mindful of the engineer's productivity monitoring – the ubiquitous cameras that follow him, heatmapping his passage across the roof.

At the end of the sixth day, the crew go out drinking without him. He sits on his bunk in their empty dosshouse, caked in dust, sipping from a tin of lager in silence, playing solitaire on his new phone to pass the time. *I could be in a submarine*, he tells himself. These are the effects of pressure. And each sip brings unwanted memories of confined space training for gas leaks – his tight mask steaming up when they pumped in the soup, a literally blind panic. A desperate climb up the inside of a three-hundred-foot chimney, a tiny disc of light above him.

I am a good team player, Shep had written in his job application to Mallory Limited. *I am fast to learn.*

He'll be out of here soon. Won't he? Maybe his sanity dangles from that promise of clean air, a better view. Get up high. Get some fresh ice-cloud packed into his lungs. Shep puts down his beer, the thought proving sticky. The beta island will be warm, and it isn't warmth he wants. But the Himalayas…

He closes his phone. He lies back and pictures a crystalline tower reaching away from the Earth. He's climbing the lattice of it, completely naked. He tops out. His lungs are close to exploding and his hands are frozen solid around a length of diamondoid monofilament. And he's happy. Cold and happy.

He lets sleep take him.

On the seventh day, Shep deigns to change his attitude. The crew is just a rough bunch, nothing more. They ignore him because they so rarely work with greens, much less trust them. Or maybe they know what he did on Clemens. It'd explain the hard glares they share, the way Shep can stop grafting for a split second and know one of them has turned to check why.

It's clear to him that the jacks have bonded despite themselves. Pressed together over the years like disparate stones at the start of a beach. How long have they gone on like this? He wonders if they've always been despatched to the margins of the country, condemned to these harsh jobs, hardened in their bones and whittled to sinew, earning the worst problems – asbestosis, miner's lung, malign tumours – along the way. Why should they accept him?

The crew break for lunch early. Shep has watched the ritual several times in that endless week. At some invisible signal, the men silently unspin themselves from the formwork and descend. They set their backs against the massive churning machines and say little as they share milk powders and canteens and rolling tobacco, and regard the roof in deep reverence. On the final day, the eighth day in a row, Shep decides he'll try and join them. He tacitly follows the crew down to the floor and stands there, hesitant under the mesh mezzanine, dwarfed by equipment. A film of concrete powder on every surface, his boots white.

He swallows and approaches the group. Their scarred and pitted knuckles. He stumbles a few metres off, and they turn to him. Shep says, 'All right?' and they blank him. He focuses on one jack in particular – a man with a perversely thick neck – and asks him, 'How's it going?' and nothing comes back. The crew look among themselves, nonplussed, and return to their pastries.

Shep gazes at the far wall. A slow seepage of shame down into his feet.

'Fuck off, then,' one of them says.

With a brick in his stomach, Shep concedes that Mallory Junior has already won.

Later that day, Shep is clipped into the roof, the span of it illuminated in sharp flashes by mig-welders. He's struggling to concentrate, fatigued and ruminating on his sacrifices – the concessions and compromises he's made to work like this, with people like these. Count them out: the small things, like forfeiting nights out, or being the last to hear about his mates' stag dos because he can never make them. Like not being messaged or called or asked after. The pains: intermittent tendonitis, weeping blisters, persistent aching in the lower back. Scuffs and swollen fingers and bruises impossible to account for. And the big things, the withering friendships. The mother he barely speaks to. Flings or relationships that fail in some way to ignite. All those second dates, when things could be heading somewhere, nice and easy and fun, until his date says, 'Let's get together soon?' and he has to say, 'I probably won't be around for another month,' and her face twitches, and her eyes, lambent over drinks, turn dull. The idea of starting a family is as remote as it is distant. No anchors. Fallow ground. Friable roots. The older jacks who rib him: 'You've not even had *one* bloody wife yet!'

By the time Shep has marked the last beam for cutting, he's ready to scream *yes* to Mallory Junior. Yes, he's learned his lesson. Yes, he'll go to the Pacific island and work to pay off his debts, if not defer his guilt. Yes, stand him there on that earth, beneath a different sun, next to the open sea, in thrall to the salt wind that puts a hardness through your hair. If only so he might arrive for a moment at the summit of the scaffold, shiver in the embrace of the cold – a welcome, foreign wind. If only to get his chance at becoming lost among the black rock and snow of the Himalayas.

Just get him away from here.

The Journalist

Late Saturday afternoon in sullen Salford. A steady whine of electric vehicles along Regent Road and Ordsall Lane. Freya waits under the awning of the McDonald's, hair frizzy and hands raw, checking her phone every other minute. It's long gone three. If Shep stands her up, she'll find him at Big Walls and stick that autobelayer where the sun don't shine.

Then a white van trundles along the drive-thru lane. Cheap white vinyl partially concealing a company name on its bonnet. Shep's at the wheel with an infuriating smile. He holds up a bag of food, motions to the other side of the restaurant. She follows him round. He parks about as far from her as possible, apparently on purpose. There's more crudely applied vinyl down the van's side.

'You're forty minutes late,' she says through the passenger window.

Shep leans over to pop the door and tips the bag of food towards her. 'Soz,' he says, still grinning. 'Chip?'

Freya huffs. A warm, sweet smell rises from the van. Shep has wires running all over the place, dodgy-looking equipment stuffed into the console.

'Traffic was shite,' he says. 'I figured you'd wait… You getting in?'

Freya shakes her head. 'Not till I know where we're going. And when I'll be back.'

'Sure you don't want a chip?'

'Tell me, please – I need to let someone know.'

Shep opens his mouth, places a chip against his bottom lip. 'Who?'

'My editor.'

'Told him it's a date?'

'He's a her,' Freya sighs. 'And no, because it's not.'

Shep nibbles the chip. 'If you say so.' Again, that proud smirk. 'Bet you told her it's a date.'

'Jesus. Are you always like this?'

He pushes in another handful of chips. 'Tell her we're going to Chorley,' he says, chewing noisily. 'Back before bedtime.'

'Chorley?'

'Don't you like surprises?'

Freya grabs the doorframe and gets in. She makes sure the door's lockpin is up. There's an army-style rucksack in the footwell, and she has to prop it between her knees. 'Can't believe I've agreed to this,' she says. She fastens her belt.

Shep pours the remaining chips straight into his mouth and turns on the engine. Solemn now – just like that. 'I get it,' he tells her. 'I'm some weirdo you met climbing. And now look at us. But don't forget you've been digging on me as well. And on Stephen. How am I meant to trust you?'

Freya reddens. 'You can.'

He nods into the passenger footwell. 'Good. And you're all right with that down there? My camera. They're decent boots, by the way.'

Freya knits her hands. 'I'm not an idiot.'

'Never said you were. Did you bring a recorder?'

'My mobile.'

'I won't say anything worth recording. But no pictures.'

'Okay…'

'What about food?'

She pats her jacket pockets. 'Energy bar. Dried fruit things. Water.'

'Sweet,' he says. 'Let's go get lost.'

They drive up the M6 in silence. Shep seems preoccupied, almost adrift, and keeps overtaking other vehicles without indicating. Freya finds his elusiveness disappointing – she questions if they really have anything in common beyond a nebulous link to Stephen. Was it an error of judgement to approach him in the first place? To agree to this? It's hard to justify how easily she got in the van. Maybe it's the same nameless compulsion that drew her to him in Big Walls… his being alone, his being oddly sexless.

She glances sidelong at him. If he notices, he doesn't care. Maybe it's his face that sits at odds with her memory. Like he's a different person. As he weaves the van in and out of lanes, it becomes harder and harder to reconcile him with the man who'd sent her those manic texts outside the library.

'You're even quieter than me,' he comments later.

Freya doesn't reply. Past Lancaster, the M6 opens out to massive skies, and Shep starts driving faster, the heater going, and the sweet smell she'd first noticed at McDonald's – petrol? – grows heady.

'Why don't you tell me about what you do?' Freya says.

'My day job?'

'Yeah.'

So Shep explains steeplejacking as basically as he can, and Freya listens. When he seems to be done, Freya presses a dot into her forehead with her forefinger. 'And even though you work in these sort of urbex-y places,' she says, 'you don't do reports on them?'

Shep smiles. Dashes of rain up the windscreen. 'Too easy,' he says. He doesn't take his eyes off the road. 'Half the buzz of a mission is knowing you shouldn't be there. When you're about to do a site, you're shitting yourself because you know, deep down, you're going to cross a border. Your heart's going like a demohammer.' He takes a hand off the steering wheel to draw a horizontal line in the air, then points to the near side of it. Is he trembling? 'Here's normal life,' Shep says. He moves his finger towards Freya. 'And here's where you shouldn't be. That's exploring. Going from one to the other. Sounds simple enough, but when you're dragged up a certain way, respecting rules or whatever, it's a big deal to cross over. Like driving at a wall and trusting yourself not to brake. You have to learn. You have to face it down. Because when the bug bites, it never lets up. You enter a parallel world. It leaves a bit of its map inside you.'

'And when did it bite you?'

Shep moves the van abruptly to the inside lane and slows off. 'My first go?'

'Yeah.'

'Why?'

'It's colour.'

Shep rolls his head sideways as if to say fair enough. 'Colour.' He nods slowly. 'Well… obviously we did pylons as kids. A fair few building sites in Ashop. But the first proper one was with a mate called Mo. Off his head, Mo was. Couple of years older than me. Climbed together all the time before he did his hip. One day we're at Big Walls and Mo goes, "Do you want to go see that big radio telescope at Jodrell Bank?" Simple as that. "And I mean see." I wasn't listening and agreed. Next thing we're blatting straight over there in our gear. The West Coast Mainline runs past Jodrell, so we leave the car in a workers' lay-by to sneak in through a trackside fence. And we're kneeling, there, right, snipping mesh with his dad's tools, and *whooomph*. A train goes past full pelt. And bear in mind I'm already jumpy, so now I've got my head right down on the verge. My hair's soaking and full of grass cuttings, and Mo's pissing himself laughing. "Mecca in't that way, chum," he said.'

'Did you get caught?'

'Did we bollocks. Legged it over the field and shinned straight up the Lovell from the back.'

'And…'

'And what? It's a beautiful thing. The trelliswork. But in the dark, big open face like that, it's a monster. It groans in the wind. The steel was soaking wet. It burned your hands.'

Freya can picture the scene. School trips with neat packed lunches.

'So, me and Mo are going up the nearest leg, and bear in mind Mo's a sprinter build, so he's well ahead of me. Well over two hundred feet of climbing, and halfway up we realise the control room is facing us with a couple of security bods in there. Fluky bastards, we are – how they didn't see us, I'll never know. Can't tell you what that feels like, either. Next news there's an almighty croak, and the whole thing starts to judder, and then we're moving.'

'Oh shit,' Freya says.

'What can you do? We're bricking it. Stuck on this beast while it wakes up. Proper bad disco-leg, sweats, all the symptoms. Forearms pumpy as anything. And don't forget this is before I was jacking, so I'm not in competition shape. When it stops, we hop off the leg and onto the dish support, and it's still shuddering a bit, but the view makes it all worth it… It filled you with this weirdness, I dunno, like you were just meant to be there, under the dish like that. Mo must've felt it, too – he said if we whispered into the dish loud enough, the whole galaxy was tuned in to hear. Soppy crap like that. Two paper cups and some cosmic string. And Mo's like a statue the whole time. Hard to imagine a lad so big with tears in his eyes. Anyway, I'm telling you all this… that's not even the punchline. We're standing there, gormless, and there's this ungodly screeching sound, this mad flapping, so loud the guards come to their window to check it out. "Now bloody what?" Mo goes. And I look round slowly, expecting God-knows-what, and what is there but a massive peregrine falcon staring at us from its nest in the telescope leg. Staring us out. And I swear – I can still see that big bastard now – I've never laughed so much or got down anything so fast in my life. By the time the guards cottoned on, we were already on the ground, running like billy-o towards our hole in the fence. It was – I dunno. It's the freest I've ever felt. And when we got back in Mo's car, I knew. I knew.' Shep taps his chest. 'I'd mainlined it right into here.'

Freya rubs her face. She can't help grinning. Shep's come alive beside her, and his excitement is infectious. It hasn't just reassured her – it's reaffirmed that this is the right thing to do.

'I thought about taking you there,' Shep says. 'It was Jodrell, or this abandoned sewage works I know. Get you wading a manky watercourse – see what you make of that. Or if we had time to go further, the Angel of the North. But that was shit to climb – too many laybacks, rockovers – even for me. Then I remembered a better one to start you with.'

'In Chorley?' Freya asks.

Shep nods. 'In Chorley.'

'Right,' Freya says. 'Well, you asked if I like surprises. I don't.'

'What do you like?'

'Spoilers.'

'Yeah?'

'Come on.'

'Can't you just wait?'

Freya turns to him. 'Tell me.'

'Why?'

'Because!'

Shep chuckles. 'Okay, okay… It's a theme park. Closed

down donkey's years ago. They're still waiting to redevelop the land.'

'Not that place, what was it… Camelot?'

'That's the one.'

'Jesus. Camelot. You've been before?'

'Course. Piece of piss to get in. Too easy, actually, so the taggers've been at it. But it's ace. Get up the coaster rails if you want. It's overgrown, like one of those apocalypse films.'

'Does it excite you?'

Shep sniggers. 'Not massively. Dibble gave up on watching it, so it's only edgy if you bump into other groups there. Never know who's camping out in a place like that…'

'If it doesn't excite you,' Freya says, 'I'm not bothered. You must know somewhere better.'

'Blackpool Tower? Suction cups for the glass? I've seen that done.'

'That's not exciting. That's mental.'

Shep laughs, but it's hollow. A sudden nervous edge.

'If Jodrell was freeing,' Freya says, 'where else is freeing?'

Shep sniffs. His demeanour changes again. 'You interviewing me? How's about you talk about what *you* do, and let me plan our date?'

'Date. It's not a date. Just tell me why it's freeing.'

'Because you don't think of anything else,' Shep says. 'Everything vanishes. All the shit in your life.'

Freya looks out the window and squeezes the chair. Falling in, losing control. And loving it.

'Do you still get scared?'

'Course,' Shep says. 'That's what I love about it. You have to use it.'

'Then that's what I want. To be scared. All of it. Even if that sounds weird. All of it.'

'That's not weird.'

'I don't want it sanitised. I don't want beginner's stuff. I want to know what Ste—'

'Freya—'

'I want to be scared.'

Shep steers the van back into the middle lane and puts his foot down. He glances across at her. There's an unsettling, intense look in his eyes, and she can't read it – or him – at all.

As if to offset himself, Shep clears his throat. 'That's your first test passed, anyway,' he says.

Freya's stomach twinges. 'Test?'

'I was blagging about Chorley,' he says. 'It's novice shite. I can't tell you where we're actually going.'

'What?'

'It's too good. It's… I want your opinion on it. Like a mini-investigation.'

And there: another twinge, lower down. A tiny electric spike. The delicate queasiness that comes when things are heightened.

She watches Shep check himself, as if he felt the same. His face in profile. His jaw muscles contracting.

Is he grinding his teeth?

'Have I got the right gear with me?' Freya asks, trying to diffuse it now, trying to cling on. Her throat squawks when she swallows. 'Will I be warm enough?'

'You'll be right,' he tells her.

Is this excitement? Pride? Shep's gawkiness has

evaporated. The purpose is back, and she finds him more persuasive. No, she finds him more attractive.

'Has to go dark before we can get in there,' Shep says. 'You telling your editor you're going off-piste?'

'No,' Freya says, tight-lipped.

'It's still a good while from here, is the only thing.'

Freya grips her seat belt. Hot and uncomfortable. It's weird to accept it, but she does anyway: the arousing unknowable. She reviews Shep in this new light – his shoulders pulled back, firm posture, slender waist – and visualises a gentle crease in the skin of his stomach. She wonders if there'd be a faint red line if she pulled up his top.

'Let's go there, then,' she says.

A single bead of sweat slides from Shep's temple. He opens his window and puts his hand in the airstream. 'Know Scafell Pike?' he asks. The heavy buffeting makes his voice distant. The land is beginning to ripple around them. The Lakes.

Freya tells him she doesn't.

'I have to start training for a big contract next week,' he says. 'Going away for a while – overseas project we've got on. And I thought, well, I wouldn't mind seeing that big lovely bastard again before I go.'

'The Lakes,' Freya says. 'Not very urban.'

'The Lakes,' Shep says. There's no denial.

The Steeplejack

Shep comes off the B-road and holds the van on the mossed slopes of a wide fell. Below lies a tarn that tapers away into austere land, starkly brown. The peaks above the water are rendered flat and featureless against the burning dusk. He pictures the range under snow, pale and somehow larger, and places Vaughan's orbital tower on the closest summit. A great lace frame, rising into the night to come.

'We go from here?' Freya asks him.

'No,' Shep says. 'I just need a slash. Thought you'd like the view.'

'It is pretty,' Freya says. 'The colours.'

It's closer to average, compared to other views Shep knows up here, but he isn't about to spoil it for her. It's enough to have her with him. Enough that she's engrossed, and to know he succeeded. To know he's this close to returning.

'It's better later at night,' he adds, 'when the water looks like fresh tar. Or first thing in the morning, with the light coming down a certain way. Mist on the water. Sometimes the peaks look like they've been cut away from the earth. Like they're hovering.'

'You always do this stuff in unsociable hours?'

Shep shrugs. 'You wanted a scare,' he says. 'There's a public hiking trail. It'd be too busy in the day.'

'Is it dangerous?'

Shep smiles uncertainly. 'If you don't mind your step.'

Freya undoes her seat belt and struggles out of her jacket. 'I want to get cold,' she says, 'so it feels cosier in here.' She gets out of the van and goes to the bonnet. She stretches, hands raised against the sunset almost piously. Shep's stomach spasms, and he turns off the engine.

Freya sits on the bonnet as he applies the handbrake and climbs out. The fells on the other side of the lake shifting to a richer purple before the half-lost sun. She smiles pointedly at him. What changed?

'Only be a minute,' he says, and relieves himself behind a bush. When he comes back, Freya is lying flat out on the bonnet, swinging her legs off the side.

'Washed your hands?'

Shep doesn't reply.

'I'll pretend you did.' She pats the bonnet. 'Space for two.'

Shep sits down next to her, feels the thin metal give, the van sag on its suspension. 'Do you usually stalk strangers online?' he asks.

Freya snorts and props herself up with her elbows. 'I'm not the one who waited outside the library like that.'

'Nah. But you came to Big Walls in the first place.'

'It was different.'

Shep pulls a long blade of wild grass from the ground. 'How?'

'You followed me in your spare time.'

'It's Saturday, today.'

'It's overtime.'

Shep chuckles. 'You like your job, then.'

'I enjoy the writing. I like having templates, making things fit. Sometimes it's a puzzle.'

'And you don't mind leaving your morals at the door.'

Shep hopes she'll laugh again, but she glances away.

'No one pretends it's noble,' she says.

'Not even when you cover war crimes? Corruption? Kiddy-fiddlers? Exposing that shit is noble.'

'I'm not really qualified.'

'So you're happier turning over dead people's lives? Taking a stick and poking what you find underneath?'

Freya flinches this time, as if to physically dodge the question.

'Slippery, aren't you?'

'I'm paid to be slippery,' she snaps. 'And no, I'm not proud of everything. But that's work. Is anybody? You have to… disengage.'

He nods. 'So you're only a minor scumbag.'

She tuts. 'You don't know much about me, remember.'

'Why Stephen, then? What's the deal?'

Freya pulls away from the view and rubs her hands on her thighs. 'It wasn't even a thing at first. Not straight away. I—'

'Fancy him?'

'Sorry?'

'The guy dies, you go digging, you get a crush on him.

186

You find me. Us lot – climbers. Because what else drew you in, if it wasn't that bugger's dreamy smile?'

'The climbing interests me,' Freya says. 'But there was something else going on with Stephen. Weird stuff, I mean. It's a hunch.'

'Urbex?'

'Maybe.'

'Must be part of it. Since you must've pulled my reports as well. Were you comparing us? Was that why you came to Big Walls?'

Freya looks shocked. 'No,' she says, emphatic. 'I lucked out. Talking to you was opportunistic. You were alone. You looked like you knew what you were doing.'

'I do.'

'Obviously.' Freya rolls her eyes. 'But I had no idea you were into urbex as well. I didn't realise so many climbers were.'

'They aren't.'

'Doubly lucky then, aren't I?'

'Pretty much,' he says. 'So, hang about: you didn't find my reports?'

'Get over yourself,' Freya says.

'Seriously?'

She sniggers. 'No, Shep. This is pure fate.'

'I don't believe in that shite.'

'No?'

Shep holds up his good hand. Flexes his fingers. 'I cock it up, that's on me.'

Freya seems to think about that. The slick road going bronze, loose stones like scattered gems. She gets off the bonnet. 'I'm cold enough now,' she says. 'Can we go?'

The van heater kicks out hot dust. Shep continues to drive the van in manual. Drives it eagerly, too fast into the corners. While Freya says nothing more, he notices her holding her chin high, eyes level, as if she's fighting to avoid travel sickness. For the first time, he thinks he can scent her nervousness.

'There it is,' Shep says.

'There what is?' Freya replies.

Shep stops the van abruptly and reverses back up the road. 'Yeah,' he says. 'That'll do it. Hold tight a sec.'

Before Freya can respond, Shep has them fording a stream and buries the van in a thicket of brambles. He notices her gripping the fabric of her seat as the van squeals deeper, cabin dark under knotted branches. When he's satisfied, Shep applies the handbrake and removes his belt.

Freya's speechless. A visible sheen on her face.

'What?' Shep says. 'Gotta do it properly. Bit of a walk from here.'

'Isn't this your company van?'

He shrugs. 'Few scratches never hurt. Can you manage?'

'With this?' She forces the door against the bulk outside. Three good shoves until there's a wide enough gap for her. 'Yeah,' she says.

'Chuck my rucksack, will you? And mind yourself down the side.'

'I'm fine,' she tells him, a little snippy. She hauls his bag onto his lap and slips out. He watches as she squashes herself up against the panelling, a hand protecting her face, her eyes tightly shut. She grows smaller in the mirror.

Shep does the same on his side. At the rear doors, he

picks a thorn out of his cheek and spits in the mud. Freya stands away from him, swaying gently. 'That jacket's too bright,' Shep tells her. 'I've got a bin bag you can wear.'

She breaks away from the view. The purpling silhouettes. 'Seriously?'

''Fraid so. You're a vision. See it as insulation.'

Shep opens the van and fishes out the roll of bin bags. He can't be sure Freya isn't studying him as he moves old rope and scrambler parts, his sleeping bag and camping stove. It gives him a twinge of self-consciousness, or self-reproach. Like he's reacting to an extrasensory signal. He looks back at her. She's biting her nails, staring blankly. She really has no idea what she's in for. But Shep isn't scared of that. He's just ready.

Freya takes the bin bag and tears holes for her arms. She flashes him an expectant look.

'Now what?' Freya says.

'Lots more sweating,' Shep says. He takes out his camera, secures it around his neck, and throws the rucksack back into the van. 'And rustling.'

'You know, I think I've got some high heels in my bag as well,' Freya says.

He ignores her and passes her a dust mask. 'For your lady lungs.'

Freya shoves him. Their first physical contact. 'Dickhead,' she says. 'Do I really need this on right now?'

Shep shakes his head. 'Soon though.'

'Soon,' Freya repeats.

'Off we trot then,' he says. And he locks the van doors and pulls a veil of brambles across them.

For a time, they trudge single-file along a winding ridge, him concentrating, her determined. The sun is all but down, the fells in rich shadow, the clouds joining up and conspiring. 'Scafell Pike's somewhere over there,' Shep points out. Bats slice past their ears, and creatures whine and yammer in the middle distance. Shep remembers his first approach to the bunker, compares it to now, his timing and all the rest of it. The beetle on the access road. The thought makes him cringe. 'You see owls out here,' he says, and takes from her expression that it reminds of her something. 'Poke me if you clock one.'

The ridge flattens and dips into a valley. They leave the main path to join a skinny dirt trail going into the shedding pines, patchy ground for the most part, occasionally given over to nettles. Shep listens to the rhythmic shuffling of Freya's bin bag in her hands. Her breathing. The air smells gamey, and he's aware of their growing solitude. Then they meet the hiking trail proper, arrowed signposts marking the easy route, stiled off. A single tyre mark crosses through the clayish mud – possibly from his own scrambler. A territorial line.

'Cut over here,' he says, pointing to a collapsed section of dry-stone wall. They scramble into undisturbed woods where the ivy has thickened and noosed the tree trunks.

'What was that?' Freya hisses.

'What?' he says over his shoulder.

'Shep.'

He turns round. She's squatting.

'It's near us,' she whispers.

He creeps back to her. 'What is?'

'I heard branches.'

Shep's back sparkles. 'A deer,' he tells her.

'It was breathing.'

He grips her shoulder. The sap on his hand sticks to her jacket. 'Forest whispers,' he says. 'Your ears are tuning in.'

'What if it's a boar? Or a—'

He stands her up. Cobwebs in her hair and an insect smeared across one cheek. For the first time, his sense of responsibility manifests as a load. A reminder of what he's done in bringing her along. He helps her put the bin bag on.

'Come on,' he says.

She touches his hand. Her fingers are sticky with sap. He loops her index finger around his, and she doesn't resist, so he pulls her with it. Then he can only hear the leaves, and her breathing.

The angle of ascent increases, and by Shep's reckoning they'll shortly meet the walking trail. He decides they can't risk the longer trek, however, lest she lose her legs for it. This way has more open ground, but it shortens the route to the bunker door.

Freya coughs, lets go of his finger, and Shep's excitement returns. This quiet addiction. Only minutes from now, Freya as witness will help Shep concede to his imagination – or give it credence.

'Really close,' he tells her.

After the next incline, Freya is breathing raggedly. Sweat on both of their faces like grease in the light. The midges are billowing now, bolder by dusk, and several times there's a *crack* as Freya slaps at bits of exposed skin.

'This can't be urbex,' she comments. Her mouth sounds full, like she wants to spit.

'You're crossing over,' he tells her.

'I'm knackered,' she says.

He pauses briefly to let her catch up. 'It's worth it.'

'Yeah,' she says. She has her hands on her knees, sniffing loudly.

Shep goes to her and retakes a handful of the bag on her shoulder. 'We'll have to get you registered on the boards after this,' he says. 'Captain Bin Bags.'

Freya gives him two fingers, then inverts them to indicate walking on. 'Unless you manage to kill me first.'

'Exactly,' Shep says. 'Or it gets too dark to see the mantraps.'

Freya doesn't seem to find that funny.

The Journalist

Shep leads her deeper into the woods, tracking unknown quarry through a dampening matrix of tree limbs and undergrowth. Soon it's too dark to see, so he puts on a headtorch and angles it low. She trails the light in dazed reverence, there in person but not properly there, as if operated by proxy. A cold nose and wet feet, and the bin bag already heavy with condensation. Her heart thuds distantly but it's full in her mouth. Her senses are blunted but sharply present in the taste of blood. The cold is getting into her bones, but her skin is slick. The ground is soft and bodily, and the air is crisp. Strongest and strangest of all is the feeling that Shep really does want to get them lost.

Beyond a clearing, humming with invisible life, Shep and Freya reach a dilapidated brick wall that bulges precariously in several places along its length. A barrel of new-looking razor wire runs along the top, secured in place with masonry bolts. Freya doesn't need to tell Shep that the wall is too tall for her. Instead, she stands there while Shep, silent and concentrating, searches for a good spot from which to try and get over.

'Here,' he says, trampling nettles. 'They forgot to join the wire.'

She's seen him hunt like this before – at Big Walls. One eye closed, he ducks low, digs in his toes, pushes in his fingertips, and lifts himself up. Graceful, like he's underwater. He pushes the razor wire aside and hops back down, silent but for a tiny boot scuff on landing. It's not just careful, it's studious. He assesses and tests and mutters to himself.

'How solid are your toes?' he asks her. He angles his head towards a pair of bricks he's worked loose. 'Footholds here. I can give you a leg-up.'

Freya smiles weakly as Shep kneels in the mud. He cups his hands, long fingers interlacing. 'Best you don't think too much,' he says. Freya steps up from his hands with a groan and feels him tense and wobble with resistance beneath her. She pushes off, not caring – not in that instant – if it hurts him. A quick sadism, cut through by the harshness of the wall on her palms. A flash of dream-Stephen climbing her body, planting his mouth above her pubic bone, working his splitting face into her lower abdomen—

Freya's on the wall. Clumsy, but up there. Shep grins up from the dim below, teeth blue in a black frame. 'Now straddle it,' he says, and the fillings in his molars flash. A lurch of fear, but she does it, one leg in the everyday and one in the new, and Shep seems impressed, eager. 'Here,' he says. He passes her a headtorch.

'Pull it on,' Shep tells her. 'Tight. Your dust mask as well. It can't be loose.'

Freya does as she's told.

'Now, recce the place. Sweep left first, the far side. Can you see anyone?'

The suggestion shocks her – does he *expect* her to see someone? And sent her up here anyway? The mask's elastic pinches the soft hairs at her temples, and its synthetic smell is awful. Glue and rubber and something else.

'No,' she says. 'No one.'

'And the rest of the site?'

She scans the plot. Tendrils of mist caught in the beam. Distant shapes, shadows on the far walls. A pile of debris, pieces of gnarled machinery. A digging machine with a clawed bucket. A rough square of missing earth. Over from that, two slanted concrete buttresses built into a mound of earth, between which is set a heavy door.

'It's quiet,' she whispers through her mask. 'A digger and a pile of junk. I can see an entrance.'

'They've tidied up,' Shep says quietly. Then, louder, 'You see the bunker door?'

A bunker? That's what this is?

'I think so,' she tells him. 'In a mound. Two big concrete bits.'

'And we're close? Coming at the entrance from the right-hand side?'

'Diagonal-ish. Shep… listen, I don't feel great.'

He takes a few steps back from the wall. 'Like how?' he asked. 'Gippy? Like you could throw up?'

She nods.

'It'll smooth out. You're rushing.'

'I'm cold,' she says. 'Look at the state of my hands.'

He bounds up the wall to join her. Breathing harder beside her. 'You'll warm up when we get underground,' he says, balancing on one foot, knee bent, his other leg extended fully downwards, ballet toes. 'This is the worst bit. See all that shit, down there?'

Freya follows the choppy torchlight. At the base of the wall there's a border of concrete covered with broken glass and ripped-up cans. She looks closer. Metal offcuts and rusted nails. 'Hang on,' she says. 'It's bedded into it?'

She turns the torch to his face in time to catch a smirk. 'Spiker line,' he says, covering his eyes, and she shivers, looks beyond towards the woods. They're so dense she wonders if they'll ever get out again.

Shep taps her. 'Jump away from the wall, right? Don't overthink it. Don't count yourself down. Like this.' And he goes.

'Wait!' she says. 'Fuck's sake.' She turns so she's facing him, both legs hanging over.

Clear of the border sharps, Shep raises his hands. 'I'm spotting you,' he says. 'So jump. Don't even think about it. Your knees'll take it. Use the momentum to roll. Land arse-over-tit, I don't care – just clear the spiker line.'

There's frustration in his tone now. Does he mean to belittle her? Does he regret bringing her?

No, that's projection. This is on her. She approached him at Big Walls. She got in his van. She steadies herself with both of her hands out-turned.

'You've got this far,' Shep says.

'Oh, piss off,' she says. And she leaps off the wall, lands heavily, and piles straight into him.

'Nice one,' Shep whispers in her ear. She pushes him away and straightens her jacket under the bin bag. Shep gestures towards the bunker. 'Now it's your turn to lead.'

'Over there? Isn't it locked?'

'Yeah. Wait in the alcove-thing.'

'The porch.'

He laughs under his breath. 'The porch. Go on. I'm checking what's down that hole.'

For some reason she defers to him, agrees to this, and sets out across the outground, keeping her headtorch angled towards her feet like Shep did in the woods. Everything glows green: a range of textures – woodchip, sponge-like soil, randomly laid paving slabs. 'What is this place?' she asks, turning back to him. He's vanished. No torchlight, movement. Her pulse running in every joint.

'Shep?'

Nothing.

'Shep?'

Freya swears. What's she doing? She continues to the bunker's porch and switches off the headtorch so she can watch for Shep across the site. Wait for his torch to reappear in the distance.

'Shep,' she says, louder this time.

He's gone. She edges back until her shoulders are flush against the cold bunker door and stares into the night, trying to pick him out. There's only empty space, the angles of the digger's simple limb. The air has taken on a thickness, a closeness, a resonance. She could almost cut a chunk from its volume.

Shep's headtorch clicks on. He's jogging, casually, towards her.

'Where the *hell* did you go?'

'Boxes,' he hisses. 'They've burnt all the fucking boxes!'

'What? What boxes? Where were you?'

'They burned the fucking lot,' he says. 'From the corridor.'

'Who did?' she says, panicking openly. 'What boxes?'

Shep huffs impatiently and pushes past her to the bunker door. 'I needed a piss, Freya. It's not a big deal.'

'Shep, what boxes?'

'Nothing matters,' he says, and for a second, she can't be sure he isn't sniffing at his sleeves, his chest.

She raises her hands and steps away. 'I'm going home.'

'You aren't.'

'What?'

Shep shines his headtorch in her face. She winces, kneads her eyes.

'Arsehole!'

'Aren't you having fun?'

'God's sake, you've blinded me.'

'We're here, see? Let me sort the door.'

Freya scowls at him. Even if she really wanted to leave, how could she? Shep is her Sherpa. She thinks of Stephen. She thinks of the strange look Shep gave her in the van.

She looks again, relenting. He's tampering with the door. Snipping, a gentle scraping sound. The clacking of a keyboard, loosely mounted. A soft pop.

'Open sesame,' Shep says, and even in those two words she can tell his mood has lifted again.

She tells herself to follow him.

'You first,' Shep says.

'What?'

'Like I said. It's your go now. This is it.'

'That was out there. Walking to the door.'

He shrugs, moves back. Against every impulse, Freya takes a step forward. Half hoping he'll bar the way, make some smart-arsed comment. Another delicate step, both hands on the nearest wall, as though she's on a tightrope. And still no word. She fumbles on her headtorch. Through the white spots in her vision, the bunker shapes up. The walls resolving in fragile lines. The smell of earth and the tang of must. The sound of trickling water, Shep's breathing. She's standing in a narrow corridor spotted with pools of fetid water, stripped out brackets and dangling wire enclosures for utility lights.

Deeper, where the torchlight deforms the angles either side of her. Her own shadow stretching ahead from Shep's torch behind.

'Expected more graffiti,' Freya says.

'It's virgin,' Shep tells her. 'They don't know.'

'It's like a tomb,' she says.

'You'd have to die for that to make sense,' Shep replies.

Freya stops. She closes her eyes for a moment. The dense earth, thin air. Her electric nerves.

'What are you doing?' he asks.

'My eyes hurt.'

'Are you loving it, though?'

'What?'

'Are you scared?'

199

She exhales. 'Yes.'

'Then use it.'

Freya opens her eyes and continues. Fairy steps now. Another doorway over there.

'Keep going,' Shep urges. He touches the small of her back. She leans on his hand, lets him guide her. She closes her strained eyes again. She'd prefer to put her fingers in her ears, like her ex did to soften jump-scares in horror films. Here, though, not looking is all she can do. How will she ever write about this? Tomorrow morning, when it's over, how will she come at it? Journalistically – which is to say coldly, by affecting a certain artificial distance, as though her mask and bin bag form some sterile barrier? Or floridly? Could she spill gleefully over her word counts? Come out with some pinwheeling stream of consciousness? She never gives much thought to creative writing – news writing being about form and concision, the doctrine that every published sentence must be a tightly bound fragment of truth, or at the very least digestible, comprehensible to anyone. This place, though, with its depths and its smells… She'd have to redraw her boundaries to do it justice. She'd have to slacken her grip.

Like Stephen did, in his posts.

Now the air cools and the sound of their feet is expansive. She opens her eyes to find they've entered a chamber with a higher ceiling.

'I reckon it was a dining hall,' Shep whispers. 'See?'

Dark marks on the floor in a pond of combined torchlight. Rubber-footed tables or chairs.

'Where now?' she asks.

He touches her head. 'Take off your mask.'

'But you said—'

'For a few seconds.'

She pulls the dust mask down around her neck.

'Smell that?'

'Rust?'

'Please.'

Freya sniffs. Her nose is freezing. 'Rust. Mould. Rot.'

Shep shakes his head and inhales deeply. A smile spreads from ear to ear.

'Shep?' she says.

His eyes turn glassy. He says, 'You don't get it,' then whispers what she takes to be 'stratosphere', which makes no sense at all. He points past her head.

'What is it?' she asks. 'What's there?'

'Can't you see it, in the walls?'

When Freya turns back to him, Shep has his camera up. She raises a hand in protest.

'Show me your teeth,' he says. And the camera flash burns white. It's like being stung. Freya trips back from him. She overbalances, hits the floor, and her headtorch falls around her neck.

'Sepsis,' Shep says, and fires the camera again.

Freya crabs backwards on her hands and her knees.

'Where are you going?' he asks her. 'Why can't you even taste it?'

A third blast from the void. Freya rolls to her front and trip-staggers to her feet; sprints into the chamber, bin bag inflating around her. She tears at it, pulls away scraps, and her torchlight bounces from floor to ceiling.

'Freya!' Shep shouts, echoless and direct. He could be right there beside her. 'Where are you going? You can *taste* this!'

Freya twists round. A glimpse of Shep standing still, body rigid, neck bent back abnormally. His headtorch pointed directly at the ceiling.

'It's perfect!' he calls, turning slowly where he stands. 'They're all here! Why can't you *taste* it?'

Freya meets the far wall at full pace, hands and face into slimy bricks. Soil fills her mouth. Vegetation flashing pus-yellow. She steps back and hideous wet things come away, crumbling into her hair. She sinks to the ground. She wants to give in. Has a tooth come loose? 'Please,' she whispers, pointing her torch with both hands.

'Don't be mardy,' Shep shouts from somewhere far away. He fires the camera again, a cone of light. A fifth time, closer: a sickening bleach.

'No,' she whispers, head swimming.

'Glanding!' Shep shouts, this time from the opposite side. 'They're glanding – for both of us!'

'Shep,' she pleads.

His laughter rings out.

'Use it!' he yells. 'It'll make you see!'

A sixth flash from the pitch. A seventh. He's hunting her with his camera.

'Stop,' she whispers.

In the corner of her eye, a long silhouette crosses the floor at unnatural speed. A broken figure on its hands and knees, like the Stephen in her dream. It's Shep, and his strong hands grip her calves, and she kicks back, connects with a cheek or maybe a throat, and draws from him a low grunt.

Running again. Iced veins and weak thighs. The bin bag a witch's cowl. Hopelessly, endlessly lost – and missing in a way it's so hard to go missing. No cameras, no transactions, no social or signal. Nobody knows where she is.

It's the bin bag. It's the sound—

Freya forces herself to a stop. There, in the wall, where the pipework forks left. She tears away another piece of the bag and follows the pipes into a corridor of naked metal shelving. If she can lose him, she might find a way back up, back outside.

'Freya,' Shep calls out, more indistinct. Behind her, the main chamber still lighting with camera flashes, like a storm out at sea. 'They're waiting.'

A narrow gap in the shelves reveals itself, and Freya slides in. A cold pressure through her clothes. She's saturated with sweat. Holding her mouth to stifle herself. There are old gardening tools on the shelves, and the smell of soil takes her back to the garden centre.

Stay right out of it—

Reaching, overreaching, Freya's fingers touch and tease down a trowel. It tips, and she catches it by hugging herself. She squeezes the handle until her hand burns. She kills the headtorch.

'I only want you to see,' Shep's saying. 'To admit it's real.'

Shep's own torch stretches the corridor, and its light catches her hand, the trowel's blade. She lowers it, but the shelves aren't deep enough to hide her. Before he can get any closer she slides out and side-steps on, trowel to her stomach like a warding charm, the other hand skimming the degrading shelves, braille-like metal running beneath her skin. Another space. Another.

Right there—

She stands suspended in total darkness, muscles burning, blinking tears. She's about to try and hurry him on – a challenge? A capitulation? – when a separate ribbon of colour flares and zeroes her attention. A shelf further along emits a luminescence. A soft light, nearly missable, almost a vapour. There's an object sitting on the remains of a cardboard box. Its sides are flapped open and dripping with a substance like syrup.

Freya swallows a breath. The colour transfixes her – monochromatic, pulsing, at its most vivid after blinking. It draws her out. It draws her closer. Within a metre, headtorch still off, her gait careful, she recognises it.

It drags into its wake proximal asteroids. It bends the also travelling light.

Stephen's nest.

'Don't,' Shep whispers. He's there with her, scent sour and metallic.

Freya lunges with the trowel. He catches her wrist, locks it off. Not forceful, more to show he anticipated it. The trowel falls from her hand.

'You couldn't smell it,' he says, his thick face in hers. 'But you can't miss it.'

He brings her closer. Inside the nest lies a knotty mass of tiny bones and feathers.

'They waited for me,' Shep tells her, edging past. 'They tried to scare me off… But that was only a test.'

Freya reaches for him. Grips his jacket sleeve so now they hold each other. 'You knew this was here?'

He shrugs off her hand. She's seething. She's distraught.

'It was always going this way,' Shep tells her.

'But they got here before you.'

Shep turns off his headtorch. 'Who?' he asks. 'There's nothing. No reports.'

'Except there is,' Freya says. 'There were two of them. Two reports. I know who posted them.'

Shep angles back to the shelf, eyes glowing. It's a chance, but Freya can't see the trowel on the floor. 'I was first,' Shep says. He extends a hand, its shape cutting into the light.

'Don't,' she says. 'I don't think you—'

'Let me,' he says. 'Let me in…'

'Stephen found it,' Freya tells him. 'With Alba. I can show you the picture he took.'

Shep's face is expressionless. He hardly reacts. 'It isn't theirs.'

'Listen to me,' Freya says firmly. 'We need to go.'

'It's *mine*. You can see that. You can.'

'We need to go, Shep.'

'They caught me last time,' Shep says, placing a finger against Freya's lips. 'Don't ruin this.'

The path for its replicants is decided, for the extremities of worlds are essential.

Shep's other hand, tangential somehow, begins to reach. It's coming from the wrong part of him, misgrown or stunted. The movement is too slow, like his hand isn't properly attached to his forearm, his steady bicep, the action of his shoulder in its socket. It twitches as he holds it up to the nest, a sudden fragility to him, and he's neither the Shep she met at Big Walls nor the driver in the van. She has no idea who he is.

'It's glanding,' Shep tells her. 'Can't you see?'

Freya just stares. Shep's scissoring fingers, the nest's luminosity on his face, his wide eye in profile, his awed smile. The glow, the vapour, expands across him.

'I'm here,' he whispers.

Freya wants to turn away, and she can't. She wants to stop him, and she can't. She gets the unshakeable feeling that Shep might want to eat her, and that interfering will only encourage him. Instead she stands there, complicit, and watches Shep grope the honeyed bones of Stephen's nest.

SUNDAY RITES

The Landowner

Sunday breakfast is a tradition in Em's house. Ted does the bacon and eggs and the girls cut the soldiers at the breakfast bar and Em sits and reads old spy novels. It's been this way as long as Em remembers, in the same way that it feels like the children have always been there, or like she and Ted have always been going out, or married, or at least living together. And it'll stay this way, she wants to think, when they've moved. Because it has to, doesn't it?

When Ted's phone goes, he throws the call to the dining room speakers. These are their Sunday rites: his mother phones at this time every week, and they each – Ted, then Em, then the girls – take turns to chat with her. The unspoken rule that as a family, they'll address the small things, report the small events, and hurry her off the line again. This way the day can run as usual, as anticipated: a walk after breakfast, probably an animated film late afternoon, an early supper, before the girls' bath time and a story.

But today marks their last catch-up in this house. Their last Sunday before they move out. And Em, clinging to the last ledge of normalcy, doesn't mind the intrusion for once.

So, it surprises them all when another voice fills the room.

'Is that Emma?' a woman says. 'Hello?'

Ted clears his throat, but Em answers anyway. The girls, sensing a difference, stop what they're doing.

'Who's this?' Em asks.

'Oh, hi—Hi there. So sorry to bother you on a Sunday. This is Tracy from Neighbourhood Watch over in Whitehaven.'

Ted puts down the knife he's using to rind the bacon.

'Are you in private, Emma?' Tracy asks.

Em doesn't know how to turn off the kitchen speakers. Ted looks at the controls and then at her, and shrugs. Em waves at him, and he hushes the girls.

'What's going on?' Em asks.

Tracy clears her throat. 'Well, I'm sure you know your security contract has a first response clause. I wanted to tell you that a young man trespassed on your property last night.'

'Where?' Em asks.

'The old shelter, our contractor says. It was a one-man job. He told us he was exploring.'

Em closes her eyes. A resigned sigh. Again? If she were more superstitious, she'd write off this land as cursed. First the 'fairy fire', as the girls had taken to calling it, still officially unexplained, but likely 'kids messing about with lighters and deodorant' if you went by the police report. Then the council's surveying drone fell from the sky and shattered in the bunker yard (even though Em suspects

Graham and his shotgun had everything to do with that). Next, the young couple that somehow broke in through the bunker's old door before vanishing the second Em tried to press charges. Then three members of some effing amateur ufology society turning up on the doorstep with all their kit, asking if they could camp out on the grounds to observe and 'take some readings', because they'd heard someone nearby had seen an object streak out of the sky a few weeks earlier.

'Was he actually in the bunker?' Em asks Tracy. 'As in, he got inside?'

''Fraid so,' Tracy replies. 'Patrol picked him up. Young lad from Wythenshawe.'

Em shakes her head. 'What was he doing in there? None of your perimeter stuff worked? The door?'

''Fraid not,' Tracy says. 'We caught him with a bag of debris. Came in by motorbike. We've confiscated some of his equipment and took swabs, which the police now have. As you know, they'll come down hard. There's only so much we can do at this stage, however—'

'What kind of equipment?' Em says. 'What the bloody hell are these kids doing in there that needs *equipment?*'

'*Em,*' Ted hisses. He's nodding at the girls. Damson is staring at her, horrified.

Em tuts loudly. 'We paid a hell of a lot to have that wall reinforced,' she says. 'And I needn't remind you that we never wanted any of that nasty stuff put down on our land, not with the girls running around. Not with the animals we get here. Are you seriously telling me it's done nothing?'

'Yes,' Tracy says. 'I know that must be frustrating. We're very sorry for the inconvenience.'

211

'The inconvenience!'

'We do recommend pressing charges…'

Ted is shaking his head. Quiet in the kitchen. This time next week they'll have moved out, and the trespassers will be someone else's problem. Why put themselves through the fuss?

'Or we can liaise with your gardener again?' Tracy suggests. 'There are some additional, more robust security measures we can put in place, I'm sure. And these would be at no extra cost.'

Ted goes on shaking his head.

'Graham doesn't work with us any longer,' Em tells the woman. And from no more than a glance, Em can already see the histrionics that are coming. Damson swivels to Ted, who puts a finger against her lips. Dolly is bolt upright in her seat, like a meerkat.

'Okay…' Tracy says. 'Well, we can file a report and include some recommendations. There's nothing else from me, unless you have any other questions. Again, I'm sorry for the Sunday call. If you have *any* concerns or queries, please get in touch. We're open twenty-four hours a day.'

'Thank you,' Em says. But the look on the girls' faces says the damage is done. Now it's about containment.

The call dies. Ted stares at the bacon. Em watches the girls.

Dolly gulps a breath, winding up. Damson is wincing. Dolly says, 'The burglar-man was looking for fairies, wasn't he, Mummy?'

Em doesn't know how to answer.

'Graham hid them,' Dolly adds. She nods adamantly. Surer than sure. 'Graham told me where he put them. Graham went away because they *told* him to.'

Ted strokes Dolly's hair. 'Let's not do this again, sweetheart. There's nothing down there at all.'

But that's not good enough for Dolly. It never is. She looks disgusted by Em, by Ted: disgusted by how they keep skirting what happened. She protests every time it comes up, and *still* her parents insist. Still they tell her.

'Graham said it gets on your *lungs*,' Dolly adds.

Damson, next to her, nods in agreement. 'And eats up your brains.'

'That's enough,' Ted says.

'But they got him!' Dolly shouts. 'They got him! He said they went inside! And that's why you made him go.'

'Girls,' Ted says. 'That's enough.'

Dolly points at Em. 'You made Graham *vanish*,' she shrieks. 'It's *your* fault he came here and now he's *gone* and the lawns have gone all long and weedy, and that's *your fault*.'

Ted slams his hand down on the hob. He catches the pan handle and the egg whites splash all over the top, all over Ted, and in the girls' hair.

Damson starts to wail, and Em rushes to the breakfast bar, stickiness on everything, and she wants to tell them, she wants to scream at them: *we haven't been lying to you*. Because Em and Ted don't know where Graham is. They don't know where Graham went.

PART II

VERTEX ISLAND

The Steeplejack

Shep has a first-class ticket from Manchester Piccadilly to London Euston. He's early for departure, and straight on the train with his gear. Carriage X, a chartered carriage on an otherwise routine service, is empty save for a guard standing by the luggage rack. 'Morning, sir,' the guard says. Shep nods as he comes along the aisle, kit bags clanking against the fixtures.

'How about this one?' the guard says, motioning to a table seat. 'Or this one, with the extra legroom. Or any you like, frankly – it's only you in here today.'

Shep stows his case and sits down in his coat, baffled and harassed. He opens his rucksack and takes out his Portsmouth literature and a small Tupperware tub wrapped inside an old hoodie.

'I'll leave you be,' the guard says, 'but if you need anything...'

Shep carefully wedges the tub between his thighs and places his head against the window. The train slides out of

217

Piccadilly, the ribs of the station roof giving way to mottled grey-blue. A soft humming in the low range as Manchester expands across the glass.

'One more thing,' the guard says, placing a carefully folded paper bag on the table. 'Enjoy your journey.'

Shep takes off his coat. The paper bag contains a sandwich, biscuit and apple, a bottle of water and a can of craft lager. A folded letter tucked in a pocket, sealed by a piece of red moulded plastic. This carries a V, with ornate curlicues flowering from both points. Vaughan.

Dear Billy, the letter starts. *Welcome to a critical stage of our not-so-little plan. We're proud to have a crew like this, which is to say a crew comprising frontiersmen and women like you, who even while testing are working to further the endeavours of our kind. With your help, we will extend the reach of our planet in pursuit of what lies beyond these bounds. Your name will be among those written about for all the years to come.*

Line after line it goes on like this. Shep reads in bemusement, remembering Mallory Junior's cynical assessment of the project, the many trials the Vaughans face.

The train passes Stockport, Macclesfield. Shep tries to read his Portsmouth literature, keep his learnings fresh, but it's hard to muster the enthusiasm. His training down there – mainly on proprietary protection systems developed for the beta scaffold tower – had been dry in extremis. His trainers were indifferent, his colleagues dull, his digs a bleak cell in ex-student halls. So instead, Shep reclines and stares out of the train, counting through container yards and hollowed factories, obsessively kept scrapyards, sidings of obsolete machinery. Past Wilmslow, a small fire burning unattended in scrubland. At Crewe, a group of neon–clad workers eating chips gormlessly. And between these markers, the countryside proper: pylon–stitched fields leading into the West Country. Undulations in the land where, after rain overnight, unmapped lakes glitter in the sun.

It's hard to be enthused by any of this. In truth, nothing much has excited him since the mission. A real sense that nothing could excite him ever again. He touches his Tupperware tub and, smiling, reflects on Freya's gift to him.

Does Shep feel any guilt for taking Freya to the Lakes, knowing what might have been waiting for them there? Not really. Or not guilt, exactly. Guilt thrives on looping specifics, and his recollections are too hazy, too abstract. Maybe the sheer intensity of being in the bunker a second time had burned holes in his mental record, flattened everything out. But apart from his numbness, it strikes Shep that he should feel bad for manipulating the situation, and Freya, to his benefit. There's just nothing to link their mission with remorse. If anything, he feels the opposite. When he concentrates, when he visualises how it all happened, the overwhelming sensation is one of warmth and intimacy. It makes his skin sensitive to the touch.

His starkest memory of the evening is sitting on the van bonnet with Freya, the smell of nettles and sweat. It turns vague after that: a hike in the dusk, going over the wall, finding the hole full of burned boxes, going inside. A strobe of colour and sound, bursting, like coming up on something, and a crescendo in which he lost time and linearity. Then an image of Freya – who'd somehow got back outside on her own – slouched against the site's perimeter wall, gaping at her feet, which were bleeding. Freya in what was left of her bin bag shawl, the plastic torn and clapping in the wind. Freya lashing out at him – cornered as she was – slapping his face and chest. Another jump forward to his van, and him driving her home in silence. A sign for a place called Dillock, a long way from anywhere. A wordless goodbye.

Shep's last reliable memory of the night is arriving back in Salford and kneeling over the van's passenger seat, savouring the perfume of Freya's fear, the petrol still in the fabric. There he'd collected all the stray hairs she left on the headrest, thankful for a way to remember their night.

Shep takes his head away from the train window and opens the Tupperware tub between his legs. He's been keeping Freya's hairs in here with the small bones and feathers of a bird, bound by a chalky substance that had started to liquefy in his fridge the day after their mission. He slides a finger inside the box and stirs the mixture. Gritty at first, but softening quickly. When it's smooth, he puts the finger inside his mouth and rubs the mixture on his gums. Even after so many days of doing this, there's still no guilt – no shame or sadness, no self-loathing or intrusive thoughts. He can't rub in the blame, can't rub in the fear. He tests it every time by recalling Gunny's confused, trauma-blown look on the stack at Clemens, the state of Gunny's hand, but his stomach stays settled. With this box he carries their night with him, and he'll salve himself like this until the box is empty. The contentment the substance gives him – its deadening of bad feeling – seems a fair price for all other food starting to taste like blood. It's like he's being replaced by a better person from the inside out, molecule by molecule. The bunker no longer frightens him, because it is him. It lives inside him, now. Going back there with Freya was part of the process.

At Milton Keynes, Shep opens his complimentary lager and downs it in one. Last time he visited London, the richness of the city was so distracting he could've starved to death just walking the financial core. Cranes, superstructure, crumbling facades – he'd wanted to climb it all. It was the layers and height and density of the place. Everything pushing down. It was the advancement, its sharp difference from home. Maybe with a fast beer in his blood, he'll just about cope.

The train reaches Euston. The guard offers him a second beer for the drive. Shep takes it happily and alights. The stickiness of late-summer London, a static charge in the air. The guard walks beside him up the platform. 'A van's collecting you,' he says, 'for Heathrow.' They crest a ramp to the station concourse, joining a flow of people and luggage, before fobbing through a STAFF ONLY door. 'It's a shame,' the guard says, leading Shep through the cable-strung bowels of the terminus, 'they don't make this place more welcoming.'

A fire door, a pavement, and London exploding upwards. A black van across the road with its hazards going. There aren't many vehicles like this in London since the ban – the wires from its bio-converted engine are secured to the exterior panels inside a carbon-fibre sheath.

'Your carriage, Mr Shepherd,' the guard says.

'Cheers,' Shep says, and slips the guard a ten-pound note.

The taxi driver, local accent, loads Shep's kit. Shep insists on keeping his rucksack between his legs. Two other men are already in the van, heads in their phones. They don't acknowledge Shep as he gets in, and he doesn't recognise them from Portsmouth. Going by the cash in their outfits, they're abseilers from the subcontracted team – and if they are, they won't have much to say to each other. Not if Shep can help it. Abseilers tend to be sparky rich kids with degrees, and the divide between their trades is enormous. *So you can rig some ropes, yeah? Fucking nice one mate.*

'You boys wanna go the scenic route?' the driver asks.

The abseilers, if they're abseilers, ignore him.

'Sure,' Shep says.

'Might need to juice up at Brentford,' the driver says. 'Here, let me check the range.'

The car's HUD reels stats in real time. The passengers' heartbeats syncopated against the windscreen's curve. Humidity is high, and air pressure hints at an approaching storm. Like the news says: London summers are only getting longer.

'We're good,' the driver says. 'Plenty of juice. We'll do Heathrow in an hour.'

From Westway they descend towards the Thames at Hammersmith, then parallel with it, the river steely and teeming with water taxis. A haziness to the light. They traverse Hammersmith Bridge, pedestrianised except for a lane of electric vehicles. A suspended cycle lane hugs the outside of the bridge – a single sheet of glass that doesn't seem attached to anything.

'Can't keep up with this place, can you?' the driver says.

Shep shakes his head.

Then nothing till the M4, when the driver pipes up again.

'On this long-haul thing, are you?'

Shep nods. He assumes the driver already knows more than he's paid to know.

'Been dropping crew all week. Similar-looking bunch. Offshore platform?'

'Installing stuff. Pack-your-spare-pants-and-toothbrush job.'

'You enjoy what you do?'

'Yeah.'

'Pay good?'

'Sometimes.'

'Beer money.'

'Yeah.'

With some relief, Shep remembers the bonus lager in his bag.

'Ever seen anything bad happen?'

Shep looks out of the window. Verges flickering. Barriers a steady waveform. He knows what the driver wants by this: action and gore. Preferably both. They always do. He reaches to unzip his bag.

'I've only got one good one,' Shep says, rooting for the beer.

The driver nods, eager.

'Packing down a crane is a pain in the arse. So, some lads I worked with found a shortcut to get the outriggers back inside. Turned out there was a little button in the housing above the leg. Press it and the whole thing retracts on its

223

own, skipping shutdown checks. One of them presses the button but doesn't move his hand in time. The outrigger jumps and takes his hand in with it... and then his arm as well. He was trapped in the mechanism, right up to his elbow, in an inch-thick gap.' He does the actions and the sounds. 'Never heard anything like it.'

The driver winces and sucks air over his teeth.

Shep chuckles and angles his lager. 'You mind?'

The driver waves him on.

'We're all there trying to tear the housing off,' Shep continues. 'But the worst thing was that his arm stopped the stabiliser mechanism closing all the way. We realised we'd have to send his arm further in before we got it out again.'

'Oh my days,' the driver says.

Shep takes a sip of his beer. Good and cold. 'We didn't tell him. We just did it. And when it came out, he hadn't broken a thing.'

'No way,' the driver says.

Shep smiles and takes a long swig of beer. 'Happened.'

Everything in order. Everything as it should be.

'Music you into?' the driver asks.

Shep goes to reply, but splutters instead. The driver laughs nervously. 'You good there, son?' But Shep isn't. His eyes are wide because there's more in his mouth than beer. Something hard clacking behind his front teeth. A mouth full of beer and something else.

Just like that, the beer comes out. All over Shep's lap. The beer and the something else. The tin can bounces off the seat, foaming out, and rattles between his boots. The driver screaming, 'You can't do that in here!'

224

Shep sits there, mouth slack and dripping, eyes streaming. The driver pulls on to the hard shoulder, a red and sweaty rage. The abseilers wake up behind, dazed and worried. Shep can't look up. On the seat, between his wet knees, there's a little brown kernel, ribbed and pitted. He picks it up. Rotates it. Like the stone of a peach or plum, but oozing from one end. It reminds him of a chrysalis. This thing that came out of him. A chrysalis.

'Get out, then!' the driver's screaming. 'Get the fuck out my cab!'

The driver's out and Shep's door opens and Shep falls out, clutching the thing to his chest.

'Christ, lad.' The driver kneels down at his side. 'The hell's the matter?' A handkerchief from his pocket, wiping at Shep's face. The handkerchief over his lips and chin. 'Let me…'

Shep palms him away. He wants to stare at what came out of him. Can't the driver see it, with its leaking shell? Can't he see all these things that say the bunker chose him, and not the other way round? The van's sliding door. A foot in the gravel. One of the abseilers leaning over: 'This dickhead dying on us, or what?'

And the driver saying, 'I don't bloody know what he's doing. Do I call an ambulance?'

Shep rests his head on the road. Cold gravel. A sign for Heathrow on a gantry overhead. For now, he's content to come away from himself. The road playing through his hands and his skull. 'My bag,' he tells the men. 'I've got medicine.' The tub will fix him. He puts the thing under his nose. A chrysalis. The faint scent of petrol. Passing traffic disturbing the air. Had he grown it? Was it meant to stay inside him? He should open his throat for it. So he does. The men try and stop him, thinking he's struggling with his tongue. He swallows. A chrysalis should be incubated, kept safe.

The Journalist

In the week following the mission, Freya tries to believe the bunker hasn't marked her. If she notices subtle changes in her temperament, a mounting frustration at all the questions she can't answer, then outwardly she blames the advancing autumn, an apathy for work that's been building for months. If there are small changes in her appearance – painful whiteheads in unusual places, new grey hairs – then she points to the sugary food her colleagues keep on their desks, to ageing. Maybe they've always been there. Or maybe she's paying more attention to the mirror.

But the physical symptoms, the deeper ailments, grow harder and harder to ignore. An especially heavy period. Blinding headaches that leave her bedridden and nauseous. When she finds the appetite to eat, her mouth fills with the taste of tinfoil.

Or it's stress, she tells herself. These bloody screens you work at.

Freya's sleeping patterns change, too. If before she resisted sleep, now it comes too easily – a dreamless cocoon that seals hermetically around her. She asks her father to buy her a baby's LED bulb for her bedside lamp, and finds herself leaving it on all night to prevent Dillock's semi-rural darkness becoming so thick, so encasing, that she's taken back to that dank corridor underground.

It's mostly at night, then, when Freya admits the bunker is inside her. A contaminant. A steady ingress. In the bungalow's pre-morning silence, she hears its ticks and leaks. Her footsteps on its floors. When she startles awake in the early hours, she sees both Stephen and Shep in the corners, obscured by shadow. When her alarm goes off, she's free for mere seconds before the events of that night compress her chest wall.

In this sense, the bunker has caused Freya countless injuries, invisible but acute. And when she submits to its damage, the echoes and flashbacks, she can tell a splinter has breached her. Deposited a foreign body that her innards have shifted to accommodate. Sometimes there's actually a sharp prick when she sits down or sleeps in a certain position.

After work – a day's writing vanishing from memory as if she hadn't worked at all – Freya comes home in fractious moods, takes early nights to escape. Over breakfast she starts petty fights with her mother. On her commutes, as cold and lonely as any she's known since the break-up, she sobs the whole way to the office.

'You can always tell us,' her father keeps insisting. 'Frey. You can just say.'

But Freya can't say much about it. What would she tell them? She eats her breakfast mechanically and stops ironing her clothes and drives away from Dillock too quickly – because apart from snatches of sleep, work is the only respite, a dam against spiralling thoughts. If anything props her up, gives her a reason, it's the job. Keep yourself busy, people told her after the split. Distract yourself, wait it out, because some things are better that way.

As she adjusts to this new routine, Freya begins to heal herself by editing her memories of the night that changed her. Her revision, gradually overwriting the truth, still has Shep and Freya exploring Lakeland mountains, stumbling upon the bunker, then discovering Stephen's nest. But now Shep never shouts or *incantates*, much less terrorises her with his camera. Shep's van, hurtling back towards Sheffield afterwards, is no longer fraught with tension or fear, but vibrant with a discussion about what they'd found.

Which is to say that, more than anything else Shep did that night, it is his pretending that nothing happened that angers her most. If the bunker hasn't changed Freya, then Shep has. And Freya despises him for what he's done. His deceit, his abuse of her trust. She's ashamed that she'd been so wrong about him. Appalled that he clings to her like a smell, like damp; that he haunts her at every turn, a ghost, a shadow under the door, a dalliance of cold air on her neck. The way she sometimes catches his expressions in a stranger's face.

What she hates even more is understanding why she can't purge him. Knowing that, without another link to Stephen or Alba, she needs to see him again. To confront him, *use* him – understand what had surely happened to Stephen, through him. To ask him, why? What drew you all down there? What made you say and do those things? What made you chase those feathers and bones? What made you take me? What makes you like Stephen?

How has the bunker changed you, too?

As the workdays come and go, opaque time, these questions drive Freya on. She tries to call Shep, texts his phone, posts in his stream, but her words bounce back with error messages. She calls various steeplejacking firms pretending to be Shep's concerned relative, having forgotten or repressed the company name partly hidden on the bonnet of his van, and is met with platitudes. When she eventually finds the right firm, Mallory Limited, a scheduler tells her he's already overseas, and will be for some time.

From there, Freya is left to hunt Shep the traditional way. For hints of him in search engines, news on the project he's contracted to. She tries vague physical descriptions, school records, even makes enquiries with a hacker about mining the firm for his medicals. Rifling news feeds with keywords like 'steeplejacking projects', or 'bunker break-in'. She scans through reviews of Shep's jacking firm's services – every recommendation – in the hope of finding his name, even a simple allusion to him. She scours the urbex forums, where Shep's reports continue to elude her, running in perfect confluence with his mystery.

Who is the real Shep? The climber she met at Big Walls – or that dread explorer in the Lakes?

Desperate, Freya also seeks the bunker itself. What's

stored down there? Who owns it? Who works there? She pirates some government mapping software to see if she can find the place manually. She eBays for late-nineties OS maps of the Lakes and pins them on her bedroom walls. There are no plots, no recognisable landmarks, no open tracts near trails and woods and water. As if the Lakes' darkness had obscured much more than their approach. Later she makes enquiries to publicly listed landowners, garden centres and landscaping firms whose staff may or may not have worked there.

Nothing comes off. No one seems to have heard of a bunker in the area.

And so, on the longest nights, she can only fill her planners. Frantic handwriting that describes the bunker in real and abstracted terms. She makes it larger, deeper, darker. The fells of the Lakes now impassable mountains. Temporal shifts. Character changes. At one point she writes twenty pages about a stretch of road covered by trees whose boughs are full of nesting birds. She describes bloodied chicks – too many to count, all pink and raw – dangling down from the branches, screaming at their approaching van. As Freya and Shep pass under the birds a rook drops to the windscreen, cracks it with its beak, and forces its way inside. *First the rook pecked holes in Shep's clothing*, Freya writes, *then it went for my eyes. If I had known what I would see later, I would have let it blind me.*

In the moment, each attempt seems to make the bunker understandable. But when Freya reviews her work over breakfast, none of it makes sense.

One morning, Freya goes into the office to find the editor sitting at her workstation. Freya's desk phone is concealed by the editor's hair, and the editor is still, obstinately still, and Freya can't hear what she's saying.

Freya stands in front of her desk. The editor doesn't budge. She goes on scratching shorthand into a Moleskine.

'Yes,' the editor says down the phone, mouth almost too tight for it to come out. 'Right.'

Freya's own scowl hardens. She puts her handbag on the desk and leans on the partition.

The editor, still taking notes, shakes her head. She knows Freya's there.

'Who is it?' Freya whispers, pessimistic.

'I'll suggest it, certainly,' the editor says, ignoring her. 'There'll be some expenses issues this side, and it's unfair of me to speak on her behalf. We'll need to unpick your proposal.'

Freya's skin runs cold. Proposal? The union, perhaps – a misconduct complaint? Or maybe it's the ethics council. Freya's done plenty to warrant investigation: if Stephen's father has kicked off, worked out who she is, she'll be out of here in minutes. Or worse – and now her stance weakens – it's the police. But then again, maybe that'd be a kindness. Get her out of this stifling office. Get her out of this building. After all, as seeing Aisha had reminded her, she doesn't have the gumption to jump voluntarily.

At last, the editor meets Freya's stare. She winks.

'Thank you,' the editor says down the phone. 'Yes, goodbye.' She replaces the handset.

'You always expect the worst of people, don't you?' the editor says.

'Who was that?' Freya's voice is throttled, and she coughs into her hand.

'You never expect anything good. You don't trust yourself. You don't give yourself any credit.'

'Why are you on my phone?'

'Because you're an hour late.'

'Am I?' Freya looks at her wrist. It's nine o'clock.

'For *you*. Your phone's been going since seven-thirty – I'm sure these bloody Europeans forget they're an hour ahead.'

Freya kneads the skin at the back of her neck. *Europeans?* She realises her mascara might be smudging, a high-shine breaking out on her T-zone. Her nylon blouse suddenly coarse against her shoulders.

'That was the editor of a French climbing magazine.'

Freya glares at the editor's lips as she speaks.

'Freya?'

'A climbing magazine?'

'Big one, as a matter of fact. *Dalle*. I'm told it means "slab".'

'They rang me? Why?'

The editor laughs. 'Why do you think?'

'I haven't pitched anything.'

'I *know* you bloody haven't. And even if you had, I'd hope you weren't stupid enough to give them your office number.'

Freya sits down on the floor, faces away from the editor. Some of her colleagues swivel to see what's going on.

The editor stands up, comes round to her. 'Remember telling me your ideas? About follow-up features?'

Freya nods.

'I pitched some on your behalf. They'd seen your Stephen piece in the *Mail*, and now they want a feature.'

Freya's stunned. 'For their magazine?'

'Yes.'

'What?'

The editor shakes her head. 'What's the matter with you? Are you sleeping?'

'Yes.'

The editor frowns. 'I'm not complaining, here. Your work rate's obscene at the moment – we've got juniors complaining of nothing to do. I'm just slightly concerned—'

Freya puts her face in her elbow.

'Well, fine, look… *Dalle* wants an essay. An investigation, I suppose. A sort of biography – the boy's climbing, the risks. Beats me, to be honest. They said it was good fortune I got in touch – they'd been keeping an eye on it all. Tight-knit scene, isn't it?'

Freya blinks at her.

'I'll forward you their brief. And if it's any good, they'll sell it on to America if there's a buyer. Their print circ figures are steady enough, but they're also growing their content arm.'

'I don't know what to say.'

'Apparently. I did mention your urbex angle, by the way. They *loved* that – had no idea he was involved.'

Freya is increasingly glad she's sitting down.

'Are you going to speak?' her editor asks.

'I just… Why would they want some English hack with no climbing experience to write it?'

'Economics. The impressions on your piece added up.

That, and I've been pitching features for donkey's years. Your ideas are fine – you only needed a kick up the arse.'

'I just don't know why you'd—'

The editor shakes her head. 'How long will you need for fifteen thousand words? These juniors will live to regret their griping if you're missing too long.'

'Fifteen? Maybe a fortnight, if I'm on other stuff.' Freya thinks of a woman and a baby without a father. A bunker. A steeplejack. The thought of writing solely about a subject she's already pursuing is heady. 'Or I can take it as holiday.'

'No, no. I think this will be good. Call it a sabbatical, with one caveat. I don't want any of your conspiracies.'

Freya keeps a straight face. 'I'll need to travel,' she says. 'To do it justice.'

'Trains? A hire car? The package is attractive, Freya. It's not *Ratler*.'

'No. Plane tickets.'

The editor baulks. 'Where for?'

Freya steals a breath. She wants to say it firmly. She wants to sound assertive. She wants the editor to agree to anything. No more leakage.

She opens her mouth. She touches her belly. She says, 'Reykjavik.'

The Steeplejack

Despite his indifference to heights, Shep isn't one for flying. Something about not being in control. So as the transfer plane taxies across a bleak Heathrow runway, he washes down a half-day sloth pill with a complimentary vial of vodka and hopes he'll see less than an hour of the flight to Los Angeles. After the trip down here – not including the taxi incident, which seems illusory now, harder to recall the more he focuses on it – he needs to rest.

The sloth pill, ordered from the recesses of the internet, is meant to treat insomnia, but it should make short work of long haul. Along with reducing appetite and slowing the digestive tract, the pill contains a thinning agent, so you don't have to worry about clots. The comedown – general aches and fogginess, sometimes the visual distortions a person with epilepsy might describe before a seizure – is worth the sensation of burning through time. When they land in LA, Shep can neck some orange juice and get on with it.

He settles in his seat. The plane's engines soothe him. He

idly scans his section of the cabin and waits for the pill to kick in. The other travellers around him weigh each other with the same curiosity. Who will they end up belaying? Handing tools to? Bunking up with?

Soon the plane receives clearance. Shep relaxes into the lurch of take-off and watches London retract, flatten. When they pierce the cloud canopy, the sun is an immense white bluff, and the plane's reactive windows darken instantly. Shep's stomach fizzes around the pill. For a moment he's sure someone says his name – but no one's looking, and everyone in his line of sight has put on their in-flight VR glasses.

Minutes later, a smartly dressed woman comes to sit with Shep. Possibly a flight attendant, or a Vaughan representative. Shep realises he can't acknowledge her properly. He's slipping away, rope out, rappelling into the throat of a warm red cavern. The woman frowns concernedly at him from above. As he comes off the conscious ridge, and his seat fabric takes on the consistency of scree, he's sure the woman reaches towards his rucksack.

He tries to stay awake. He tries to fight back to the surface.

'Is it in here?' she asks from the distance.

What? he wants to ask.

'Your child. Is it in here?'

The woman flickers. Holographic, almost. How can she know what he's carrying? Shep has no choice but to let go of his rope. The woman smiles and gets up. Dank animal musk. A wave of sweet petrol. Maybe it doesn't matter what she knows, he decides. Not really. Same goes for if she's even there or not. After the bunker, the real and imagined have long since converged.

Violent turbulence drags Shep from the sloth-hole. He pats his face, dry as bone, and is alarmed to feel bright and alert. His stomach is rumbling, which isn't supposed to happen, and his mouth tastes clean, a hint of peppermint.

Noticing Shep's movement, the window blind slithers into the trim, and the glass lightens. The western seaboard greets him, a textbook Californian night vista. Pastel-purple sky, gradated into deepest black. On the ground, the LA megalopolis itself – an endless, intricately woven tapestry of light, impossible to process by dint of scale and sheer population. It's like the biggest oil refinery he's ever seen. Clemens times a million.

'Awake, are you?'

This was a passenger in the next row, a man in his mid-forties. He's wearing a pair of army surplus cargos, a camo jacket. He has the complexion, the waxiness, of someone with a chemical dependency.

'They'll be screening us the second we touch down,' the man says. 'You daft fucking prick. They'll sling you on the next flight back.'

Shep rubs his eyes. Sloths are blood-soluble, won't leave a trace. And anyway, it hardly feels like he took one at all. He blinks and focuses on the man's mouth. A cold sore. Uneven stubble.

'You what?' Shep says.

The man shakes his head. 'How'd they let a squeaker like you on this flight?'

'I'm not a squeaker,' Shep tells him.

'No?'

'No.'

'What's that boner about, then?'

Shep gazes down. His erection is visible through his trousers. He covers himself and turns back to the window – starfield Los Angeles. 'Jesus Christ,' he whispers. That's not meant to happen on sloth pills, either.

'Disgrace,' the man says. 'Absolute disgrace.'

Shep keeps his face to the window.

Soon the jet banks, loops the grid to start its descent. The landing gear engages, the lights of LAX blur into hard white lines, and Shep continues to question his alertness. The clarity of thought. He should be ill, or bleary, or both, but the only physical marker is a mild tingling in his forearms.

The jet touches down. The airbrakes roar. When the roaring stops, someone in front actually claps.

'Welcome to Los Angeles,' a synthetic voice announces. 'Local time is 4.20 a.m. On behalf of the Vaughans, we wish you a great layover in LA.'

The belts come off. Groggy passengers stumble from the cabin. The grizzled man who'd reproached Shep makes a point of shoving past him. Shep finds it hard to care. He steps onto the skybridge and smells America.

Opposite him stands the woman who sat down next to him during the flight.

'Feeling better, sir?' she says.

'You sat next to me,' Shep says. 'After take-off.'

The woman's expression doesn't change. 'Sorry? I don't understand.'

'You did. You went in my bag.'

Now a look of awkwardness. Her colleagues have started listening.

'You snored from the moment we left,' she says. 'We did try to wake you for refreshments. We thought you'd stopped breathing at one point. You were... writhing. Like you had a fever.'

Shep is dumbfounded.

'But you're okay now,' she says. 'Aren't you?'

'I don't know,' Shep replies. 'I don't know.'

LAX expands into a lattice of control. They've thought of everything. Even the armed surveillance drones, dallying above the fine mesh overhead, emit calming birdsong. At the passport stiles, a squad of border guards pick through the jet's hold luggage. Shep's case has been emptied out, Tupperware tub on top of his kit-roll. He drops his rucksack into the hand luggage chute and heads through various bombproofed cells, bulletproof tunnels and body scanners. At the far end he's invited forward by a woman wearing what looks like an industrial worker's exoskeleton.

'Hold baggage?' the guard says, passing over his rucksack.

'Yeah,' Shep says, pointing to his open case on the conveyor. A large yellow sticker has been added to its side.

'Wait there,' the guard says, nodding to another guard who points his maser at Shep. The guard seals the case and brings it back to Shep, carrying it effortlessly on the last joint of a mechanised finger.

'Please come with me,' the guard says. Shep follows her to a brushed steel countertop.

'Does this case belong to you?' she asks.

'Yeah,' Shep says.

'Did you pack it yourself?'

'Yes,' he says.

'Are these yours?'

A set of overalls.

'Yes.'

'And this?'

The Tupperware.

Shep nods unsurely. His bowels squirm. He'd added a concealment liner, a reflective weave that fires innocuous shapes back at security monitors, but it's a cosmetic. If she decides to open it—

She opens it.

The moment dilates.

'Come with me,' she says. Voice restrained. She strides to a room lit by a single harsh bulb. 'Stand in that corner,' she tells him. 'Do not speak.'

Shep stands in the corner.

'Turn away from me,' she says. 'Hands open.'

Out of the rucksack come his belongings. The slam of his keys. The snap of his wallet. A pack of tobacco skittering over the floor. The crackling blister pack his sloth pills came in. The wadded Portsmouth literature with a weighty slap.

'Is this all yours?'

Shep turns back. All his things are out on the table. His boots and tools. His Stillson and his podgers.

'What's this?' the guard asks.

'Gear,' he says.

'For what?'

'Work.'

Eyebrows furrowed. 'And this?' The tub again.

'Food,' he tells her.

The guard removes the lid and casts it aside. Her suit's servos sound precise in the smallness of the room. She shakes off the exoskeleton arm so she can use her own hand to hold the tub closer to her face. She tilts it back and forth so the contents slide around.

'It's disgusting,' she says.

'I'm on a diet,' Shep says. 'For my joints.'

The guard tilts the tub.

'Try some,' Shep says.

The guard glares at him. 'You can't take this with you.'

Shep tenses.

'Sir…'

Before he can think more about it, Shep comes off the wall. He pulls the tub from the guard's real hand, slopping it over the table, his clothes and tools. He pours what's left into his mouth.

The guard's exo whines angrily as she re-sleeves her arm. With her other clawed hand she snatches back the dripping tub and clamps Shep by the throat, scooping him almost clean off his toes before driving him into the wall. Shep coughs a clump of wet hair down his chin, a bone fragment onto the guard's front. His lips are on fire. The guard locks his wrists together with her spare hand.

'What the fuck are you *doing*?'

Shep forces down a breath, tonguing the mixture into the gullies of his mouth. The taste is sweet and sharp, and there's an unlikely mass pressing into his gums. Freya's hair and sweetened bone. Marrow and jelly. He can feel tiny abrasive nodules working against his tongue, his saliva flowing.

'I don't have time for this,' the guard says. She shakes her head, revolted, and liquefies Shep's tub with a single blast of a device on her arm.

Shep wants to laugh. He wants to shout at her, tell her how perfect it all is. How light and alive he feels. How nothing can change this now. He won't fail his bloods. He won't fail anything. Not today, or tomorrow, or probably ever again. Not now.

'Put the rest of this shit away,' the guard says, 'and get out of my airport.'

Shep swallows what's left in his mouth.

The Journalist

Freya piles through Manchester Airport, a woman on a mission. Her shaking hands betraying the urgency behind her ribs. Call it nervous excitement, call it release, but for the first time in a long time she isn't churning with dread. Not running from something, only towards it. For the first time since her break-up, since what happened in the Lakes, there's a vividness here. A breathless contentment, pulsing vessels, her teeth set. A fizzing at her bony edges, her shins and fingers, her skin sensitive to even the lightest touch. Drawing her on is a mental image of her final article published in *Dalle* magazine – the thing written and rewritten and subbed and flowed in elegant type. *Dalle*'s editor calling to congratulate her on its quiet power or startling insight or—

'Steady on, Frey,' her father might say. Because, of course, the work is still to be done – a living thing to carve from her planners and Dictaphone recordings, and intimidating because it's still impossible to see its final shape or tone, the sense of its ending. While long features are usually written after the fact – planned, paragraph to paragraph, argument to counterargument, within tight parameters – this is a story without constraint or oversight. And that's it, in essence. To actually own the blank page is exhilarating. For the first time in her professional career, Freya has the opportunity – is being *paid* – to write about what obsesses her, to properly engage with it. If Stephen and Alba and Shep posed the question, *Dalle* allows her to respond. She needed it, and now she has it.

Before she knows it, the man at the plane door wants to see her boarding pass. She's come all the way through the terminal shops, the flight gate, right up the stairs to the plane itself, with no recollection of doing so.

'Getting too used to autopilot in my car,' she says, smiling a little. And she scrabbles through her bag and flashes the man her phone screen.

'Sure,' the attendant says.

Then – then Freya's mood crashes. Stalking up that plane aisle, alone, the situation collapses in on her. *Nothing goes this right for you. Here you are, you sneaky bitch.* And as she stows her bag and sits down in her empty row, the self-doubt glimmers and grows. As much as Freya has control – can take responsibility for her final draft, owes to her editor and *Dalle*'s commissioning editor a standard of quality that justifies their faith (never mind expenses) – she wonders if she's setting herself up for failure. Today, she's up and away. Tomorrow she might come unstitched entirely. It matches up with a familiar dejection: the fear of writing she has to manage every day, made worse by her growing distrust of the outside, of the dark. The fear she's missed a signal, a clue; that she's getting too deep, too infatuated; that she doesn't deserve this job at all. That Alba and Oriol don't deserve her invasion. That Shep's grinning face will be watching through every blackened window. That the earth at her feet will only give way.

Sneaky. Bitch.

Freya wants to get off the plane. But the belt sign is on, and how the hell has she already reasoned herself out of feeling so good, out of being giddy that the world might not be as unkind or cold or cynical as she usually reads it?

Because you're you, she thinks. When her friends call her down-to-earth, they're lying. When her editor says she only expects the worst, she's right. Freya isn't down-to-earth at all. She just knows how to poke holes in her own wings.

The plane readies for departure. Freya opens a novel pinched from her mother's bedside table. The writing is smooth and tidy, very matter-of-fact. Nothing much seems to happen, though in the second chapter a woman describes her joyless affair to a friend until they both fall asleep on the settee, holding hands. It's quite a powerful scene, Freya reckons. Fiction being pat like that.

The plane reaches cruising altitude. Freya closes the book and then her eyes. Her thoughts turn to her own affair, her joyless tryst with the photo editor. She winces, a hot blister of remorse. Freya's ex must never know their relationship ended for so little satisfaction. A few shags that, in the beginning, occurred through raw opportunity and circumstance – late nights in the office, stress, caffeine – and only then when Freya was ill, or a bit down, or felt like a boring local hack with no prospects beyond the walls of the sixties block they worked from. Her ex's faults – his sour-smelling jogging bottoms, the way he chewed, left an inch of cold tea in his mugs, resented going down on her – never even figured. Freya betrayed him consciously and without excuse.

'Causality doesn't even *apply* here,' her ex spat when he found the text messages. 'You're just fucked up.'

The photo editor was single and quietly egregious and an enthusiastic kisser, and Freya liked him droning on about cameras and photo sales because it was white noise. All she really wanted was the smell of someone else against her, a different body, skin with a different tone, elasticity. Electrified she'd even allowed herself to try.

But then? After that? Empty in the office, as those beige walls came back into view?

Freya opens her eyes. The man in front has reclined his seat and Freya's tray is digging into her belly. If there's anything to glean from the whole mess, it's that the affair's pointlessness can't hurt her ex now. The truth is sealed up in Freya, and she'll make up for it in her own way.

Freya closes her eyes again. The commission. The commission from *Dalle*. 'Pull your socks up, Frey,' her father might say. Be grateful for the editor's kindness and this opportunity. 'Crack on with it,' her father would say. Be grateful the editor is one of the few people who know what she screwed up for so little gain, and still gives her time. Then she's on to Shep, where he might be now, and whether he's climbing some tower, infected by the bunker and drinking himself into oblivion, climbing a scaffold gantry and falling to his death—

247

Freya wants to be there to watch. To find him lying in his viscera and slap him and ask him: What did you do to me, you bastard? What did you open?

As the plane starts its descent towards Iceland, Freya decides she'll spend her first night in Reykjavik getting so drunk on expenses that the financial controller will have no choice but to go beyond appalled to impressed.

The Steeplejack

Shep and the crew see the space elevator's beta scaffold before the edges of Vertex Island emerge from the horizon. Through the helicopter's curved glass, the scaffold is an impossible spire, so thin and strange that it looks pasted onto the sky. Closer, a considered silence in the cabin, and its details resolve: a latticed obelisk with four tapering sides and a pyramidal cap, a platform at its apex, standing a kilometre tall.

The sun swings behind the tower as the transfer helicopter nears. Even at this altitude – two-and-a-half thousand feet, and dropping – they fly in the tower's long shadow. Down on the ocean surface, the tower's fractal twin spreads across azure and emerald. The spectral outlines of reef formations create a third, darker layer beneath.

Shep is at the front of the cabin, dead centre. A happy fluke, given the view. The chopper's pilot is only slightly ahead of him. A number of others, including the abseilers who shared his taxi back in London, are piled in behind him.

'We're only ten out, folks,' the pilot tells them. He has a soft southern American accent, dry and deliberate, and teeth that had positively shone in the hangar. His cheeks ripple as he speaks. 'Time we did some facts.'

The helicopter tilts forward on its Y-axis, nimble despite its bulbous fuel tanks, and the pilot switches on a panel above Shep's head. A nosecam feed, slaved to the pilot's helmet. The island's rugged form fills the panel as well as the chopper's chin-bubble. The scaffold blinks with lights and beacons. At various heights of its frame, the tower sprouts immense guy-lines that stretch down to evenly spaced points on the island's rim. These cables alone must count as marvels, and it reminds Shep that hundreds, if not thousands, of people have been on site already. He tries to imagine the lifters going up and down the tower's central stem. What the same journey would be like on a snow- and wind-blasted peak.

'Unlike the gold site, Vertex lies in US territory,' the pilot says with reverence. 'A small but perfectly formed atoll of the equatorial Pacific, only two miles north of the equator and three thousand south-west of Hawaii. I know you'll have come a ways for this project, but I call it a home from home.'

'A ways' is an understatement. From LA it was another six hours inside a cramped chartered jet to Honolulu, Hawaii, where the plane was refuelled and sent on to a second, unnamed island. By the look of it – outbuildings, security fencing, military and support vehicles – it was a navy staging post, whose workings were never fully revealed. Here they were disembarked and marched inside a hangar, fed what might have been rations, and given an hour's rest on bunk beds before they boarded their transfer helicopter. The whole journey seemed purposely dislocating, as if each leg was designed to further alienate you from civilisation itself. But it didn't matter. To Shep, it didn't figure. He might as well have floated here.

Scaffold feet aside, the island is a concrete reservoir, terrainless and flat. No sandy beaches or verdant shores, only scrubby green fringes that stop abruptly and drop into water. The effect is stark, as if the island's edges have been sliced clean away. Innumerable cranes, masts and antennae stand in conference. A runway teems with cargo containers and support vehicles. Docked ships bear enormous sections of formed steel and equipment. An unlit pyre of hacked vegetation the closest thing to a natural feature.

The helicopter is noticeably lower, and the beta scaffold looms. Soon only the patterns of steel formwork fill the windscreen. Then the pilot says, 'Entering isolation volume,' and points off to one side. 'We're under navy watch, now. Big-ass destroyer out there on control. You can't see her, but she's always there. Give us a signal if you're listening, gang!' The pilot grins to himself. 'Now – see under the south face of the tower? The runway? Vertex was once a staging base for the Pacific campaign, and that old concrete has kept its core, God bless – it could still take a Hercules. And over to your left, see the warehouse? That's the navy's drone hangar.' The pilot chuckles again. 'I hear some of you guys are charged with making sure the Vaughans don't have to pay DARPA any compensation...

'Next up, the western dock,' the pilot goes on. 'Deliveries

arrive by boat once every week. Parts mostly, and food when we need it. Tropical storms occasionally disrupt shipping routes, though we're well adapted for rainfall on Vertex. There are no freshwater sources here. Seawater treatment happens offshore on desalination vessels on the east side. They're some big ships, oh man. Big.'

'What about the nightlife?' someone chirps from the back. The crew sniggers.

The pilot clears his throat. 'How you like roaches, son? We got those. Invasive exotics in most shades, come to that. You're better off-structure. The reef is mostly healthy. I snorkel when I can.

'Latterly we have your sleeping zones, out there by the sat and radio masts. That's your village. The quarters. What do you Brits call this shit? Garrison? The Vaughans shipped two goddamned Michelin-starred chefs to your rec-room...'

Inside, Shep is ecstatic. But not about the food or fauna. The beta structure has an odd magnetism that plays in him like abstract music. It shifts between his legs and ears. It fills him with childish awe, a giddiness, just to look at it. It isn't just the bones of an orbital tower; it seems to him, as a climber, as an explorer, the perfect mission. He wishes old Mallory could see him here. That Mo, his partner for Jodrell Bank, could know what lust seizes him now. Because if you actually scaled this thing, if you somehow got right to the top, what would you actually see? He stares wide-eyed. The air around Vertex has taken on a heavenly brightness.

'All you pale guys,' the pilot says. 'I hope you brought hats.'

• • •

Shep sleeps roughly during his first night in the cabin, possibly owing to a delayed comedown from the sloth pill, the bunk's hardness, the bitterness of mosquito spray or even simple jet lag. Since their transfer touched down on Vertex he'd dealt with waves of nausea, a nagging pain in his wrists and chest, and several times he's staggered to a toilet block expecting diarrhoea. The island's intense humidity doesn't help. Even though it drops to the mid-twenties by early evening, the air pressure is disparaging. Even with the air-con going, the constant perspiration makes it hard to get comfy. Harder still to get himself back out of the bunk when his bowels grumble. As the night lumbers on, he can only stare at the roof and try to make sense of his journey – comparing over there with inside here, the gulf between. He feels now like he has been teleported. Like England – and everything there – has vanished forever.

He tries to order the day. Earlier that evening, the transfer crew had driven Shep to the cabins on this, the 'civilised' side of the tower. They'd handed him a keycard and cabin number, told him to drop his stuff and make hay before collecting his contact sun-lenses, harness, helmet and hydration packs. There, Shep had walked between the parallel ditches left by heavy plant, the ground rubbly from whatever was cleared to make way for their accommodation. Pillboxes or concrete fortifications. War echoes.

The cabins would clearly have no shade come the morning. On the roof of his cabin stands a barometer and weather station, a flaccid windsock. He'd opened the cabin's sheet-metal door to campsite grade sleeping quarters: a space a few metres square containing a bunk, a rack of hooks in a flimsy wardrobe, a plastic one-piece bathroom pod complete with a sink, shower unit and toilet. The floor is covered in sawdust, whose bleachy smell mixes with the island's elements: heat, steel, salt. A large mosquito net across him on the bunk.

After he signed for his harness and helmet, Shep sat on the cabin doorstep as the sun slipped beyond the tower. The whole structure glowed, backlit, more impressive than any chimney he'd looked out from, any stack he'd climbed. Its impermanence made it all the more surreal. It was hard to think this whole thing might be pointless, a fake, a Babel sprung by a family with more money than sense. When the sun was gone, Shep went and sat on the toilet until he felt sure he was empty.

The next morning his cabin door rattles at eight o'clock sharp. Shep opens it to a man in a leather Stetson. The sun is up and already powerful, and the scaffold is glistening.

'Billy?'

Shep rubs his arms. Despite the net, his arms are riddled with mosquito bites. 'Shep,' he says weakly.

'Billy,' the man repeats. 'I'm Eddy, your foreman. You're rota'd for beacon installs with me.' Eddy has a clean English accent, like an army officer.

'Right,' Shep says, and coughs.

'Get yourself together while I round up the others,' Eddy says, motioning to a little electric cart on the path. 'Labour pool going this morning.'

Shep dresses and pushes in his sun-lenses. The cabin dims. When he opens the door again, Eddy is waiting for him in the cart, the Stetson pulled down to his brow.

'Thought I had more on your block,' he calls. 'Lenses in? Mood killer, aren't they?'

The foreman drives to the base pad beneath the beta with Shep leaning out of the cart with his mouth open. On stepping down from the cart he immediately stumbles, too busy gawping up into the guts of the scaffold, a bewildering mesh of platforms, ladders and joists. He sucks on the line from his hydration pack to try and control himself. Near the top of the tower – where the weave tightens – the connections look like gold thread. Eddy says nothing, like he understands.

'How long did it take?' Shep asks. He speaks out of the corner of his mouth, still sucking on the tube.

Eddy shrugs. 'Three years?' He lights a cigarette, points at it, then cups it close. 'Don't grass me up.'

Shep shrugs. They stand in silence until the foreman points over his shoulder. 'You're late!' he shouts. Shep turns round to see the rest of the team pulling gear from a luggage tug.

'Get a move on,' Eddy shouts. 'We're way behind.'

Six more men and two women join Shep and Eddy on the pad. Shep shuffles into the shade of a support beam. He recognises no one from training in Portsmouth. Their darkened sun-lenses make them all look dead.

'That makes nine of you,' Eddy says, tallying them. 'Where's our tenth?'

Shep is also scanning to see whose height and body mass best match his. Working out who he might be paired with. To install the drone warning beacons, you need a partner to manage a specially made belay-and-brake system designed to lock you on to the guy-line, so you won't slide off if your main protection fails. They'd nicknamed this new system a *biter* in Portsmouth, where Shep trained with a guy who kept reeling off the beacons' features – 'ultraviolet pulse, echo ping, chaff-splash for emergency proximity aversion' – like a salesman practising his patter.

'We'd better crack on,' Eddy says, pacing. 'I trust you've prayed to the Stack Gods this morning. This may be your first ascent, but we don't have the luxury of time. The navy's low-level tests start in a week, and our service level agreement says we should be halfway by then. Full tests start the week after, by which time we'll be done. I can't imagine…' Eddy trails off and adjusts his Stetson. The group look among themselves. The foreman stares past them. 'Joining us after all?' he says.

The crew turn in unison. The latecomer is crossing a patch of bulrush remains, sand crunching under his boots. A stringy man, chipped-at and leathery, with a gait that makes him seem taller than he really is. He has a canvas kit bag over one shoulder, a cantina of water on his toolbelt, and his harness already secured at the waist. Its many dangling carabiners and attachments make it look like a mechanical hula skirt.

When the man takes off his sunglasses, Shep's stomach twinges. It's the man from the plane to LA.

'Alarm didn't go,' the man announces. The way he stands – legs wide, chest out – says he doesn't care whether the engineer believes him or not.

Eddy shakes his head. 'What's your name?'

'Kapper,' the man says.

256

Shep recognises that, too. The lead jack at Manchester Airport had mentioned him.

The foreman stares him down. 'Kapper. Want to apologise to your crew?'

Kapper spits heavily on the dry earth and drops his kit bag.

Shep steps out of the shade. He wants Kapper to see him. Even in the heat, with his back wet and temples running, the weakness in him, he wants Kapper to notice.

'Sorry, lads,' Kapper says.

One of the women tuts.

Shep coughs a laugh into his fist. Kapper stares at him – pretends to stare straight through him.

Shep turns away at the perfect moment. Conceited as anything, like the beta is his. And suddenly the sickness, his cramps, have gone.

'What's up with you?' Eddy asks, meaning Shep. 'What's funny?'

Shep doesn't answer. He smiles. He loves that Kapper's still staring. Cocky green Shep on the island. Cocky green Shep who's going to run rings round you all—

Shep's ears start to buzz. A steady whine. The pain in his wrists comes on strong. His bad finger throbs.

'Enough dicking about,' Eddy says. 'Helmets tight. There's a lot to get through.'

Kapper shakes his head.

'You two,' Eddy says, gesturing to the women, 'will partner up and work ground today. No ifs or buts – the referee's decision is final. Get these winches prepped and divvy up the beacons. For kick-off I want four teams on each quadrant to cover from here to a hundred metres up.

257

Rotating daily like this will improve our work rate. This goes to plan, you'll get a day's leave before the second test flights in a fortnight.'

'But—' one of the women protests.

'You and you,' Eddy says, ignoring her and pointing at two of the men. He goes round the group. 'You and you. You and you.'

Shep swallows.

'And you two,' Eddy says, motioning to Shep and Kapper.

'Fuck's sakes,' Kapper mutters.

'Billy?' the foreman says. 'You with us?'

The buzzing in Shep's ears turns to a roar. 'Shep,' he says, holding out a hand for Kapper. The bites on his arm look wretched.

'Don't fuck this up,' Kapper says, leaving Shep hanging.

Shep and Kapper enter their quadrant through a tight access hatch. As the senior, Kapper has the scaffold schematics and a temp monitor on his watch. He knows where they are, where they get out, and when they should top up on fluids.

'I'll go first,' Shep says at the load-point, keen to prove himself. Kapper grunts, so Shep slides in and starts climbing. There's no natural light inside the ladder tube, and no let-up. While the rungs are rubberised, the sun-lenses make it even harder to see. Shep closes his eyes and climbs by feel alone, satisfied to hear Kapper's laboured breathing beneath him.

At sixty metres, the wind begins to whistle through the tube enclosing them. 'You train at Portsmouth?' Shep shouts past his boots.

'What?'

'Portsmouth. On the alpha.'

'Can't hear you.'

'For this job. Biters? Beacons?'

'Piss off,' Kapper says. 'What do you think?'

The hundred-metre hatch brings them into harsh sunlight. They stand sweating in the bounds of a cube-shaped opening in the beta scaffold's face, boundless ocean below. They take off their helmets at the same time.

'Clip in, then,' Kapper says.

Shep snaps his fall arrest to the railings that line the inside wall of the platform. Kapper leans out over the edge protection to get eyes on the first guy-line they're rigging with beacons.

'You'd think they'd have realised,' Shep says.

'What?'

'Could've just integrated the beacons and saved a packet. Could've had the flights out sooner...'

Kapper glares at him. 'No one knew the navy's specs till they started the build. That's the whole fucking point. Testing. Don't you listen?'

Shep takes out his sunblock. The staging creaks under their feet. Shep senses the load of the tower bearing down. A hint of the climbing still to come. If only he were wearing a headcam to capture the water's sprawl. Some distraction from the draining humidity.

Bag open and tools laid out, Kapper double-checks his

helmet and reties his boots. 'You're going on first,' he tells Shep. 'So we can find out how useless you really are.'

Shep grins as he slathers his face and neck in cream. Then he unclips his own bag from his rear carabiners and unpacks his beacons, cable clamps and tooling. The biter from its moulded foam at the bottom.

'Sharpish,' Kapper says.

Shep nods. All harnessed up. Checks and rechecks his tools. Slings a rack of beacons over his shoulder like a bandolier. Puts his helmet back on.

'Have at it,' Kapper says.

Shep comes off the railing and clips into the anchor points on the platform's edge.

'Rope out,' Kapper says, and the height becomes tangible, a thing you can almost taste. Kapper has the biter controls slotted in next to his main belay device. With both systems together, he now protects Shep's life in two ways: standard drop protection and fine controls for the biter. When Shep's out there on the line, these systems will be all that keep him from pancaking it.

Shep edges out from the platform until only his toes are left. He opens the biter's mouth and takes up his starting position. He swallows and leans back, legs like a bipod, lines good and taut. Kapper feeds out rope until Shep stands fully horizontal off the platform lip. The sun on his bare arms is close to unbearable.

'Holding,' Shep says. 'Guy cable's two metres down.' And he commits one sole to the beams that support the platform, heart raging. Past his excess rope and dangling gear, the tower's first hundred metres taper gracefully into the base pad. The merging blue–gold horizon out to sea. Eyes up, and he almost can't stand the beauty of it: a shimmering curve rolling up, up, up for another nine hundred metres into the heavens, his angle giving it the appearance of a solid blade. The rush is acute.

He thinks of altitude sickness. He thinks of slipping, falling. He thinks of jumping deliberately, like on the motorway when you realise how easy it would be to gently rotate the wheel towards the central barrier to meet the oncoming traffic. Seventy miles an hour to zero – just like that. He could shrug off his lines and go for it, right then and there. What does falling that far feel like? If you jumped from the scaffold's very top, it'd take about fifteen seconds to hit the base pad, or the ocean, or the island's sheer edges. The effect would be much the same. Those unlucky enough to be in earshot would talk about the sound you make breaking for years to come. But after the sudden lurch, the strange heaviness in your lungs, wouldn't it be blissful?

'Are you on, or what?' Kapper says.

Shep nods to himself. 'Solid.' With his legs wrapped around a beam at the knees, Shep arches back and applies the biter's mouth to the guy-line. The biter chews through the protective grease and into the metal. He asks Kapper to check the jaw pressure.

'All gravy,' Kapper shouts. 'Oh – what weight are you again? Haven't factored.'

To emphasise the point, Kapper gives both fall arrests a playful tug. Shep's guts drop. He can hear Kapper laughing on the platform.

'Twat,' Shep whispers. He takes a breath and shuts his eyes and starts to shimmy down the first metre of cable. It's a complex slippery braid about as thick as his leg, and he relies on the biter to chew and release as he goes. He has three beacons to space at five metres apart, out to fifteen metres. He thinks of Gunny as he slots in his first beacon at the five-metre mark, wincing as the connection is made, grateful for the cable's rigidity. The ten-metre install is harder – not least because Kapper has a better view of what might kill him, and the wind is gusting. As he edges down to the fifteen-metre mark, the sweat is relentless, and the cable's slickness makes his hands ache from gripping. What he'd do for some chalk. For a cold rain to break overhead as it always seems to when you're out on gritstone.

'Keep shifting,' Kapper shouts from the platform. This far away from the beta, Shep can see his partner. Kapper's stare is laser-precise, a disdainful look of concentration. He's hardly holding the belay, but his stance gives Shep confidence.

Shep secures the last beacon. Taps it triumphantly.

'Done?' Kapper shouts.

'Yeah,' Shep shouts back. 'We're hanging tough.'

Kapper nods, seemingly satisfied. 'Nice one,' he says, like he means it.

Shep starts back up the cable towards the platform. Metre by metre, bite by bite, more cautious now the task is done and the adrenaline has waned. At around twelve metres out he pauses to wipe his brow on his sleeve. A smear of sunblock, cable grease and sweat.

'All right?' Kapper asks.

'Yeah?'

'Billy?'

Shep's face tightens. He's hot and his ears are ringing again. Forearms cramping slightly. He takes a sip from his hydration tube, then starts the routine again.

'Billy,' Kapper says. A distance between them now. Shep notices Kapper has taken one or two steps forward, and that the anchor lines securing Kapper to the platform are straining. Kapper's face is also different. His lips are moving but Shep can't tell what's coming out.

'Can't hear you,' Shep says. And his own voice is muffled, too. Like being underwater. He tries to swallow, but his throat has closed.

Ten metres out. Kapper is past confused – he looks frightened. Shep edges up the wire towards him, unclasping and clasping the biter. His lips are burning. The metal too hot in the sun. He notices the way Kapper's boots are protruding from the platform edge. How, for some reason, Kapper is leaning back towards the access shaft like he's being pulled over and trying to stop himself.

'What are you doing?' Shep calls.

Kapper continues to ruminate. Opening and closing his mouth, eyes blank and wide. For a moment, Shep swears he sees a hornet flit across the platform and coil a figure of eight between Kapper's legs.

'Whatever you're doing, you need to fucking stop,' Shep tells Kapper. 'You need to pack it in.'

But Kapper's boots are casting longer shadows off the platform and down the supports, and he's unspooling the main protection to give Shep more slack.

Shep stops again. Arms weak. Nausea and petrol. The beta scaffold glowing again. He has the biter's mouth up by his face, but doesn't remember taking it off the cable. The sky is so blue. The hornet reappears by Shep's face. He swats at it, and then he weighs nothing. He cries out. The guy-line is suddenly a long way above him.

The fall ends before he knows it's started. Shockload, violent and disorientating. A shattering *crack* as the main safety line runs to full extension, where at its limit Shep pitches right over, sky-then-ocean, whiplash-quick, and hears the rope snap back on itself, a second *crack* deep inside his head. He spots a tool – *that's my Stillson!* – pinwheeling away from his belt, flashing silver before it's impossible to tell it apart from the dazzling ocean surface. There's a groan, either Velcro tearing or his throat, and all the alarms are going off on his harness. In that bonded bubble of time, Shep notices the sleeves of his overalls have ridden up. He looks at his wrists and thinks there's more blood in them than there ought to be, that his veins are much darker than they ought to be, and he vaguely understands that he's dangling off the scaffold with his ear yanked right into his shoulder, clamped against it.

The answer comes from without:

– the safety line's round your neck –

Next thing, the arrest line tightens. He's rising, vision clotted purple, a sweet smell and a taste he knows. A muffled voice: 'Billy! Billy! Shep, you fucking cabbage! Look at me!'

'It's all right,' Shep says drowsily.

Someone grips his leg. An arm there, knotty with muscle, veins like shoelaces. At the end of that arm is a shoulder half-out of its socket, a straining neck and frothing mouth.

Why's Kapper out on the guy-line?

But he is. Kapper is flat along the wire, feet down past Shep's head. His anchor lines are all stretching the wrong way, and his fancy belay device is smouldering at his waist.

'Brake on,' Kapper tells him, nodding urgently at the biter. 'Brake *on*, son. Use the biter. *Now*.'

Shep reaches up with the biter, mercifully still attached to his wrist. He depresses the trigger, watches the teeth chew in.

Kapper's voice is clear at last. 'You're okay,' he's saying. 'You're not going anywhere.' The jack has a hand jammed between Shep's throat and the rope, while Shep is suspended in thin air, the friction wet and stinging, and it's such a long way to fall. 'Can you move your head?' Kapper asks. Shep can, and he does, and the rope drops away and his head lolls back. Complex pain explodes in his neck.

'When I say,' Kapper says, 'you grip my harness and brake off. Your protection's shagged but you're quickdrawn on to me – look.'

Shep spots the linked carabiner, umbilical. He still doesn't understand it entirely – this says Shep's main safety line is no longer running through his partner's belay device. That only the biter is protecting him from the drop.

'*Go*,' Kapper says.

Shep releases the biter and grips Kapper's harness at the shoulder. Kapper slips an inch, another inch, then holds fast, and there's a gruesome whine as Kapper presses the switch to retract the platform's anchor lines. After a clunk, a juddering hesitation, both men accelerate up towards the platform. They're smashed against the edge and dragged across the floor to the access hatch. There they roll apart and lie coughing and moaning.

Kapper starts laughing first.

'Fuck me. You trying to die on me?'

'There was a hornet,' Shep says, gasping.

Kapper slumps against the railings and clips on with the last of his energy. Extending his legs in front so his toecaps touch and he's half-sitting like some petulant child. 'You were tugging the main line,' Kapper tells Shep, 'like you wanted to come back faster – it was pulling me off the platform. There aren't any frigging hornets up here.'

Only that isn't Shep's version of it at all. There was a hornet, a taste, and he was gone. 'I thought it was you,' Shep says. He sleeves away the sweat. 'You were slacking out—'

'Yeah, you prick,' Kapper says, 'if I didn't, you'd have taken us both down.'

Shep nods. 'Sorry, man.'

Kapper shakes his head. 'Don't apologise. Save it for the paperwork. But that weird shit you were babbling out there, you need to keep that to yourself.'

Shep can't reply. What did he say? His head is full. He can't bear the absent spaces. The idea of a lapse.

Kapper starts repacking his gear, shaking his head, as though a minute ago they weren't staring down a long drop. 'At least you went pretty fast with the beacons,' Kapper adds. 'I dunno. Maybe it was just a bad rush. Helmet too tight. I'll need a new belay before the next batch, so you

might as well get your head checked. Of all the things...
Christ almighty. That was a fucking shit-show.'

Shep doesn't know what else to say. He inspects his
mechanical biter, the fibres snagged in its teeth. An image
of Gunny's burst hand on Clemens.

He catches Kapper's eye.

'What?' the jack asks. 'You've not popped another
fucking boner, have you?'

The Journalist

A cold bedroom and a scratchy blanket. Then a smell of the sea and, fainter, condom latex. To Freya's right is a bright square of a window, morning light warm on her arm. She rolls to one side. The man is snoring softly, chin angled away from her. A funny whorl of stubble at the hinge of his jaw.

Freya is a little hung over, and the man will be too. Perhaps he doesn't snore when he goes to bed sober, or alone. She picks the sleep from her eyes and watches the bedroom clock roll on.

Reykjavik has surprised Freya. The city is flatter than she expected, yet even under grey skies it avoids drabness through playful colour – building roofs and iron sidings are brightly painted, garlanded with scrappy bunting. It's also small, very walkable, and sedate. Even with days being so short at this time of year, the locals don't rush at all. It'd rained non-stop the evening before. It was so heavy at times that the man she met fell about laughing as she struggled to keep her hair from curling.

'I wanted to see the Northern Lights,' she'd said.

'Too wide,' he'd replied, meaning the cloud. 'And it's not cold enough, even if we go somewhere empty.'

It was chilly enough, though. November in the north of England wasn't a bad analogue for Iceland in autumn, which made Freya think of her parents' bungalow and the colour it turned on a wet morning, and knew she'd packed the right clothes. Her mother's old ski jacket kept out the wind and the damp. Her brogues kept her toes dry.

'Take me to see some music,' she'd slurred to the man after the third or fourth drink. He was probably ten years older. She'd nodded too enthusiastically when he said he patrolled the coast for illegal trawlers. His eyes were sharp, and his lips were slightly chapped, which seemed enough to prove it. When he first went to kiss her, he licked them first.

'The smell is like bad eggs,' he'd said over Freya's shoulder in the late afternoon. That had been his first line to Freya, who was sitting in a tiny cafe browsing for things to do locally – thermal spas, city tours, ice bars, interesting food. Anything to distract herself from what she planned to do the next morning.

'The spas smell of egg,' he explained.

'Really?' she'd said back, playing ignorant.

'You are a Londoner, are you?' The man leaned on her chair in a way that would've annoyed her if he wasn't grinning. She'd immediately liked the scruffiness of his hair: a same-length fuzz that might have grown out from a number one all over.

She shook her head.

'Then where?' he'd said. 'I don't believe it.'

'Near Sheffield and Manchester.'

The man had shrugged. 'I think they have nice mountains near Sheffield and Manchester.'

'Hills. They're just hills.'

'You will have to explain.'

A seeking half-smile. 'Okay,' she'd said. 'But it'll cost you a beer.'

'Of course.' And he'd half-winked in kind.

Their sex had been slightly disconnected, more of a secondary act to the way they kissed. Salted caramel, indefinable heat, wine.

After breakfast with the man, polite and nonchalant, as if they hadn't met by chance and allowed their lives to helix briefly, Freya says goodbye to him with a peck on the cheek. She sees herself out of his flat, wondering if being here was made all the more inevitable by the mystique of a new city, a new face. But last night wasn't only about distraction – it was procrastination. And now, this morning, the task is at hand.

It's drizzly outside, the clouds a heavy alloy. Freya diverts herself past the Hallgrímskirkja, a Lego rocket ship of a building tipped with a dainty crucifix. She stands in the rain and takes some pictures and posts the best to her stream. Proof this trip has really happened.

After that, she goes in search of food and a toilet. A little shelter. She finds a homely cafe not far from the Hallgrímskirkja and eats a pastry in a window seat.

Hi, I'm Freya. I knew Stephen. Could we chat?

She doesn't even know if Alba will be in. What if she's at

work? What if she's already left the address Stephen's father gave her?

Gulls are calling. Freya puts down the pastry. She can't swallow her mouthful.

Alba's apartment occupies a nondescript block around six storeys tall. The building's modular fascia is coming away from its battens, and underneath, in the shadows, Freya makes out the old walls, stained and furry where moss grows in the mortar.

In the building's foyer – there's no lock on the front door – Freya loiters until a resident collecting his post goes outside. She checks the communal post boxes. The labels are filled with handwritten characters and names. Alba's sits in the fourth row: *A y O.*

Freya takes the lift to the fourth floor and walks into a windowless corridor that smells of wet mud. She stops outside what must be Alba's apartment, straightens her jacket, clears her throat, and forces a yawn to prepare her mouth. Then, shoulders back, she knocks.

Alba opens the door looking taller and narrower than Freya anticipated. The space between the two women shifts like a weather front. Alba's expression is impassive, her hair gathered into a half-hearted topknot. Dark eyes, naked lashes. Wisps of fly-away hair. She's wearing an oversized woolly jumper and clasps her baby to a wet towel on her left shoulder. The baby is naked and making little snuffling noises. Beyond Alba is a messy room strewn with small clothes and blankets. A sleep monitor hisses gently.

Directly facing the door is a framed picture of Stephen.

'Hi,' Alba says.

'Hello,' Freya replies, surprised to notice her breath condensing on the second syllable. 'Alba?'

Alba considers Freya's clothes and nods. 'From the police?'

'No,' Freya says. 'Not with the police. Is now a good time?'

'He has fed. If you don't mind, I must wind him…'

'Of course.' Freya waves her on. 'And then do you think we could chat? I'm okay to wait out here while you sort him.'

'Chat?' Alba says. She pats and rubs her baby's back. After a few seconds he burps wetly, and Alba strokes his cheek as if to congratulate him. 'About what?'

'England.'

Alba glances behind her. Back to Freya. She bobs gently. 'England.'

'About… yeah.'

'What about it?'

'Stephen,' Freya says.

If Alba reacts, she hides it well.

'Who?'

Now Freya weighs the situation. 'Stephen Parsons,' she says. And her next words come even more slowly. 'Your partner.'

Alba pulls her son into her chest and holds him there beneath the towel. The baby relaxes. Alba draws a long breath. 'Okay.'

Freya crosses into Alba's apartment, careful not to tread on the blankets and muslin squares strewn across the carpet. It's desperately cold.

'Please take a seat,' Alba says.

Freya swallows her guilt and sits down in the stream of an air-conditioner. 'Thank you,' she says, hugging herself.

Alba settles on the couch opposite, still unperturbed. She holds her son against her belly. 'How did you find us?'

'Stephen's father,' Freya says quickly.

Alba gives a little backwards nod. 'And you are Freya. You searched for me online.'

Freya doesn't break eye contact. 'Yes.'

Alba looks at the baby, unbothered by the chill, and says, 'Do you hear that, little man?' She swaps him to her right shoulder, allowing Freya to catch his face in profile, milk-drunk and half-asleep. In person it's hard to say who Oriol better resembles – one of those babies who takes features from both parents, and looks different in every picture.

'I wanted to offer a drink,' Alba says. 'But...' She glances at Oriol.

'No worries at all,' Freya says. 'Maybe I can fetch you something?'

Alba shakes her head.

Freya's smile tightens. Unsaid things starting to press on the seams.

'Little man,' Alba says to her son. 'Can you say hi to Miss Freya? She wants to know about Papi.'

Alba turns Oriol so he's facing Freya. Pudgy legs over her knees. His eyes wide and startling green. His smooth skin makes Alba's face look drawn and haunted.

'Hey,' Freya says, leaning forward.

Oriol gurgles and squirms. He seems a happy baby, animated and excitable, and his motor control hints at a preternatural awareness. Having made himself comfortable, Oriol sits bolt upright, regarding Freya with keen focus. Again, Freya sees Stephen in him. That milky smear on Oriol's chin could almost be climbing chalk.

'He's cute,' Freya tells Alba, trying not to shiver. Trying not to hint by looking at the air-conditioner.

Oriol continues to gawp, head perfectly still, eyes locked to Freya's own. She feels that stare right down inside her, and in there with it, in the tumult of her stomach, there's a barb of Shep, Stephen, the man from last night. Would Freya's son look like Oriol if she and Stephen had conceived him? In adolescence, would he develop those same long fingers?

Freya makes herself tiny in self-disgust. Shoulders rolling in. Then, as a way to appear normal: 'How many weeks is he now?'

'I don't remember,' Alba replies.

'Tiny Oriol,' Freya says, and her stomach gives.

Alba laughs coolly. 'Stephen said it like you. Never right. His own child!'

Freya crosses her wrists over one knee. 'Oriol,' she repeats. 'Oriol.'

Alba waves her spare hand. 'Do you think we better go for a walk? You look cold.'

Freya nods, almost too forcefully. 'But could I be really cheeky and use your bathroom first?'

'Yes,' Alba says.

Freya stands up, out of the air-conditioner's draught.

'It's through there,' Alba says. 'Be careful on the tiles.'

• • •

274

Alba's bathtub contains a smaller tub of still water, fitted with an infant support seat. An orange flannel has sunk to the bottom, and three plastic frogs float on the surface. When Freya's done, stands up to flush, she realises what's causing the peculiar shadows playing over the tub's base, the support seat. The water is full of ice cubes.

The women descend in the lift in silence. Alba has dressed Oriol and strapped him to her in a carrier. He faces inwards but constantly looks around, seemingly interested in the lift-car's corners, the high-contrast details.

On the street, on neutral territory, Alba says, 'We can go to the family park. Oriol enjoys to watch other children. It's not far.'

Freya nods, trying to appear calm. She rubs her hands as if she'd plunged them in the ice-water herself. She can't shake the feeling that Alba might run away, even if the carrier appears to restrict her hips.

They walk past rows of Reykjavik's gaudy buildings, down quieter streets, until fields and dense treeline disrupt the pattern. Small talk, minor diversions, as they go. If she were more detached from the situation, Freya would like how Alba speaks English: relaxed, not completely faultless, and with a slight adenoidal quality.

At last Alba points towards a park entrance. Freya looks at her mapper: *Fjölskyldugarðurinn*. They cross a small bridge, and the atmosphere immediately brightens. Children and parents running amok beneath the open sky. There are dozens of fist-sized drones in the air, flashing and whining while making cartoonish bombing sounds.

'Lovely place,' Freya says. And it is, despite the racket. Even under cloud, the park's grass is unnaturally bright.

Alba's disposition has also shifted. She's... what, more involved now? Passing a small playground, Alba stops and leans sideways on the railing so Oriol can watch the children on the roundabout. He coos appreciatively, a spluttering laugh.

'So, you are a private investigator? Is that how you call it? You never actually said.'

'Sorry,' Freya says. 'I'm writing a story.'

'Oh. Like a book?'

'An article for a French magazine, about climbing. Their biggest one, I think – you've probably heard of it. *Dalle*.'

Alba thinks about that. She shakes her head. 'And you really come here to see me?'

'Yes,' Freya says. 'I did.'

'All this way from London.'

'Near Manchester.'

'Manchester, right. The library address. You're crazy, you know. You're crazy people.'

In the carrier, Oriol pushes his head into Alba's chest and starts to suck his fingers noisily. His face has turned red. It might be the shade, but there's an unusually dark and prominent vein on his forehead.

'Why did you?' Alba asks.

'Did I what?' Freya replies, staring at the vein. It pulsates like a newborn's fontanelle.

'Come to here. To talk about Stephen.'

'I...' Freya hesitates. 'He's the focus, I suppose. I'm writing about climbers, and urbex.'

Alba blinks. Freya grips the playground railings.

'You weren't at his funeral, were you?' Freya asks. 'You weren't mentioned, is all... and you're out here with his son.'

Alba shrugs. 'Is a free world.'

'But—'

'You knew my Stephen?'

Your Stephen. My Stephen. Our Stephen.

'Not very well.'

'Did you date him?'

Freya's gums hurt. She's caught, full glare, in Alba's gaze. She gets by with, 'No,' and it's hardly decisive. Like Alba can see inside her head.

'And still you went to his funeral?'

Freya's top lip quivers. 'There's... after he died, I did a piece on what happened. Then my editor wanted to know more. And through my investigation I found his profile on an urbex site.'

Alba smiles sadly. 'Ah,' she says. 'So it's the picture.' She shakes her head. 'I tried to delete it.'

And Freya tries to catch her breath.

'What can I tell you, Freya?'

'You had a bet with him.'

'You saw that?'

Freya nods. 'What was the bet?'

Alba laughs. 'Really?'

'I'm not—'

'It was a bet on who will die first. Couples do these things, don't they? And what else? We are okay here. We survive.'

'I can tell.'

'Then I am confused. His climbing? Or his exploring?'

A drone buzzes overhead. Freya lets go of the railings. The ground feels soft. 'I thought… yes. It's the picture. You could tell me more about his exploring. If it won't upset you.'

Alba snorts. 'You found his travelogues! You already know. I cannot speak for the dead. He always said his pictures helped him understand his life… Maybe that's stupid.'

Freya still doesn't believe Alba is annoyed, despite her growing bluntness. If anything, there's a sense she wants the release. At the same time, Freya has imposed on their family space, and is being careful. It's not like Alba is wrong to be suspicious.

'I suppose I'm trying to understand his life as well,' Freya says.

Alba shakes her head sadly.

'We can talk off the record,' Freya adds. 'No quotes, nothing like that. It's more like… colour. It helps me grasp stuff.'

'Like what he did? Or why he did it?'

'In a way.'

'Tell me what you know,' Alba says. Her face has set hard. She stands away from the fence, which makes Oriol's finger-sucking more intense. He peers at Freya. 'Because,' Alba says, 'you are not telling me everything yourself.'

Freya takes a breath. She wills Oriol to blink. 'There's a place,' she says. 'An old bunker.'

Alba rears back, and Oriol protests at the sudden movement.

'It's okay,' Freya says. 'No one else knows.'

Alba sighs, and Freya suddenly sees how tired she is. How

desolate it must be to lose a partner that way. How Freya might not even appear as real to Alba at all. If Alba wakes to a fresh wave of grief tomorrow, will she even believe Freya visited the day before? She wouldn't blame Alba: Freya herself is beginning to see their meeting as another surreal event in this strangest of years. If her life was dredged when her ex finished with her, the silt is yet to settle.

She looks at Alba with her son: how can she not know his age?

'I need a drink,' Alba says.

They sit on a bench outside a cafe deep in the park, their feet on the border of a lawn, both toying with the cardboard sleeves of their coffees. Shared silence some concession to the situation.

Oriol is sleeping against Alba's sternum, the vein on his forehead now settled.

'I lost someone recently,' Freya tells Alba. 'Though not like you lost Stephen,' she adds quickly, 'and thank God, because I can't... I can't imagine. I mean I lost someone – through my own idiocy – so I get why you'd want to escape.'

'So now you chase another man across the world?'

'What? No, I—'

'You have a word in England. Rebounding.'

'Alba, no.'

'Then what?'

'I was unfaithful.'

Alba shrugs. 'People are stupid. We do stupid things. I say it again: you are not here for your story only, are you?'

'No,' Freya says. 'It's the bunker. The picture I saw. It's…'

'Miss Freya, you are confused.'

'I've been there.' And there it is. The confession. An exposure of that mythical journalistic objectivity. Freya's been part of this story all along, and there's no getting away from it.

Alba's eyes narrow. 'When?'

'Not long ago.'

'Did you touch it?'

'The nest?'

'Ha. Call it as you want. Nest.'

Freya looks into her cup.

'We were stupid, too,' Alba says. She nods. 'I pushed him to go. I heard of it through someone selling images on the message boards. A drone man. I wanted to keep my own body… my pregnancy was hard. Stephen agreed, for my sake. We found your nest there.'

Freya's arm hairs stand up.

'We were arrested,' Alba says. 'Security. Still, it was too late.'

'Too late for what?'

'Did you touch it, Freya?'

'No.'

'Someone else?'

'I can't be sure. I think so.'

'Who?'

Freya closes her eyes. The memory has the force of an avalanche. Shep in that dour corridor, his hand reaching out. Things splitting and dividing.

'Stephen touched,' Alba goes on, 'and he takes from it.'

'What happened?'

'Nothing. Nothing. And then... I don't know. How to say... *estado maníaco*.'

'Stephen's dad told me his behaviour changed. His parents can't accept how it happened.'

Alba nods. 'We had more fun in those weeks after than we had ever had. He is so smiley. Excited for our baby. Excited for the family we are making. Happy.'

Freya grips the bench. 'And – and he wasn't like that usually?'

'Not like *this*. He laughs all the time. He laughs all the day he goes to Leeds...'

'And you? Afterwards?'

Alba smiles. 'After he went? Or the bunker?'

'Bunker,' Freya says.

'Me, I caught the dreams. You must have caught them too.'

The dreams. 'No,' Freya lies, and thinks of consumption, contagion. Her headaches. She's shaking. 'What are they?' Freya asks. 'The dreams?'

'Tell me who touched it,' Alba says.

'You can't ignore—'

'Tell me.'

'I don't know where he is.'

Alba's face changes completely. 'He'll need you,' she says. 'I have my guardians. But he may not.'

'What does that mean, guardians?'

Alba smiles as if to a passing stranger. It's like Freya hadn't said anything at all. 'Do you want to know more about Stephen?'

'Please don't ignore me, Alba.'

'Stephen was a good photographer,' Alba says, 'because I took most of them.'

'Alba, what are your guardians?'

'Stop it,' Alba says, direct. 'If you want to pretend to talk about your story again, why not ask how we meet? Ask me things that will honour him. Ask me what he told me in our bed in the middle of night when we are the only two people in the world. That is what you should want. But you came about your nest. Not about Stephen. You came here for you.'

'That's not true,' Freya says. 'I just want to know.'

Alba sighs. 'What does it matter? We were not very careful. He didn't want to go. But this is my body, you understand. I am pregnant. Not him. Not him.'

Freya is blindsided. Of course Alba went out there, climbed that wall, ventured deep while she carried Oriol in utero. Where some of her friends had used parenthood as a reason to seal themselves off, Alba kept – keeps – Oriol unshielded in the tangle of living, the mad stew of it.

'Did *you* touch it?' Freya asks. 'The nest? Is that what you mean by guardians?'

'No,' Alba says, more abrupt, even hostile. 'Now ask me a different question, or I'm leaving.'

'Your dreams,' Freya says quickly. 'Stephen changed – you said you dreamed. Caught the dreams. What dreams?'

Alba inhales. 'A glacier. Every night. We are there. Stephen, then me. I am always pregnant. We wear crampons and carry picks. The same every direction: only white. Very, very cold. We walk on it for hours, no talking because

282

it hurts for us to say anything. No animal comes to us. He holds my hand, I hold his. We lay down on the ground together and wait. It does not scare me. It tells me things.'

Freya blinks. 'Like what?'

'That I should be cold to have our baby. That I would be happier with a baby in the cold. That my boy needs the cold.'

'Happier.'

'Yes. Cold. For Oriol.'

Freya looks at Oriol. His resting face.

'And you still have this dream?'

Alba shakes her head. 'Not every night. It changed when I came here. But it brought me through Stephen's leaving. I was thirty-nine weeks pregnant when he went. I was sure I would lose my baby as well. And the dream soothed me. It's how I could keep sleeping.'

Alba's phrasing, as if Stephen had simply transitioned, makes Freya's eyes hurt. His coffin in that dank church. His brother Toby's voice catching in his throat. It dawns on her: Stephen never met his son.

'Is this what you wanted to hear?' Alba asks.

'I don't know,' Freya says. Again to Oriol, who has dribbled a thick mucus down his chin. 'I'm grateful you can open up.'

'Did your friend take something from inside?'

And Freya shakes her head, because if she opens her mouth the tears will spill.

'Because if he did, he will need help,' Alba goes on. She puts down her cup and rolls up her sleeves. 'See?'

Freya wishes she couldn't. Dark veins run across Alba's forearms, the skin barely containing them. The whole

283

vessel network has risen up to sit just under the surface, like a tattoo. One thick section by Alba's elbow writhes slowly. An odd, sweet scent rises. It reminds Freya of being in Shep's van.

Alba turns her toned forearms. They're completely hairless.

'Their map,' Alba says. 'I think they are charting us.'

'What is it?' Freya manages.

Alba gives a backhanded wave, casual if not outright dismissive. 'We are happy here, remember,' she says, gently pinching at her wristbone. The muscle beneath stays taut but the skin is too elastic. 'And so is my son.' She looks down at him. 'This,' she adds, meaning her arm, 'is what I paid with. It is what Stephen left to me.' She touches a line down Oriol's forehead, where the vein had been. 'What he left to us.'

Then what price had Stephen paid? If Shep really pulled something from that nest, what did it mean for him? Dream-visions? Manic states? The same impulse that made Stephen climb the scaffolding of a Leeds building site?

Yes, their bunker incursion has marked Freya. Unseen but inevitable. It follows that she's already paying her own price. A fear of Shep, but an inextricable binding to him.

'What was the writing?' Freya asks. 'Under the picture? The symbols on Stephen's post?'

Alba smiles. 'It was in the EXIF data,' she says. 'The picture was taken with a used camera. To begin with, we thought the last owner did changes to the firmware. It was Stephen's job—'

'There were two versions. Symbols and non-symbols.'

284

Alba stares at her. 'Stephen translated it for us.'

'Why did you post it?'

'Because it was funny! Because I wanted to. Why do we share anything private? Where is your friend now?'

'Away,' Freya says. 'He's a steeplejack. He's somewhere overseas.'

'And he uses the message boards?'

'Yes, I think so—'

The lights in the cafe behind them snap off, begin to flicker. Alba spins on the bench and pulls a face.

'You don't have long,' Alba whispers.

'What?'

Alba turns back to her. 'They want you to go.'

'What? Who does?'

'Yes,' Alba says, measured. 'I think they want you to leave.' She puts a hand on Oriol's head. He's woken up. A low whimpering. 'You should find your friend,' Alba says.

Oriol begins to wail, twisting wildly in the carrier.

'I don't…' Freya starts. 'Who's here?'

'Oriol wants to feed,' Alba says flatly.

Freya stands up. The horizon tilts. The cafe lights are strobing. She thinks she might be sick. 'I shouldn't have come.'

Alba has already slipped Oriol out of his carrier, uncovering a black-veined breast for him.

'It's not my decision,' Alba says, helping Oriol latch on. 'You understand? They do as they do.'

Freya doesn't understand. But she can't turn, either. The dark vein in Oriol's forehead has risen again. Whatever happened to Stephen – whatever's happening here in this park – must be no clearer to Alba than it is to Freya.

Whatever was in the nest has got into Stephen, and so into Alba and Oriol. It has likely got into Shep, too.

Carry it for us, the caption under Stephen's photo had said.

Freya turns to leave. 'Your boy is beautiful,' she tells Alba.

The Steeplejack

Vertex consumes Shep in the days after his fall. The island charges his sleep, his waking hours, his sunburn, with terrible purpose. On shift, his life is reduced to the quadrant he works with Kapper, to wire-walking and installing beacons. After his shifts, stinking and dehydrated in the canteen, Shep barely has the energy to lift a fork to his mouth, let alone miss anybody or anything back home.

As they work on the uppermost guy-wires, Shep and Kapper avoid discussing their near miss, though a new caution is established in certain movements, their piously kept-to safety checks. At this level, the wind roars through the scaffold's negative space with a ferocity that's hard to fathom on the ground. At its gustiest it's hard to see, move or speak, much less think. Nor does Kapper repeat any of the things Shep apparently said as he came back up the guy-line before he slipped. Progress is all that matters; the past being irrelevant, and talking about it more so. Besides which, they're actually getting on. Despite their initial clashes they've made peace through a shared work ethic – and a silent competitiveness that plays out as they take turns to belay each other on the wires.

Food eaten, Shep will usually limp back to his cabin and lie outside on the parched earth through dusk, watching the miniscule lights of technicians starting night shifts deep in the beta's lattice. Sometimes these technicians test-fire the beacons the crew have installed that day. Shep finds these times especially peaceful, absent of pressure. Home, with its refineries and red-brick chimneys and Friday night drinks, a bound-up state a whole planet away. So maybe it's inevitable that in this peace his old hobby should start to creep in. He starts taking photographs of the scaffold with his phone, cropping and colouring each picture differently for effect. When the commsat dishes rotate his way with a fleeting connection, he uploads pictures to a thread on the urbex forum with no explanation, no captions, no reports. It's not that he's trying to affect mysteriousness – it's more that the scaffold speaks for itself.

When the first drone test session comes around, Eddy seems confident in the quality of the crew's handiwork. From one hundred to five hundred metres, at which point you need to use the lift to go higher, the beta scaffold's quadrants are fully rigged.

Walking towards the base pad that morning, Shep and Kapper acknowledge the rainbow forming over the runway where navy ground crews are hosing down the hot macadam. One end of the rainbow putters out by the radio masts, the other above the wings of a Merlin drone. The rainbow has gone by the time they meet the rest of the crew. They strap on their helmets, apply fluid to dried-out sun-lenses, fidget with nervous energy. It rained overnight and now their boots are heavy with a thick elemental paste.

'Reckon we ballsed-up the microclimate,' one of the jacks says to break the silence, pointing up the tower. His knuckles are tattooed with DEMO MANC. 'Keep getting these freak clouds.'

On the other side of the base pad stands a group of abseilers, both strange and strangers to Shep. They're fresh off the chopper and curiously innocent by the looks of them, like a group of visiting schoolchildren. It makes him realise how easy it is to recognise people who've been working on the island for a while. Little signs that make the distinction simple: raw skin, the smell of used overalls as they draw past, a willingness to discuss constipation, treacly piss. The intense nightmares they all seem to have about falling. And never mind the grey hairs sprouting on Shep's face since he last shaved.

Eddy eventually shows up, Stetson on tight. 'Now then,' he starts, beaming, 'how about we grab ourselves a view for take-off?'

The crew shuffle to the access hatch of the runway-facing quadrant. Before it's his turn to slip inside, Shep stares out to sea. Visibility is decent most days – a good ten miles to the horizon, more up top – but the clarity of light is exceptional today.

'You coming, cabbage?' Kapper says.

Shep nods. A single drone signaller on the runway

continues to rehearse. Kapper has taken to calling these signallers 'scarecrows' on account of the arms-wide semaphore they use to calibrate the drones' sensors. In this there can be no error margin, and so Shep is excited to feel part of the process. All their work on Vertex has been building to this flight.

'Not nervous, are you?' Kapper asks Shep as they prepare to climb the ladder. He claps Shep on the shoulder. 'Because I'll eat my harness if that thing spoons it on our lines.'

'Not nervous,' Shep tells him.

The engineer wants the crew staged between all five maintenance platforms so they can each get a view. Shep, Kapper and two of the others are sent to the two-hundred-metre mark, with Kapper on point.

Shep has been up and down this tube dozens of times, but the climb is no less cramped or humid. Lactic acid is a pacer, and even without the biter to carry, Shep is relieved when Kapper leads them back into light.

The four jacks squeeze onto the platform. A vibration deep in Shep's chest cavity. He writes it off as excitement and clips on to the railing. Then a surplus of saliva and a sensory surge: sea air, filth and degraded rubber on his palms, the lattice cocooning them. The edge calling him forward. But Shep doesn't speak. He swallows all the spit and leans right out from the barrier to stretch his back and shoulders. The tower curves sickeningly into the pad. The island's edge is razor sharp. Birds wheel lazily beneath them. That urge to jump is powerful.

Kapper touches Shep's arm. 'Laddy,' he whispers. 'Shut the fuck up.'

'Eh?'

'You're doing it again.'

'What again?'

'Babbling,' Kapper hisses under his breath. 'They'll think you're bloody tapped.'

'I didn't say anything,' Shep protests.

'No? Then where's this hornet? Where? You copped for sunstroke, or what?'

'Leave it out,' Shep says.

Yet even as he tries to read Kapper's face, something moves in him. He fixates on the sensation and his stomach cramps hard.

'Shep?'

Shep bends over double, staggers towards the platform edge.

'Shep!' Kapper shouts. 'Fucking hell. Someone get Eddy on the line—'

Muffled, Shep hears Kapper asking the others to share their water tubes – feels them poking at his chin and lips. The tower's formwork has doubled, separated out. His stomach cramps again and he falls to his backside. He manages to brush away someone's tube before he vomits fleshy string onto the platform, choking hard to get it up, purging himself. The way it drops through the mesh is grimly fascinating. Slow, sinking squares that are torn out to sea by the wind. Then hands are all over him, and his bowels empty out, and he's dragged to the access hatch and held down.

'I'm okay,' Shep keeps telling them as he comes round, sees three jacks with wide eyes. 'Guys – I'm fine.' And he's sure of it. So sure, he pushes them away and shuffles to the platform fence, his overalls dripping, and throws his soiled legs and filled boots over the side, ignoring them all. The hornet buzzes around him. A cloying metallic stench. The view, this island, a weightlessness. The drone scarecrows, tiny figures down on the runway, with their paddles waving madly. The hangar door is fully open and a second Merlin noses along the apron to join the first. Both machines readying for take-off, the whole scaffold tremulous with anticipation.

Shep doesn't know what Kapper is saying urgently into his watch. Couldn't tell you if this, the first test day, might also be the day his friendship with Kapper is cemented and cracked all at once. He doesn't care if the other jacks are cowering against the platform railings, hands clamped over noses and mouths at the smell of him. He doesn't. All of Shep's concentration is given to the Merlins as they clear the runway then rise, smooth and dark against the sky, heliophobic paint rendering each craft a dull, flat stone – like the kind Shep would try to skim from the banks of a lake somewhere in the northern uplands, in the past, in an old life.

The hornet hovers at his shoulder. It watches the drones with him.

The Journalist

While it's still unwritten, Freya's planned piece on Stephen is now seriously at odds with the detachment of her local reporting, the far-too-neatness of an obituary. It'll be rigorous, sure, and of a certain quality – she hopes – but written with some new, much more personal emphases. Alba was right to say Freya's story about Stephen is equally about her. So after leaving the park, Alba's warnings in refrain, Freya goes directly to the airport and pays for an earlier flight home with her own savings. Just to get out of there. Just to start writing this thing out of her.

What's the alternative? The idea of infection, a transmission – psychological or biological – is now too credible to ignore. Imagine another night in a hotel room, or this terminal, with no respite from Shep – Shep who's surely suffering somewhere, changing beyond his comprehension; Shep whose living experience is surely the key to the mystery of Stephen's death. Shep who'll plug the holes in Freya's project, and whose health now feels like

Freya's responsibility – as if through some bizarre inversion it's her fault he did what he did that night. As if he was only showing off because she was with him.

No, Freya can't stay here. She wouldn't cope with the frustration. She'd only sit and chew herself up. The obscene cost of the early flight is worth it, cushioned slightly by her trip expenses being covered. That, and the man she spent the night with had given her his drinks receipts.

What had Alba called Stephen's pre-death behaviour? *Estado maníaco*. A shift in mindset that led him towards arrogance, to risk-taking. To climbing a scaffold in his going-out clothes.

And Freya wonders: was Stephen silent as he fell? Or was he still laughing?

She holds her face. Her eyes are burning and nothing helps. Why is Alba so serene in her new life, even if something was clearly skewed or unbalanced there? And the boy – the cold in the flat. That unforgettable vein.

What does she have to stop Shep doing? And how can she, when he's so out of reach?

'They want you to leave,' Alba had said. These guardians of hers. It makes Freya shiver. What has infected them all?

Freya checks the departure boards. Not long till the flight. She picks her nails. She thinks, *If I'm not lonely, then I'm adrift.* It means a lot to feel wanted, to understand your place in another person's world. Who is Freya to Shep? Who is Freya to anyone? God, how simple it can be to miss the easy comforts of cohabitation. The familiarity of touch, a particular bed linen. Bobbly pillows. A well-travelled route between foreplay and sex – this being your side of the bed, this being mine.

Anonymous in the departure lounge, Freya finds herself scrolling through her contacts for a number she should've deleted. Then she swipes red on the second ring. She opens a new message and puts, *Sorry, sat on it.*

When she presses send, the screen locks up. He's calling back. He's giving her permission.

'Hello?' she says.

Dickhead's voice is faint. 'Had a call off this number?' Wind in the background. Brash voices, traffic wash. He's snippy. ('You in a mard with me?' she used to ask him, when he came in from work under a cloud.)

'I sat on my phone,' she tells him.

'Didn't catch that,' he says. Sirens passing. 'This is—'

'Are you keeping all right?'

'Sorry, who's this?'

'It's me,' she says. 'It's Frey.'

'Freya?' Practically shouting into his phone now. 'Did you say it's Freya?'

'Yeah, it's me.'

The background noise drops. Suction as a door opens into a foyer, maybe. Then the crackle of his beard rubbing the mic.

'I'm in town,' he tells her. 'What's up?'

'Nothing,' she says. 'I thought I'd call. See how you are.'

'Oh.'

'Oh,' Freya repeats.

'You abroad?' he asks. 'Dial tone was funny.'

'I'm in Reykjavik. For work.'

'Iceland? Time is it there?'

'Same time it is there.'

'Are you drinking?'

Freya shakes her head. 'Same time zone. And nope.'

'Well, I'd better get on with this shopping.'

'That's fine. I just wanted to—'

'Bye, Frey.'

Freya's next words are right there, suspended. But he's already hung up.

It's dark when the taxi drops Freya at her parents' bungalow. The lights are off and there's a fresh pallet of whole milk on the breakfast bar. A note nearby: '*Gone to Tescaldi to complain about fridge. M+D x*'

She finds a portion of lasagne in the oven but can't face eating it. Instead, she sits there with a sugary tea and browses her social feed. Her shot of the Hallgrímskirkja has been reposted by a savvy Reykjavik tourism firm, and it's netting hundreds of likes and comments. Normally she might feel proud of that – that something she'd created so quickly could travel so far in so little time. Not tonight.

She finishes her tea and goes to run a bath. She undresses and runs her phone's torch over her skin. Her arms glow pinkly. Her fingertips light up red. She perches on the bath edge in the curls of eucalyptus steam and does the same with her stomach. What does she want to find? Bruise-like blotches, darkening veins? To be like her – like Alba? In the absence of Shep, will that help her get closer? Help her move on?

As she eases into the bath, she pictures Stephen and Alba

having sex. Standing up, their dark hair pressed together. Passing the bunker between themselves.

Freya's skin, however, is clean. No physical changes. No hints. The bunker still hiding inside her.

Shep, though, is out there. Away with work—

'*Sodding* milk,' she hears from the kitchen.

Freya wakes with a start. Her father's voice. She's sitting in a cold bath.

'Freya?'

Her mother at the bathroom door.

'Are you decent?'

'Bloody hell, I'm having a bath. Hang on.'

Freya stands, takes a towel and covers herself.

'Okay,' Freya says.

Her mother barrels in. 'What's going on?'

'What?'

Freya steps out of the bath and sits on the edge.

'Where've you been?'

'What?'

'We've been trying to get hold of you.'

'I did say – Reykjavik.'

'What, in Iceland? What on earth for? You look *terrible*.'

'Work? I told you. I've got a feature to write.'

Freya's mother puts a hand to her forehead. She seems very old. 'You didn't say a word.'

Freya knows this isn't true. And so what if it is? She has every right to disappear and reappear.

'Pretty sure I did,' Freya says.

'You can tell your father over supper.'

'Seriously? Do you want to get me chipped? Is that easier?'

'Our house. Our rules.'

Freya snorts. 'You know what you sound like?'

'I mean it.'

'I'll piss off, then, should I?'

Her mother swallows. 'Be our guest,' she says. 'You haven't spent… haven't spent a *bean* on board or food while you've been here. We took you in with… with unspoken conditions.'

Freya glares. These are her father's words.

'You've wrecked one household,' Freya's mother adds, and now her voice is trembling. 'You're not – you're not doing it here.'

Freya shoots up from her perch on the bath. The towel comes away. She's naked and the chill is hideous. She's only a little taller than her mother, but she leers down at her with a straight back and feels like she's towering.

They stand there, looking at each other.

'Freya,' her mother starts.

'Get out,' Freya says. 'Give me some fucking dignity.'

Her mother picks up Freya's towel, eyes down. 'No more,' she says. And she leaves.

Freya turns to the mirror. Fever-cheeks. She dabs the towel across her brow, beading with sweat. She's never sworn at her mother before. She looks at her neck, her shoulders, her belly. She scowls at herself, desperate to see it, then: to see *them*, to have her own testimony. But there are only red blotches from the shower's heat, and an angry flush on her chest that rises to her neck and ears.

She wraps herself in the towel and returns to her bedroom. She slams her door as she did at twelve, as she always did when she wanted her parents to get the message.

● ● ●

As her parents sit for crackers and cheese, Freya shovels in the lasagne for lack of anything to say. If there's accord, it's because her parents daren't speak either. The only noises are their chewing, the exaggerated way her father clears his throat as if he's ready to announce his terms.

When she's done, Freya gets up. 'Can I use the computer?'

Freya's mother settles her knife.

Freya's father looks at Freya levelly.

'What?' Freya says.

'Apologise to your mum,' he says. 'And you're welcome to do whatever you bloody well like.'

Freya glances at her mother. There are faint stripes of grey down her cheeks. Freya looks back to her father. 'I'm going to move out,' she says. Then she flounces back to her room.

Before she knows it, Freya's tablet is open, fingers responding mechanically to the security prompts. A few likes on her picture of the Reykjavik church from friends she hasn't spoken to in years, like someone else's anecdote now; a notification to say an anonymous user in Iceland has viewed her stream; and a direct message from the man she'd slept with: '*Good luck with your fairy tale.*' She swears. How much had she told him? She opens her email. The usual spam. The airport asking her to review her time there. The airline and hotel in Iceland doing the same.

She selects the lot for deletion. She stops.

A knot. An email whose subject line is made from squares, which would've been deleted as spam just weeks

ago. There in the sender field is a single world: *freighter*.
She opens the email:

> Miss F,
>
> It was interesting to meet you and I am sorry we did
> not say goodbye in a helpful way. I find your details
> on the news sites. I email now because I have
> searched and there is one man who has written about
> climbing being his job before. It is the same way on
> his social profile, where we are friends (as you know).
> There are also scouting pictures (I have sent these)
> of the place he is now.
>
> Of course he may not be your friend. You may
> confirm this for yourself. I am emailing because in ten
> days there is a press visit to this place. I cannot tell
> how I know, I think you may guess.
>
> I must feed O now. Hungry boy!!
>
> Good luck.

Replying is pointless. Freya's anti-hack plugins, synced
when she signed in, report Alba's IP as masked. The email
has been routed through an otherwise dormant botnet.

Freya opens the images attached to the email. Despite
their poor quality, she recognises the background colours of a
big urbex forum in each screengrab. She studies the pictures.
Their subject is at first glance an old-style electricity pylon,

300

decorated with lights. She soon realises the scale is off, and she's looking at a kind of mesh pillar with a square cross-section, supported by cables that come off it at staggered heights. It's like scaffolding, except vastly more complex. The structure is crowned with a fine-mesh spire. In one of the images, workers in helmets are walking by.

Freya rubs her face. Whatever it is, she can't imagine a more tempting figure to an explorer – a climber or a steeplejack. Or both. It has that presence. But what is it? *Where* is it?

Freya rereads Alba's email. These are Shep's pictures. No question. Tomorrow morning she'll call Mallory Limited again.

The Steeplejack

Shep won't remember it, but in that Vertex night, the windsock flapping above his cabin, the throttled cries of terns overhead, he wakes to a delicate tinkling that seems too close to his head. He sits up in blue light, drawn to a shadow on the window: a section of the beta scaffold, projected there by the night workers' floods. He watches this crisscrossing shadow, the flow of it, and Freya is almost beside him again, taking off her coat in his van.

When the tinkling stops, Shep sees a mosquito flying away from his body. He wriggles, realising he's pushed a section of bare arm through the mosquito net. He withdraws and lies flat. The mosquito, a big one, continues to circle him, perhaps hoping for another go. He'll wait for its wings to stop, try to slap it in time.

Then its ungainly loop is cut short, as though it's been swatted, and the mosquito pops against the cabin roof.

Shep, too tired to consider it strange, lies back and closes his eyes again. Light friction on his eyelids tells him he's left his sun-lenses in. That he was seeing things.

In the morning, bleary and hoarse, Shep makes porridge on the camping stove Kapper loaned to him. It's already a bleak picture – a contractor alone with his ways, hands clumsy with fatigue – but as he stirs the gruel, the left side of his face starts itching painfully. He pinches his cheek, and it stings. It's a bite, a big one. He puts down the spoon. It's so swollen it's like there's a patch of whiskers missing from his cheek.

Shep goes to the bathroom for some antiseptic gel. Digs it out of his washbag and turns to the mirror.

There's no bite. No swelling. But he was right – the skin is clear. The bristles in that spot are totally gone. How? It wasn't like this before he went to bed. He decides he'd better shave the rest of his face. He lathers up and takes a disposable razor from its pack, and starts.

When he comes to the underside of his chin, he finds another patch of hair missing. He drops the razor. His neck and torso tingle. He drags off his T-shirt. He doesn't understand. The mirror shows him where a patch of chest hair has also vanished. A patchy ladder formed from negative space runs from the nobbled gully between his pecs right down to his navel.

Shep picks up the razor, turning it. He touches the hairless flesh. A picture, now, with shaving foam everywhere, his brow puffy. The nude skin glossy on his face and body. No rashes, nicks, razor marks. It's just clean. He leans into the mirror and angles his face to study the absence on his cheek.

The absence is spreading.

Shep leaps back with a sharp yelp. He clutches his face. His hair is disappearing. Going missing. He searches himself. Is it the contacts? Is that it? He pinches his eyes until they begin to water and redden. No – he's tugging at naked cornea. Panicked, he leaps into the shower and turns it on full blast. The heat and steam quickly engulf him and he claws at his features, his sunburnt neck, and holds his face up to the showerhead as he turns the dial beyond the red line. The water hisses as it comes through, and above the peal in Shep's ears, the heater grinds as it struggles to keep up. He winces and whinnies and chews his tongue. He wills himself to stand there for as long as he can bear it. The heat is a horrible balm, each jet of water a cutting torch. He knows he'll go all the way to passing out, to lasting damage, before he pulls himself back.

The system trips. The heater dies. The water turns cold.

Shep squats on the shower floor in a miasma of chlorinated steam. A trickle of icy water spattering his back. The plughole between his feet and the cool air over his skin. More lost hairs, drawn like iron filings to a magnet, bunch together and skirt the plughole before they vanish. With a slow hand he traces his cheek. The tingling has stopped. Has the hot water worked? Stroking the gaps, he vividly remembers having sunstroke as a child, a night on his uncle's spare room floor, delirious and scared, patting moisturiser onto a blister that slowly spread across his shoulders—

Someone banging on the door pulls him back to Vertex.

'Shep? You up?' Heavier thuds, perhaps a foot. 'Billy?' Kapper's voice. More banging.

'I'm up,' Shep shouts, shakily. ''Sakes, Kap – I'm having a dump.'

The banging stops. Shep comes out of the shower and turns back to the mirror. He scarcely recognises himself. He splashes his face with cold water and staggers to his bunk, dizzy and uncoordinated. Miraculously he hasn't scalded himself, though his cheeks and eyes are swollen.

'Won't be a sec,' he says to the door.

'Too late,' someone says. Not Kapper, this time – it's a woman's voice. 'You've missed the test briefing.'

Shep knows about this test. Yesterday, six days after the first test – six days after being consigned to the infirmary with symptoms of an 'episode' for which tests yielded no results – he and Kapper rode the tower's central lift car to the beta's topmost maintenance platform, eight hundred metres up, and got on with installing the last of the beacons.

Or was that yesterday? He's overtired. He can't account for the time elapsed. It could've been six weeks for all he knows – Vertex swallows you like that. And what if the second test has already happened and the woman means a different test, a third test? What if the navy's programme is delayed? Shep racks his brain. He's cracking up. The cabin warps around him. Has the test been postponed? He... he doesn't remember. What if he's been in the cabin all week – subsisting on scraps, living the same day over and over and over?

'Shepherd?' the woman says. 'Are you coming?'

Shep starts for the door but stops at the bedside. A hazy flashback. A tinkling noise close to his head. A mosquito in half-sleep... He looks up. There it is – the splatter. His arms break out in goose bumps. There's a slimy, cold substance under his bare foot. He looks at the floor to work out what he's spilled.

'There's a press trip arriving tomorrow,' the woman goes on.

There's also a translucent substance on the floor, skinned like custard in places. A slug trail? Vertex has its creatures, but this would be an enormous slug – at least an inch wide. He wipes his foot on yesterday's socks and follows the trail. It circles his bunk and runs into a tiny gap between the bunk frame and the wall.

'You're an ignorant sod, aren't you?' the woman shouts.

Shep hops over his bunk. The trail resumes between the bunk leg and the wall. It seems deliberate. Here the trail changes direction – goes upwards over the bunk frame, and onto Shep's mattress.

Shep follows the mucus line, shinier on his sheets, towards his pillow. He holds his breath. He closes his eyes and grips the pillow at either side, tears the pillow away. The sheet underneath is a little damp, a little see-through.

Shep flips the pillow. Tears back the sheets. Stray hairs, dead mosquitoes, fluff.

He jumps on the bunk, ripping away the sheets, the harsh wool blanket, trying to find a trail away from his pillow. It goes nowhere. It stops beneath his pillow. The mucus trail stops under where he puts his head.

'Shepherd?'

Shep goes to the door. '*What?*'

'You're late!' the woman shouts. 'Kapper knocked half an hour ago.'

But it can't have been five minutes. He was just here.

'Are you opening up for me?'

Shep unbolts the door to that beta scaffold sheen, night lamps still weakly on, the drone beacons blinking. The woman has her hands on her hips. He's never seen her before. Not a contractor, either, because she wears a sort of safari expedition outfit: lots of hi-tech stuff, breathable fabrics. A comms loop dangling loosely from one ear. At a push she'd pass for a cycle courier. The right build, the urban war kit. The weary countenance.

'You're Billy Shepherd?'

He nods.

The woman grimaces over his shoulder. 'What's this about?'

'What?'

'What've you been doing in there?'

Shep turns around. Bare bunk, mosquito net, clothes, camping stove and pot, helmet. Harnesses and tools by the door.

'It's my cabin,' he says.

'The… paper?'

'What are you on about?'

'Are you all right?'

Shep pulls the door towards him, leaves a gap big enough for his face. 'No,' he says. 'I'm not.'

'Ashamed of yourself? Do you live like that back home?'

'Like *what?*'

'Gear up,' the woman hisses, 'and get over there. You're pushing your luck, now. Big time. Insurers see the state of this, you're on the next supplies ship out of here. I don't

307

even want to know what you're playing at. No wonder Kapper's asking for a new partner.'

Shep's lost for words. Is it better to laugh, or shrug? Or to retreat inside and into himself? The woman's terseness, her responses, seem false, contrived. Being accused of something with no defence is frustrating enough, but none of her reactions match with reality.

'Well?' she says.

'Five minutes?'

'You've got three.' She nods sharply and marches off, an automated quad bumbling up the path to collect her.

Shep focuses on the tower. He'll be up there soon. Everything makes more sense up there. He closes the door. He dresses facing the window so he doesn't have to see the slug trail. So he doesn't have to think about it. He puts in his sun-lenses. They burn a little – more than usual. No bother – that's what you get for trying to scrape your eye out. It's only when he notices that his hands are wet that he remembers where he left the carrycase. He opens it. It's filled with the same substance he found on his bunk.

A kind of glamour is lifted. Shep falls backwards. An imprint on the flesh of his eyelids: the completed tower, crafted from gold sheet, a daedal spire. He stumbles over the bunk end. A hornet by the light bulb. A hovering Merlin. A flash in a corridor from which a winged creature emerged.

How long have I been on Vertex Island?

When Shep opens his eyes again, the cabin has changed. The floor is covered with streamers of twisted wet toilet paper. Here and there it's plastered to the walls. It's been rolled out from the bathroom, spread about in a way that tells him more than one attempt has been made to cover the floor between the bathroom door and his bunk. In one corner of the cabin is a pile of ashes. He stoops to it, and in the ashes there are dozens of twisted insect legs, tiny probosces. A pyre of mosquitoes, left like an offering. At the very top of the pyre lies a cracked case – a chrysalis. From it, half emerged, is the carcass of an enormous hornet. Except it isn't exactly a hornet. It has the body of a hornet, but the head is an unfamiliar shape: a ring of eyes, an array of glittering tendrils where the legs or antennae have been pushed out or excised. It twitches when he breathes over it.

Like the beetle he found in the Lakes, the hornet has been hollowed out.

Shep pushes himself to his feet. The bunk has changed, too. His sheets are soiled and stinking. A tightly wound spiral of slug trail curls out from beneath his pillow into the centre of the mattress.

Here, a single word daubed neatly in brown.

STRATOSPHERE.

Shep rubs at the word; it flakes under his fingertips. He understands it perfectly. The mucus, the trail, still damp around it. Still drying. A separation occurring: the detachment of mind and memory from body and being. Not so much frightening as freeing. His stubble, his hair – was that all dreamed? Had it really happened?

He touches his denuded cheek. There's a bright prick of pain in the tip of his finger. He sucks it, noticing a deeper, richer pain in his palm and wrist. He remembers: this finger has been hurting all night. All this time. It'd flared up the moment he witnessed the stubble being eaten from his face.

He pulls the finger from his mouth. It's weeping plasma from a rusty-brown clot. He looks at the word on the sheets. It was him. He wrote this. He wrote this message to himself.

That Shep wants this Shep to know – *this was you*. This is an instruction.

Our blood ladder.

'Stratosphere,' Shep says.

He sits down on the bunk to tie his boots.

The Journalist

Freya leaves for work before the windscreen has fully demisted. There's a ground frost, and from the scarps behind her parents' bungalow rolls a low mist that gives the hills above Dillock a temporary appearance.

Freya yawns. She's been churning all night, as she often does the night before a deadline, or had in those endless hours after she admitted things to her ex. In this case, she's been anxious to speak to Shep's firm and charm her way to the right information. She'd lain there, willing her alarm to go off. Waiting to make that call.

To stay awake, Freya sets the car to manual drive and listens to an old mp3 stick full of bland indie rock, up louder than the system can handle. Each bass kick makes the speakers cough static, the treble a painful wash. She doesn't turn down the music when houses and streetlights appear and the speed limit dips to twenty. She stalls on a tricky junction because she can't feel the clutch biting with the speaker vibrating by her foot. Nor does she hear the drivers leaning on their horns behind her. For the next few miles she ignores the irate white-van man hanging off her rear bumper. The onboard nav keeps whining, so she kills that as well.

Bleaching it all out is the plan. Deflect the terror of half-revealed things. Numb it, smother it, until she gets to the office and does what she needs to do with the details she gleaned from Mallory Limited's scheduler. Little else matters the way these answers do. Only doing will keep her sane now.

She parks and storms into the office, straight over to the editor's door.

'Come,' her editor says.

Freya goes. Outlined by the warmth of a desk lamp in the far window, she catches her reflection, wild and botched. Her hair tied back but her ponytail lopsided. A lump of hardened toothpaste down one jacket lapel.

The editor stands up from behind her desk. 'Freya? What on earth are—'

'Morning,' Freya says brightly. 'I need your secure line.'

The editor studies Freya. A halting look. Feigned shock that someone would dare acknowledge what the phone is for. But Freya knows – they all do. It's an unmonitored VOIP system built into an old black Bakelite unit, data encrypted via the parent company's private satellite. When you see the editor using it, you know big news is about to drop.

'What for?' the editor asks coolly.

'I don't want anyone to hear,' Freya says.

'Not good enough. You work with journalists.'

'Not at the moment, I don't. Not technically.'

The editor tuts.

'I won't beg you,' Freya tells her.

'Are you in trouble? Is that it?'

Freya shakes her head. 'No.'

'I've been around long enough to know I've seen that face before. Do we need Legal up here? Have you been silly?'

'It's not like that,' Freya says.

'What, then?'

Freya puts a hand on the editor's desk. 'If I call from my desk phone,' she says, talking low, 'and you or Diligence check the records, you'll think I've lost the plot. So will the rest of them. I want no dial-backs. No trace. It's too sensitive.'

'And you really can't go outside and use your mobile?'

'Not really,' Freya says. 'But you can stay and listen if you want. That's fair enough.'

The editor touches her lips. 'I'm not sure I *want* to listen. Frankly, I'm not sure about a few things going on here. You look tired, Freya—'

'You're fine with me using it, then?'

'What's your game? I'm not being—'

'—funny? You know it's about Stephen.'

'Of course it's about Stephen,' the editor says. 'It's been about him for a while now.'

'I need to call the coroner.'

The editor comes round her desk, hands on her hips. 'Why?'

'I need to know what they found inside him.'

'Bloody *hell*, Freya.'

'It's for the story.'

'And that wouldn't be gratuitous at all? Unethical?'

'It's colour,' Freya says.

'*Colour?* What the hell do you think they'll have found?'

313

Freya shrugs.

'Don't be so bloody childish.'

'Fine,' Freya says. 'I think he had…' She breaks off. What's more plausible? A disorder? A disease? Admitting she believes Stephen contracted a parasite that made him terminally overconfident?

'He had a tumour,' Freya says. 'On his brain.'

'That's awful,' the editor says. 'Nobody knew?'

'I don't know what anyone knows,' Freya says.

'But surely the coroner would've found a tumour.'

'I don't know about that, either,' Freya says. Then, after a pause, 'Maybe the injury from the fall concealed it. Maybe it was so powerful an impact… Or maybe it was new? A tiny thing.'

The editor picks up the special handset and grips it. She taps it against her forehead. 'How can you be sure?'

'I've been putting it all together.'

'But what difference will it make? If it really was? Apart from the fact that the coroner has, what, not done their job properly?'

'I'll tell you afterwards,' Freya says. And like that, she has a new hook. The editor's intrigue is so palpable that any headline suggesting his inquest could've *missed* something will be a puller.

'Be quick,' the editor says.

Freya breezes past the coroner's front desk with a few rehearsed lines about delays in medical waste supplies. It isn't luck: she knows they'll burn through consumables from one day to the next, and it's always easier to reach a decision-maker if the story sounds innocuous to a receptionist but potentially worrying to the higher-ups.

The front desk connects Freya to a distracted technician who quickly palms her back into the internal menu tree. This gives her options including the head coroner's direct line.

'Derek speaking,' the coroner says, slight Yorkshire inflection. 'Hello? Justina? I'm in lab.'

When Freya doesn't answer, the coroner repeats himself.

'Morning,' Freya says. 'This is Amanda from Civil Liaison, Greater Manchester Police.'

'And?'

'I'm chasing a post-mortem report,' Freya tells him. 'My team's seconded to the uni over here and we're collating inquest data. Traumatic brain injuries, mainly. A prevention study. I believe you recently signed off on a young man who died on your patch.'

'And it's his report in particular, is it?'

'A man called Stephen—'

'Parsons,' the coroner finishes. 'Yes. I ruled misadventure.'

'Misadventure,' Freya repeats.

Derek sniggers. 'And you hope I'll send you the report by email, for convenience? At some time today? Amanda?'

'Yes,' she croaks.

A pause, then: 'Are you sniffing for the national rags or plain old click-whoring? You've done better than most, I'll admit – TBI! Ha! – but your mistake is to think we haven't already had a line of bin-riflers queuing up to sniff the poor sod's body. You're like flies.' His voice falters then, revealing the fullness of his anger. 'You bloody *people*.'

315

Freya hangs up. The editor stares at her, holding her face with both hands.

'Part two,' Freya says flatly. She dips inside her coat and removes an envelope.

'*Now* what?' the editor says. She gestures to her office window. Between the blinds, the whole floor is gawping at them.

Freya puts the envelope on the desk. 'There's a press junket,' she starts. 'These are the times, with my business justification. If you can pull some strings, I'll be your copy-monkey forever. I don't care about my salary. Use the *Dalle* fee. Fire me afterwards if it doesn't work out. This is literally the only way I can file.'

The editor opens the envelope. 'Good God,' she says, scanning the page. 'You want to go *where?*'

From the office, Freya drives straight up to the cemetery. A kind of pilgrimage, decided on without hesitation or the need for navigation.

The road inclines for the church hill, and the roof slate rises into view. A grubby St George's cross flying above the tower, before the church emerges from the rock, Manchester in the basin beyond.

Out of the car. The smell of wet leaves. The wind is up, and the memorial garden's silver birches spasm with every gust. Freya crosses the church path, lost names filled with lichen on the limestone beneath her feet. These graves are the oldest on the plot, their inscriptions worn shallow by acid rain. The masonry style changes between rows and ages, growing increasingly worse in condition as she nears the church door.

Freya stands there and hammers on the wood, a courtesy. Nobody answers, so she doubles back towards the memorial garden and pulls her blazer tight around her. She searches for Stephen's grave in the fresh plots, between the pristine headstones, but none give up his name. At the very edge of the cemetery, two graves are laid open, earth piled on green felt bisecting them. No headstones yet, though someone's left a posy between the holes. Dead flowers in bright acetate.

A car crash, Freya thinks. *A double murder. A suicide pact—*

Freya walks down into the memorial garden. The birches are all at different stages of maturity so she moves for the youngest. There's a degree of acceptance in this, an odd calmness. The wind is more settled here, and that's some comfort.

The newest silver birch isn't Stephen's. Its neighbour, however, is. The plaque is elegant, S. PARSONS, and Freya pictures him beneath the restful earth, bacterial processes already under way. The roots of the birch will spider deep to recycle what remains of him. She touches his plaque lightly.

'Where are you?' she asks.

Freya steps up to the trunk. The leaves underfoot feel oddly familiar. Already the trunk has a wonderful grain and finish – a cracked sheath of greys and browns and blacks, speckled with tiny fungi. She reaches to touch it and registers a low tinkling, so close as to be inside her head, but unmistakably there. Almost like a bell ringing. Did the tree just shiver? It could be the wind, of course, but the grass around her stands still. She peers closely at the bark.

She holds her mouth.

There are signs in the tree trunk. A network of lines. She knows this pattern: the black vein markings on Alba's skin, her hairless arms. Her exposed breast on the park bench. And there's more. About Freya's chest height there are puncture holes in the trunk, minute perforations whose edges curl outward. As if something has burrowed out.

Freya allows herself a word. A single word. A word she almost can't bring herself to say. She says it before the church, the man in the ground, and a fresh gust sweeps through and takes the word with it. She realises what's strange about the leaves on Stephen's grave. They're skeletal, stripped of their flesh.

A car door slams in the car park. Freya burns up with discovery, the fear of being caught. She quickly takes a picture of the tree and pulls her scarf to her nose. Her phone displays ten missed calls. Lastly, there's a text notification from her editor that she only half-understands on first glance:

Dalle will pay.

Freya darts away from the memorial garden, eyes running from the cold. She doesn't acknowledge any of the mourners or well-wishers passing her on the church path. She can't bear the thought of recognising them, or they her. Let them notice her bloodshot whites and think her lost in sorrow, drifting. Let them think her madness isn't vindicated. Because Freya knows. Now Freya's sure. Whatever had possessed Stephen, whatever lived in him and changed him, made him drink to his end – whatever that was, it has left him again.

The Steeplejack

Shep leaves the cabin in full kit. Away from the mosquitoes, the hornet husk, towards the base pad, from which the scaffold calls him. The heat draws sweat instantly. It's already a sour, suffocating day, and owing to Shep's sensory faults, the slime that's lifted his veil, it's harder to know if the scaffold is even there at all. Streaks of a vile colour backlight the clouds, and the clouds resemble the death mask of Harold the yard mannequin, mouth-slit parting, Mallory Junior's hidden camera, a probing tongue moving slowly from side to side. Harold's dead eyes search the sky dome before he speaks down to Shep – 'Stratosphere!' – as his face bursts into rain. The smell of the yard slop-bucket hits Shep.

Shep holds up a hand to shield himself from Mallory Junior's inspection. 'The absolute state of you,' he hears.

What is the state of him? Shep is wearing his toughest clothes, right enough for snow at the tower's tip. Right enough for cold. Because the island is the mountain now, and the tower is complete. That's what Shep believes.

'You need a word with yourself,' the mannequin says.

At the base pad, Shep finds another mountaineer.

'Shepherd?' the man asks.

The tower is more tangible here, attenuated and thin. But the diamondoid ascender cable is live, running up from the top.

'Shep, mate.' The mountaineer taps him on the shoulder.

If he could see himself – bowl-eyed, slack-mouthed.

'Where's the trail?' Shep says.

'We need to get you back to medical,' the mountaineer says. 'Come on, pal.'

But the mountaineer can't hold Shep. He'll find a route. His perception shifts again. A sudden appreciation of humidity, the wetness in every line on every surface, and it's fine, good, to be standing here, pregnant and willing, and to know the tower wants him. There's fresh sweat under his pack straps, tool belt, the weight-bearing points of his harness. He likes this harness – it's sophisticated. Though his tools won't do for rock and ice, they'll manage this mountain in particular.

'Look,' he urges, to nobody. Here's a heavy spanner with a fine motor built into its head. Here's a pack of tobacco. Here are things an explorer should carry. His hands are engorged, don't seem to be his own.

'Shep,' the mountaineer says. 'Have a quick sit while I call you a quad.'

Shep shakes his head and darts towards the tower, leaving the mountaineer grasping. He's on the base pad, directly under the tower's summit, where looking up reminds him of the first time he saw *it* in the bunker: a flash, a lacy shape in his peripheral vision. A nexus: the extreme detail of some fault-block spike, a ziggurat. As he stares, the whole structure appears to sway and flicker, the tower solid with beautiful markings scoured into its beams.

He thinks: *They'll be here longer than I will,* and he doesn't know why. But he does understand that his brain is oscillating between the real and the not. Some powerful stimulus isn't being decoded properly: there's a barrier inside him. He stands there to observe the tower-hive, nesting birds flitting in and out. It knocks the breath from him. He could touch its apex, even from here. All around him is the Pacific, and here he is, waiting to be swallowed.

Shep closes his eyes. He keeps them that way, and he listens: the creaking and buzzing, the arc-welders crackling, drone engines burning in the hangar. He's never taken hallucinogens, never thought it necessary since the real world gives him so much to admire, and yet he's surer and surer, rushing for the surface, that his visions are authentic. This is a new boundary line. He stands halfway in, halfway out.

He opens his eyes. The tower scaffold and nothing more. Even his cabin melting into irrelevance. In his sleep or not in his sleep. His stubble and his body hair. Toilet tissue and ash piles and bells ringing. Messages in blood.

Then the mountaineer's back there with him, attaching Shep's harness to a thick rope, frowning when Shep challenges him. The mountaineer faces away to the scaff.

'You shouldn't be out here,' the mountaineer says. 'You're meant to be in bed.'

The sun-lenses are gritty; Shep blinks away the uncertainty.

He squeezes out the tears, and the base pad is alive again, teeming with contractors. He chokes up to see fellow jacks surrounding him, the heave and push of flesh and fluorescent clothing. 'Where's Kap?' Shep asks the mountaineer. 'Where's my crew?' But the mountaineer has gone, and his crew have gone up to watch the test without him.

Stratosphere.

Shep makes for his quadrant entrance, bouncing off people on his way through. A woman takes him by the shoulders then lets go in disgust, stares in horror at her hands like they've been stained, like there was too much give in his flesh. She flashes a threatening look and says, 'Chill out, man.'

'Kapper,' Shep tells her. 'Where's Kapper gone?'

'Kapper?'

Shep dips under the stile outside the ladder tube. The accessway. He stumbles into a small crew sorting camera gear, a micro-drone. The lights inside the ladder tube flickering. He stretches onto it, climbing quickly until he grazes his head on the hard soles of another contractor's boots.

'Kap!' Shep yells. 'Is that you? What's happened?'

What's happened, of course, makes no odds. It's still happening, and Shep, in shortening spells of lucidity, is beginning to grasp that.

He comes off the ladder at the hundred-metre mark. There's a huddle of contractors on the work platform, a few with their legs dangling over the edge, the rest against the railings. All of them are clipped in.

'You'll miss the fun,' Shep says to those at the wall, scanning them. No one acknowledges him. 'Kap's up here somewhere,' he says, and they ignore him again. 'Twats!' he shouts, and crawls back into the cage, back to the ladder.

One-fifty, then two hundred metres, then two-fifty. Kapper isn't on any of those platforms, either. A safety warning on one crossbeam shouts EGRESS WITH CARE, with a markered-on note: UV SUITS REQUIRED ABOVE THIS POINT.

He only pokes his head out at three hundred, and at three-fifty he does the same. Still no Kapper. The cold expanse. He gulps every breath. The wind is screaming. The ladder is a cage, a long cage, and in this thinning air it's squeezing him.

At four hundred metres Shep finds them. Kapper and Eddy against the railings, cross-legged on the platform. The two women from his crew setting up what might be a telescope.

'Kapper,' Shep says firmly. 'What happened?'

Kapper's eyes go wide to see Shep there on the platform. A deep red that makes his ears glow.

'Who let you up here?' Kapper asks. 'Who?'

Eddy giggles nervously. Shep's insides twist and lock. For all the things he has or hasn't seen on the ground, in his cabin, Shep is certain that Kapper and the foreman are sharing a look of resignation.

'I know I'm late,' Shep says.

'Shep…' The foreman clears his throat. 'You're not meant to be… Why are you out of bed?'

Shep clambers out of the hatch fully. 'You knocked,' he says, pointing to Kapper.

The foreman seems puzzled. Looking Shep up and down. 'No, he didn't. He's been up here since dawn. You shouldn't be—'

323

'Why?'

'Don't back-chat,' Kapper says, standing up.

'It's fine, Kap,' the foreman says, then pinches the bridge of his nose in thought. 'Ladies – we've got a spare winch-line, haven't we?'

'A winch-line,' Shep repeats. 'I'm right here. I can hear you.'

Eddy comes right to Shep's side. He unclips a quickdraw, holds it about hip height. 'Listen,' he whispers, and snaps the quickdraw to Shep's toolbelt. 'Where's your protection? Your helmet?'

Shep follows the foreman's gaze to the empty loops on his harness. He realises he's climbed here ropeless, and that he's been dropping tools on his way here. The only things in his toolbelt are his Stillson and fraying knife.

But that can't be, either. He dropped his Stillson a fortnight before—

Eddy notices the knife and takes Shep's arm. Applies enough pressure to stop Shep's jitters. 'You're cold. You know you shouldn't be on here without gear.'

'Course,' Shep says, and he bats away the foreman's hand. 'I want to see it through. I want to know we did it – me and him.' He nods to Kapper. 'That the Merlins'll fly safely.'

'No,' Eddy says. 'Bed rest. That was the deal. Your head isn't straight.'

'Bed rest?'

'Come on, Shep,' he says. 'Let's not go over this again. You know we had complaints. Your bloods…'

'Stop saying my name like that.'

The foreman swallows.

'Kap,' Shep says. 'Tell him. You were at my door.'

But if Kapper hears Shep, he doesn't acknowledge it. He's standing back-to, bent at the waist and leaning out over the platform's edge protection. The snub stings badly.

'He knocked on my door,' Shep tells the foreman. 'Then a woman came…'

'Who? Your nurse?'

Shep touches his cheeks. They're slimy.

'A woman came round. To my cabin.'

Eddy sighs. 'Let's lash you to the railings at least.' He turns to Kapper. 'Grab the ropes. We'll abseil him down when the test's done.' Back to Shep. 'Pick your moments, don't you? You know Vaughan's here on a tour this week? So, let's compromise: you can stay here if you're safe, if you behave, as long as you listen to me. But Christ, man, you needed your gear on for this.'

Shep senses the others' gaze. He hears one of the women whisper to the other: 'Won't have a pissin' clue where he's been tomorrow.'

'No,' he says. And he draws his knife and slices once, twice, into the quickdraw fabric before pushing hard against Eddy. The foreman's Stetson flips off his head and blows right off the tower. Kapper rushes over with his fists raised to his face.

Shep swings hard and misses. Kapper doesn't flinch, but looks amazed. It gives Shep time to slip towards the access hatch, where he squats and thrusts his feet backwards until his heels meet a rung, boot soles squealing. He unzips his top layer, pulls it open. The air rushes in.

'Shep,' Kapper says, appalled. 'Don't—'

Shep pulls his arms out of his sleeves, drags down the overalls to reveal his naked torso. The jacks on the platform gape at his patchy chest, the black lace on his skin. A single word sears across Shep's lips:

Stratosphere.

And Shep gives in to the word and the word engulfs him, and the air above Vertex crackles. He lifts his arms, each dark and swollen. He pulses hard against the crotch of his overalls, tearing at them until only the ankle hems hold them on. He wrenches his knees up, legs out, upper body juddering at the hatch. Kapper and the others back away, hands raised.

Shep reaches down with the knife and slices at the material trapping his boots. He wants to be colder than this. He needs to be. He lets the overalls fall away down the ladder tube, fully naked now apart from his boots and toolbelt. Slick with sweat and something thicker. Shep leans back into the ladder tube and grips the nearest rungs, staring up to the five-hundred-metre point, the lift access platform halfway up, and beyond to the very top.

'I'm glanding,' he tells the jacks on the platform, and with one last jerk he kicks away his boots.

From here he takes the ladder in great leaps – no protection, no helmet – missing rungs with his feet where shins and knees will do. He suffers the start of every bruise, every scrape, every blow of his penis on the rungs, and he doesn't break pace. He passes the lift access at five hundred metres, and starts on the tower's gantrywork itself. He'll get there now, he'll crown this tower, stand a kilometre tall. Even as his breath shortens, he goes on. Even as his nerves lose the capacity to report and as the sunlight blinds him, he climbs on.

Closer to the summit, he breaks momentarily to look down. A labyrinth between his toes. Perfect geometry with no end. He shimmies out across a beam to lean out of the structure to where the wind shear is at full force. His body black-veined and raw. Through his tears, the tower is shivering silver, vanishing point deep in the ocean itself. It appears unstable, unconnected to anything. The island is a hard lake, its cabins and service buildings no more than flotsam. All activity – all life – has been extinguished by perspective. Shep stands alone. He could explain God's ignorance. He looks up. He's nearly there, the height a revelation; in this sun he'll release his burden. Absolution. That's clear now: they tell him from the inside, these surfacing things, these lives between his synapses. And for the last length of ladder, land and soil turned into distant ideas, the burden teems, roils and burns him. Icy holes open in his wrists and fingers, and through his molecules flows a vision of the future, the goal – and Shep at last remembers the bunk, last night, the sequence that led him here.

He'd woken to bells above his cabin, a clicking under his pillow. The hornet had crawled from her cocoon. She whispered to him as she had before, the night he returned to the Lakes with Freya. She the siren, and he her sailor. She'd whispered to him as he ate from her nest, filled his tub. He remembers when she spoke to him again, hushed and hypnotic, his mother's voice or someone else, someone dead. A lament he understood in the moment and would forget by morning: *We have met before. You, little vessel. Before the stratosphere you will bring us. Carry us.*

'Stratosphere,' Shep whispers. Her scheme is bare now, exquisite. *Ingress*. Shep stands there at the top of the beta scaffold surveying the prize with a conqueror's smile. The rich Pacific looks infinite. His skin breaks out in crystalline formations that creak as he studies his hands. An innate sense of dying, an exertion that might have already killed him. Then irrelevance. His wrists and arms are completely hairless. He raises his hands, stands on tiptoes. His penis is so hard it's aching. He isn't in control, but it feels very natural.

The beginnings of an exodus.

The sun contracts to a dot. The chill that follows is so severe that Shep's mouth is welded shut, and the toolbelt on his belly freezes, grafts itself to his skin. His toes begin to fuse to the metal joists of the platform, here at the very point where the orbital cable might one day meet the earth and complete the Vaughans' moon-link. There comes a pain in his fingertips that makes him come and vomit simultaneously. He opens himself like his ribs are hinged, pulling at his skin. The things inside hatch and spread outwards, particles of dust in the light, many connected together in long mobius-like filaments. A smell of ripe fruit and semen. A perfect, intoxicating taste. They shouldn't be visible, he realises, but they're letting him see, they dance and play and explode around him, satin against his face. He marvels as they shoal and spin against his damp skin, gemstone particles in antigrav, bronze and lilac flashes, motes of slate and cerise. The wind is stilled, the horizon is burning. He has no name for them, can think of none, but they're alive and livid, frenetic yet harmonious, vibrant and fizzing, pouring out of him to seed the island and the ocean that holds it. And Shep knows that even if their queen died in his cabin, the brood isn't vengeful. Her children play with their father, and he stands there on the beta scaffold and lets them, lost to total, obliterating serenity, fixed in this point between sun and concrete. Shep's grateful, most of all. He's found the vertex itself. The fractal hive he saw in that corridor all those weeks ago. The cold he sought.

The Journalist

The private annex in Manchester Airport isn't Freya's idea of the North. She rarely sees this side of the job, being more used to dreary shops opened by Z-listers in damp town centres, packed press conferences for weary-sounding detectives, tearful parents, and stifling court waiting rooms whose wooden floors hold in the peppery smell of old rubber.

It's the decadence, mostly. From the luxurious car that collected her from the bungalow, to the velvet bedroom she waits in now, the organisers want Freya to know that no expense has been spared.

Freya included, there are twenty journalists and photographers at the airport. They were marshalled inside by white-teethed chaperones wearing identical uniforms and security guards whose faces never betrayed an emotion. After an initial briefing – a self-satisfied speech – they were each given a keycard to a ritzy suite overlooking the private jet paddock. They were told to relax, to enjoy a good night's sleep, to help themselves to room service.

After eating, Freya showers before visiting the bar for a nightcap. It's not that she wants to socialise, much less craves a drink. It's more that Shep is within reaching distance – and she doesn't want to feel angry or excited. To think of him now is almost painful: she's so close to the full truth, and the most selfish part of her needs him to show her, to unlock everything. To give her closure.

At the hotel bar stand five or six journalists loudly discussing foreign policy with a security guard. As Freya skirts them, she overhears a comment about Iran. Another man saying, 'That was before the fall, wasn't it?' A reply, huffed out by a know-it-all in olive drabs and a camo snood: 'You youngsters know bugger-all about war.'

Freya orders a double whisky on ice and smiles politely as the bartender starts pouring.

'Bit of a sausage-fest,' the bartender says.

'Sorry?'

The bartender smiles. 'These lot. Didn't plan to be with them, did you?'

Freya grimaces.

'You'll be fine,' the bartender says. 'They'll give up when they realise you don't want to suck them off.'

Freya snorts. The bluntness is refreshing.

'Who's treating you, anyway?' the bartender asks, putting down Freya's drink. 'You're press, right?'

Freya takes a sip and tilts the glass so the ice slides across the bottom. 'Heard of the Vaughan family?'

The bartender couldn't care less.

'Doesn't matter either way,' Freya says. 'I'm only a

jumped-up court reporter. Still waiting for them to realise their mistake.'

The bartender pulls an earnest face. 'Don't have to be a travel journalist to travel and write about travel, though. Who cares?'

'Yeah,' Freya says. 'Who cares.'

'Can anyone go?'

'I was commissioned,' Freya says. 'A climbing magazine. It's a secondment – I don't think they're bothered about what I get up to.'

'You into your extreme sports?'

'A bit,' Freya says. 'These guys say what they're doing?'

'Sure. Tosser in the army get-up was giving it all that about "futurism". He showed me pictures – space lifts? A big tower. Won't even open for decades, will it? Himalayas? And then what?'

Freya takes another sip of her drink.

The bartender leans in, conspiratorial. 'Lap it up, I say. They want you impressed. As long as you bang a few hits in the aggregators, return on investment… You gone through your literature yet? I was told to ask you all.'

Freya shakes her head. It's disarming that the bartender has all the right words.

'I don't blame you,' the bartender says. 'I had to. And it's not that it's dull – it's *mental*. This big dick-swinging tower they want you to gush about. Touring with Daddy Vaughan while he drags his mouldy old bollocks around, playing Alpha Male. Sure, love, but I'm there for the canapés and maybe I'll bang a contractor or two. Know what I mean?'

332

'You're working for the Vaughans?'

The bartender laughs. 'Everyone in this frigging airport is, tonight. And I'm only making your drinks!'

'Sorry,' Freya says.

'Oh,' the bartender says. 'Me too. But anyway. Would you?'

'Would I what?'

'Bang a contractor.'

Freya smiles and takes another sip of her drink. 'It won't be so bad,' she says. 'Surely.' She nods backwards. 'Unless I'm sitting with one of them on the plane.'

The bartender makes a different face. They can both imagine that all too well. Then the bartender swears and draws up a tablet from behind the bar. 'You seen this?' A screaming headline: NEW FOOT AND MOUTH STRAIN SPREADS.

Freya downs her drink. *Transmission. Infection. Proliferation.*

'You want one?' Freya asks, shaking the empty glass.

'Nah,' the bartender says. 'But you plough on.'

Freya takes the press literature to bed. True romance. Out of its sleeve, it's a perfect-bound volume, presented like overwrought brand guidelines for a corporate. The first page has a full-bleed shot of Mr Vaughan playing golf, the entrepreneur and visionary at leisure. The copy beside it is unreadably pompous – a litany of space metaphors finished with a clunker: 'What if, this century, we could reach the stars without rocket fuel?'

Her drinks have hit the mark, either way. Drowsy, head dulled, one eye shut, Freya flips through the book and takes in technicalities between lengthening blinks: 'nanothread', 'core size', 'anchor station', 'vortex shedding', 'geostationary orbit'; a flowery description of the island, once mined for guano deposits, now a 'uniquely terraformed base of operations'. Details of 'deep synergy' with the US Navy, who are testing drones on the island.

She manages to stay awake for the section on 'threat assessments', and finds herself twitching to read about what could go wrong when the tower is built in the Himalayas. Orbital debris, terrorism, megastorms – it's already under siege. She drops the book and starts to drift off, half-dreaming of standing on the shore of the island. A legion of frogmen, a thousand in blank masks, marching from the swell with bolt cutters in their hands. Her body convulses, that weird primitive release before proper sleep, as one of the frogmen taps a beam with his tool. He takes off his mask and his face is Oriol's, webbed with black veins.

She opens her phone. She writes a text she knows will bounce:

> You're ill, Shep. Don't do anything stupid.

She hits send and sets her alarm. *Tomorrow*, she thinks. And before long she slips down through island sand into the warm ocean.

The Steeplejack

Lying this way should feel wrong to Shep. As he drifts, encased in a white box, he thinks about that, wondering if an injustice has been wrought against him. It's good to realise he doesn't mind. How content, how relaxed, he is.

He's definitely restrained, though. A mechanical paralysis, a pressure on his body. Vague shapes move across his white box, but it's impossible to interact with them: he occupies a no man's land, nothing to climb or pass over. The only thing he can control is emptying his bladder, and he isn't sure where it goes.

When Shep opens one eye a crack, the white box takes on fuzzy detail. A cheap suspended ceiling, a curtain, a metal-framed cot. Owing to a sore neck, examining his body takes effort. He lies in a sort of bivouac, wired into machines purring by his head. Pins and needles rage in his feet. There's a cannula in his hand. His arms are wrapped in bloodied bandages. His skin feels tight.

At some point, a more solid shape appears and hovers at the end of his cot.

'You awake?' the shape asks. With a strain, the shape becomes fleshy. A face. It's Kapper.

'Shit man,' Kapper says, 'you are awake. Don't speak – you've shredded your larynx. Nurse says your tongue's fucked as well.'

Shep tries to give his partner a half-nod. Kapper stares at him. No easy openers. It's Kapper who breaks the tension. 'Can't believe you made it down,' he says. 'I swear, Shepherd. No suit, nothing. I figured the cold must've preserved the bloody cloth between your ears. But the sensors all said it was boiling up there. Strongest UV the climate crew has on record this *decade*, and you, you silly bastard, you had no protection. Sweet fuck-all!'

Shep twists in his cot. Each breath feels badly interrupted, like a morning stretch cut short by a cramp. He tries to sit up, but his body won't fold. He turns his face towards the window.

'Shep?'

In his mind, Shep occupies a jungle. There's a bird with incredible plumage out there on the sill, pecking at moss. A shocking view, as though the end of the world has been and gone, and a rainforest has overtaken the island.

He focuses farther afield. To make certain he's awake. The beta scaffold has the matt-green finish of oxidised copper.

He comes back to Kapper. He slowly brings a hand up to his face and lets the image settle. Two of his fingertips are missing, and his three remaining fingers are deep grey.

'What happened?' Shep croaks. Not that it matters: he'd

topped out. A strange frost had coated his body, metallic sweat reflecting the sun from every pore. There'd been a whispered memory, excerpts from some sleep-conference with a queen, an entity... but from where? He smiles. In exchange for her children, she altered him.

Kapper puts a hand on Shep's foot. His pins and needles give way to liquid heat.

Shep opens his eyes fully, conscious of a shift.

Kapper is naked.

'The navy still had the Merlin up,' Kapper tells him, apparently oblivious. 'We had teams on every platform. And the drone hovering there. Max range, and this Yank comes over the relay: "There's your guy. Summit of the rig." And you *were* there, Shep. You just were. Stark bollock naked.'

Shep swallows; his tonsils burn. He can't speak. He can't say: *But why are* you *naked*?

'Time we had enough crew with slings to get you down, you were gone,' Kapper says. 'You'd hooked your Stilly in a big hole in the superstructure, even though you had nothing on you to punch a hole through the platform like that. By the state of your fingers, you wouldn't have managed to wedge it afterwards.' Kapper breaks off to shake his head.

'Kapper...' Shep tries.

Kapper ignores him. 'You had all these symptoms. Frostbite, hypothermia,' he says. 'It was impossible. First the heat, and second because you'd have to be five miles up to be affected that way. Maybe it was climbing the whole tower, maybe that did you in? Skipping the lift and that, like you did. *Exothermic*, they said... but I don't know, Shep. And your eyes. They found growths on your corneas.'

337

'Why aren't you wearing—'

'You're going home soon, see? Eddy bagged you a space on the next freighter. Tomorrow, or day after, weather depending.'

Shep moves his head fractionally. 'I can't,' he rasps.

'The tests are done,' Kapper says. 'The navy's already packing up. Beacons worked. You can get some proper rain, a pint down you. Nurse says the Vaughans' insurance covers transfer and private care back home. You'll be on the mend in no time.'

Shep considers his damaged hands. Thinking of the fingerboard at Big Walls.

'Prosthetics are pretty sweet,' Kapper says. 'If they upgrade you, I'd get a wet chip while you're at it.'

But Shep doesn't want upgrading. That's not how jacks do it. You retire early with a big pile of compensation to blow...

'Either way,' Kapper says, 'you're their first inpatient. When Big Vaughan's tour arrives this afternoon, you'll probably get a hi. Mallory says he'll ring in from Blighty, too.'

Kapper steps away from the bed. 'Speak of the devil,' he says, looking at his watchless wrist. 'I'm meant to be on the welcome committee – best get cleaned up. Who'd want greeting by this godawful mug?'

Shep tries to protest. Kapper smirks and parts the curtains. 'Don't be a dickhead. And for the record,' Kapper says, 'you were never shite.'

Shep lurches as far as the cot will allow him.

Kapper pauses halfway out of the bay. Lines of life-earned muscle. His dark pubis. 'What are you doing, you daft twat?'

'Kap,' Shep says.

'Your hair? Is that it? I don't want you jumping off something when you see it.'

Shep holds his fingers to his head.

Kapper coughs. 'Shep...'

Shep touches his crown. His hair is all but gone. He rubs his scalp, finds the matted little tufts that remain. No pattern to it: only nature. It's a process. The way it's been all along. If you disturb a nest, you take responsibility for its children.

Shep understands what he's done to the island. What's happened to them all. What's happening to Kapper. The way Kapper's body will swell, shed hair, like his has.

The big man's nose scrunches up. 'What?' he asks. 'What's up?'

Shep clears his throat. 'You can see it,' he gets out, throat boiling. 'My hair.'

'Course I can. You're fucked.'

'Ta,' Shep says.

'*Ta?*'

'I haven't lost the plot.'

Kapper comes back to the cot. 'No one's said that. And I saw that hornet, you know. In the end.'

Shep reaches over with his hand. Holds it open, fingers splayed. Unsure what else to do.

Doubtful, Kapper takes it. A slow interlacing. Another moment to clasp. This close, Shep can see how Kapper's skin is already lined with black filament, that the hair on his wristbone is vanishing.

'I'm sorry,' Shep says.

Kapper shakes his head and squeezes. No accident this time. 'It doesn't matter,' he says. Now he's Shep's brother by blood, not only through jacking.

The Journalist

They approach Vertex Island by mid-morning, darting through cloudless sky towards thousands of flashing red lights that describe the scaffold's bulk. But rapt as Freya is, there's no time to admire the view. The plane dips sharply for the short runway; Freya kneads her thighs and wishes she were religious. Even the cabin crew look worried by their angle of approach.

The rear left wheels connect. The jet sticks in, distorted crops of the scaffold flashing through her window. She bumps shoulders with an otherwise silent woman next to her.

When the plane brakes to a halt on the runway, Freya exhales.

'Welcome to Vertex,' the pilot says. 'Local time is ten-thirty. Current temperature – pretty bloody warm.'

Two long flights in twenty-four hours have all but finished Freya. She's lethargic and senses a grimy film on her body, and almost can't stand.

'I need a beer,' the woman says, drawing photography

equipment from under her seat.

'Long day,' Freya agrees. 'I wouldn't say no.'

The photographer hauls herself up. 'If we don't drown in sweat first.'

The flight attendant opens the door. Hydraulics and sliding parts. The suffocating heat collides with a bizarrely moreish ocean and chemical smell.

The plane stands on a recently surfaced runway, and the runway lies in the gossamer shadow of the tower scaffold. Off the plane, half-blinded by brilliant light, Freya stands in awe, neck craned, following the tower's silhouetted form from base to shining apex. It's exactly as Shep's forum pictures showed, finely wrought yet brutalistic in sum. As the other journalists alight and crowd around her, cooing similarly, Freya counts weldspark flashes in the structure's sides. She thrills to spot red and yellow blobs up there in the mesh – a crew at work.

'All that cash,' the photographer comments at her shoulder. 'Madness.'

'It is,' Freya says. But truthfully, it's not the investment that amazes her. It's the craft. The will of it. Where would you even start? The scaffold tower's height is already intimidating, and yet the tower in its final form will be monstrous. This, the 'beta', is the smallest Russian doll in the set that will encase it, layer up around it. And when the lift cable is actually attached and the satellite anchor goes into orbit, it'll be more overwhelming still. How many cranes had it taken? How many people? How many individual rivets had been driven through its body?

It might just be impossible to write about. It might be that she has to write *around* it.

'Would you do it?' the photographer asks.

'What, sorry?'

'Work up there.'

Freya doesn't know. Maybe she'd have to stay long enough to grasp the tower's effect on her psyche. Going by the press literature, she'll be closing on eighty years old when it starts running. Does feeling so insignificant before it – so short-lived – not make this tower even more oppressive? She gulps, and a bubble of panic pops in her gullet. *Alien.* The word that keeps popping up from the edges. The word she can't bear to think, valid as it is. The scaffold is already so vast, so intricate and deliberate, so artificial, that it's otherworldly. Like a crash-landed spaceship, or an upended alien city.

'This whole place stinks,' the photographer adds thoughtfully, 'like baby shit.'

And the plane they arrived on screams away.

After a short wait, a four-by-four pulls up to the runway. A glum-looking woman in designer sunglasses climbs down from its passenger side. To Freya she's every bit the PR: dark two-piece suit, feline contouring, hair scraped into a tight bun. Bright yellow heels nauseating against the blasted scrub. Freya admires her instantly: here's a woman deliberately at odds with this island. And practical or not, the shoes are fun.

'Good morning,' the PR says. She's swaying a little, which Freya finds distracting. 'How're we all feeling on this lovely day in paradise?'

The group murmurs a response.

'You'll spend the next two days in my care,' the PR says, before telling them all about Vaughan arriving this evening 'for supper' after a guided tour. Sweat rolls from Freya's fringe. She wonders where Shep and his crew are right now.

'If you'd like to follow me,' the PR says. And the whole group goes along with the charade, the photographers discussing loudly which of their lenses will get the whole tower in shot.

They pass no workers on their way to the next stop, a 'bar and restaurant' made of two shipping containers whose fenced-off 'roof garden' is accessed by steel walkway. Like the PR, the building is out of place on Vertex, doubtless installed for the junket in some nod to luxury, an abstraction of urban living. Freya can't pinpoint why, but it makes her uneasy – a feeling that only grows when they go inside to find three exhausted-looking staff handing out paper fans. Ten minutes later, the same three staff stand mixing breakfast cocktails behind a kind of faux-rustic bar. The youngest actually looks ill – he has sores around his mouth and is sweating profusely.

As technical videos loop on the container's ribbed walls, Freya sneaks away from the group and climbs up to the sparse roof. She sits on a scrap of fake grass beneath a parasol. The shade here is pleasant; the view overlooks the runway, the tower's base pad. A moment of quiet, a chance to reflect on the fact that, tiredness aside, she's actually made it here, to admit to herself that Shep is somewhere close.

She spaces her fan and wafts it around her face. Would she spot him, or he her? She's hopeful for many reasons, but

344

if the island really counts as a city, then in cities you only ever bump into the people you never want to see. What are the chances of him just appearing? In two days? She'll have to look for opportunities.

Freya is about to finish her drink when the PR's heels ring in the stairwell. She looks on, bemused, as the PR comes across the roof and dallies at the edge. Here the PR reapplies lipstick, before circling Freya and sitting down. She pushes her sunglasses up onto her head.

'Taking a moment?' the PR asks.

Freya swallows. The woman's lipstick is smeared all over her cheeks and teeth. Her eyes are glassy, distant.

'All this... bullshit,' the PR slurs.

Freya tries to humour her, but a fake laugh isn't enough.

The PR isn't fazed, either way. She yawns and asks where Freya came from. 'Actually, hold that thought,' the PR adds. 'I need to piss.' She stands, hutching up her skirt. Freya winces as if the PR might do it right there.

The PR notices herself, grimaces. She says, 'Maybe later. You should steal some toilet tissue and hydration sachets from downstairs, by the way. I haven't passed a shit for three days now.'

'Right,' Freya says, and taps her cheek. 'I don't mean to be funny, but you've – your make-up's run.'

The PR grins oafishly. Pads her face. 'Oh,' she says. 'We can fix it.' She returns to the stairwell, skirt still up round her waist.

Freya sits there, staring into space, wondering what just happened.

• • •

From the bar, the PR lolls towards the tower's base pad, the junket in tow. Freya tries to distract herself by taking in the scaffold's construction, conjures the sense of climbing it. Hard metal. Cold metal. Cutting metal. How would she record how it looks and sounds? Closer to its formwork, the similes come easily: Eiffel, Burj Khalifa, Freedom. Babel, if she had to nail the cliché. But close up, the similes start to break down. The tower isn't there to be admired, doing that fetishizes the work of the people involved. Instead, it's a totem to their labour. It's taken dedication, planning, precision to get this far. Sacrifice, no doubt. Very often, Freya knows, climbers have to suspend beds high up on mountains. Does Shep do that here? Is he up there right now, making tea and taking photos? Taking a slash off the side?

No sooner than she's pictured him, made some element of the tower understandable through him, the crocodile of journalists veers away. A small commotion has broken out ahead. Even from a distance it's clear that something has happened under the tower. Except it's like no one else has noticed, much less cares. The rest of them, in their bright red helmets, are too distracted by the interplay of light and steel above.

Freya drops to the rear of the group to try and get a closer look.

'I've... I've been told we'll now take you up for a viewing at last light,' the PR tells them. Her voice isn't solid enough and the disquiet spreads – everyone in the press junket glancing at each other. The PR woman smiles. 'It'll be worth the wait. Now, if you can follow me on to the

346

crew quarters, we'll demonstrate how a blend of advanced catering solutions and state-of-the-art building services has created a comfortable living experience for our hard-working colleagues. If you'd like to share any pictures at this point, please be sure to tag Vaughan Holdings' construction partner, Vertex Management. There's free Wi-Fi inside.'

Freya stays at the rear, peering at the base pad. A group of workers stand around a lump of equipment on a sheet of blue tarpaulin. The heat-haze makes it hard to see their faces, but they're jeering and shouting, and most of them are topless, some stripped right down to their underwear. As she watches, they take it in turns to kneel down and slap or punch the tarpaulin, before standing up again, covered in oil or paint, which they smear across their bodies.

Freya carefully steps away from the departing group. They're not only smearing themselves in this stuff – they're *dancing*. One of them, a short man, has removed his helmet and is tugging violently at his hair.

Someone grips Freya's arm, spins her away. It's the photographer from the jet.

'Don't,' she hisses, dragging Freya back into the group. And Freya turns cold.

'What?' Freya asks. 'Why?'

'Shut up,' the photographer mutters. 'Act normal. Wait.'

Freya feels slow. Dread-weighted. As the group swallows her up, she looks back. It might be the haze, the light. It might be the heat. Something about the bulk of the equipment on the tarpaulin had seemed wrong, as if it wasn't mechanical at all.

· · ·

The crew cabins are neat and numerous. Stacked in rows, padlocked from the outside, many with neat red crosses taped across their doors. A worker sleeps on the cracked ground outside one of them, hardhat tilted over his face. Freya can't help concentrating on his chest to check he's actually breathing. She doesn't see it rise, but tells herself to stop being paranoid.

The group marches up to a large teepee-like structure attached to an outbuilding, generators running at the back. The photographer looks distracted, and Freya is desperate to ask how she'd overreacted.

'An army marches on its stomach,' the PR says, 'so Mr Vaughan hired Michelin-starred chefs to design a high-energy, super-nutritious diet for our workforce. In turn, we keep smiles on their faces.' She pauses then, well-rehearsed. All Freya can picture is Shep chewing with his mouth open. 'Let's go inside, shall we?'

After the canteen, the journalists bunch into an immaculate landscaped garden. It's obscenely out of place – an effect topped off with a KEEP OFF THE GRASS sign.

'Here,' the PR starts, 'we'll give you a quick tour of the crew kitchen. Designed in collaboration with the University of Wales, this facility boasts vanguard technology including the latest advances in automated cooking.'

The group piles inside, and Freya seizes the chance to confront the photographer.

'What's going on?'

The photographer's eyes are red. 'I saw him,' she whispers.

'Saw who?' Freya stumbles.

The photographer tilts her head to the tower.

'Who did you see?' Freya urges.

The photographer wipes her eyes. Her strong body odour takes Freya back to fever-dreams on some ancient holiday. Possibly her last with the girls before she'd moved in with her ex.

'Outside the bar. Before. When you were… oh God, I saw him. Falling.'

Freya grabs the doorframe. 'He fell? From where?'

'He' – the photographer sobs it – 'he was looking at me.' She lowers her face. 'He was laughing.'

Freya takes the photographer's hand. 'Are you sure?'

'How did no one else hear?'

'Why didn't you tell someone?'

'I did. The PR. I tried.'

'What did she say?'

'I was lying. That I'm jet lagged.'

'Bloody hell,' Freya says. 'We need to find someone else – now.'

The photographer drops her kitbag to her knees, reaches inside. 'I was shooting the tower. Here.' She loads an image on the back of her camera, enlarges it with two fingers. A crop of the tower, and dead-centre, blurry but discernible, a streak of blue.

Freya wrests the camera from her. She spreads two fingers and the image magnification increases. She holds the camera up. She hands it back. 'Maybe it was loose tarpaulin,' she says. She has to believe it. She has to believe that the tarp's contours, the way it's falling, don't make it look like there's somebody inside.

. . .

The smell of the kitchen worsens Freya's faintness. Her knees are watery. At the front, by the ovens, the group has folded around the PR. Off to one side, the photographer is in a worsening state. Freya motions at waist level for her to go back outside.

'What's the matter with her?' another photographer whispers.

Freya ignores him. She's looking for someone, anyone, to alert. The PR droning on about square meals a day, about the logistics of their operation. 'Supplies reach port every few days, and your trip happily coincides with a ship arriving tomorrow morning, weather permitting…'

Freya notices an arrowed sign on the wall. INFIRMARY. There'll be someone in there to help, surely.

A fresh surge of adrenaline. Freya mumbles an apology, some vague allusion to the toilets, and breaks away. She moves through overlit rooms filled with shrink-wrapped equipment, glinting surfaces. It's difficult to adjust to the contrast, the sterile grey. She follows a corridor, shoes slapping polished floor, and calls 'Hello?' and still there's no one. No signs of life. And now a ward whose bay curtains are all drawn. Light sluicing in from slats in the roof.

All of the bay curtains, she realises, but one.

Freya's world accelerates. It takes an admission to step closer to him, one hand up in lame defence – another to see she's already too late, that she's failed him. Like Stephen and Alba before him, Shep being wired into this cot is confirmation enough that the bunker has done its work.

Alarmed cries fill the ward around her. She's magnetised now, and they won't – they can't – stop her. She's nearly by his side, and someone is shouting more aggressively, and Freya shakes off a grasping hand and trips, nearly crashes over Shep's bed. This is how to end her story. This is how she understands. Centimetres from him, where Shep's condition brings a momentary relief – he can't have been the person who fell from the tower outside. He lies depleted in a sack, sewn with monitoring equipment. His face is sallow and patchy with bristles. His hair looks hacked-at, the scalp raw, with stains like birthmarks splotched from his forehead to his crown. A knot of dark veins over one ear.

'Shep?'

He smells deathly sweet, and Freya knows the smell. It was the same at Stephen's burial tree.

'Shep!'

But Shep is unconscious, and when she's sure her fingers will brush his face, rouse him, the security team are on her.

Later that evening, Freya lies awake on her cabin bunk, reading her notes. She's been sanctioned, segregated, locked in. Grounded, literally, as the rest of the press group are taken up the tower.

In a way – beyond the heavy-handed security guards shutting her in here until morning – Freya's situation is simple. If only she'd left things exactly as they were: *a man dies after heavy drinking*. If only there'd been enough roots down to keep the ground from shifting. Her infatuation has become an obsession, and writing her notes is compulsive, like listening to the same piece of music over and over again. She's moving towards a conclusion she doesn't understand but hopes to expose, and she doesn't yet know what she's sacrificed to try. Is she a different woman? Is she redeemable? And there he is again – Shep. Shep, so forbidding and dangerous on this island; Shep who, in different circumstances, would've been a glancing acquaintance. What would she be doing if they'd never met? If she'd followed Aisha down to London all those months back? Would she have read about Stephen's death with a fleeting sadness, then moved on? Would she have noticed at all?

'You're ridiculous,' she tells herself.

But so is all of this. And even if denial has displaced Freya's anxiety – surely those workers weren't dancing under the tower; surely the PR was simply overtired when she did her lipstick; surely the photographer was mistaken about a worker falling from the tower – then Freya's rational mind is fraught. The alternative – that all of these things happened, and are true, have been *caused* – is too much.

She puts her head in her hands. She should sleep. Faint buoy bells on the water. She slaps the cabin wall, surprised to hear it echo around her. She does it again. The sting is satisfying, the sound rich, like being in an empty room. She raises her hand, taken with it. Her fingers are hot. She swings, but there's no echo. Instead, the whole cabin starts to rattle. Her heart skips. She touches the cabin wall, horrified. The wood is humming. The window darkens with a presence. 'Hello?' she tries, frozen on the bed. It catches in her throat. She pulls her hand away. The rattling gives way to a keening, then there's a wave of pressure that makes her ears pop. The cabin flexes. A force tugs on her. She turns her head to find the door resting on its corner, top hinge popped. She gets off the bunk. There's a triangle of dirty ice in the gap. She pushes on the door, which falls open. A snapped chain and broken padlock lie in the dust.

A thought of Oriol in his ice bath crosses her mind. A whisper of cool breath across her skin. The air is cooler, a gibbous moon hanging low. This must be what they want. But how would the explorers do this? Stephen, Shep – Alba with Oriol in her belly? They'd move close to the ground, as Freya does now. They'd move furtively, as Freya tries to. And next thing, she's beyond the cabin block and in the open. The tower, silvered and creaking, work lights flaring in the dusk, dew rising. Her skin charged and hot.

As Freya picks her way towards the canteen and infirmary block, a low siren begins to wail across the island. From cover – a driverless forklift left in the open – she watches a huge warehouse door sliding open. Out comes a group of armed figures wearing rubber suits and masks, guns raised, torches on. They take positions on the warehouse perimeter. They pace. They go back inside and start again, as if they're drilling the movement. She can make out the nose and fuselage of an aircraft just inside the warehouse, its black carapace glistening. Another gang of people attend to it. A visible crate reads US NAVY.

When a masked guard swings a torch in her general direction, Freya dives low. If this were a film, she might expect gunshots, shouts. In real life there's nothing. They haven't seen her. They weren't looking to start with.

They're on with something else.

Tall fencing conceals the rest of her route to the canteen. She sneaks through the main hall, echoless, a smell of eggs. The chairs are stacked on the tables. The breakfast bar empty save for a single deflated croissant. She leaves through a fire exit, across the lawns that connect the canteen and the kitchen. There's nobody outside and the kitchen door is locked. She tabs the wall around the side until she's sure she's next to the infirmary. Several windows have been left ajar, so Freya jimmies a frame until she can slide her head and torso into the gap, then heaves outwards so the latch breaks and the adjuster slips out. She scrambles inside.

Freya finds herself in a store cupboard full of medical collateral. Bedclothes luminous in the moonlight. She opens the door in time to hear soft footsteps – perhaps a staffer on their rounds.

Freya ducks back into the cupboard. The window mechanism breaking must have alerted someone. 'Shit,' she breathes. There's no explaining it. *Try to use your fear.*

The footsteps are close. A squeak of plimsolls on laminate. Was that a tut? The storeroom door stays closed.

Freya waits for another minute, then checks. A glimpse of a nurse's coat flashing round a corner. Freya moves on. At the opposite wall she fights for breath, tries to moisten her lips. She leans round the corridor.

The ward.

Freya sprints for the bed, head pounding. Shep is there, sleeping. His peace catches her off guard. Like it's difficult to accept her restlessness as one-sided. She could slap him, kiss him, scream in his face – any of those things – and he might never know she came here. She wants him to be awake, to understand right now what he's put her through... but he's a wreck.

She slumps in the chair by the window. Cheap leatherette, a recliner. Her face sits level with his. It's all so wretched; the way his throat rattles when he inhales. He hardly looks like Shep at all.

But he's still alive, she tells herself. He, like Alba, has survived what Stephen did not.

As night crawls towards morning, Freya whispers into her Dictaphone a single meandering paragraph that describes the empty ward. Every hollow follicle of Shep's head; every thread of the bay's curtains; every last beam of metal she can see of the tower, the silent sentinel waiting outside.

The Steeplejack

Shep opens his eyes to find his two lives – the working and the hidden – have merged. Freya Medlock asleep in his bedside chair, a personal recorder teetering on her knee. She's a different colour to the wall, patterns against grey. Outline soft. Traces of perfume, a more caustic scent: hairspray or sweat. She has her thumb on the red dot of the recorder.

It takes a lot to touch her. His hand looks like a burnt glove on a stick. She comes to with eyes bulging.

She searches his face. 'I'm too late, aren't I?' she asks.

Shep shuffles in his bed, trying to get up on his elbows. The bivouac wrinkles and traps him, causing an alarm to sound.

Almost immediately, a nurse appears at the ward entrance. 'Morning,' she says, before her expression turns stoic as she swings full-stare to Freya. 'Who the hell are you?'

'She's visiting,' Shep croaks. 'Navy attachment.'

The nurse comes closer. A clipboard and a handful of

drip bags. She looks dishevelled, like she hasn't washed or slept properly. 'We don't do visiting hours,' the nurse says, frowning as she works to deactivate the alarm. 'All visits are suspended while the navy are on operations.'

'She's fine,' Shep tells her.

'I don't *care!*' the nurse barks. 'I'll ask you one more time before I call security: what are you doing here?'

Freya clears her throat. 'I'm a liaison officer,' she says. 'Just making sure everyone's accounted for.'

'She's grand,' Shep adds. 'Honestly.'

The nurse thinks about this, then appears to accept it. 'Right. I was told not to… it doesn't matter.'

'Are you all right?' Freya asks.

'He's meant to be resting,' the nurse says, ignoring her. She gestures to the machines near Shep's bed and taps her watch. 'You've got another sleep due soon. And a scan in a couple of hours.'

'Scan?' Freya repeats.

'Fifteen minutes before your next shot,' she says, wiping her forehead. 'Ideally you'll be alone by then.' And she leaves the ward.

Shep turns to Freya. Her eyes on the wires running into him.

'Good at lying, aren't you?' he says.

'Don't start. She looked awful.'

Shep raises an eyebrow. 'Local rag really paid you to be here?'

'No,' Freya says. 'I'm writing about the island.'

'I *bet* you are.' He puts his head back on the pillow.

Freya sighs. She's trying to look stern. Trying to hide

357

herself from him. 'I wanted to see you,' she says. 'To ask some questions.'

'About what? My accident?'

'Is that what this was?'

Shep taps his bloated temple. 'If you want. Nice here, though, isn't it? What's that word? You'd know. Plush.'

'It's not plush,' Freya says.

'Plush. P-l-ush.'

'Shep.'

'I thought you were interviewing me.'

'I said I wanted to.'

'There you go, then.' He tilts his head towards the window. 'I see flowers. The beta changes colour when I look at it. Everybody's losing their minds – haven't you noticed?'

Freya swallows. 'You know there are no flowers, Shep. There's nothing.'

'The sun's up.'

She glances out of the window. 'It's overcast.'

'You aren't looking hard enough.' He yawns. 'What are you milking me for?'

'You know that's not what I'm doing.'

She's tired. She's pretending to be detached. He could just stop talking and return to oblivion in ten minutes.

'The bunker,' he says.

She shakes her head. 'Not yet. Tell me about your accident.'

'I was stranded.'

'Stranded.'

He glances at his cannula. The window.

358

'This isn't getting us anywhere,' she says.

Shep tilts his head. 'It's keeping me busy.'

'Okay. What if I tell you something?'

'Why?' Shep says. 'You saw it all. What's done is done.' He folds his arms. Covers his wounds. Freya's recorder makes a grinding noise.

'Does it hurt?' she asks.

'Not any more.' He smiles. It's all so formal and stilted, and her face is thinner than he remembers. A slender necklace. A nose smaller from the front than it is from the side.

'Go on,' he says. 'What else?'

She looks away. 'The thing is,' she says, 'I don't have many questions.'

'What?'

'You conned me,' she says quickly. 'You used me.'

He takes a breath. 'Ask me about the island.'

'But Shep... you have to understand—'

'Ask me. Ask me – what it looks like from the top.'

'You climbed it?'

'Or... what it smells like up there? When did you know you had to do it?'

'Shep, I—'

'They're good questions. I'm not answering stupid ones. Make yours good. Then get yourself off this island. Go home.'

'I'm trying to think,' Freya says.

'You asked why I'm in this bed.'

'I did.'

'But you know why. Look at me.'

She nods. 'And I feel responsible. For not stopping it.'

Shep laughs. It hurts his stomach, his face, but he can't help it. 'You missed me, didn't you?'

Anger flashes across Freya's face. 'I resent you.'

'If that's meant to be a professional response...'

'No,' Freya says. 'I didn't miss you.'

'So, you're not just a liar. You're a bad liar.'

Freya stands up and leans on the windowsill. Head haloed in the light. 'That's not what you said five minutes ago.'

'Then I'm a better liar than you.'

Silence.

'I've got another one,' Freya says. 'A bigger one.'

'Go on.'

'You know how dogs can hear things we can't?'

'I guess.'

'What if there are things we can't see or feel that, I don't know, put a kind of pressure on us?'

'Right...'

'Like pheromones,' Freya adds.

'I don't worry about it.'

'I mean, what if something got inside you, made you do something. Against your will. But it also made you enjoy it.'

Her tone is direct. It isn't even a question – not the way she puts it.

'They're here, aren't they?' Freya adds.

The ceiling tiles. The ward's white walls. The bay curtain.

'I met Alba,' Freya says. 'Alba and her son by Stephen – Oriol. I went to Iceland. She called them her guardians. Can you see them, Shep? Are they here, now?'

Shep inhales, holds it down.

'I tried to help,' she tells him.

Shep shakes his head.

'And yeah, I admit it. I wanted to know. Why you did what you did to me. We didn't speak afterwards.'

Shep chews his lip. How to explain what he lacks the words for? What he saw at the top of the scaffold?

'You took stuff from the nest,' Freya says.

'Now you're skipping ahead,' Shep says back.

'No. It's important. You did. After I ran. You stayed.'

Shep cocks his head. 'So?'

Freya makes a point of stopping the recorder. He realises that whatever she's discovered since they explored the bunker, the full truth is just out of her reach. She's collected scraps, glimpses, hinted-at fragments – but he's been all the way. Which means only living it will explain it to her now. Stay here on Vertex, and she'll get her answers. And so Shep pities Freya. They're both to blame. He opened his secrets to her, brought her in. She came happily. But that was then. Nobody can ever understand his landscape: the spires and light arrays, harnesses and lines, his chimneys and roofs. The places they can take you. The purity of a parallel world. It was always a mistake to believe otherwise.

Freya looks out of the window, at the scaffold. 'You're happy like this, aren't you?' she asks.

'I've never been happier,' he says.

The Journalist

The new Shep is a mess. His hands say it all – there'll be no climbing or working or exploring for a while, if ever again. As she speaks, Freya is conscious of the walls between them. There's self-preservation, too – the same face new reporters are trained to pull when they ask bereaved parents if they'll sell anecdotes from their dead child's life.

Or is that wishful thinking?

When Shep coughs, his ribcage clatters. Polluted blood moves visibly, slowly through his temples. She's haunted by the possibility of being watched, observed, by the same unseen monitors that had followed Alba and her to the park in Reykjavik.

She starts where Shep wants her to start. She tells him about Alba's recurring dreams of a glacier. How it calmed her. That without her dreams, Alba wouldn't have been in Iceland at all.

Shep's chin touches his neck and rises again.

She tells him Alba was still pregnant when she got the call

about Stephen. She asks him to imagine being convinced you'll lose your baby to the stress of it. She says, 'Could you live like that?'

She tells him that Alba's dreams inspired her to move somewhere cold. Shep blinks and smiles at this, and Freya sees through the smile for its knowingness, for what he's hiding. Clearly a similar impulse had gripped him. It must have.

'She was a remarkable woman,' Freya says. 'I turned up out of nowhere. She invited me in. She didn't care. No defensiveness. Their baby, Oriol – he's so lovely. And he's infected too.'

Freya pushes wet hair away from her forehead. The chair squeaks. Her shadow shrinks on the far wall.

'Remember,' Freya says, 'when we were by the nest, and I told you Stephen had been there before you? That he'd been arrested?'

'No,' Shep says, yet she can see he does.

'A drone operator tipped them off,' Freya says.

Shep smirks. 'Course,' he says. 'Course he did.'

'Alba told me Stephen was giddy in the weeks after they'd been down. Took more risks, behaved arrogantly. She called it a manic state.'

'Yes,' Shep says.

'Did you notice any effect?'

'No.'

She looks at his head. His hair. His arms. 'No?'

'I don't remember.'

'Migraines or sickness. Impulsiveness.'

'I don't think so.'

Freya rolls her eyes. 'And deciding to climb a kilometre-tall scaffolding tower was…'

Shep starts laughing.

That the nest effects biological change is clear. But Shep doesn't *seem* to consider himself different, other than being, what, reduced somehow? Maybe he doesn't care what Freya makes of him. But surely here, after whatever had happened on the tower, he's also in a kind of remission.

'Alba's forearms had healed a bit,' Freya tells him. 'They looked less like yours. There was a presence. I think – I think it might've opened my cabin. Tonight.'

Shep exhales through his nose. 'They're everywhere,' he says.

Freya gives a short nod. 'And you can see them?'

Shep shrugs. 'You ever notice a light flicker and wonder if it was really the light, or if you'd just blinked?'

Freya remembers how Alba reacted when the lights snapped off in the cafe. The way Oriol wailed. 'Do they frighten you?'

'Why, do you want to rescue me?' he asks. 'Will that be a happy ending for your story? Will it make you famous?'

'Shep.'

'You said you wanted to help me. I think you wanted to see how I'd cop for it. Like Ste. And here I was thinking we got along.'

'We did,' Freya says, 'until you took me to that bunker. But I still have to know.' She takes a breath. 'And if you say, "What next, Freya?" I'll say I'm going home. Today, tomorrow. Maybe I'll go climbing more regularly. Try and figure out the rest for myself.'

Shep doesn't reply.

'I realise now that I should've stolen from the nest as well,' she adds.

'You came all this way to work that out?'

'No.'

'You can't help me.'

Freya stands up. Sighs. 'Do you reckon they might be...'

'What?'

'I think it's a kind of parasite. A kind of virus. It gets right down inside you.'

Shep shrugs again. 'I think they turned up here, and now they just are.'

'Just are,' Freya repeats.

His half-nod. 'Like me and you.'

'If that's true...'

'I don't care if it's true or not. Who'll believe us anyway? Tell me how to explain all this to my landlord when I don't make rent. The rest of Mallory...'

He's right, of course, and the fact of it stings her. She can't submit proof with her *Dalle* piece, and not just because the story is already beyond her, bigger than her. The facts are right here, and they're horrifying. All she can do to stay calm is deny the scale, evoke her editor, tell herself it's conversations like this – the human angle – that will help her to share what's happened on Vertex. *Colour.* The relatable stuff that stands up against speculation.

'Does it hurt?' she asks. 'Do you hurt?'

Shep shakes his head.

'Will you be yourself again?'

But he can't answer that, and she knows it.

'You should get going,' Shep says. 'Before my jab.'

Freya pictures herself lying on his bivouac, just holding him. Or throttling him.

Shep sniffs indifferently and spreads his gnarled fingers across the bag's outer layer. Tentatively, she reaches over and touches the ends.

'When's your flight back?' he asks.

'Tomorrow.'

He sighs. 'Okay.'

'What?'

'Nothing.'

Freya frowns, strokes the back of his hand. The grazes between his knuckles. Is it forgiveness? Or shame? She shakes her head. 'Where do I start?' she asks. 'How do I tell people?'

'You're the hack,' Shep says.

Freya looks at the ceiling.

'Start like I do. Ignore the map. Cross a boundary. And don't get caught.'

His machine timer clicks off, and an automated syringe draws up liquid.

'Hopefully see you around,' Shep says. And he squeezes Freya's hand and gives her a smile. There's sadness in it.

The needle slides into Shep's thigh. His eyes flare and ease shut. Freya strokes his face as his body relaxes, draws a finger across his patchy stubble, the crags of his cheekbones. She cups her hand under his nose like she's trying to collect his breath.

She leaves him with a tap on the forehead, walking in rhythm with the anesthetiser's compressor. She exits the ward into the infirmary garden. She sits on the flat lawn in the shadow of the tower. Soon, the other journalists will be up to watch the supplies boat, and she'll go and join them at the docks. She'll apologise for yesterday evening, try to explain herself. Every outlandish detail, every theory. It's all here, see. Go and visit the man in the infirmary.

The panic rises again. She lies back on the grass, dew in her hair. She has the compulsion to write in one of her journals. Stephen and Alba and Oriol's story. Or Shep's story. It might be pleasant, that, sitting cross-legged on her bed. Her mother bringing in the odd cup of tea, moaning about their malfunctioning fridge. But she knows it wouldn't be enough. Writing her stories about the bunker was never a means to process what she saw inside it. It was a way to evade it. Here on Vertex, it's inescapable. The bunker is contagious, and now Freya has to prove it.

Cross a boundary.

Freya clutches the Dictaphone through her pocket. A sensation like falling out of orbit. She stands up, dizzy. She'd only need a head camera. A good rucksack. Dark-coloured, decent waterproofs. And a map of the Lakes. A drone operator from a forum could show her the way…

She brushes the dry grass from her backside. High cloud has given way to a heavy bank the colour of gritstone. Vertex Island smells a little like petrol. She runs back to her cabin as warm rain starts to fall. On her bunk, surrounded by clothes, hydration sachets, and with rain against the cabin window, Freya buries her face in her pillow and cries. She knows how to break the story. She knows exactly where to go when she gets home.

• • •

The next morning, Freya is the only person at the dock. There was nobody in sight coming over here, not a soul working at any stage of the tower, not on the base pad, not in the outbuildings or by the drone warehouse. No transfer jet waiting. The PR, in her unmissable shoes, is conspicuously absent. Freya stands at the island's sharp edge and holds her hair off her face.

They were meant to meet here this morning, and here she is, having missed the show somehow, alone and fatigued, and frightened. No boat. No sign of a boat – nor its cargo. Only a pile of Vaughan-branded umbrellas.

Freya walks along the artificial coast. The path has been depressed into the sloped concrete that forms a kind of beach. Heaving waves for company. She checks the tower, stands there for a time, wet hair and lashes, face in the spray. This solitude – even the gulls are missing. Maybe it's the weather after all? Maybe the supplies boat is struggling out there, in the pall, slowing off until the weather eases. Maybe she ought to go back to Shep's cot and wait.

She calls: 'Hello?' Polite at first – cheery almost. Then louder, coarser. 'Hello?'

Freya can survive in her own company. What's difficult is to feel vindicated but isolated with major information in another time zone, trying not to succumb to panic. She reminds herself that when you're an adult you can't be lost like the little girl in a supermarket whose parents have taken too many turns; that as an adult, she's accounted for and missed; that she's here on Vertex and a paper trail marks her spot. Someone will come along this path any minute, and the whole episode will be forgotten in an instant – a warm drink, a fake laugh. *Silly Freya*.

'Hello?' she calls again.

This time there's a reply. It comes from above – as if the sky tears open to respond. Freya gasps: three black aircraft pass over in a tight V, banking hard before they start looping the tower at different heights. Closer and closer they circle the scaffold, like spiders wrapping their prey in silk, before they spread out to follow the island's outer edges.

Hypnotised by their terrible elegance, she doesn't call again.

Now one of the drones dips and buzzes the ground at dangerously low altitude – close enough for Freya to see the star on its belly, the US Navy markings. It makes another circuit of the island. She wonders what they're doing. What they're for. Why there's still no one else here to see.

The three drones return to a holding pattern: an evenly spaced wheel revolving the scaffold tower's peak. How long they'll stay there, she can't begin to guess. They remind her of scavenging birds, graceful but menacing, strangely languid.

The rain begins to clear, the heaviest front rolling east. Freya turns from the drones. Visibility has improved out to sea, and she spots a set of green and red lights flashing just this side of the horizon. Red to her right, green to her left. Relief: this must be the supplies boat coming in.

The old sirens from last night whir. Time to welcome the crew. Freya expects the port will fill with dockers. A lot of action. But as the boat closes, takes on a more defined shape, the port stays empty. Pieces of paper turning over in the calming wind, fresh heat as the sun starts to burn through.

Freya checks behind her. The drones are still up. Then back to the supplies boat, which has altered its course slightly, turned sufficiently to starboard that only its port lights, the red lights, are visible. If it stays on that course, it'll miss the island completely.

Freya stands on tiptoes, as if the extra height will make sense of things.

The ocean flashes, and a second later a terrific pressure wave sends Freya sprawling to the ground.

There's another boat out there. Another boat, much larger, grey and low in profile, spined with antennae, is crossing the sea laterally. Flickering light springs from its bow. A flat, percussive roll – a firm shove in her solar plexus – and the water close to the supplies ship erupts in spray. The supplies ship is turning hard to starboard, and the darker ship is cutting it off. It's a warship, she realises. It's firing on them. And as if arriving from the sun itself, the three navy drones are out at sea.

There comes a staggered, high-pitched rattle from the air. The navy drones are also firing on the supplies ship. The ocean surface is seamed along three straight lines. The warship bears down, implacable. The supplies ship carries on turning as the Vertex sirens blare.

Freya breaks for the edge of the island. Her shoes are gone, and her legs can barely carry her.

The supplies boat's red and green lights have swapped sides. It's facing the horizon. The supplies boat is going away from her. But don't worry, she tries to reason – this must be routine. Training, or a drill? The navy testing countermeasures? And isn't she early, anyway? Their transfer plane hasn't arrived yet, and the rest of the press attachment must be tucked up in their cabin bunks, enjoying childless lie-ins, lazy mornings, extra rest to compensate for island time, for jet lag…

She tells herself the other journalists can't all be padlocked inside their cabins with those neat red crosses taped over their doors. She tells herself that the old man in the garden centre was making threats, not warning her.

She watches the departing supplies ship, the approaching navy drones, the hulking navy warship, and tells herself not to turn around when heavy-sounding boots reach the concrete shore behind her. The click and squeak of uniform, weapons. These are the workers. The dockers. They're as confused by this as she is. The supplies ship will turn back in a moment, and the drones will come in to land, and the press tour will go on. Tomorrow, after two long flights home, her father will collect her from Manchester Airport, and her mother will have tea on the table for seven. She'll apologise, and they'll accept it, and she'll tell her story. She'll tell the world what really happened to Stephen Parsons.

'Ms Medlock?' a man says. It's an American voice, muffled by breathing gear.

She turns to him. The air is still. She turns back to the ocean. The reality of the situation finally inundates her. Vertex Island is already lost. What Shep carried here has contaminated all of it. She considers jumping into the water, then – swimming after the supplies ship in the hope it might see her before the shelf drops away and the water turns cold.

She doesn't begrudge it for leaving – we have to look after ourselves. It should've been more obvious, after all. No press. No plane. No supplies boat.

Quarantine.

How foolish, how blinkered she's been. How wilful.

'Ms Medlock,' the American says, much closer. 'Did you come into physical contact with Billy Shepherd?'

Freya sits down on the concrete lip. The breaking waves send foam over her feet.

A heavy glove on her shoulder. 'Ma'am?'

A bird is drawn to fruit and gorges happily. The bird doesn't ask why the tree offers its treats. But the carrying of a seed is a process. It's how the tree lives on.

'I had this,' Freya says. 'I had it.'

The American pulls Freya up and away from the water. The breeze draws her requiem from the steel of the tower scaffold.

HOME BY THE SEA

The Landowner

Em and Ted move their little family to North Wales, new bearings fifty miles along Anglesey's coastal path. 'The market's really developing here,' the agent tells them. 'Your money'll go a lot further.' And it does go further: an overinflated payoff from the council nets them a charming beachfront cottage with whole-bay views, a handsome garden. A rickety workshop is taken up by the previous owner's loom, but easily convertible – a granny flat for Ted's mum, say.

So the Irish Sea displaces Lakeland forest, and with it the girls forget their Seelie Court between the trees downhill from the old garden. It turns out there's plenty to distract the girls out here, and they take instantly to the beach. It helps that Em and Ted bribe the girls with a rescue dog – a dopey mutt the girls insist on calling Dragon. Dragon, this great daft animal who tries to eat the sea foam and brings great clods of beach into the house when you've walked him.

Some afternoons, Em will stand at the edge of the garden

and watch the three of them playing in the breakers – the girls rolling about and kicking the water and laughing at each other, the dog sprinting gamely over the flats. The mountains of Snowdonia, shrouded, out of reach, always over there. These are the times she questions whether the council's compulsory purchase order was so bad after all.

Ted, though, is slower to adjust. He's often sad, occasionally angry. In the swell of his mood swings – between the sad smiles and silent, barely contained rages – Em senses his resistance to their new life. When it happens, Em endures withdrawal; knows their hearth is still in the Lakes, that their taken-away land is still the crux and the crutch of her. While Ted goes on denying it, there's no question he feels that way, too.

So it's all they can do to try and forget. Overwrite the place. Suppress their pangs for it.

Still, by the time the girls have started at their new primary school in September, Em is adjusting nicely. To the sea and its reach. She likes the way the waves follow you back inside: that brisk, fresh spray at your heels, the stubborn grains of wet sand in your boots, on your scalp, under your watch strap. The colour of the bay in the early morning. Buoy bells ringing as the whole family lounge about and barbecue in dreamy light, late summer, as she and Ted learn to rinse the sand from the girls' clothes before they put them in the washing machine. Dragon, lying down in the patches of sun that waltz round the garden.

And even Ted, struggling Ted, seems to be getting his head around things. A peace about him, where before the same quietness was a symptom of what he probably saw as capitulation.

So it goes, then, that something should happen to rupture this delicate state.

The blank postcard comes early. The reverse addressed to the girls in crimson ink. Em is the one to scoop it from the welcome mat.

Em skim reads it there in the hall with a hand on her chest. She takes it to the kitchen and reads it again, slower, colder, and this is appropriate: the stamp in the corner depicts a polar bear adrift on a tiny floe, and it's postmarked Svalbard, Norway. Vaguely, Em remembers the name. Up in the Arctic – that's the one. One of her spy novels concerned a plot against the Global Seed Vault.

Em puts down the postcard. No doubt about its sender, its veracity. The round body of the initial – the G that signs it – is the very same G she'd seen on their gardening invoices. But she doesn't understand how he'd have their new address. Why he'd wait so long to get in touch. What he's doing in Svalbard.

Em reads the postcard back. One more time, whispered aloud. Her response isn't relief but crawling flesh. Her neck and back. Under her skin.

Ted comes in to find her hunching over the breakfast bar. 'Morning, trouble,' he says.

'Hey,' she says, with a quick, habitual hand squeeze.

'What's burning?'

Em can't smell any burning. She looks at the toaster, the Aga. The sockets. Then at her palms.

'Em?'

'It's… we got a postcard.'

'Oh?'

Em turns it on the breakfast bar. 'From him.'

'When?'

'This morning. Sent six days ago, the postmark says. From Norway.'

'*Norway?*' Ted gapes. 'Have the girls seen it?'

'Still in bed.'

'Let me.'

Em pushes the postcard tentatively across the tiles. She scrapes the hair out of her face. It's not yet six-thirty and she could murder a drink.

Ted reads the postcard. Enunciates the lines. 'It doesn't make sense,' he says.

Em's holding her face when he finishes. 'All those ideas he put in the girls' heads last time… And if he writes again, what's to stop them seeing? I can't do this, Ted. We can't. You know what it did to Damson, all that bloody stuff and *nonsense*. How the hell's he got our new address?'

Ted starts to read the postcard aloud:

The girls never did lie. There's a queen for me and a queen for you and a queen for all of us. They want most of all for cold. They can breathe, then. They make you want for cold. The cold's all right. Have to like it, this line of work. Em, your girls did not lie. But they are not fairies. You watch. G.

Em's shaking when Ted puts down the postcard.

'He's gone,' Ted says. He touches his temple. 'In the head.'

Em takes back the card, turns it over. 'And the thing is—'

She stops. There are more words imprinted on the picture side. Not with ink, but as if pressed in with an empty nib. Like he'd written another letter while leaning on it. She holds the card to her face.

'Oh my God,' she whispers. 'Ted. Look. It's the girls' names. Over and over.'

Ted comes closer. Pulls Em's hand, the card, into focus.

'Overwritten,' he says. 'Another note to someone else. A separate postcard, maybe?'

Em can't accept that. And Ted won't have it, either. She saw the thing burning in the greenhouse, the line scoured in the grass. She can see what's happening here. *Damson. Dolly. Dolly. Damson. Damson. Dolly. Damson. Dolly.* Em rubs the indentations.

'What's that on your thumb?' Ted asks.

Em looks at it. Brownish. The initialled G has smeared, and she's surprised to find it powdery to the touch. A deeper colour than the red ink of the rest of the message. Em scratches lightly and more of it flakes away.

'What?' she asks, looking at her nail.

Ted stands there.

'He's not signed it in—'

'Don't,' she says. Because why? Why would he? Proof of life? Some sort of cruel joke? That Graham's had some sort of breakdown is plausible. But to sign… No, worse, to do it so *neatly*—

'He must be in a bad way,' Ted says.

Em shakes her head. 'What are we supposed to do?' she asks. Graham never spoke of family or friends, and his flat was repossessed shortly after he absconded. Ted had kept various court processes at bay for months, but slowly gave up as the chances of Graham resurfacing diminished.

'I don't have a clue,' Ted says.

'I'm scared,' Em tells him.

But Ted isn't scared – he's angry. 'Give it here,' he says. 'I'll fucking burn it. Then – then we forget about it. It didn't happen.'

'Till he sends more,' Em says. 'My *God*. It's like he's back here.'

'Well he isn't,' Ted says. 'Only thing I can think is that he's reaching out. Some people, you know, before they take their own... some people, they, ah... they get ready. You know? Writing to their nearest and dearest. Settling accounts. You know?'

Em stares at her husband. 'What? How can you go there—'

'I mean... he was always a *bit* off. Wasn't he?'

Em shakes her head furiously, welling up. She looks over one shoulder. 'Dragon? Dragon! Come on. We're getting out of here.' And the dog pelts into the room and puts his front paws on Em's knees.

'Don't wake the girls yet,' she hisses at Ted. 'And wash your *hands*. It's the card that stinks. It's that fucking card.'

In the back garden, towards the hardy scrub of the beach, the shale and sand, the swell. None of the neighbours are up yet, though there's an old tent and the smouldering remains of a fire some distance around the bay.

Dissatisfied, livid with the run of things, at Ted's

indifference, Em walks for a while along the beach fringe, holding Graham's postcard by the corner so it flaps noisily in the wind. She remembers the nights she'd bunked down with Dolly, reassuring her that Marigold and the fairies weren't coming back, that they weren't watching the house from the woods. All those long, long hours staring at the plastic stars covering the ceiling in Dolly's room.

Dragon gallops ahead, chicaning in and out of the foam. It's about degrees of plausibility, Em supposes. The greenhouse, the girls' obsessions. The visits from the ufologists. Those damn trespassers in the bunker. But the question lingers. If they weren't fairies, then what had the girls seen that day? Or what, at least, was Graham's postcard driving at?

You watch, it said.

Em squats in the sand, steadies herself with one hand. A pull in her gut, like an old pregnancy pain, and the faint sound of tinkling on the water. She looks out to sea, back to the house. Maybe some ghosts can travel with you.

ACKNOWLEDGEMENTS

Certain aspects of the Vaughan family's space elevator plans were inspired by Sir Arthur C. Clarke's 1979 novel *The Fountains of Paradise*. Some of Shep's past urbex missions, as well as Stephen and Alba's forum profiles, were inspired by posts on 28dayslater.co.uk.

This project owes almost everything to my brother Alex, whose steeplejacking stories and photos got me started (and whose technical advice I mostly ignored).

Endless thanks to those who read drafts and shoved me along: Anne, Chris, Ed, James, Jayne, Mark, Mike, Nina, Penny and Steph.

Huge thanks also to my agent Sam Copeland, editor Gary Budden and everyone at Titan Books, especially George Sandison, Tash Qureshi, Dan Coxon, Lydia Gittins and Polly Grice. Extra special thanks to Julia Lloyd for the beautiful cover art.

All my love to Suze, Albie and Felix.

ABOUT THE AUTHOR

M.T. Hill grew up in Tameside, Greater Manchester, and now lives on the edge of the Peak District with his wife and sons. He is the author of *Zero Bomb*, *The Folded Man*, and 2016 Philip K. Dick Award nominee *Graft*.
Find him on Twitter @matthewhill